*Moolelo o Kalola*

# Moolelo o Kalola

## Maui's Sacred Chiefess

MARILYN WHITEHORSE

ISBN: 0692718583
ISBN 13: 9780692718582
Library of Congress Control Number: 2016909943
Marilyn Whitehorse, Honolulu HI

# Dedication

*In Loving Memory:*
*Blanche Bernard Sharpe*
*Anne Lowenkopf*

# Acknowledgments

Without the help and support of kind folks, this project would not have been possible. My warmest *aloha* and *mahalo* extend to Allison Chun, D. Dillon, Al Lagunero, Lani Lofgren, Lynn Louise, Lani Murray, Ron McGaughey, Puakea Nogelmeier, Susan Rummerfield, Michael Ryall and Jane Wheeler. Research made available through Bishop Museum archives, Hawaii State Public Library, Hawaii Pacific University, the University of Hawaii, Manoa and the University of Hawaii, Hilo.

Although this book is based on real events and real people, it is most definitely a work of fiction.

# Prologue

$\mathcal{S}$ ome say….
Some say….

But this, I know…

…the rhythmic beating of the women's *kapa* mallets, the background sound of any Hawaiian village

…roosters crowing as the chicks scurry after the hens that cluck and peck their way across the compound

…dogs stretching out in front of the doorways of the *hales*

…men's muscles rippling across their backs as they bend over the wooden pallets, their hands gripping the stone *poi* pounders as they knead our staple food, *kalo*, into a purplish gray paste

…trade winds rustling the fronds in the coconut groves.

Toward evening the men lean on their digging sticks and pick their way down the trail from the hills, streaked with mud from wading in the *kalo loi*. Others come from the upland garden patches, bent with the weight of the nets of sweet potatoes slung across their backs. Kihawahine, the *mo-o* goddess and our family *aumakua*, guarded the fishponds so that there was plenty to eat. Our island of Maui was at peace.

By a white man's calendar, it might have been the year 1736, but the foreigners to our shores were years away yet, and still a myth of the Lono priests. Each day melted into the next under the glaring sun. I look back now and realize I was but a child. I didn't know to count the days, nor understand that they would add up to all these years.

# *One*

## 1736

*M*y father's sickness came on suddenly. To this day, I know in my heart there was some power sent from afar; that some *kahuna*, some black magic sorcerer, completed his ritual, tipped back his head, and blew. "Whooo…" His breath traveled straight to my father, *Alii* of Maui. Although much subtler than hundreds of warriors making a landing--their polished lances gleaming and their coconut helmets revealing only their dark eyes--the curse hit its mark as true and as crippling as any spear. By sending an illness on the breeze, there was no guard on the hillside to light a signal fire and warn of the danger, and certainly no way for my father, Kekaulike, to escape. Actually, it was very clever of Alapai, the ruler of Hawaii, to answer my father's recent raids on his land by sending sickness instead of losing any more men in battle.

My father was perhaps sitting too quietly, having let his guard down in order to enjoy a peaceful moment with me. He had just come down the steps of the *heiau* after having consulted with the priests at his newly built war temple. He had left instructions for them to conjure up spells against his enemies and was returning to our compound, his retainers carrying the *kahili* standards before him to announce his presence. He spotted me sheltered deep in the shade under the broad branches of a *kukui* tree and came to bask in the comfort of the afternoon breeze, settling down beside me, his eldest daughter.

Being so sacred--the daughter of a half-brother and sister mating, descendants of the first man and woman, Wakea and Papa, brother and sister themselves--and my *kapus* so strong, I was seldom allowed outside the compound during the day, but this day I begged to go out, and my mother finally acquiesced. "For just a bit," she said. If I wouldn't have asked; if she wouldn't have given in...those thoughts have haunted me for years. Neither mother nor I could have guessed we were carrying out the wishes of an unseen force. I dangled my feet over the edge of the lava stone wall, looking out to sea and to the island of Hawaii in the distance. Looking back, I wish I could have done something to change those moments, although deep in my heart I know there is nothing I could have done. But still...perhaps if I had said something to make my father turn his head slightly, perhaps if a rooster crowed, a baby cried, dog trotted through the compound—his attention diverted somehow. I distinctly remember looking up as a gust of wind ruffled his gray hair. Such a peaceful moment—not even the sound of a bird chirping interrupted the stillness.

Silence, the warning...

All at once the ripple of a breeze came from nowhere and tousled his hair. Then, it was as if it had found its mark and his hair stood straight up. His eyes rolled back in his head. His teeth chattered. He shook so hard his bones rattled. White spittle foamed on his lips. His tongue protruded, then rolled back and disappeared into his mouth. He fell backward and began to gag. In a flash, his retainers threw down the feather standards and fell upon him, pinning him to the ground. One man shoved his finger in my father's mouth and pulled out his tongue. The man held it between his fingers and shouted for someone to hand him a stout stick. Father writhed on the ground while the retainer held his tongue for dear life. It seemed like it took forever--but it must have been only a matter of a few seconds—before one of the men found a stick. The retainer pressed down on my father's tongue, shoving the stick between his teeth so that he would not swallow his tongue and choke to death. Other men held my father's arms and legs down until he stopped shaking.

"Get the priest!" they shouted at me as they held him still.

I scrambled to my feet, teetering on the edge of the wall, unable to move.

"Run!" One of them bent down and shouted in my face. "Run!"

I came out of a daze and scrambled up the path to the *heiau*.

Being female, I could not enter the sacred fortress of the priests. I had to stand outside the wall and shout for the old half-blind and deaf *kahuna*. Dismayed that someone had interrupted his afternoon prayers, he tottered to the entrance, ready to scold the culprit. When he saw it was Kekaulike's daughter, he softened. Then he peered closer and realized how distressed I was. "Come! Come!" I beseeched him as I turned back down the hill. He followed, hobbling along as fast as he could, for in his hurry he had forgotten his walking stick.

By the time we reached my father, his intense shaking had stopped. The priest insisted my father needed to be watched over and kept under his direct supervision, so the retainers picked father up and carried him to the *heiau*. The men broke *kapus* by touching their chief. Weak and terrified father did not protest. Priests from the district were called and soon were murmuring healing incantations, appealing to the gods for help. Those who came from afar accused the local priests of not following proper protocol during the morning prayers at the *heiau*, but the priests soundly denied that idea. Others suspected it was the shaking sickness brought about by something my father must have eaten. His food tasters were summoned but all presented themselves in robust health. Still others suspected a deeper conspiracy and conferred among themselves.

"Maybe it was the retainer who is responsible for the correct disposal of the chief's bodily functions," one man suggested.

"Yes!" another chimed in. "He traded the sacred spittle from the royal spittoon…"

Another man interrupted, "Or transferred some fingernail clippings…"

The priest calmed them down by saying, "Since the destruction entered from his hair, the guilty man must have been gathering stray hairs from the chief's whale bone comb and slipping them to enemy spies."

They all agreed they had seen a recent visitor from Alapai's court in our village and that the retainer had been seen talking to him. And with that, the retainer's fate was sealed. Truly, it seemed the only possible way for the spells to have fallen on my father—payback from chief Alapai for father's raids upon his lands in Kona. Father was guilty of devastating villages along the Kona coast the last time he raided Alapai's homeland. On his way back to Maui, father ordered his men to cut down a grove of coconut trees, which was an open invitation to reprisal.

The retainer, who had slipped away and headed for the hills at the first mention of his involvement was hunted down and brought before the chief. The priests ordered him taken to the bay and drowned so that he could be offered up as a sacrifice in the hopes of easing father's convulsions. The offering seemed to ease father's anxiety, but only for a short time. The next attack came within days. *Kahuna laau lapaau,* those who specialized in herbal medicine, were consulted. Many remedies were suggested, and one after the other tried, but in the end the priests remained baffled and could not bring about a cure. The seers gazed deep into the water of their calabashes to see where and what and who, but the water remained as murky as if it had been muddied by sacred *awa.* With no help available from his *kahunas* or insight from his seers, father weakened and folded in upon himself. He was no longer a chief strong enough to call himself *Alii.* His time to rule had passed, brought down not by a spear, but on the whiff of a gentle breeze. Alapai had sent the sickness that the priests called *kamakahukilani*—eyes drawn heavenward. Overnight my strong father became a doddering old man.

Naturally, when one man falters, rumors fly, even if another qualified man is in line to take his place. Father turned the rule of Maui over to my elder brother, Kamehamehanui, son from our father's highest-ranking wife and our mother, Kekuiapoiwanui. The sacred ceremony was performed at Mokulau near father's compound, for in his weakened condition, he dared not travel. In that way, my brother became the new leader of Maui, and my keeper. At the insistence of father and his priests, my brother's first order of business was to send spies to Alapai's court, not only to find out the source of father's illness, but also to keep an eye on the cunning chiefs of the island across the channel.

Although in his right mind when not besieged by epileptic seizures, father felt gravely threatened when he heard that his old enemy, Alapai, had moved his troops directly across the channel to Kohala. That news sent father into a state of panic. He sensed that whatever Alapai had in mind would not bode well for him, his son the new ruler, or the commoners who depended on both of them for strong leadership. It was early spring and the Makahiki season—the time for feasting and revelry—had just ceased. The god Lono had been retired to the *heiau* and the war god had taken its place.

Sensing the end of his days, father drew upon all the strength he had. He called for his wives, children, war leaders, and other chiefs. We assembled in haste and were hustled onto his double war canoe, Keakamilo. Warriors, spearmen and counselors were separated: some traveled in ten-man canoes as part of the fleet, others headed out overland, planning to rendezvous with us up the Maui coast at Maalaea Bay.

The warriors raised the *lauhala* sails and the canoes departed.

The farther we traveled, the sicker my father became.

"I'm dying!" he whispered to his priests. "I can see the end!"

The priests consulted my mother. "Apparently the chief's life force, his *mana*, is draining out of him the farther he travels away from his home at Muolea in Kaupo."

I sat beside my mother as she held my father's hand. She asked, "Is your spirit near enough to hear me? What do you wish, my husband/ brother?" She bent over him in order to hear his reply or to catch his last breath, whichever was necessary.

"I command you—with what little breath I have left—do not let me die at sea," he begged her. "I must die with my feet on the *aina*. It is what I know; it is what I have fought for. It is what I love."

"I will see to it," she said and reported his final command. The men set the sails and turned the canoe toward shore. There was discussion among the chiefs because we had not reached the landing spot they preferred, but mother remained adamant, so we pulled ashore on the sandy beach at Kamaole. Mother ripped off her skirt and insisted it be used for the sling of the litter the men cobbled together for my father. Defying all *kapus*, she walked completely naked beside him, holding his hand and praying softly.

Men vied for the honor of carrying their chief's body, trading off as they trudged up the hill to a *heiau*.

My father's breathing grew shallow.

Mother commanded, "Stop!"

The men stopped and laid the litter on the ground.

Father shuttered; the death rattle came. His last wish--to die on land—had been fulfilled, but alas, he passed before reaching the resting place of our ancestors in sacred Iao valley.

We sat quietly on the hillside watching his spirit gather itself, then soar into a grey cloud that hovered above us. Rain soaked us through and through, then a rainbow arched over the far ridge.

"He is gone," my mother said.

By that time, messengers from our village had caught up with us, reporting that they had hurried to find us because the men with eyes of a hawk who were stationed in the lookout posts had seen Alapai raising the sails on his war canoe. Upon hearing that news, the priests insisted that no time be lost and led us in the sacred *Waimahoehoe* rites in order to purify my father's body. The priests sent my brother, surrounded by his guards, away from the retinue immediately. It was imperative that our father, the dead chief, not defile my brother's *mana*. We vowed to meet at Iao in ten days.

The priests were certain that, if discovered, my father would be desecrated—that his sacred bones would be used for fish hooks and his skull used for a spittle container—an insult to his person like no other. There was nothing else for us to do but proceed as the priests directed. Amidst cries of lamentation and great wailing, the priests commanded the warriors to collect themselves. "Do not fall victim to the chaos," the *kahunas* warned. "It is induced by the enemy so that the *Alii* will not find his ancestors."

The warriors collected themselves, putting down their spears in order to follow the priest's directions. Some were sent to collect dry wood; others dug an *imu* pit with their bare hands. After the wood was laid on top of the pile of stones, the priests rubbed sticks together and lit the fire. We gathered round and watched it blaze while we wailed for the loss of our great ruler. After the fire burned down and the rocks were sufficiently heated, my father's body, wrapped in banana leaves, was lowered onto the rocks. More banana leaves were laid on top of the body. Some hours later, the smell of roasted meat hung in the air. With great ceremony, the priests directed the men to peel back the leaves and separate my father's flesh from his bones. A few trusted men were sent to the bay that night to call the sharks in order to dispose of the meat. My father's bones were wrapped in fresh *kapa* cloth, and my mother given back her skirt, which she did not change until his bones were safely deposited with our family.

Our procession started overland, everyone anxious to take their turn carrying the still-warm bundle of his *iwi*, his sacred bones, which were less of a burden than his litter had been, allowing us to travel much faster. We returned to the canoe, boarded and sailed to our original destination, Maalaea Bay. The news of their chief's death had spread to the villages all along the way. As the *kahili* bearers waved the tall feather standards and called out "*Kapu Moe! Kapu Moe!*" the commoners prostrated on the ground, wailing as we passed, showing veneration for the bones of their *Alii*. The priests conducted the sacred ceremonies on the run as we fled across the isthmus of Maui. At last we stopped near the mouth of the valley where the solemn priests of Iao met us. They took the bundle and departed for the back of the valley, safely tucking my father's bones away in the sacred burial cave, Olopio.

Hard on the heels of my father's canoe was Alapai's army, his fleet landing at Maalaea about the time that my father's bones were being carried deep into the valley. Upon learning from the villagers that the old chief was dead, Alapai decided not to attack, but rather to pay his respects to his sister--my mother--wailing with her and the rest of the family. He assured us he did not wish to declare war on my brother, for he felt that to fight against his nephew at a time like this would have assured disaster via the gods. Instead, he took the high road, carefully sidestepping the responsibility for the death of my father. He claimed he sent the chiefs Kalaniopuu and Keoua as a favor, but we were aware they were acting as court spies during the ten days of grieving. Many chiefs shaved all but a swatch of their hair, knocked out front teeth, or tattooed their tongues. Everyone carried on as wild animals in heat, seemingly paying no attention with whom they mated. After ten days, the wailing ceased and my brother, Kamehamehanui, returned. He called for the royal court to be convened. Instead of war, the days at court were a joy. The utmost courtesy was paid to my mother and to my brother, the new ruler of Maui.

# Two

## 1736

My brother had not been ruler for many days before he faced rebellion. As was to be expected, Kauhiaimokuakama, our half-brother—my father's eldest son, but whose mother was a woman of lower rank than our mother—decreed that he deserved to be the ruler. Of course it was the *kahuna* at the *heiau* of Wailehua who stood to gain the most. He nudged and prodded until Kauhi saw things his way. Kauhi's priest insisted that his time and energy would be better served by going to war against my brother instead of carrying stones for the building of the new *heiau* my brother had begun. In truth, it did not take much for Kauhi to gather support from the *makaainana*, the local men, who had been forced to build the *heiau*, for they were not thrilled with carrying stones any more than the man who not-so-secretly wanted to rule. It only took days until the priest got his way and Kauhi was able to incite the men of the village to put down the stones, conscript them into his army, and hand out spears. In Kauhi's first act of war against my brother, he looted the sweet potato fields at Alamihi, leaving the commoners under my brother's care without sustenance. Soon a riot broke out and the conflict quickly escalated. Some men joined my brother's army for the love of battle. Others joined because they had to. Basically, men were left with few choices: death in war, fear of death if they headed for the caves with the women and elders and were discovered as deserters, or starvation. The women packed whatever food they could scrounge, grabbed the children, and fled to the safety of the hills, as they always did in times of war.

Kauhi and his army proceeded south to Kahili in Hana. While Kauhi sent for reinforcements from Peleiohalani, chief of the Ewa district on the island of Oahu, our family counseled and made our own plans. Alapai had just returned to his own island, and Kamehamehanui sent messengers to our uncle across the channel to seek his help. Alapai had been my father's old enemy, but after my father died, my mother--fearing an attack by her clever sibling--declared Alapai to be her favorite brother and welcomed him openly into our family. My brother also thought of Alapai as his favorite uncle because, after he had been warmly welcomed back into the family fold, he had refused to go to war against us. Whatever the convoluted relationship, Alapai came to my brother's rescue, returning to Maui with troops and becoming my brother's military advisor and, ultimately, our family's savior.

Even though I had been around the court all my life, I was still young. The warrior's swirling feather capes, each chief with their own brilliant red, yellow and black design, scared me out of my wits. My brother was a giant of a man, and with his *mahiole*, his red feather helmet, arching over his head he was well over eight feet tall. When he bent down, I feared his hawk-like headdress would peck my eyes out. I can see his warriors to this day: their brown arms shining from *kukui* nut oil rubbed into their skin to make it slick so that in hand-to-hand combat their foe could not easily grab them. The men's white *malos* flapped between their legs, their gourd *makini* helmets their only protection. Although fascinated, I knew enough to know they had worked themselves into a battle frenzy and to be afraid of their heavy *koa* spears and the carved wooden weapons that had edges lined with one or more rows of serrated teeth from the tiger shark.

"There is no need to fear," my mother assured me as she patted my shoulder. "It is just a family quarrel and it will soon blow over. Surely the men will come to their senses before too much damage is done. My brother, Alapai, has sent many skilled warriors. They will make quick work of the disturbance."

I wanted to believe her words, but I saw the deep line between her eyebrows and I knew she was as worried as I.

"They will surely stop before too many men's lives are lost," she said, more to reassure herself than me. Then she pulled her hair back, wrapped it round and round, and stuck a turtle shell comb through the bun to hold it tight. "Besides, you and I won't be anywhere near the battle. We will view it from a safe distance."

I nodded agreement, but I was still not convinced.

"The men will hurl insults at each other and maybe throw and catch a few spears," she mused. "There is nothing to be concerned about at all."

Even though we were far away from the battle at first, as my brother's army began its hasty retreat, the fighting swiftly stretched in our direction. My brother's men were soundly defeated—slaughtered brutally right before our eyes. Mother grabbed me and dashed for the shoreline. We dared not blink or look over our shoulder or we would have been killed too. Splashing through the shallows, we dove under the water, coming up a few yards later, but not yet out of range of the men's spears. We swam out to Alapai's waiting canoes, leaving the slain on the battlefield—our kinsmen all.

My mother and I were hauled aboard one canoe, my brother and uncle, seeing our canoe full, climbed into another waiting vessel. The paddlers turned the canoes and fought their way over the breakers to the outside of the reef, out of the range of the spear throwers that were lined up on shore. Our warriors brought the canoes together long enough for mother to shout across the waves, "Our family is separated—it is the will of the gods. I will take Kalola and go to Molokai—to the priestess Kanealai--where we will both be safe."

"But what about…?" My brother began.

Mother raised her hand, assuming command, and did not allow my brother to finish his question. "You go with Alapai and regroup. When you are ready, take back what is rightfully yours." Both mother and my brother turned to Alapai, seeking his approval.

My uncle nodded agreement.

"Kalola and I will not return until you have taken back the island. Only after you have secured the *aina* and established your court, only then may you send word and we will return."

It was as my mother said: the gods had willed it. As soon as our paddlers turned our craft away from my brother's canoe, a strong wind came up from behind, causing our canoe to slide down the steep slope of a wave, separating our canoe from the group. I looked back over my shoulder, wondering if I would ever see my dear brother again. Already our canoes were much farther apart than I thought was possible, for it seemed that it had merely been a beat—maybe two--of my heart since we had parted. Before I could catch my breath, our paddlers headed across the Pailolo channel to the safety of Molokai. How quickly the tide had turned--Kauhi was now the ruler of Maui, and my mother, the former chiefess, and I, the sacred daughter, were refugees hoping to be taken in.

From that moment on, time became a slippery eel—something that I would not be able to grasp again for many, many moons.

Even before we landed, the old chiefess Kanealai, a seer who could divine the future, had made her way down the hill behind her *kihili* bearers and was at the shore to greet us when our canoe landed. When my mother stepped from the canoe, Kanealai chanted a warm welcome. Mother returned the welcome, chanting her lineage and our appreciation.

"My sister / wife—and her beautiful daughter—I welcome you to my home," Kanealai said as she leaned forward on her staff, touching my mother's forehead with her own. The women shared the breath of life. Then mother picked me up and I, too, took in the aging chiefess' spirit, and she, mine. After mother put me back on the ground, Kanealai turned to her men and told them to hide our canoe and take our men into their homes for a few days until proper shelter could be built for them. Because she was elderly, her male retainers carried her back up the hill as we walked behind, thankful to have our feet on solid ground again.

When we had settled, she came to see us in our *hale* near Iliiliopae *heiau*. Instead of staying inside, she invited us to join her under a tree, looking across the channel to our home island. The clouds hung on the horizon, turning pink, then gray, as the sun set.

"The *kahunas* saw danger in the clouds. Is my *hanai* son Kamehamehanui safe?" Kanealai asked.

"For now, he is safe with my brother, Alapai at his court at Kawaihae," Mother answered.

The perfect hostess, Kanealai talked with mother late into the night.

For a little while I was able to stay awake and listen, but I had lived through the recent troubles they were discussing. Eventually my attention wandered. I found myself counting stars and soon dozed off.

---

$\mathcal{I}$n no time at all I felt like Molokai was my home, although from our hawk's nest on the hillside at Waialua I could look across the channel and, most days, see the land of my ancestors. If mother was homesick for our island, she did not let on. She took advantage of her time with Kanealai and spent many hours with her sister/wife in the women's *heiau*.

When I began my first bleed, mother invited me to go with them to the women's hut. After the bleed had ceased, she led me to the women's sacred temple to teach me the traditions of the *Hale o Papa*, the women's *heiau*, imparting her deep understanding regarding my special position, not only in my family, but also the duties and tasks I was to assume as the *kahu*, the keeper, for eventually I would be responsible for the care of the rituals and tradition of Kihawahine, the *mo-o* goddess, for my people. She and the elder Kanealai stressed that it was my duty to honor my guardian spirit, goddess of the fishponds. They explained that I had grown from the toes of the *kiha*, up the legs and into the actual body of the *mo-o*. "Your family has been placed near the goddess, and you will be treated as such, it is true," Kanealai told me. "But that nearness is paid for with a dear price: there are many *kapus*, and they are there for a reason."

"You are responsible for performing the correct rites to bring continued sustenance to the people. If you fail in your duties, all will suffer," mother warned. "Our family is especially blessed. Kihawahine was once our physical ancestor. Her name was Kihawahine Moluhinia Kalamaula Kalaaiheana."

"The lizard woman?" I asked, drawing upon the stories I had heard of my long-deceased relative.

"Yes. She was born on the birthing stone of Pohaku Hauola at Makila beach at Apuakehau," mother said, beginning in the middle of my name chant, linking me to my royal ancestors. "She was a royal chiefess, some say an *eepa*, a special one, transformed into a goddess upon her death. We are from the Ulu line. With one of her husbands, our ancestor began the Maluna line. It is prophesied that the last of her line will be the final chief and chiefess of the islands. She is the giver of abundance. She is the landholder—those that have land, have plenty. Worship her because, my dear, that is our honor, but also our responsibility of power."

"But the men kill to gain power…" I began.

Kanealai held up her hand and interrupted me. "Yes, men gain by killing, but that is not the best way. War means destruction. The way for everyone to flourish is to provide for each other. You provide well for the *makaainana* through prayer, and the *makaainana* will provide for you in return. Always remember Kihawahine is the land keeper, which means that we are the caretakers." She studied me, her eyes probing deep into my soul. "I asked the *kilo*, the seer, to look into your future, my dear. Your destiny is great."

As befits the young, I was curious about my future, and asked, "What did she see?"

Kanealai looked at my mother, "You haven't told her?"

My mother shook her head.

The old woman smiled and said, "I will tell you enough now to curb your curiosity for a time." She reached for my hand and held it in hers, all the while looking over my head at my mother, careful not to reveal more than I could understand at the time. "You will spend your life among chiefs."

# *Three*

## 1737-38

*T*ime on Molokai at the court of Kanealai was a fluid thing, but eventually I realized we had not heard from my brother in a long time—it could have been weeks or months—I had completely lost track. When I questioned mother, at first she seemed not to care—she spent her time in the women's temple with Kanealai--but as the months wore on, she became concerned. Finally, she declared she was sending an emissary to her brother's court. I had grown bored on Molokai, and at the thought of seeing my older brother I begged to be allowed to visit his court. At first she said no, but then she relented. I don't know what made her change her mind—maybe Kanealai looked into her calabash and saw something mother hadn't seen; maybe she wanted more than one report, for as a young woman I would be more likely to see things at court as they were and tell it innocently. At any rate, the most trusted men were chosen as my escorts and I prepared for the trip.

---

*A*t first I was thrilled to be at my uncle's court. I was pampered and coddled—Alapai's many wives saw to that. I learned that my brother and our uncle had not been idle for they had spent the whole year of planning and regrouping. Legions had been sent to the mountains to fell trees and deliver them to the canoe builders at the shore. Every day fishermen had been sent out beyond the reef to catch sharks. Far into the night, as the men gathered around the fire, they wove cordage from the fibers of coconut and then lashed the shark's teeth to their carved *koa* weapons. They drew detailed maps of Maui in the dirt and planned their attack. My uncle was positive my brother would regain Maui again. Any man that voiced opposition heard my uncle bellow, "Traitorous talk!" The man was whisked away and fattened up for sacrifice. My brother smiled when yet another addition had been made to his sacrifical pool—he had learned many things from our uncle's leadership.

"I feel like I don't know you at all," I said to my brother. "Once upon a time you were as gentle as the summer breeze. Now…"

He took my hand and led me to the edge of the compound. "In truth, I am as nervous as an eel slithering between the rocks, looking for a safe hole," he said as soon as we were far enough away from prying ears for him to speak candidly.

When I heard him say that, I looked deep into his eyes and realized how much stress my brother had been under.

"But what I have to do is so much bigger than just me. It is the security of our family and our island. You must understand that you will face the same pressures when you are older. That's probably why mother sent you to me—so that you could see what strength it takes to defend our island and our family."

After that I began to watch my brother and my uncle closer. Alapai did not dissuade my brother from seeking to keep himself safe, even advising him that as the ruler, his life would change beyond anything he could imagine and that he would soon learn to be on guard every minute, waking and sleeping. "After all, look what happened to your father," Alapai said and then caught himself.

I did not say anything at that moment, but when I looked into my uncle's eyes, I had a strong suspicion he had been the one who had set the *kahuna's* prayers in motion.

The longer I stayed in the court of Alapai, the more I grew to loathe the island of Hawaii and its people. I wanted to go back to my mother. I wanted to bask again on the sandy beaches of Maui instead of the lava strewn rocky coast of Hawaii. I wanted to go back to the sweet potato patches and the *kalo loi*. My tender skin baked under the blazing sun on the barren lava fields of Kona. Even more, I missed the breezes that I'd grown up with on Maui: the sea-cucumber eating wind of Kaupo, Ailoli, and the gentle trade wind, Kaiaulu. I felt lost that I could not name all the winds of Hawaii. I only knew the southern Kona wind, which brought the heat of the volcano and its poisonous sulfur fumes.

Kamehamehanui kept a close eye on me—closer than I had ever been guarded before. I was under strict watch, always with armed men surrounding me, especially when Alapai's chiefs were present. I was sacred—I had been told time and again since birth—but now I was beginning to understand that I was the object of desire by the two chiefly brothers from Kau. Although much older than I, they hovered around, eyeing me, flirting a bit when they were allowed to get close enough. I was beautiful, but when it was rumored that I had bled for the first time and was now capable of producing an extremely sacred child who would be a certain heir to any chief's court, the two brothers hovered like plovers guarding their nest. I had never been under that much strain—I was a pampered child no longer. I became distraught and cried hopelessly, begging to return to the safety of my mother.

It was then that the priests declared the omens were favorable and that it was the perfect time for victory. Alapai's army cheered. The next evening, all was deemed ready.

We were ushered into the canoes and headed back across the channel, traveling far out to sea under the light of the crescent moon so that Kauhi's guards along the coast line would not spy us, although how they missed such a big army was always something I never understood. We did not land until morning when we came ashore at Lahaina.

Runners fled to Kauhi, telling him of the invasion, and soon battle lines were clearly drawn. Peleiholani, from Oahu, came with 640 of his best warriors to help Kauhi. My brother had Alapai's reinforcements of well over 8,000 men. Although greatly outnumbered, Kauhi's warriors defended their land. Each day the loss of men on both sides was staggering. After several days of battle there was still no clear victor on either side. Retreating in order to plan anew, Alapai elected to try a different strategy. He had his men divert the streams, drying up the *kalo loi,* thereby starving the country people who supported Kauhi. The women of the *ahupuaa* near the battlefield bundled up their thirsty children, dogs and chickens and headed for the hills the same as they had done a year before. If nothing else, the women were practical and knew survival skills: they would feed their children the ferns of the forest before letting them go hungry due to another *Alii* war. In a day or two, the warriors and their camps were the only remants left in the abandoned village on the hillside.

What transpired next was "not fit for children's ears or eyes," my brother said, but I heard and saw it nonetheless. In fact, the whole camp witnessed high chiefess Kamakaimoku's temper tantrum, aimed directly at her husband Alapai, after she heard about yet another day's carnage. "I will not have my sons killed due to your recklessness in battle!" she screamed as a large calabash flew out the door of the *hale,* thrown so hard that it smashed against the coconut tree trunk and shattered into small pieces. "You poisoned my husband and now I refuse to have you use my sons for your faltering schemes!"

Alapai fled his wife's rage, ducking out the door before she could launch another calabash, her final words echoing in the night air. "Let Maui fight their own battle!" During my time at Alapai's court, I learned that Kamakaimoku was Alapai's third wife, having been absorbed into his court along with her sons, Kalani and Keoua, after the death of her former husband, whom many believed was poisoned by Alapai. The next day, the rumor around Alapai's court was that she had good cause to be upset. She was worried about the safety of her sons who stood on the front lines of the battleground. Those words stung my uncle. It was never good form for a chief to have one of his wives upset. Alapai minced around, seeking counsel from one chief, then another. I saw with my own eyes how the spears of words could wound as deeply as an enemy's lance.

Alapai turned to his trusted advisor Naili, his angry wife's brother, and begged him to help calm her down.

"Do something!" Kamakaimoku screamed at her brother when he went to hear her out. "I demand that you find a way to stop this senseless massacre!" The chiefess would not be quieted and let no one in the compound rest the next night either.

For several days, couriers and retainers shuttled back and forth between Alapai's court and the Oahu chief, Peleiohalani. The daily battles continued, but at a slower pace, each side hoping for a resolution so that the men could go home to their fields, to their fishing nets, to their wives and children. Eventually, Naili procured a clever genealogist who was able to weave peace into both family lines, for in truth the *alii* of all the islands had intermarried and were plaited together as tight as a rope made from coconut fiber. With much chanting and unraveling, and much discussion over cups of *awa*, Naili was able to come up with a plan to stop the fighting that was agreeable to both chiefs, without bringing shame to either side.

It had been agreed that on the battlefield at Puunene, Alapai's warriors would surround the Oahu troops, with the brothers from Hawaii, Kalaniopuu and Keoua, leading the attack. All was going as planned. Led to believe that he had bested his enemy, Kalaniopuu raised his club above his head, ready to deal the fatal blow to an older chief and win the war. Suddenly Peleioholani called out, "My son, Kaleiopuu!" and pointed to Kalani's *lei niho palaoa* necklace. Only Kalani's true father would have been able to recognize the unusual sperm whale bud that hung from Kalani's neck. Kalani dropped to his knees, his war club clattering to the ground, in surrender to his father. Seeing their chief bow down to his enemy, the warriors on both sides paused. Kalaniopuu rose to his feet, the two men embraced, and the battle ceased.

Without delay, Alapai ordered Kauhi drowned so that there would be no further trouble, and my brother, Kamehamehanui, was declared ruler of Maui. Runners were sent to the caves to bring the women and children home to the villages. Immediately, a canoe was launched for Molokai to bring my mother back. After Kalaniopuu feasted with his biological father, he and Keoua headed back to Hawaii with their uncle, Alapai. Peleioholani retired to Molokai for some months before returning to Oahu.

My family was, once again, at home on our island of Maui where my brother, Kamehamehanui, was now ruler with the chiefs of the other islands in agreement about his supremacy. He settled down at his court and his gentle ways returned. Above all, he wanted peace, and because of that, all the people loved him. He was generous to the commoners because he knew happy farmers and successful fishermen would allow him to reign in peace.

For a time, life settled back down. The farmers returned to their *lois* and planted *kalo*. After the fishermen repaired the fishponds, they took the canoes out for some deep-sea fishing. The bird catchers left for the mountains to bring back *o-o* feathers for the chief's royal capes. The steady pounding of the women's *kapa* beaters once again became the familiar sound of daily life. Children ran from *hale* to *hale*, chasing chickens when they tired of chasing each other. Shy young girls wove mats in the afternoon, their sudden outbursts of laughter scattering when their favorite *kane* strolled by.

Although I was a chief's daughter, I had the curiosity of any young girl. It was in my heart to join the *wahine* under the shade of the trees, but I knew that I couldn't because my sacred *kapus* kept me inside during the day. I understood that I was special; and that both my mother and brother had definite plans for me. "You are no longer a child," my brother kept reminding me as he gazed upon me in a way I did not, at the time, understand.

If she were around, my mother would place her hand on his arm and say, "Not yet. Be patient. Wait." I did not have any idea what she was asking him to wait for, but a few months later I was to find out another meaning of the word womanhood.

In the daytime I stayed with my mother in the compound reserved for the *alii*. My *kapus* were so severe that I dared not reveal myself lest some unsuspecting commoner, crossing too close to the chiefly quarters, accidentally let his shadow fall on the walls of my *hale*. For that infraction his punishment was death, plain and simple. Mother always taught me that it was my duty to guard my sacred body so that an innocent *makaainana* would not lose his life over my carelessness or inattention. But at night, when the sun went down and my shadow was no longer a danger, I spent more and more time enjoying the hula, chants and *meles* at my brother's court. As the night wore on, I was fascinated by the rowdy games that resulted in varying sexual liaisons among the women's retainers and the chief's guards.

Keoua, one of two *hanai* brothers from my uncle's court on Hawaii, visited Kamehamehanui's court often. Handsome young chief that he was, Keoua could have had any woman in court, but more than once I caught him glancing in my direction. I was allowed to watch the beginning of the games, however my brother made sure I could never participate in the outcome. My virginity, my most sacred possession, was closely guarded. When the games built in intensity, I was hustled from the court. It was then that I noticed my brother also staring in my direction. Other men noticed too, and from then on, every man began to look differently at me, and I, differently, in their direction.

Kamehamehanui was the ruler of Maui but I was, in many ways, the most important member of his court. "Soon you will understand just how special you are," my brother repeated over and over to me. It did not take me long to understand that he was thinking of ways he could use me, the virginal sacred woman, to gain favor with the other chiefs. The thought scared me even though I had been groomed from childhood to know what was expected of me. Now I was no longer a child, but instead a budding young woman—one whose beauty was as sought after as any prize--even more worthwhile was my pure bloodline. It was expected that I would lose my maidenhead to my brother to keep that bloodline in tact and the sacred *mana* flowing strongly in our family line. I was the favored at his court. A healthy offspring was any man's desire, but if my brother and I had a child, our child would be *naupio* –a sacred *alii* offspring from full brother and sister, the most sacred child in all the islands. If the child was a boy, he would become ruler of Maui—of that there was absolutely no question; if the child a girl, she would become a sacred seer and a high-ranking chiefess. It was my duty to keep the royalty in our family as well as give the *makaainana* the assurance of the most direct route to our guardian spirit, my *aumakua*, Kihawahine, the *mo-o*. The more I thought about it, the more I came to understand I was part of plan that stretched back generations--a plan much bigger than myself.

And so I waited, biding my time, until one day I was summoned to my mother's *hale*. "Your monthly bleed is regular," she said. "It is your time."

———◆———

*T*he retainers were given precise instructions in order to prepare me for my full blossoming into womanhood. I was pampered even more. Only the gentlest *lomi lomi* practitioners were allowed to touch me as they rubbed *kukui* oil into my skin, kneading and stroking every inch of my body with their strong hands. Others ran their fingers through my dark wavy mane, anointing my hair with coconut oil until it shone. Through the doorway of my *hale* I glimpsed the women *kapa* makers beating *wauke* bark, passing it on to others who stamped decorations of the sun, our sister Hina the moon, and the many stars in the night sky on the soft, finely made cloth. Still others wove *hala* into carrying baskets and sleeping mats. All this was in preparation for me—only for me--for I was to be further initiated into the *Hale o Papa*, the *heiau* where only women worshipped.

At the end of my coddling and training, I was the talk of the royal court. My brother sent his runners all over Maui to invite the strongest men to test their skills against each other. He summoned his paddlers and had them push their canoes from shore, sending them to the outer islands, calling the all the chiefs to assemble at his court. Every day more warriors gathered and displayed their manly arts. Even though they knew I was not to be their prize, there were plenty of other women at court who would be entranced by their strength and bravery. In order to feed the growing crowd, my brother commanded the hunters to foray deep into the mountains and bring back only the largest wild pigs. When the fishermen learned that the hunters had been sent off, they came to court offering the choicest mullet. *Opihi* pickers lined the rocky cliffs and risked being swept away by rogue waves as they plucked the small black shellfish delicacies in order to win the chief's favor. *Kalo* was gathered in increasingly large bundles from the fields and pounded into *poi*.

---

The afternoon shadows lengthened on the first night of the full moon, *Akua*. The *makaainana* spent the final hour of daylight hustling about the village, rounding up their hens and roosters and shoving the squawking birds under calabashes to keep them silent. The commoners pulled down the *kapa* cloth covering over the doorways of the *hales*, muzzled their dogs, and huddled their children next to them so as to maintain complete silence. Those with small children fled with their babes into the upland caves to be away from the strictness of the *kapus*, for a child's cry or innocent misstep would endanger the whole family. As the final rays of the sun set over the horizon, the priest's guards stood watch. The standard bearers, holding the long turtle shell handles in both hands, waved the *kahili* to warn of our movement through the village. As we moved to the women's *heiau*, *puloulou*, taboo sticks, were put in place to announce the night-long rite. Any living thing that made noise would be put to death—crowing rooster, whimpering dog, crying child—even a man who sneezed.

In the *heiau*, drummers stood behind the huge *pahus*, carved from the trunks of coconut trees. The reverberations from the taut sharkskin drumheads echoed down the valley and rolled like thunder to the sea. Soon it seemed the sounds of the throbbing drums came from every direction.

"Are you nervous?" my mother asked, whispering in my ear as she stood beside me. "These ceremonies are as important as the day you were born. The priestesses have been waiting for you all this time."

I trembled with excitement as I followed my mother down the path to the women's temple to be honored and welcomed into womanhood via more sacred rites. Deep into the night the women chanted a special prayer for conception. At first I gorged myself on the eight broiled *kanawao* fruits and two eggs I was offered. Many goddesses walked among us that night, whispering secret after secret into my tender ears. The women chanted and brought our family gods to earth with the *pule* to increase our family line. For five days I remained at the temple with the priestesses, eating nothing but the sacred food and repeating the prayers until I had learned all the sacred movements and prayers by heart. Only after the women were satisfied at my knowledge did they remove the taboo sticks from in front of the women's *heiau* and released the *kapu* on the village.

The next night the royal court convened. I, rare and delicate, like *ahinahina*, the silver sword plant that grows at the heights of Haleakala and nowhere else, was ripe for the plucking. The firelight highlighted my perfect skin and I glistened as bright as the star *Hokulea*. Little did I understand that, like the voyagers that followed the star, my journey was only beginning.

# Four

## 1740

After a brief ceremony, my brother, chief of Maui, and I joined in *niau-pio* rites wherein I became my brother's wife. Maybe it was because Kamehamehanui was my brother and he really cared, maybe it was because he wished our child to be conceived in the best possible way, maybe it was the sacredness of our blood joining with that of our ancestors—who is to say? Most of that night and those that followed remains a blur to me even now, but what I remember and know from the very bottom of my heart is the fact that I was absolutely certain the moment our child was conceived.

Even though both my retainers and I assured my brother that I had kept my sacred vows and invited no other man to my mat, Kamehamehanui had guards stand at my doorway night and day to make sure. After a few months, when the priestesses determined my pregnancy viable and it could be proven there had been absolutely no other claims to fatherhood, I was fussed over. The more my belly protruded, the faster my every wish was granted. My brother, the proudest man in court, strutted like a rooster, for no matter whether the child was a boy or girl, he would be the father of the most sacred person in all the islands. We had fulfilled our duty to our family and ancestors. Our bloodline remained pure—it had always been so.

Even though every woman told me what to expect, and were there to help me in every possible way, I was young and this was my first child. I was terrified when the first labor pains began. The priestesses calmed me with their chanting, beginning my genealogical chant with Papa and Wakea, the first woman and man, so that I might understand to the very roots of my being that birth was a natural process and that this child was fulfilling my family's destiny. My mother held my hand. Thankfully the goddesses saw to the birth, and anymore, the details remain fuzzy.

"The pure children are the most difficult," my mother whispered in my ear. "I should know--I had you and your brothers. If I can do it, you can do it."

All and all, it was a very long night on the birthing stone. In the hour before dawn, my daughter, Kalanikauiokikilo Kalaniwaiakua Kekumanomanookekapu, the chiefess whose head is held high in the daytime, slipped into this world. From the very beginning, I knew she would not be mine to raise. She was so sacred and her *mana* so strong that she was given to the priestesses to bring up in the bosom of our ancestors. Love her, I most certainly did, but she was a child of Maui and not mine to care for. Like all my family, she had the birthright of the prostrating *kapu*, *kapu moe*, which meant that none of the *makaainana* must ever see her face. Everyone in my family had that *kapu*--we knew our retainers and most everyone at court by their backs, not their faces. To Kalaniakua also went the sacred-fire-burning-at-midday *kapu*, which meant that during certain times of the month, her head always had to be positioned toward the sun. She was destined to be a *kilo*, a great seer, because she was of the highest rank and closest to the gods. She would be a heavenly summer-star gazer: one who would look into the heavens and see the future. Her *aumakua*, of course, was Kihawahine, the *mo-o* goddess of the fishponds, who brought prosperity to all who worshipped her.

# *Five*

## 1745

*A*fter being assured by the women in the court that I had regained a full year of regular menstruation after the birth of my daughter and that my young body was sufficiently recovered and healthy, my brother carried through with his plans. There were only a few men in all the royal courts in the island chain that were of high enough rank to be considered suitable mates for me. In truth, I would have preferred being sent to our cousins on Kauai, far away from the conflict and strife that seemed to be building between Hawaii and Maui.

One day my brother called me to his court. He sent away all his retainers, leaving only the guards at the door. "There is only one place for you," he began. "One place where you can do the most for our family and for the *makaainana*—for it is by their prosperity that we, in turn, prosper. You do want to live out your destiny to the fullest, don't you?"

"Of course," I assured him as I bowed my head in subservience to the chief. What else was there for me to say? Even though I was still somewhat innocent, I understood the wiles of the court well enough to know there was little I could have done to avert whatever plan he had made.

"I know it's going to be a lot to ask of you, but I ask you to be a peace of-fering in order to avert a war." And then, seemingly without a thought for my own wishes, he revealed his plan to marry me off to the brothers from Hawaii.

"They—and particularly Keoua, the handsome younger brother who has spent so much time at our court--have shown intense interest in you. Now that you have proven your worth by bearing a child…"

Although I knew Keoua's manner to be gentle, and observed that he was well loved by everyone…still… I did not want to leave my island. As for his elder brother, Kalaniopuu, I found him, in a word, severe. Even though Kalani followed protocol faithfully, his mean-streak was often rumored, so much so that it was no longer a rumor, but had been firmly established as fact. From his birth the honor of ruling chief was bestowed upon Kalaniopuu, and he had been trained as a fierce warrior and groomed by our common uncle, Alapai, for the job. Keoua had a much easier time of it, and his personality had developed along more amiable lines.

When I became aware that the Hawaii chiefs and my brother had seriously discussed plans for my future, the only thing I could think of to do was throw myself to the sharks.

Somehow my brother must have sensed my inner thoughts. He increased the number of retainers, ordering them to watch over me night and day, and true to their duty, they never left my side. When I went to the bathing pond—the one place I could have been alone--guards surrounded me. Maybe they were there to protect my womb from intruders, my brother having promised the brothers that I was ready to bear another child; maybe they were there to see that I didn't take action on the suicidal thoughts that swirled in my head. But how could he read my inner mind? Was he capable of such a feat, or did he have the priests probing my thoughts? I never knew. Maybe my mother knew—maybe she could feel my thoughts when we stood at the women's altar during our daily adulations. I had heard stories about my ancestor, Kihawahine, who as a young woman was transformed and became a *mo-o* guardian at her death. Maybe if I were to take my own life, I would be considered a suitable sacrifice as well, and I could help my people from the other world… maybe…maybe…

I lay awake nights staring out the doorway at the swirling stars and fretted until I made myself sick.

After awhile my mother noticed dark circles forming under my eyes and intervened. "What are you worried about, my dear?"

"Maybe it would be easier to be eaten by a shark," I cried, feeling relief at having released my fears into my mother's bosom.

"You have a life to fulfill that is far greater than you know," she assured me as she patted my back and dried my tears. "And you have a grave duty to your people."

"You sound just like my brother!"

"You cannot take your responsibility lightly—more people than you can imagine depend on you daily. And even more will depend on you in the future."

I shrugged her off. Even though I had been raised to honor the gods and knew that was my destiny, I was young. My thoughts strayed more to myself than how I could be of help to others.

Mother could tell I was not convinced. "Maybe I shouldn't tell you this yet—maybe it's not the time for you to know." She stopped and waited to see if she had peaked my curiosity. When I lifted my head, she continued, "The seers have predicted you will be the mother of a great chief."

My head swelled with pride. Suddenly it all made perfect sense to me, and I understood my destiny. There was, of course, the status of the assured purity of my royal blood. Still, there was the nagging thought that my brother was using me to court favor, using me as trade goods, although my budding arrogance assured me I was certainly trade goods of the finest kind.

The next day I snuck out from under the watchful eyes of my guardians and met Kamehamehanui on the path as he headed back to his *hale* after finishing his morning prayers with the priests. I stood in his way, my hands on my hips, and confronted him. I was so arrogant in my righteousness that he must have been amused. He was a large man, over seven feet tall. He stopped and looked down on me, his kind eyes twinkling as I exclaimed, "You're using me."

"You could say as much," he murmured, deflecting my pointed statement.

His thinly veiled answer fanned the flames of my rage. "To you I am nothing but a white *keokeo* in the game of *konane*," I shouted. "I am but a small white pebble being moved around in a game between chiefs. You have no regard for me or my life!"

"You are playing a very costly role…"

"Costly?!" I screamed and stamped my foot. "Costly to whom?"

"Costly to me," he shot back, his voice dripping with anger at my insolent behavior. He glared at me, but then softened, "And costly to the *makaainana,* for they are the ones who have to fight. And they are the ones who will be kept alive to suffer if they should lose the war." He stared off into the distance. "Me? They will sacrifice me immediately and use my bones for fish hooks." He took my hand and walked with me to the edge of his compound. He sat down at his favorite resting place and gazed out over the fertile *kalo* fields. He patted the stone beside him and I sat down. The cerulean waters of Kahuli Bay shimmered in the distance. "The chiefs of Hawaii like to fight. Kalani and his brother sometimes call the people on their own island enemies. Can you imagine? Their plan is to take over that island and they are succeeding. Now I fear they look across the waters to us. I can feel they are hungry."

"So, we will feed them," I said innocently. "We have plenty of food."

"It's true—they are probably not as well cared for on their island as we are here, but they're hungry in a different way. They are hungry for our fertile lands. Like sharks, they circle at the smell of blood. And like sharks, eventually they will open their mouths and gobble up everything that swims in front of them. It is better for everyone that I should retain the rule of our island and not go to war. It is my fondest wish to remain at peace. With peace, everyone wins." He glanced at me to see if I understood. "Everyone keeps their lives." He patted my knee. "But I must give the men of Kau something to distract them. I chose to give them the sweetest gift I could possibly think of, my sister / wife."

"But ..."

"The task I ask of you won't be easy. Keep the peace, if you can. It will take all the courage and intelligence you have. The people of this island are depending on you. You are being given the most important job on both islands."

"But they are Keawe," I argued. "The men of that family have spilled their seed all over the islands—*alii* and *makaainana* alike. Their blood is not pure."

"All the more reason the sacredness of your pure blood is important to them," he said. "It will increase their *mana* tenfold—maybe more. You have no idea how precious you are."

"But I am..."

"Play the game well and you will be the mother of a chief," he assured me.

"That is the second time I have heard that prophecy. How dare you keep me in the dark! It's my life! Why was I not told years ago?"

"Because it was of little consequence then," he said, dismissing my question with a flick of his hand, something as inconsequential to him as a fly that buzzed too near his ear. "But now it is. Time will tell." He arose, and then looked down at me. "My advice is to always pay attention to the priest's prophecies. They are never wrong."

---

*A*nd with that, Kamehamehanui sent an emissary to Hawaii. In a few weeks the canoes returned laden with presents for me, and thereby the deal was cinched. All the gifts really were not necessary; I, truly, was the prize. In the meantime, I looked at the men in my brother's court as if a new light shone upon them. Suddenly I found many young men to my liking. Of course I flirted, and the men flirted back, but my brother allowed no close contact with those who flocked around me at court. And truthfully, even though some were clearly interested, none of them wanted to risk their lives for a short dalliance with me. My brother placed guards who curled up like dogs on my doorstep each night. Everyone understood my destiny.

---

*T*he same as it always had, the sun rose, glowing like a brilliant yellow blossom on the *hau* tree. Roosters let loose from their overnight cages pranced around the village, crowing to lay claim to their territory for another day. Village dogs padded across the compound softly. Men stood in the doorways of their sleeping huts, rubbing dream dust from their eyes and then stretched to greet the day. Fishermen hefted their nets and headed for the shore, the carefully woven webbing dangling down their backs.

It was a day like any other, and yet, for me, it wasn't. My mother, who usually called to me to deliver my brother's morning meal, did not call. Instead the high priest came to tell me my brother was deep in prayer at the *heiau*. "He sends his *aloha*. Until then…" he said as he blessed me. "Fulfill his wishes. They are not only for him, but for the well-being of all the people of this island."

"But…"

The old priest smiled. "He said to tell you to fulfill his wishes and it won't be long until you are safe in his court again."

My mother, braver than my brother in many ways, came at last to bid me farewell. She held both my hands in hers, and then pulled me close as she touched her forehead to mine as she inhaled my breath. "Be strong, my sweet. You are exalted and will bring blessings to many." With that, she retreated to her *hale*.

Tears streamed down my cheeks as the priest ushered me down the hill to the beach. He walked right behind me and kept me from turning my head to look over my shoulder. "I must be brave," I whispered to myself over and over, but I did not believe a word I said.

The canoe was prepared, the paddlers waited. There was nothing for me to do. I gripped the gunwales on either side of the canoe as it was pushed from shore. Then the paddlers dug their blades into the sea and we sailed over the breakers into deeper water. The men took up a steady rhythm and the canoe gained speed, cutting straight through Kahului Bay. Great sobs stretched up from deep within my *naau*. I tipped my head back and wailed, piercing the air with my cries. There was no one but the paddlers to hear. The spirits of the air gathered my screams and fed them to the wind, which carried them far out to sea. I hung over the side of the canoe and let the tears roll down my cheeks and drop into the sea, but my puny tears only rippled the surface and did nothing to make the the vast ocean wetter. The paddler behind me splashed me and I turned to berate him. He jerked his head over his shoulder, pointing me to the lush *kalo* fields of Wailuku. "Look carefully and remember, my chiefess," he said, not missing a stroke.

My heart was breaking. I could not breathe. And yet I soaked in the scene, memorizing every rock, every field, and each *puu*. Gone were my mother and brother; gone was life as I had known it. Would I ever see home and my precious island again?

Down the eastern coast of Maui the men paddled, past Piilani *heaiu* and the sea caves at Wainapanapa. The men had their orders and kept their silence.

My knuckles turned white from gripping the sides of the canoe. When the time came to relieve myself, the man sitting behind me first had to pry my fingers loose. He averted his eyes as I hung my bottom over the side of the canoe, but he did not stop paddling. The sea became rougher after we left Nanualele Point at Hana and headed across Alenuihaha Channel. The chop splashed over the sides and one man's job was to drop his paddle and use half a coconut shell to bail when the water in the bottom of the canoe came up to our ankles. As the sea swirled about us in the middle of the channel, I became nauseous. I bent over the side of the canoe and vomited, my throat burning as I heaved up the little I had eaten. I was so sick I could no longer hold on to the sides of the canoe and I slumped forward. I just wanted to lie down in the bottom of the canoe, longing for the sloshing water to splash in my face, offering welcome relief.

The man behind me put down his paddle, reached over my seat, and pulled me upright. Not only did he break a sacred *kapu* by actually touching me, but he also, once again, broke his silence, "My chiefess. You must sit up. It is worse down there."

I groaned, barely able to utter, "You have no idea how sick I am."

"You must sit up," he repeated as he wrapped a coarse coconut rope around each wrist and tied me to my seat. "This is for your own good. Spot something in the distance—focusing on the horizon line will help—and keep your eye on it."

Easier said than done. When we reached the top of a wave I could see land, but as we surfed down the slope of the wave my stomach lurched upward, finding its home somewhere at the back of my throat. As we began the arduous climb up the other side of the swell, my stomach settled briefly. When we balanced for a moment on the top of the wave, I could catch my breath and spot the cliffs of Kohala in the distance. Then we'd plummet down the churning water on the other side of the wave, only to begin the assent. I was certain that at any moment the ocean would open its deadly maw and swallow us whole: the men, the canoe and me.

It really didn't matter what I thought or felt. The men paddled on.

After what seemed like several lifetimes, we were across the channel and nearer the shore. At least having the safety of land closer eased my mind. The sea still slithered by, but the fact that I could see land, pick out individual trees, and focus on each deep valley helped to settle me down. As we traveled down the Hamakua coast, the men pointed out the six valleys: Palolu, Honokea, Ohiahuea, Waikaloa, Kaimu, Waimanu. Just as the sun went down that evening, we turned toward shore at the seventh valley, sacred Waipo.

The canoe rode the breaker all the way to the beach. The men jumped out on the sand at the last minute to pull the canoe over the rubble past the high tide mark. The man behind me untied my hands, gently pried my stiff fingers off the seat, and lifted me out. I thought I would be so glad to have my feet upon solid earth, but to my surprise, it didn't feel that way at all. My body had become so accustomed to swaying with the canoe that my legs collapsed under me as soon as he put me down. I could not take even one step before my knees buckled. No one seemed to care that he broke protocol again when he lifted me up and carried me to the visitor's hut. He laid me down on the mat and instructed the women to massage my arms and legs until feeling returned. Food was brought. Although I was hungry—or thought I should be—my stomach turned over at the sight and smell of it, and I pushed most of it away without so much as a nibble. I tried to sleep, but every time I laid my head on the mat, the room swirled and I had to sit up. The night wore on. My retainers, who were in little better shape than I, moved my mat so I could lean against a post. Sitting up, I finally nodded off and got a few hours sleep.

In the excitement of the night before, someone forgot to put their rooster under the calabash, and his crowing woke the whole village up before dawn. The women insisted I eat something, saying it would help settle my stomach. Although I was past the point of being hungry, I complied. As we came out from under the shelter of the ironwood trees toward the beach, I saw black sand for the first time. I bent down and picked up a handful of the coarse grain and let it sift through my fingers. Had it been there last night? Surely it had, but I had been so sick I had not noticed. Better that I pay attention, I told myself. As I climbed into the canoe and took my seat, my only prayer was to ask the powers that be for a day better than yesterday.

The men stood ready next to the canoe. The man behind me held the cords that he had used to tie my hands to my seat.

I glanced down at the red welts on each wrist and could not bear to be shackled for another day. "No!" I shouted when he reached for my wrists. "What will happen to me if the canoe capsizes? Will you be the one to answer to the chief? Will you be the one to tell my brother, or the chiefs of Hawaii, that their most precious one drowned?"

"She doesn't want to be tied down," he said as he looked up at the rest of the crew. The men consulted each other, deciding I was right—perhaps I was in more danger tied than free. They shrugged their shoulders in resignation and waited while he helped me get settled in the canoe. They pushed off from the sand, the last man piled in, and we were on our way.

We spent an easy morning riding an offshore current that pushed us southeast. As we neared each new geographical feature the man behind me called out its name, which meant nothing to me for I was not acquainted with the island at all. The dense jungle hung from the cliffs and seemed familiar because it reminded me of my homeland on the windward side of Maui. But farther inland I could not see sharp ridgelines and valleys, but rather the gigantic slope of a mountain that seemed to spread out forever. Thus we journeyed all day, the vast mountain on our right. The man behind me said we were fortunate to see Mauna Kea because it was usually covered in clouds. He told me myths of the fire goddess, Pele, and her sister Poliahu, goddess of snow, to distract me.

I was not intimately acquainted with the goddesses of this island. Of course I had heard stories since I was a *keiki*, but suddenly I realized the stories were not just stories to amuse a child, but legends about actual places, and I paid closer attention. For me, now, there was no sense looking back over my shoulder. With each dip of the paddles, the thought occurred to me that it was the farthest I'd ever been from my home island. The past was receding. I could only look ahead to the future.

We passed Hilo far from shore, but I could see the village spread out along the beach. I begged to visit, thinking that we could be guests for a few days. I was certain the people would be thrilled to have royalty such as myself at their court. Truthfully, it was not that I cared so much about visiting that particular village, although I had heard of it for years, but simply because I wanted to feel land under my feet.

Traveling along the Puna coast, we were caught up in a swift current that swept us further and further from shore. The land changed from the lushness of jungle to miles and miles of dark gray lava. I had seen lava before of course, but nothing like the flows that stretched down the slope. I was entering a foreign land. Not even a bird flew out to greet us. The men had their orders and, like the desolate, craggy rocks, kept their silence as they bent over their paddles, their muscles straining from two long days of travel. I knew it would be dangerous if the current carried us out of the sight of land. I tried to sit lightly in the canoe so they would not feel my weight as a burden. Toward late afternoon they maneuvered the canoe out of the strong current as we rounded the eastern-most tip of the island.

"Kumukahi," the man behind me said, pointing with his paddle. "The point where the day breaks first on the land."

We stopped for the evening at the warm, soothing springs at Ahalanui. Like the men, I was so relieved to soak my weary *iwi*, battered as I was from two long days of voyaging and not much sleep. I slipped into the warm pool and stretched out. I would have gladly spent several days there soaking the ache from my bones, but our journey was not complete and I was roused from my sleeping mat before daybreak.

The tide had gone out during the night and the ocean was calm. We made good time. As the sun came up on our left, the winds and the sea awoke. The paddlers fought their way through the rough water along the southern coast of the island.

I looked shoreward and saw trees in the *kipuka* aflame as lava coursed down the side of Mauna Loa, the long mountain, from the crater at Kilauea. Great walls of steam rolled out to greet us where lava poured into the sea.

"Only breathe when the air is clear," the man behind me instructed. "Don't breathe when the clouds roll by. The vapor is poison."

Stories and chants told around the fire at night came alive for me at that moment. I had not really believed such things existed until I saw them with my own eyes. It was as my brother and mother said--the world was much bigger than I had ever imagined. At times I thought I could see the body of Pele twisting in the steam, her sister, Namakaokahai, writhing in the foam as they battled for control of the island. All day long the men paddled as we watched the sisters clash. The sun sank below the horizon and I began to think we were never going to land. The men seemed unconcerned as they journeyed on, but I was afraid that we would spend the night at sea. The rising moon glinted on the water and I sensed, rather than saw, that we'd rounded yet another point. Nudging the canoe closer to the shore, the men slowed now and then, as if searching for something. I looked over their broad shoulders and tears filled my eyes. I saw the light of welcoming fires on the shore and heard people shouting as they guided the men in the final sprint over the reef toward the beach.

When the canoe pulled up on the sand, the men's families gathered to greet them.

I tried to stand, but once again my legs buckled under me. That same man (although I never knew his name, I thought of him as my savior) gently lifted me from the canoe and hustled me away to a *hale*. He barked at one of the women, who eventually brought me a meager meal. Though by this time I was ravenous, I could not eat; even water did not stay in my stomach long. I was left alone with my retainers, some of whom had been seasick themselves. They gathered around me in the middle of the room.

"We are in Kau," my calabash bearer informed me. "At the southern end of this island." She did not say I was as far away from home as I could possibly be.

Even though I was on land, I felt weak, and if I turned my head too fast in either direction I became so dizzy that I had to reach down with both hands to steady myself on the mat. I had never felt so strange—so out of place.

"You must be exhausted, my chiefess," the women said as they fussed and soothed me.

At last I could keep my eyes open no longer.

"Rest…" I heard someone say as they propped me up against a *hale* pole. "And tomorrow will be much better."

The next morning, I was allowed to sleep until I woke up. A woman—a stranger-- waited just inside my door, bowing low when she saw I was awake. I rubbed the sleep from my eyes. "Where are my retainers?"

"Gone."

"Where have you sent them?" I inquired foolishly.

"Back to Maui, where they belong." The woman turned and summoned those who were to be my new retainers.

I swallowed my feelings and pushed them down deep, hoping my fear would not show, for I was now alone among an island full of strangers. I pulled the mask of indifference down over my face and somehow got through the day. Since I was dizzy when I moved about too much, I was left to doze. Every time I opened my eyes, strange women stared at me. I waited until I was alone that evening before I cried my first bitter tears. That night I dreamed I was flying over the canoes that carried my retainers across the channel. I wished I were with them—far from this alien land.

I awoke the next morning no longer so wobbly. My battle with the sea was replaced by another sickness that lodged itself in my bones. I was undeniably homesick.

I wanted the familiarity of my own retainers, the warmth of white sandy beaches, and the supreme comfort of looking across a stretch of water at another island in the distance. What I had was strangers, black sand, and the vastness of the sky and ocean. Instead of the lush verdant valleys of my home island, I found myself staring across undulating fields of barren lava. Instead of bathing in a clear pool beside a waterfall and sunning myself on soft warm sand, I cleaned myself with brackish salt water and stretched out to dry on a hard, charcoal-colored rock. No more could I see Haleakala, nor even the clouds that surrounded it. Instead I looked out across a desolate landscape at an endless cloudline bunched along the horizon.

Nothing.

Forever.

Wherever I turned my head, emptiness surrounded me. Pahulu, the god of nightmares, crept under my *kapa* night covering and lay beside me. He brought me visions of molten lava rolling down the mountainside, engulfing everything in the village. Night after night, I woke up screaming.

"You will get used to it," I was told and left alone to calm myself.

During the daylight hours, I grieved in silence for my home and family, beseeching the gods, "Will I ever see my family again? My own island?" And, night after night, I cried myself to sleep only to be accompanied by more hideous dreams.

"You must bury your homesickness. It is the source of your pain," I was told by an older woman of the court who tried to help me. She was kind, taking pity on me as she would a child. Of course in my own selfishness, I thought she did it for me. No doubt she had her own reasons—she was tired of being awakened at night by my screams. The ladies my own age, unusually hard-hearted I thought, said nothing. At the time I did not know the ways of the world and did not understand their silence for what it was: jealousy. Were it not for me, one of them might have been chosen to be in service to the handsome and highly popular high chief, Keoua, or be wed to his brother, Kalaniopuu, the one who had been groomed to be ruler over his land. I vowed that when I gained my rightful position in court, I would remember the treatment of both the kind and the cruel and model benevolent behavior.

"Keep the peace," I heard my brother and mother whisper in my ear each time my temper threatened to flare. "Keep the peace. You are a child of Maui. You are sacred. Your job is to keep the peace."

By and by I became used to swallowing my words. I did as they said: dulled my feelings and dried my tears.

"This is your new home. This is your island," the women of the court assured me. "Turn your thoughts to the future and new life, for soon you will bring it forth."

I had little doubt the words the women were saying would prove to be true, for I knew my destiny was to be the mother of a chief.

The brothers were, of course, anxious to wed, but they yielded when the women told them I was not fully adjusted yet. I had the idea that the longer I made them wait, the more they would want me. Whether that proved to be the case or not, I'll never know. Finally, the older women told me they could postpone the anxious chiefs no longer and the wedding would have to take place. Much to my surprise, they had been preparing for the event all along, and I had very little to do with it. The *punalua* wedding was held and I assumed my place in the family as the wife of both men. I will never forget that day—it should have been one of the happiest days of my life, but for me it was one of the saddest.

The first night I lay under the mat with the older brother, Kalaniopuu. Since up to that point I had only been with my brother, the ceremony with the priestesses and then his gentle, loving way was what I had expected. Imagine my shock when Kalani threw the *kapa* covering back and descended upon me. He pursued his endeavor with rigor, which was the way it was to be with him thereafter. After several weeks, the women finally noticed my increasing haggard condition, took pity on me, and stepped in to relieve me of his proddings. They assured him there would be plenty of time and got him to calm down, thus giving me a few nights of much-needed rest.

———

*W*ithout the safety and comfort of my family, honored at court though I was, it took some time to be accepted into a new family and homeland. I was but an outsider—a foreign fledgling introduced to the Keawe family nest. Within the limits of my *kapus*, I was free to move about the compound provided for me, but of course I could not leave during the day lest my shadow fall on the unexpecting. Nor was I free to move about the island, which really didn't matter because I had no idea where to go. I looked at the hillside and sensed that even if I tried to escape, I would not survive long in this unforgiving land. There was no water, no shade--nothing, it seemed, but endless mounds of undulating lava. I knew that if I were to set out on my own, I would become lost in no time. I pictured myself starving to death in the middle of a sea of rock. I asked myself, 'Who are these strangers?' Having heard stories of jealousy and treachery from the earliest days at my father's court, and seeing it exhibited in this court, I trusted no one. I had never felt so alone.

# Six

## 1748

Homesickness crawled in and curled around my heart, making itself at home and settling in for a long stay. I remember one of the many nights I visited the marriage hut with Kalani. "With you it is like planting my *o-o* in dry ground," he complained.

"The soil is softer after a gentle rain," I answered, hoping that he would understand the subtlies of the marriage mat, but to him, it meant he should plant twice as deep and he rammed his digging stick harder. After he finished spilling his seed, we lay together under the double *kapu* mat. He looked down at me. "Are you crying because you're so happy?" he asked.

I dared not tell him the truth. I tucked my chin to my chest and nodded the briefest assent. That was all he wanted to know—that I agreed with him. I knew then that it was only the first of the many lies I would tell him, for he was the kind of man who was easily satisfied with lies rather than be bothered with the truth.

Not so much to show his concern for me as to show his incredible strength, he picked me up and carried me to my sacred hut where I lived surrounded by strangers. Bronze-skinned warriors encircled the compound that was enclosed by a tall, spiked fence. I was not allowed to leave, for under the sacred nuptial rites, I would be a virtual prisoner until the priests were satisfied I was pregnant with his child. I prayed for release—either by death or by fertility.

There was nothing for me to do but pray. I prayed for the people, for the land, for good fishing—for some relief in this desolate land. While I was praying, Kalani was also praying—for a child. He consulted with his priests who performed many rituals of insemination. They had calculated my body rhythms in relationship to the moon and knew exactly when to send him to pump me full of Keawe seed. All were excited when I announced to the women that I had missed my bleed—a clear sign I was pregnant. By announcing the answer to Kalani's prayers, I thought I would be released. But no-- I was kept secluded longer— surrounded, yet alone. As closely as both the guards and the retainers watched over me--never mind the intense scrutiny of the women of the family--there was absolutely no doubt that Kalani was the father. Only when it was obvious that I was *hapai*, pregnant--that Kalani had firmly planted his seed, the sprout was growing, and that a sacred child was definitely on the way--was I allowed more freedom of movement in the family compound.

The priests were quick to predict a son. I did not know whether they actually had some secret method of influencing the gender of the child. Maybe they had seen a shooting star, or the water in the calabash had revealed the secret, or whether during one of their many rituals a pig's entrails had shown signs. Maybe they simply told Kalani what he wanted to hear, figuring they had a fifty-fifty chance and hoped for the best. I knew in my heart the child would be a son because of the prophecy of my brother's priests: I was to be the mother of a chief.

As my belly swelled, so did Kalani's chest. He strutted and crowed like a rooster that boasted at dawn, his whole torso inflating with regality. The thought of a new ruler of the southern region of the largest island was heralded with much pomp at court. I must have been somewhere between eighteen and twenty years old when Kiwalao was born, although inside I felt much, much older.

The *makaainana* were as thrilled as the king himself. Everyone understood that he was to be Kalaniopuu's heir. Kalani set out to make his son a warrior in his own image. Seemingly the gods had answered his prayers, but the first time he held his son Kalani did not bother to look deep into the child's eyes. Instead, he pulled back the bottom of the *kapa* cloth the child was wrapped in and closely checked to make sure this manchild had an *ule* and two *hua*. As soon as he saw Kiwalao had been delivered with the proper equipment, Kalani was satisfied, pulled the cloth back down across the child's loins, and handed him back to the child's nurse. In his excitement, he had not looked into his son's eyes to see what kind of a person he had in his hands.

I admit I had the advantage of forming our son's personality in that I had been living with the child for months as he grew in my *opu*, and I had done some praying myself. Kalani may have gotten the physical child he wanted, but this child's soul was not one of a warrior. I can vouch for that—I did not form the child in my womb to be a fighter. I did not mold his temperament for those ends. I molded exactly what I wanted: a calm, gentle soul. I could see into the child's spirit and I knew deep in my heart his soul was a reflection of my own. I willed this man to be a peace seeker.

Kalani called for his most esteemed warriors, the Alapa, and made his captains promise to teach the child *lua*, the art of bone breaking, as soon as he was old enough.

"Stop!" I told him. "The child has been in this earthly body for only a few days and already you're making him a man killer. Just stop! I don't want him sent away to the caves like your nephew, Kamehameha, because of the chief's fears. If anyone is going to kill anyone, let it be the guards who are entrusted with our son's safety."

That statement brought Kalani up short, reminding him of the chiefs who wanted his nephew killed because they feared his inherent power. Thereafter, Kalani stationed extra guards around the compound—all the time boasting of the importance of his son.

After the end of the day, when I was finally allowed to hold my son and quiet him for sleep, I smiled to myself. The prophets were right: I am the mother of a chief. As the nurse took the sleeping child from my arms, I dropped off into a deep slumber, dreaming of how our two families could unite to build a legacy.

# *Seven*

## 1750

*I*f I had understood how tender Keoua would prove to be and how much he wanted to please me, even before our lovemaking, I would have welcomed him to the marriage bed sooner. Quite unlike his stormy brother, Keoua was like the gentle rain that nourishes the land. So it was no surprise to me that not long after, from my loins a daughter was born. Fatherhood was granted to Keoua because the child was a girl, although, truthfully, it could have been either brother. Keoua was thrilled at the chance to claim her, just as he claimed fatherhood for Kamehameha, the boy being raised in the caves—the one who had been named after my brother, Kamehamehanui. Keoua bragged that his new daughter and the boy child they call 'the lonely one' would someday join and have a *naupio* child. It hardly mattered to me at this point—let the priests and chiefs battle it out later. Actually Keoua's happiness from claiming a child did my heart good.

This beautiful girl was named Kekuiapoiwa--"one who was sought for a lord"—in this case, the lord being Keoua, the seeking having been done by both brothers. She was named for my mother, but I called her Liliha, "heart sick" because, much as I tried to feel otherwise, I was simply that: heart sick. I could hardly bear being so unhappy.

At first the women assured me it was just because I was still so young. They told me that as I grew older and had more children I would become accustomed to childbirth and its accompanying mood swings. I tried to be cheerful for the sake of my daughter and my growing son, but sadness enveloped me like a veil pulled down over my eyes and I could not fight my way clear. Some of the women advised me that, given time, my mood swings would subside.

I so longed to nurse my daughter, but I am a chiefess. I had to hand over the care of my children to the nurses. My breasts ached as my milk came in. When I was allowed to hold her, milk poured out, gushing down as heavy rain, unleashing a heavenly torrent. I know that she sensed my milk was different than her nurse's because when I was near, she screamed and then lunged for my breasts. Sometimes I could not help myself and I insisted on holding her. Liliha's loud sucking noises made my milk flow faster. It broke my heart not to let her suckle as long as she wanted, but I was not allowed. Before the retainers could take her from me for the last time, I rubbed her face in my milk as it oozed from my nipples. I longed to have her soak in my smell; I sobbed as she was taken from me, her tongue licking her lips, lapping up my sweetness. She knew—she knew I was her mother. In the night when she cried and the nurse comforted her, my milk gushed and it was all I could do to choke back my jealousy. They took her away and didn't bring her to me—not even allowing me to hold her—until my milk stopped flowing and my breasts dried up. Eventually my feelings abated as well, leaving my *naau* with an echo as hollow as a bell stone.

Halfheartedly, I resumed my daily prayers for the health and prosperity of the people, for the *makaainana* in this barren land feared famine above all.

Sensing my indifference, one of my retainers suggested I might be happier if I took my children home to Maui for a short visit. "To meet their grandmother," the woman counseled, knowing no one could refuse the right of a chiefess to see the next generation.

I jumped at the idea, playing on Keoua's gentle nature and childhood on Maui when I made my request. "I wish to take my children to meet her Maui relatives. My daughter is named after her grandmother and it is time for them to meet."

"I admit, sometimes I am lonesome for the gusty winds of Hana," he replied.

"So you will join me?" I was elated at the thought. "You will be warmly welcomed at my brother's court."

"We will introduce our daughter to the warm sands of Wailuku," Keoua smiled. "I understand. I, too, have been away from Maui far too long."

Kalaniopuu granted permission for Kiwalao to accompany us on our journey, but made us promise we would return to Hawaii the moment he sent word.

For me, a ray of sunshine poked through the dark clouds and I felt I did not have to hold my breath any longer. I drew deep, cleansing air into my lungs. My heart, hanging so heavy in my chest, began to lighten as the men gathered to outfit the canoe and prepare for our travel.

Keoua insisted that a double canoe with a platform built across the hulls be used instead of the single outrigger canoe that brought me to the island years before. He even insisted on overseeing the small *hale* built between the hulls, our protection from wind, waves and rain. "Nothing is too good for my daughter," he said.

Every day I went down to the beach to observe the progress. Instead of dreading the long trip, I counted the days until we would be launched off the bleak rocks of Kau on Hawaii and deposited on the sparkling sands of Wailuku on my home island, Maui.

---

*A*ll Keoua's fussing had been worth it; the double canoe rode much easier on the waves and the trip was actually enjoyable. The sails caught the wind and we sped along. It was as if we were two *iwa*, two frigate birds, skimming over the water. I hardly noticed the island passing on my right. At Upolu Point the sails strained against the wind, thus the channel crossing to Hana was swift. Up the windward coast of Maui we glided. When we rounded the point at Pauwela, we were far enough out to sea that I spied the *heiua* of Pihana on the hill. It was just as I had remembered it that day I looked over my shoulder on my way to my new life. I burst into tears when my foot first touched the soft white sand at Wailuku, so thankful was I to be home among my own people.

My family clustered around us. Liliha and her brother, Kiwalao, blossomed under my family's care, the same as I. My brother welcomed Keoua to his court, plying him with every kindness. Keoua enjoyed his time as much as I did, but the day came, as we knew it would, when the canoes arrived on the shore. His brother was calling him back.

"I must return. There is no other way," he said as he reached across our sleeping child and touched my face tenderly.

Keoua sensed I was in no hurry to go back. I could not control myself, and wept. My heart was torn. Which should I choose, the father of my child or the land of my heart?

In the morning, my mother read my mood exactly. "Stay a little longer, my dear. Then return." To my husband she said, "See how the children flourish--and your wife as well? What is good for the mother is good for both children. Let her stay a little longer. Allow her to return to the backbone of her family from which she gains her strength."

So sweetly did my mother ask that he relented without the slightest hint of protest. He had seen that his daughter was a favorite of everyone, especially of his esteemed host, Kamehamehanui; he had seen how the women of the court lavished care on her. No one could resist that child—particularly her father. "I must go. I have been called to Hilo, but I will assure my brother in Kau that you will return," Keoua said. It was an order, really, but he was so gentle about his demands that I said yes without thinking. "Return when you are ready," he assured me, "But don't wait too long. I don't want to miss out on seeing my daughter grow."

———

A veil of calm and prosperity enveloped Maui, for my brother's island had been at peace for many years. It was such a contrast to the constant bickering I had escaped from at Kalani's court that it took me several weeks just to regain my balance. I could finally breathe again and let go of the constant vigilance I had embraced while in that foreign land to the south. Every day I gained strength. When I opened my eyes in the morning, I felt like I was waking up from a lingering nightmare. But after a few days I was able to allow my roots to embrace Maui soil again. Every day I felt myself getting stronger and slowly I began to regain my balance. Although I did not normally go out during the day, it was so wonderful to see the *kalo* leaves brushed by the breeze that I could not resist asking my *kalihi* bearers to accompany me to the *loi* occasionally just to drink in the lushness and peace. The farmers smiled when they heard us coming, and willingly abandoned their backbreaking work for an hour, leaving me free to wander and meditate. In fact, the farmers begged me to spend time in their *loi*, claiming the *kalo* recognized their chiefess and grew faster. In the afternoons I listened to the gentle trickling of water flowing over the stones as I soaked in a private freshwater pool.

Days turned into weeks, then weeks into months. I witnessed brother *kalo* grow from sprouts to the mature plants that sustain us all. As had been true since my brother had become ruler, peace prevailed on Maui. He believed that healthy, well-fed people were the most content. He understood that a man's proudest accomplishment is providing for his family, and that satisfied men and women invariably increase the wealth of the *alii*. My brother encouraged the farmers to wade up to their knees in the *loi*. He came out of his compound when the shadows lengthened at sunset and gazed at the fishermen throwing their nets out across the reef, hauling them in full. Kamehamahenui praised the men who paddled out to the deep water and came home with canoes loaded with *ahi*. He cheered when the hunters came down out of the mountains swinging fat pigs tied to the branches slung between their shoulders. He sang the praises of the bird catchers when they returned from their stay in the mountains, sacks full of precious feathers on their backs. At other times he would stop just to listen to the sounds of the village: the rhythm of women beating *kapa*, the squawk of the chickens when the toddlers gave chase. All his people were precious to him. Many are the times I saw him lean against a coconut tree, a smile slowly sliding across his face. "Healthy," he would nod and chuckle, and then move on to the temple for his prayers.

———

*I* performed my spiritual duties with renewed vigor, following closely in the footsteps of my mother and aunts as they tended the women's *heiaus*. I learned even more chants and gained more *mana*. I asked for rain at the appropriate time so that the *aina* would provide. I prayed to our *aumakua*, Kihawahine, for protection of the fishponds so there would be continued plenty for all.

Months folded into a year as Kiwalao and Liliha grew. Kiwalao joined the priests and began learning the chants and rituals. Liliha was strong-willed, but a darling child. Not even the severest priest could resist her smile and cheerful laughter.

Because Keoua had been passed over as supreme ruler, due mainly to his older brother's aspirations and birth order, he was able to leave court and travel back to Maui to join us occasionally. Keoua loved his daughter and missed her, but put up no arguments about us lingering at my brother's court. Although he didn't say, I think he felt blessed to be able to get away from the aggravation of court life in Hawaii and let the gentle breezes of Maui caress him. He could see both children were thriving; he knew I was happy. So even though he had to return to Hilo, he allowed me to continue to extend our stay.

———

*S*everal days after Keoua left, my brother emerged from a lengthy session with his *kahuna*. Liliha toddled across the compound to him. He bent down and plucked a delicate white *aluha* flower and tucked it behind Liliha's ear—something I would never have believed if I hadn't seen it with my own eyes. He wrapped his arms around her and lifted her up. She circled her arms around his massive neck, holding on tight. The softness in his eyes told the whole story: he was totally captivated by her.

"Oh, Liliha, you're like a little *opihi* clinging to the rock. Don't squeeze your uncle's neck so tight. Don't be a bother. He has important work to do," I said, taking my time as I strolled across the courtyard.

"Nonsense! She is no bother." He smiled as he shifted her to his hip.

"Take her now," I said as I waved for her caretaker, who bowed low as she took the child from the chief's arms. "We have things to talk about." I took my brother's elbow and led him to the courtyard where we could sit in the shade and be alone. "I have a proposal to put to you, my brother."

"And I one for you," he said.

"You first, then. You're the chief."

"I wish you could stay here on Maui and remain in my court…"

I was so thrilled at that news I almost bent over and kissed his feet. It felt like he had relieved me of heavy burden of underlying stress and I stretched my shoulders. In my enthsiasm I did not realize I had not let him finish his statement. "I would be honored to be in your court," I gushed.

"Before you agree to that, you must know that I want something in return." He sat close to me and took my hand.

"Anything," I said, as I squeezed his hand. "I mean it—anything."

He shifted, dropped my hand, his smile fading from his face. "What words do you hear from Kalani's court?"

"It's business as usual. Canoes are being built. The men fashion daggers and spears. There is continual gossip at court—alliances being formed and betrayed before they have a chance to blossom," I assured him. "They fight among themselves for every scrap of land. It's the same as always."

"I want to hear every detail. Tell me about Kamehameha. He seems to be a favorite with the women at court. He is still but a young man…"

I shrugged. "Those women's calabashes do not have lids. They are always open and anyone may dip from them."

"Keep the roosters jealous of each other, then. If the women can keep them far enough apart, they will spend their time posturing and crowing instead of fighting," he chuckled, but then became serious again. "Do they not know the advantages of peace over war; of food over famine? Must it always be carnage with them?"

"The gentle breezes of Maui do not flow in their blood," I replied. "They are spurred on by a force I can sense, but I cannot name. If I could change it, if I could control it, I would. Do you not see me lingering in the peacefulness of Maui? They are all men of great ambition, and they breed the same kind of man. Those that gather under their banner are anxious for favor and rewards."

"Then you must go back and find a way to keep their struggles against each other confined to their own land. If the lust for blood runs in their hearts so strong, let them kill each other over there. In the long run, it will save me much bother." He took my elbow and turned me toward the canoes that were being loaded. "Do not let them come here."

"But …"

"You must go back to Hawaii. I need you in the court there—I need to have someone near the chief."

"But…you just said…" The sun that had been shining on my shoulders suddenly dipped behind a cloud and I shivered. "No," I said, but immediately knew I had uttered the wrong word. Of course I had to go back—it was my duty. I could not bear to think of the loneliness I felt there—the barrenness of the lava at Kau seeped under my skin until my bones felt parched. I started to argue, but before he could say, 'Who do you think you are?' or 'You have responsibilities that are beyond your private desires,' I swallowed hard and whispered, "I gave that island two children. Isn't that enough?" I could not hold my tears back any longer and I sobbed. When I finally could gather myself again I begged, "The thought of going back again is unbearable. They have never been my people. I can do nothing to change them. Please let me keep my daughter at home on this island. If I am here, Keoua will visit often. He loves his daughter. Of that, I have no doubt. And, truth be told, he loves this island as well. Has he requested my return?"

"It is not necessarily my desire to send you back, my sister, but news has come to me from Keoua's court in Hilo." He lowered his voice and tenderly said. "Your husband is dying. You and his daughter must return."

"No!  Not Keoua!" I shrieked as the tears streamed down my cheeks.

# Eight

## 1752

*I* gathered Liliha and my retainers and hurried to Hilo where Keoua lay dying. I sat by his side, wiped his brow, and watched him wither away. Such a handsome man—gentle Keoua—still in his prime. At first, I denied what was happening in my attempt to nurse him back to health. I said to myself, "This cannot be." But after several days, I saw that he grew progressively weaker. I said to myself, "It is so."

Every time I looked out the doorway all I could see were grey clouds hovering over us. I knew there was a mountain beyond the village, but the clouds were so thick it was as if the sacred mountain didn't exist. In my heart, sacredness didn't exist anywhere. Keoua of the gentle rain was slipping away. The rain would no longer be gentle; it came down in torrents. Was it the rain, or was it my weeping for Keoua? After awhile I didn't know; after awhile I didn't care. Sheets of water fell until it seemed as if the very clouds were sobbing as Keoua slipped from my grasp. I finally understood why the roof was so thickly thatched—at least while I was inside I was able to remain dry. But when I stepped outside, I sank up to my ankles in mud that made a sucking sound with every step I took.

And then one day the rain stopped, the wind blew, and the clouds parted. As soon as the sun came out again, Keoua sat up and called for his older brother, Kalaniopuu.

"My dear, you know he is in Kau," I whispered.

"Send for him!" Keoua insisted.

"Of course," I said. I patted his arm to quiet him.

"Now!" Keoua batted my hand away. "Now!"

I sent for Keoua's fastest runner and told him to take the shortest route. "Go over the top of the mountain at Kilauea. Skirt the goddess Pele at Halemaumau. Drop down the mountainside and find the king's brother."

"My chiefess," he argued. "That is the most dangerous route. The poisonous gas…"

"I don't care what you have to do. Take several men. Maybe one of you will make it. Hold your breath if you must," I insisted. "Just head to Kau."

Keoua was restless as he waited for Kalaniopuu to come. Every footstep he heard outside caused him to raise his head with the hope that the person entering the *hale* would be his brother. It seemed an eternity, but in truth it was only a matter of a few days.

Finally, word came from a retainer that Kalani had arrived. I left Keoua's side and went to Kalani. He wanted to rest and bathe before he saw Keoua. "No! You must see him now. His breathing grows weak. I know he has been fighting to stay alive, waiting for you. There isn't much time." I took his arm and hustled him to Keoua's side.

Upon seeing fragile Keoua, Kalani let out a piercing wail and dropped to his knees beside his brother.

Keoua opened his eyes. "I do not have much time," he whispered. "There is no time for us to lament. I worry that our uncle, Alapai, will kill my son, Kamehameha." Keoua took Kalani's hand and pulled him near. "Our uncle threatened to 'cut the sprout before it could grow' when my son was born. I beg you to take him into your court. Care for him as if he were your own."

"But Alapai has asked for the boy at his court…" I began. "Why would Kamehameha be in danger? Wouldn't Alapai be glad to have such a strong young warrior? After all, he lifted the Naha Stone…"

"Hush woman! You don't know what you are talking about. Can't you see that Alapai is killing my brother?" Kalani interrupted. "If you'd wipe away your tears and open your eyes you'd see the prayers of death are circling all around him."

Keoua coughed and spit up blood.

Kalani scowled at me as he helped Keoua to sit up, leaning his emaciated body against the house post. "To you who did nothing to stop the prayers of death-- hush, I say! This is a matter between men," Kalani hissed. "If anyone should know about the powers of the prayers of Alapai and his *kahunas*, it should be you. After all, everyone knows that Alapai had your own father prayed to death years ago."

I staggered back and held on to the *pili* grass wall of the hut before I fell. I sank to my knees and then sat down. The day of my father's sickness came back to me--the day the sickness came on the breeze, when my father's eyes rolled back in his head and he fell to the ground trembling. There had been rumors, of course, but I had been too young to understand. Later, I dismissed the tales as idle gossip at court. Now Kalani had pulled back the veil and exposed the truth. Now there was no doubt.

"Take the boy," Keoua urged his brother. "He has no one else to care for him. He will be a fine warrior. You will need his strength in the days to come. I can see the future unfold as I cross over to the land of Po. Our uncle kept us near after he killed our father. He has never had any love in his heart for either of us. He will do anything to remain the ruler of this island."

I scooted across the mats and reached for Keoua's hand. It grew cold as the life force drained from his body.

"After Alapai is finished with me, he will come for you, Kalani. Take the boy and raise him beside your own."

Kalani bent down and assured Keoua, "I will do as you say, my brother."

"Flee then. Go now, while you can. We will see each other no more," Keoua murmured.

Kalani left immediately. It was only a matter of a day—maybe two… when I reached over and closed Keoua's eyes, sending him alone into the darkness to greet his ancestors.

---

*K*eoua died at Piopio near Wailoa in Waiakea, Hilo district. The rumor that Alapai poisoned him, or perhaps had a powerful *kahuna* pray him to death, circulated for a long time, and I did nothing to stop it. Perhaps the retainers started the stories because that's just what people did—they fed each other with rumors. Perhaps the news was carried on the wind, just as the prayers that had caused Keoua and my father's death. Perhaps it was that others had been subject to the intrigues of court even longer than I. Maybe some believed what their bones told them. "A *kahuna* prayed him to death," was always the charge when a healthy young man became severely ill and died for no apparent reason. I knew the dangers of being a chief, and the tricks of the *kahuna ana ana* as well as anyone. No *kahuna* ever admitted responsibility for the act of praying anyone to death, but then none who wished to save his life would; it would always remain a closely guarded secret. Many questions, and few answers, were batted back and forth in the royal court. Would Alapai have poisoned Keoua because he had a child by me, sacred *alii* of Maui? To me, that hardly seemed a reason for a man to lose his life, but still the question was put to me more than once. Would Keoua have been poisoned because he did not conceive with his wife Kekuiapiowa II? Some claimed that her son, Kamehameha, was the product of my brother Kahekili, although Keoua had always claimed the child as his son. But, the rumors persisted. Those who argued that Alapai had nothing to do with Keoua's death stated the fact that Alapai had taken both brothers, Kalaniopuu and Keoua, into his court and raised them as his sons after their father died, and gave both young men great responsibility as his war chiefs upon reaching young manhood. Of course there were others who said Alapai had, indeed, poisoned their father and that Alapai brought them to court to keep them close so they would not form a *hui* and rise up against him. To me, the question remains: why would my uncle, Alapai, spend all that energy and effort to raise them and then poison one of them? To this day, it remains a mystery. However, the fact was that Keoua was dead, and all the rumors flying about would not bring him back to life.

As was my duty as Keoua's sacred wife, I spent my time praying and doing what I could to see that Keoua's soul was at rest. Kalaniopuu had sent word that he was back in Kau and had begun the three-day ritual for turning the death prayer back on the sender. He was, for now, without Kamehameha. Since Kalani stood to inherit his brother's lands, he could not be present during the time Keoua's body was slowly roasted on the *imu* and his *iwi* stripped of flesh. The priests wrapped Keoua's bones in the finest *kapa* that had been dyed with sacred symbols of his family. After all the preparations, his *iwi* would be secreted away in a sacred cave in the cliffs above Kaawaloa.

When all was ready, I sent a runner to Kau to fetch Kalani. All the royal courts gathered for the final rites of the great chief. I could not believe it when I saw my uncle, Alapai, in attendance. He carried on as if innocent, even though he was well aware of the rumors. He had brought Keoua's son, the young Kamehameha so that he could pay respects to his father's spirit.

Kalaniopuu attempted to keep the promise he made to his brother on his deathbed: to wrest his nephew from Alapai's grasp. Whether Kalani was genuinely concerned about the boy, or whether he wished to honor his brother and keep his vow, or whether he simply wanted Kamehameha's superb strength and fighting acumen for his own purposes... maybe for all those reasons... Kalani's impulsiveness came to the fore. He risked his own life--and Kamehameha's--in his attempt to liberate his brother's son.

As the family and chiefs gathered, Kalaniopuu used the assembly of the council of chiefs to ask for persmission for Kamehameha to move to his court. Alapai flatly refused, stopping the issue cold, allowing no discussion. The chiefs, ever mindful of which way the royal wind was blowing, and all quite aware of the recent consequences of seeming to be in Alapai's disfavor, supported their chief's decision. What started out as a funeral dirge for a fallen chief ended in a shouting match.

This was yet another lesson in learning about Kalani: when his schemes failed, they failed miserably. Instead of leaving with his head held high and his nephew tucked under his protective wing, Kalani ended up running for his life, pursued by angry chiefs, any one of them his potential executioner. He fled for a canoe that his guard, Puna, had waiting offshore and the two men barely made it out of Hilo Bay with their lives.

———————

*I* received a message to rendezvous with Kalani a day later. After escaping at sea, he had concealed the canoes and headed inland to meet up with the troops he had hidden in the hills. He knew as soon as he reunited with his troops he would be followed on his way back to his homeland of Kau on the southern tip of Hawaii. Alapai's army caught up with us and ambushed our small band. The warriors battled their way south along the coast all day. His instructions to me were to fall far behind—that would be my safety, he assured me. Meanwhile, Kalani led Alapai's army farther and farther into his familiar homeland in the desolate lava fields. The master of revenge, Kalani picked the perfect place to attack. Under the cover of night, Kalani slipped half of his troops out of camp. In the morning, the remainder of his army led Alapai's unsuspecting soldiers up a narrow trail. The steep slopes kept Alapai's men contained in a single line. As they slowly cleared their way through the low hanging branches and underbrush, Kalani's warriors bore down on them front and back.

At one point, Kalani's foot slipped on the smooth *pahoehoe* lava and two of Alapai's men seized him. Although not a large man, Kalani was exceedingly strong, both in body and temperment, for he had been trained in the secret art of *lua*, bone breaking. Without blinking an eye, he picked each man up over his head, brought him down on his knee and snapped each man's spine. He hurled the men, one by one, over the side of the cliff to their death.

In battle, as in life, Kalani saw the world in terms of the *koane* game: white was an ally, black the enemy. For him, that day was not a battle so much as a slaughter. When the news reached Alapai that his army had been destroyed, he gathered more troops and hurried back to attack Kalaniopuu again, chasing him further down the Puna coast. The armies skirmished the whole way, but Kalani soundly defeated his uncle's army for a second time, and what little was left of Alapai's troops withdrew as Kalani reached his homeland of Kau.

There was no longer any doubt about Alapai's intentions: what Keoua had insisted on his deathbed had been right. But, there are always two sides to any story.

Those who sided with Alapai believed that it was Kalani who had started a rebellion against the aging chief now that his brother was dead and he would no longer have to share the wealth of his brother's inherited half. It was said that Kalani demanded his *kahuna* to begin chanting death prayers for Alapai as soon as he safely reached his homeland. Kalani defended himself against the rumor, swearing again and again that he had not done so. On the other hand, everyone knew he was not the type of man to let bygones be bygones. By him not admitting to the death prayer after he had gotten home was a masterful stroke in stretching the truth. Knowing that Keoua would be dead within days, he had started the death prayer against Alapai immediately. By the time he was accused of starting the death prayers, he had already finished, and was telling, on the face of it, a semblance of the truth. And who was there to say different?

Reports came to Kalani that what was left of Alapai troops had regrouped and then moved away from Hilo, heading up the Hamakua coast to the scared Valley of the Chiefs, Waipio. Kalani's spies reported that Alapai stayed in the valley for some time, and then headed inland to Waimea where he fell ill at Lanimaomao. Kalani chortled when he heard that news, but made no other indication that his own *kahunas* were still hard at work on the death prayer against his uncle. Alapai was finally able to make it back to Kawaihae on the leeward side of the island where, in a ceremony at Mailekini *heiau*, he named his son, Keaweopala, successor.

# Nine

## 1754

*K*alaniopuu's head priest had not been able to save Keoua from the death prayer of Alapai—he claimed he had been summoned too late. But, with a great deal of effort, and substantial encouragement by Kalani, the *kahuna* had been able to reverse the prayer that Alapai had used to kill Keoua and use it against Alapai, or at least that's what Kalani and his *kahuna* both claimed. It took more than a year, but the *pule kuni,* the prayer of one sorcerer against another, was successful. When the runner arrived in Kau with the message that Alapai was dying, Kalani donned his feather cape and swept through the village, startling the dogs and waking babies with his rooster crows of victory. Thrilled that he had finally settled the score with his uncle, his *laho* swelled up full of his manhood. In the days afterward he hardly left me alone. For him, revenge for the death of his beloved brother and father was sweet.

In the dividing up of Alapai's land holdings it seemed, much to everyone's surprise, that the old chief had thought more of his nephew Kamehameha than he did of his own son, Keaweopala. Although he had given the right to rule to Keaweopala, he bequeathed much land to Kamehameha. Even before Alapai's body was wrapped in banana leaves, the wrangling over land started. Although Alapai was given all due respect, the chiefs of Hawaii bickered and quarreled. Former alliances collapsed and the chiefs circled each other like sharks in a feeding frenzy. Ever the hothead, Alapai's brother, Keeaumoku, formed a warrior unit and attacked his nephew, Keaweopala. Small but formidable though the unit was, they were quickly defeated. Keeaumoku swiftly retreated to his canoe and fled to Kau. Cunning man that Keeaumoku was, in his besseching cry for help, he referred to Kalani as 'the mighty chief,' which further stroked Kalani's already swollen ego.

"Do not trust Keeaumoku," I advised Kalani. "He has been simpering around my brother's court for years, looking for an opening. His reputation is that he is heartless and cunning. He is a man who only looks out only for himself."

"He is looking for an opening, and when he finds one, he'll take it," my husband parried. "All men do that." He turned his back to me, his rebuff made swiftly, quelling any argument I might have made. "I, myself, would do that. What's the matter with it? He is a strong fighter, and that will always be welcomed at my court."

"He changes sides like a bird flitting from flower to flower, gathering sweet nectar wherever it can."

"Every man does that too—whether it's the nectar of women or the satisfying smell of enemy blood." As an afterthought he mentioned, "And though Keeaumoku's army is small, he has trained his troops well."

I threw up my hands. "I relent," I said. "There is nothing more I can say." In truth, there was nothing I could do. Once again, Kalani had put me in my place. I had momentarily forgotten I was in the land of men who settled everything with clubs and daggers. Seemingly, among the chiefs who still seemed backward to me, might always prevailed over reason. For a time, Kalani was able to say, 'I told you so' because Keeaumoku proved himself to be more of an asset than he was a liability.

Kalani was quick to seize upon any person who was willing to go to battle, especially if that meant Kalani could break up what remained of the old guard of chiefs at his uncle's court. It wasn't enough for Kalani that Alapai was dead. He still had in his mind to draw Kamehameha closer to him—partly from the promise he had made to his brother, and partly to gain control over the lands his nephew had recently inherited. From that time on, it seemed Kalani was obsessed with fighting. He loved war better than any man I have ever known.

He was ruthless and left his enemies begging for mercy. Of course that can be said of any man who wished to best his adversary, but I have seen Kalani's bitter cruelty with my own eyes.

———

The two men, Kalani and Keeaumoku, quickly gathered their armies on the southern coast at Honomalino Bay, then headed up the Kona coast, knowing that somewhere along the way they would meet Keaweopala's men. The land where they came together was on a rugged *a-a* flow, full of holes and razor-sharp rocks. The first battle on the uplands of Keei went to Keaweopala, who sacrificed the dead at Kauluwai, the *heiau*, on land that belonged to Kamehameha.

Kamehameha's mother, Kekuiapoiwa, was in residence with her son and was furious when she heard about the sacrifices, claiming that Kamehameha had been slighted and protocol broken. She argued that since the land was given to him by Alapai, her son should have had the honor of sacrificing the enemy to the gods, not Keaweopala, and that it was her son's right to be instilled with the *mana* inherent in the sacrifice of a rival chief. She was quite miffed and commanded Kamehameha to leave Keaweopala's court and join Kalaniopuu. Of course everyone close to Kalani knew that he had been looking for the opportunity to gain his nephew's favor. In her shrewdness, Kekuiapoiwa knew that Kalani would gladly extend the sacrifical rites to Kamehameha. My half-sister sent me a private message, assuring me that by Kalani welcoming Kamehameha to his court, Kamehameha would declare his undying loyalty to Kalani. I knew her well enough to know that she believed Kalani would emerge the victor in this latest land battle, and that I was to hold my tongue and not oppose my husband's rise to power.

The next evening, when plans had been drawn up for his nephew's safety in approaching, Kamehameha snuck into his uncle's camp to declare his loyalty. Honoring his mother's wishes, the young warrior pleaded to be admitted to Kalani's court. Kalani feigned surprise, but graciously accepted Kamehameha's loyalty. Kamehameha assured him he could be trusted because he felt slighted by Keaweopala. Even though I understood the loyalty of family, I shuddered as Kalani gathered the young man into his open arms. By accepting Kamehameha as a son, he had not only gained a strong young warrior and the troops that followed him, but he also added a large section of land to his domain. I should have been grateful. Now Kalani controlled the whole southern third of the island: the lands of Puna, Kau and South Kona in this latest masterful stoke of conquest.

I was beginning to understand how much Kalani loved everything that had to do with war. I had never seen him so elated—his eyes sparkled as he celebrated with Kamehameha. Long into the night, the two huddled together, whispering as the *awa* cups were passed.

My shrieks woke the whole camp before dawn. I dreamed I had been on the battlefield and had seen warriors falling on the front lines, spears flying past my ears, and women wailing over their dead husbands/ brothers/ sons. As the years passed, my dream proved correct on all three counts. I, who had come from the court of my peace-loving brother, did not understand how many times I would witness those scenes—not as a reoccurring nightmare, but as actual battles.

All Kamehameha had asked for was permission to change sides. Thankfully he did not stay at our court. He assured Kalani he would return when he could bring back his mother and retainers. He left on the tail of my nightmare, when it was just light enough to see the trail. On his way he met the messenger who had been sent by his mother to tell her son that she had suddenly become ill and was afraid she was being prayed to death for causing trouble at Keaweopala's court. Kamehameha sent the messenger on to us to relay the news while he ran down the hill to his mother's side.

Kalani felt the tides of war shifting and sent for his *kahuna*, Holua, of the Paao heritage, saying he wanted to draw the battle to a close--naturally not before claiming victory. Holua, who had been at Alapai's court with Keaweopala's *kahuna* Kaakau, saw the opportunity to have his old rival eliminated. He declared that Kaakau was responsible for prolonging the battle, and quite possibly for Kamehameha's mother's illness. Holua said all it would take to win was to see that the rival *kahuna* was killed. Once that priest was gone, triumph over Keaweopala would be assured.

I thought to myself that it did not take the wisdom of a *kahuna* to weave those stories together, but I kept my silence, knowing better than to point out the advantage to Holua of doing away with his competitor.

The very next day Kalani returned his men to the battlefield and told them to keep a close eye out for the unsuspecting priest. As soon as Kaauka stepped onto the field, he was cruelly slain and ceremoniously baked in Kalani's *imu*. Within hours, the same fate befell the chief, Keaweopala, who joined his *kahuna* on the sacrificial altar. The remaining troops, sensing their fate, quickly surrendered.

Kalani returned to his homeland of Kau once again victorious. A few days later, Kamehameha came to our court permanently. He was in deep grief at the time, for in the melee, the gods had claimed his mother's spirit. Kalani felt sorry for his nephew who was now orphaned, and spent many hours consoling him and making sure the young man felt welcome.

The news of Kalani's quick dispatch of Kaakua and Keaweopala sent a strong message to all the chiefs of the island. The meaning was clear: no one dared challenge his supremacy, making Kalani the undisputed ruler of the island.

For a time, we were at peace. Kalani busied himself with affairs of state. I didn't think much about the fact that he had men carving canoes on the beach— I assumed he was thinking more of the upcoming deep-sea fishing season than war. Nor was I paying attention to the village men who were busy shaping spears and fashioning shark-tooth daggers. When I thought to ask, Kalani assured me those were the affairs of men and none of my concern.

In truth, I always felt like I was looking at the village life through a veil. When I said my daily prayers at the women's *heiau* in what to me was still a foreign land, my visions were not always clear. I always wondered if the fumes coming down the mountainside from Kilauea were what fogged my vision, or maybe it was the water, for in Kau the water was sometimes brackish and did not taste sweet, but rather had the aftertaste of volcanic fumes. The sulphur fumes also seemed to cloud my eyes when I looked for visions in my calabash. I mulled it over many times, but never came to a definite conclusion—all I know is that it was so. I could not penetrate whatever it was, and thus was less than helpful to my brother and kinsmen on Maui.

The messenger from my brother's court came in secret one night and I asked permission to visit my family on Maui. Since we were at peace, my request was granted, but Kalani's last words, "Do not tarry" haunted me the whole time.

# Ten

## 1763

Although he was always glad to see me, my brother gave me a few days to get settled and relax in the white sands of Wailuku before calling me to his court.

He hurried through our formal greetings, and when I questioned him about his urgency, he got right down to business. "The priestesses say our daughter, Kalaniakua, has had her first bleed and is now of the age to give birth. Her first child should be for our sacred lineage. Since she has no full blood brother with which to mate, her first child should be with me. I'm trusting that you will see to the sacred ceremony."

The formal procedures did not take long to prepare for everyone was anxious that it was to be. My brother and his daughter lay under the sacred *kapa* cloth together, and because it was the will of our gods, it was not long before she was *hapai*, with child. Everyone in the court was thrilled—another generation was to be established. I sent word to Kalani informing him that I would be staying through my daughter's pregnancy and the sacred child's birth.

For once, all of my children were with me at home on the island of my heart. The clouds scuttled by, the rains came and went—I was at peace again. I was with my family. I was going to be a grandmother. I couldn't have been happier.

Unfortunately, my daughter's pregnancy was not an easy one. "Maybe it was because she is still so young," the *pale keiki* suggested when Kalaniakua's time came. "And it is her first," she said as she rubbed Kalaniakua's belly, hoping to ease the child into the world.

"It's because she's birthing a chief--a man child who will be a ruler," I snapped, remembering what my own mother had told me when I gave birth to my first sacred child, the one who was now becoming a mother herself. I was certain I was right, but I softened my response to the midwife so as not to upset my daughter. "Giving birth to a boy is the hardest. The girls seem to already know what to do."

The midwife rubbed Kalaniakua's stomach harder. Kalaniakua's labor pains were intense.

I was afraid my nervousness was of little help. I wiped the sweat from my daughter's brow, then from my own. "Just a little longer," I assured her. "You're almost there. Push one more time."

Kalaniakua leaned back against the birthing stone and pushed. The child's head crowned.

The midwife bent over in order to catch the baby. "Breathe—*ha*," the midwife said. "Breathe. Now push."

I shoved the midwife aside and put my hand under the child's head. "One more push." Into my hands a sacred son slipped into the world. I was thrilled and cuddled the baby to my grandmother's heart as tears spilled down my cheeks. A peace came over me as I held that child—this man-child of the next generation made everything complete.

But, I should have known better. That is to say, I have been led astray by the sweetness of life before...

———————

The guards in the outlook on the hillside warned the village when they spied several canoes bearing Kalaniopuu's banner rounding the point and approaching Kahului Bay. Everyone felt the tension as my brother stepped out of his *hale* and walked to the shore in order to greet the canoes as they landed. I had already started packing, knowing the message I had been dreading had arrived: Kalani had firmly established his rule and he was summoning us back to his court. The messenger relayed that he had been instructed to wait several days until I gathered all our necessities. It was clear that I would not be returning to my brother's court. There was really no choice.

On the night before our departure, my brother and I sat together in silence for a while before he spoke. "The safety of our island and all your kinsmen depends on your willingness to complete your life's destiny."

"You know that my heart isn't really in it," I replied. "But I know what I have to do."

"It is not for my sake; it is not for the sake of our family. It is for the sake of the people on both islands."

"Yes, I understand," I nodded and sighed. "For the sake of the people."

"As before, keep the peace."

"If I can…"

"We need you to do better than that. We need your supreme effort."

"I will do my best."

There was never enough time to properly say goodbye—as if I wanted to say those words to my brother or my eldest daughter at all—and now the next generation. The only word I could say to my grandson was *aloha*: hello, goodbye, I love you, I honor your spirit. With a heavy heart, I held him close to my breast, knowing that when I next saw him, I would be a stranger to him. I gave advice to my young daughter as the women at court smiled. "We are all mothers," they chided. "We will care for the sacred one." I knew that they meant both my grandson and my daughter; still, a mother's love is fierce and she always wants to be the one to protect her own.

At the last minute, my brother came to the shore. He whispered, "Keep the peace." We touched foreheads and took in each other's sacred breath, not knowing when we would see each other again.

Liliha, Kiwalao and I got in the canoes. I kept looking over my shoulder as the canoe skimmed over the surface of the sea, my spirit stretching behind me as the paddler's blades sliced through the water. My heart was clouded. I felt it dragging like an anchor, stirring the sand along the bottom. With great reluctance, I turned and sat facing the front of the canoe. I had to let go of what I could not control.

As we reached the point at Nanualele and started across the Alenuihana Channel and were in sight of Kohala, I saw what I had feared: war canoes pulled up on the beach. As we pulled closer, I witnessed warriors milling around, tense with anticipation as they waited for their orders. Kalani did not bother to meet us at the shoreline. He was busy going over the last minute details of his plan with his chiefs. I felt sick to my stomach, knowing my kinsmen on Maui were about to be attacked. I tried to think of some way I could get word to them, but there was nothing I could do that would not endanger my children or myself. I no longer had a cadre of friends surrounding me. Except for the *keiki*, I was alone.

Kalani broke away from his army and walked up the hill toward us.

It was all I could do not to spit in his face when he stood before me. Instead, I turned my head and spit on the ground, screaming at him, "You have no regard for my family. This is the first time I have met with such an evil person wishing to harm me."

"Harm you? No, not harm you," he answered calmly. "I brought you over here so that you would not be harmed. But regard for your family? Why should I?"

"You act like attacking a family member is the most natural thing in the world," I screamed at him.

He shrugged and shook his head. "You forget whose island you are on," he mumbled as he turned to trudge back down the hill, his attention being drawn back to the final loading of the war canoes.

My children and I were ushered to the shade of a *kukui* tree where all we could do was watch, helpless to get word to our people across the channel. I recognized the chiefly red and yellow robes of Kamehameha and Kekuhaupio, Kalani's trusted war leader, but neither came near. That night we were given food, but left alone in a hastily built hut. At dawn we were awakened.

"You'll come with me," Kalani ordered as he took me by the arm.

"My children...."

"The others will follow," he barked as he twisted my arm and forced me aboard his war canoe. Kalani stood at the forward mast, gave the signal, and his crewmen raised the *lauhala* sails. With a ferocious war cry, he urged his warriors on. Answers echoed back from every canoe. We crossed the thirty-mile channel even faster than we had the previous day. I could not count the number of canoes and men, but I guessed that Kalani had brought all his forces. Of course the guards on Maui saw the canoes coming and sent a runner to alert my brother in Wailuku, but he was too far away at that time to be of any immediate help. The men in the sweet potato fields dropped their tools and ran to protect their homeland, but they could not keep the canoes from landing and taking the fort at Kauwiki, Hana.

My brother, Kamehamehanui, did his best to rally troops, conscripting farmers from their *loi* and drafting fishermen who abandoned their nets and picked up their spears. He sent messengers all over Maui, and to neighboring Molokai and Lanai for reinforcements. None of the chiefs on the other islands wanted their lands to fall to the fearsome Kalani, so they sent help as soon as they could.

Within days, the Maui army gathered. Skirmishes, and then battles, broke out all over the southern part of the island, from Makaolehua to Akiala. The men from Maui fought hard and were willing to risk everything because the safety of their families and their precious *aina* was at stake. Eventually Kamehamehanui tired of fighting, for he was not one driven to wage war like Kalaniopuu. My brother did not want to lose any more men and was satisfied to have gained back most of the southern lands. He figured the fort at Kauwiki was insignificant and abandoned it to Kalani's men, thinking it would prove hard to defend and not worth the time and effort. He knew he would get it back at some later date. Kalani's *kahuna* was left in charge. I was forced to return to Kau. The *kahuna* soon lost control of the fort to a man who outsmarted him, but the fort itself remained under the control of Hawaii, not Maui.

# *Eleven*

## 1765

Then it seemed like things happened all at once—they didn't, of course, but to me it all ran together. The seasons were that of grief. My brother, Kamehamehanui, had started on a trip around his island and was meeting with his chiefs in Kawaipapa in the Hana district when he fell ill. As the winds of change blew over the land, he called for me.

"Over and over," the priest told me later. "But you were not there."

Every chief knew that by rights, and certainly by their own decree, I should have taken over rule of the island. I was next in line—a woman, yes, but women rule the people sometimes better than men because the love of battle is not in their hearts. The chiefs of Maui would have gladly given the island to my care—I was rightful heir and there would have been no war of ascension. I had been trained in the sacred ways alongside my brother, but most of all, because I had been trained to keep the peace, I was noted as a fine diplomat. The *makaainana* of Maui cared deeply for me: I was their beloved *alii* of the purest blood. They trusted my judgment and knew my daughter Kalaniakua would be by my side, using her skills as *kilokilo* to see into the future. But Kalaniopuu, clever man that he was, insisted I stay at his court in Kau.

Whether my brother was prayed to death, poisoned, or simply died of old age, I can never be sure, but I swear I know the minute he passed over into the land of Po. My heart heard the people in Hana wailing their lamentations, even if my ears could not.

At any rate, as far as the chiefs of Maui were concerned, there didn't seem to be any chance of Kalani releasing me from my duties as his sacred wife, so there was nothing for the family to do but make my younger brother, Kahekili, ruler. He had lived his life at court, of course, under the wing of Kamehamehanui, but never in his wildest dreams had he ever thought he would rule. He had always been thought of as the younger brother and had consequently been trained as a warrior, not a negotiator. He was hotheaded, and did not have the temperment or training of a diplomat.

My two brothers could not have been more opposite. Kamehamehanui had many wives and was devoted to his children. He loved the festivities and pomp of court and gathered the *makaainana* around him to celebrate often. He knew that people with full bellies were content, and so he had made planting and fishing his paramount objectives. Kahekili, a much simpler man in some respects, had taken only two wives. When he became soverign, he shunned his wives and became a recluse. He had his *hale* built on a hill and lived alone because he said he needed all his power to rule. His favorite pastime was to leap off high cliffs to the sea below. Some say he did it to show off; some say that he did it to establish his rule. He had done it since he was a child, so I knew that if he was not necessarily showing off or posturing. It was just who he was—a risk-taker in all things, willing to risk his subjects lives as well as his own.

I begged Kalani to let Kiwalao, Liliha and I see to the disposal of my elder brother's bones, but he refused. "All of you leave Kau at once?!" He snorted. "Definitely not! I will not allow that to happen again."

"Just me go, then. He was my dear brother," I cried. "And the father of my daughter, the sacred Kalaniakua."

Kalani did not even consider it for a minute. His answer was swift and sure. "No! You will all stay here. If I let you go, you will establish the rule over Maui and never come back."

"And would that be so wrong?" I asked him. "We could be rulers together: you over your island, and me over mine. What would be the matter with that? Between the two of us, we could rule all the islands and have our own empire."

I knew in my heart that my destiny was to be the mother of a man who would rule an island, but no one had ever made mention of me being a ruler of my own island. But with that right, I could see to it my own son became ruler. Maybe that was what the gods had in store. It was worth a try.

"That is exactly what is the matter with it," he groused. "I've had to fight my way to rule, many hardships, much bloodshed, many men lost. Yours is handed to you without bloodshed."

"Does it matter how one becomes ruler?"

"Yes!" he said and turned away from me. "My destiny is to rule these islands and I will not share my rule with anyone! Not another man, and certainly not with my own wife!" he yelled as he stomped out of my *hale*.

"What I really want is to see that my brother's bones are safe," I said as I followed him to the door. "As a chief, surely you can undersand that."

He pretended not to hear, but I know he did because he stumbled, but then quickly righted himself. He glanced over his shoulder to see if I had noticed. Surely he could imagine the horror of this own bones being used for fishhooks. When he got to the gate at the edge of my compound, he turned and shouted, "What do you take me for? A fool? If you think you can trick me that way, it is you who are the fool."

I did not reply. There was no need. Everyone in the compound had heard him, and that would make him the fool—or at the very least, foolish--in their eyes.

Certain that the priests would take their time with my brother's bones and that they would expect me to arrive in time to see to the ceremonies, I waited a couple of days for him to calm down and then called for a canoe. I needed to attend to my brother, and Kalani knew it. He did not try to stop me. I knew that because he did not stop me, he fully expected me to return. I hated to leave my children, but by leaving them with him at Kau, Kalani would see that I intended to return.

My dear brother and husband, Kamehamehanui, lay for some time at Pihana *heiau* in Wailuku so the *makaainana* could pay their respects. There, above the turquoise blue of the bay, above the waving leaves of *kalo* that he had been raised on, near to the heart of his people that he loved beyond all measure, he rested in peace. After the *kahunas* had properly conducted the ceremonies, his body was removed to Moanui on the island of Molokai. Since the priests on that island had nutured and trained him as a boy, it was fitting that his bones were tucked away safely in the caves along the southern coast of that island.

# _Twelve_

## 1766

After my brother passed, Keeaumoku left Kalani's court and made his way to Maui. He lost no time in swooping in on my brother's widow, my half-sister Namahana. Everyone assumed Namahana would have joined Kahekili's court, he being her brother-in-law and the new chief, but his austere ways did not suit her. Without bothering to observe the proper protocol for grieving, Keeaumoku recklessly pursued her favor. After a swift courtship--before anyone could counsel her otherwise, certainly before she had any idea of the sort of man he was or what she was getting herself into--they married. It was a daring move on both their parts, and a stunning slap in the face to my brother, Kahekili.

When Kahekili realized Keeaumoku's actions for what they were--an act of rebellion against our family and his new rule--he was outraged. Kahekili and his thunder god roared their diapproval. For days and nights, shafts of lightening halved great trees in the uplands. Bellows of thunder bounced off the mountainsides, their echoes grumbling down the valleys. The _makaainana_ huddled in the _hales_ for safety, letting the anger of the god and his emissary run its course. Eventually the storm, both in the mountains and in my brother's heart, blew itself out. The clouds parted and the wind whisked the last of the billowing vapors far out to sea.

Kahekili established himself in his new role and, for a time, he continued to let the new couple reside in Waihee, for after all, those lands were Namahana's where she had been living with her mother and some chiefs from Molokai. Although Kahekili was annoyed, he felt that Keeaumoku posed no real threat, and his half-sister seemed to be happy, so he allowed the interloper to stay. It is always the last fish that tears the net, the new log shoved on the fire that causes the smoke to rise. This time it was not even Keeaumoku who caused the actual trouble. Instead it was Kahekili's *hanai* son, Kahahana, who was being trained as a soldier. The young chief donned his feather cape and helmet. He set off to kill three of Keeaumoku's men, claiming perceived slights over not receiving his fair share of fish from the daily catch. All the chiefs voiced disgust that there was fighting over baskets of food. There was absolutely no need to fight; the sea was teeming with fish and there was enough for everyone. People pointed to Keeaumoku, the overseer, saying that if he had paid closer attention, everyone would have had a proper share to take home to their respective families, just as it had been done for years. But, no—trouble was already brewing and the basket of fish was just the excuse they all needed. The confrontation was inevitable.

My brother and I had been with the priests on Molokai, ceremoniously laying our elder brother's bones to rest. Word came that there had been an uprising at Waihee and Kahekili sent word to his troops to put an end to it. Keeaumoku's small band fought back for a couple of days, but they were outnumbered. In the meantime, Kahekili decided he should return to Maui, leaving me on Molokai to see to our brother's final placement in the cave.

———

Seeing that his small group of warriors had no hope of winning against the might of Kahekili, Keeaumoku gathered up Namahana and the priests from Molokai that had been living in their village and fled over the mountain to the western shores of Kaanapali. Some of the Molokai priests abandoned Keeaumoku's faction and did not board canoes for Molokai. Instead they scurried back to their chief's court when they heard that Kahekili's double canoe had been spotted heading across the channel between the islands and down the windward side to Wailuku.

Keeaumoku beat a hasty retreat across the Pailolo Channel, landing on the leeward side of Molokai, where the interloper's canoes were permitted to land only because the *kahunas* were with them.

As soon as Kahekili heard that cagy Keeaumoku had outsmarted him, his ire rose and he sent war canoes back across the channel. Keeaumoku drew the peaceful planters and fishermen of Molokai into his battle only because he used his slippery tongue to convince them they needed to defend their island. After a short skirmish, the men of Molokai laid down their weapons, declaring they were not looking for trouble with Kahekili and that they were definitely not willing to lose their lives over strife that had been started by men on another island over a fish. The men of Molokai turned on Keeaumoku, who was, once again, forced to jump in his canoe and flee. This time none of the Molokai chiefs accompanied them.

He and Namahana were almost alone.

I say almost—for at our brief meeting, Namahana had whispered her secret to me. She was *hapai*, pregnant.

# Thirteen

## 1766

When I finished with the ceremonies of putting my brother's bones to rest, I returned to Hawaii. Left on my own, I would have remained on Maui indefinitely, but I knew that Kalani would send for me soon, so rather than cause problems, I returned to Kau on my own—before he had to send out forces to bring me back.

I was shocked when I heard that Keeaumoku was back in Kalani's good graces and was living with my sister in the lands Kalani had captured from my elder brother in Hana. Kalaniopuu never told me exactly why he let Keeaumoku back into his graces and return to his court, but I imagine it was because the rumors were true: Keeaumoku had promised Kalani undying gratitude and loyalty, swearing that he would do anything Kalani asked—anything at all—even suggesting several underhanded plots. Perhaps Keeaumoku's promise of loyalty felt desperate enough to Kalani; perhaps it was because Keeaumoku and Namahana settled in Hana and did not ask to come directly to Kalani's court in Kau; perhaps Kalani thought Keeaumoku would remain true because they had the same enemy, my brother, Kahekili.

Imagine my surprise when Kalani actually asked my opinion about that rogue, Keeaumoku. What could I say? I had already expressed my doubts about trusting him, and related the story of all that had transpired in Waihee and Molokai.

I assured my husband I would never change my feelings about Keeaumoku. "He changes sides like a sail trimmed to catch the most favorable wind," I said. I told Kalani that my half-sister came to me in private and begged me to protect her while she awaited the birth of her next child.

Kalani, of course, cared nothing for the child and scoffed at my concern.

"Women's business," he said gruffly. "I will let them stay as long as neither one of them causes trouble. Keeaumoku can keep his eye on the rascal, Mahihelelima, who chased my *kahuna* out of the fort."

"One scoundrel watching another, I scoffed. "How appropriate."

———

*K*eeaumoku and Nahamana settled down and things were quiet for a time, although by the time their daughter was born, it was not surprising that war had broken out again. Their daughter, Kaahumanu, was born at Mapuwena in Kauiki, Hana. Because of the battle, Namahana fled with her midwife and gave birth in secret, tucked away in a small cave near their *hale*. The afterbirth was buried at Kaniamoku above Pihehe in Kawaipapa. She was named using part of my brother's full name-Kahekilinuiahumanu—for hers. Maybe our shrewd grandmother, Haalou, had something to do with that—the naming, of course, but also the prophecy that this babe would be a ruler some day, which of course pleased Keeaumoku. Secretly, I thought it very wise to name the baby after her uncle, making sure that Kahikili would finally be appeased. Haalou later whispered to me that naming the child was a way for Namahana to extend her sincere apologies to the family.

Outwardly, Kahekili was ambivalent.

I shrugged as well, knowing there are more reasons to do things than a person has time to explain, and sometimes actions are taken without anyone understanding their motives, or the outcome, until much, much later.

# Fourteen

## 1767

It was inevitable that father and son, Kalani and Kiwalao, would disagree. Their personalities were as different as night is to day, as black is to white, as the *mano*, the shark, is to the *io*, the hawk. Although neither my son nor husband ever told me the source of their dispute, I could have told them both. The two sapling boys that were growing into manhood were jealous of each other: Kiwalao, the son, and Kamehameha, the nephew who was being raised as a son. Kiwalao was tired of vying for his father's attention. The blood son would never be able to please Kalani, no matter how hard he tried. On the other hand, Kamehameha basked in the glow of finding a mentor in his uncle, someone who appreciated and understood his skills as a warrior. Many of the chiefs said that it was as if Kamehameha and his uncle, Kalaniopuu, had been marked with the same *kapa* design. It was clear to everyone at court that there was trouble brewing between the two young men, and one day tempers flared.

The boys had quarreled before, but I had always been the buffer and managed to get them to come to terms. They were no longer boys—yet not quite men. However, they were old enough to fight like men. At the time, I was again on Maui and not there to step between them and keep the peace.

Kamehameha easily mastered every warrior skill and was praised by Kalani, an old master himself. Kiwalao, try though he did, would never be the warrior his cousin was. After winning yet another sham battle on the practice field against his cousin, Kamehameha turned to see if his uncle was watching. When he saw he had Kalani's full attention, he strutted up and down the field, proudly declaring his loyalty to Kalani, "I am his umbilical cord, his navel, his bones, his blood."

"Everyone wonders who your father is," Kiwalao's angry words hung in the air. "You think your father is dead, but in truth, your father lives. He is *my* uncle, Kahekili, the Thunderer, Chief of Maui."

"You've been listening to your mother too much," Kamehameha retorted.

For Kiwalao there was no backing down. He dared not attack Kamehameha— he had just lost the practice session and knew he could not best his cousin. And now having his mother's name drawn into it had wounded his pride. He did not attack his cousin, but rather turned his back and walked away. He waited for nightfall and snuck out of camp, heading for the northern end of the island. Of course his retainers followed him, but soon he stopped and admonished them to follow at a distance. "I want to be alone," he declared.

The next morning, upon being informed that his son had deserted and that his nephew was the cause of his flight, Kalani confronted his nephew. Kamehameha hung his head and admitted having words with Kiwalao after battle practice. Kalani was furious. "My son has run away! It is all your fault," he yelled. He grabbed the nearest spear and shook it in Kamehameha's face. "Go find him and bring him home."

Who is to say whether Kiwalao moved fast or Kamehameha moved slow? Whichever way the story is told, Kamehameha did not catch up with Kiwalao until they were both in the land of Kamehameha's birth, Kohala, at the northern tip of the island. In fact, Kamehameha arrived just in time, for Kiwalao had commandeered a canoe and paddlers. The way the story was told by those who saw, when Kamehameha was certain that Kiwalao was ready to board, he raced down the hill and met Kiwalao face-to-face. Kamehameha told his cousin that Kalani had sent him and urged Kiwalao to return with him to Kau.

"Go back yourself! You are his favorite. *You* take care of him! I choose to live with my mother." And with that, he jumped in the canoe and crossed the channel. Soon he was on my doorstep. Of course I welcomed him, as did my brother, Kahekili.

The two men—nephew and uncle--met for several nights. Much discussion and consultation ensued. In the end, I was invited to a lengthy initiation ceremony where several pigs were sacrificed by the *kahunas*. After all the rituals were completed, Kiwalao began the process of having his body marked with tattoos. It took a month for the extensive work to be completed. My son marked his back with the power of the thunder god, the same designs as my brother Kahekili. My brother and I were both pleased, for with these markings, Kiwalao declared he was a true son of Maui.

---

On Hawaii, Kamehameha had no choice but to return to Kau without his cousin. Kalani brooded a little, and then called for the fearsome warrior Kekuhaupio, the best on the island, to finish Kamehameha's training. Those two formidable men were favorites of the ladies, who fawned over their sleek strong bodies. At night both men took advantage of their circumstances, but spent their days practicing in sham battles until they were in top form.

After Kalani was completely satisfied with Kamehameha's accomplishments, he called for a feast to celebrate the end of his training. Somehow, Kekuhaupio's pig was spoiled as it cooked—whether someone did it intentionally or it was an accident, I never knew--while Kamehameha's pig roasted perfectly. That night at the sacrificial altar, perhaps because of the pig, the *kahuna* predicted Kekuhaupio's death in a sham battle and Kamehameha's eventual rise to rule.

I should have known when the spies told us of Kekuhaupio being invited to Kalani's court that my husband was up to his old tricks, but I was so thrilled to have all my children together that I didn't give a second thought to what might be transpiring. I assumed that Kalani would do nothing to endanger either his sacred son or his brother's daughter, both who remained with me. For a time, all was calm and peaceful. Neither my daughter nor I foresaw the trouble brewing, even as we scanned the clouds for omens every day.

# Fifteen

## 1773

For many years, Kalani sent troops to steal the sweet potatoes that the Maui farmers planted in the verdant fields of Kaupo, the alluvial fan that spread out from the outpouring of lava from Haleakala. It was the perfect soil for dryland crops, specifically sweet potatoes. Every year Kalani raided the fields; and every year he was defeated, but not without making a mortal enemy out of my brother, Kahekili. Kalani returned to Kau after his yearly retreat from Kaupo, and although he brought back food, it always took some time for him to get over the sting of defeat.

Meanwhile, Kahekili turned his attention to the north and wasted no time in seeking my advice. Of course I knew that just because he sought my counsel, it would be unreasonable of me to think that he would take it. Those were two different matters; nonetheless, I appreciated being able to have my say.

"My spies have returned from Oahu with the news that Kumahana is a cruel chief and is alienating both the *makaainana* and the other chiefs," Kahekili reported.

"How can that be?" I asked. "He is a son of Peleioholani. He was raised under the same feather cape as Kalaniopuu. He knows as well as any man what it means to rule."

"Evidently he has forgotten." Kahekili shrugged. "They say he maims and kills the commoners for no apparent reason. He is stingy—not thrifty—stingy. And lazy, refusing to carry out his duties. The chiefs have advised him to change his ways, but he turns his head, deaf to their pleas, and does what he wants."

"He has been on Oahu for several seasons. Surely he knows…"

"Instead of paying attention to his people, they say he spends his time wandering on the Ewa plains shooting rats." Kahekili smiled—something he rarely did. "He will soon be dispossessed. If he is lucky he will live. If not…"

"How can you be so sure?"

"Because not only do I hear from my spies, but I received a visit from the chiefs of that island. They begged me to release Kahahana from my court in order to be the ruler on Oahu." Kahekili's chest swelled with pride.

It was true—Kahekili had done a good job raising his *hanai* son. Kahahana was a handsome young man with dark curly hair and striking features. I was proud of the young man too. "He has earned his place at court," I said. "And he has the *kapus* of Maui…"

Kahekili held up his hand, shook his head and chuckled, "Unfortunately while you were with Kalani, Kahahana made like the gods with a lesser woman and has been stripped of the *kapus* that were bestowed by his association with this court: *Ahi* (Fire), *Wela* (Heat) and *Hahana* (Extraordinary Heat) are no longer his."

I clutched my breast and bowed my head. The pain of his indesecrations stabbed my heart. "He had such a brilliant future," I muttered. Afraid of the answer, I asked, "Do the Oahu chiefs have any idea that he is no longer considered so sacred?"

"I kept no secrets from them. I told them everything. I held back nothing. They said the *kapus* from this court were mostly a bother to them. After all, those *kapus* were bestowed by our priests, not theirs. In truth, they waved the *kapus* off as if they were swatting at flies. I guess to them it really didn't matter."

"If it doesn't matter to them, then…" I hesitated. "Still…"

"The power of the *kapu* seems to be on the wane."

I could hardly believe my ears. My *kapus* were such a part of my life I could not imagine living without them, but here was a young man, stripped of his *kapus*, and about to be anointed ruler of an island. Like sand under my feet, the traditions of my people were shifting.

"They say if I will agree to let Kahahana come to Oahu, they will release Kumahana and not offer him at the *heiau*. I guess they don't think the gods would accept such a sorry example of a chief for their sacrifice."

"What are you going to do?"

"I do not care about Kumahana. He should be punished for abusing his people. But, that's in the hands of the priests of Oahu. If they choose to let him slip from their grasp, that's their business, not mine." His eyes twinkled with mischief. "I want the Oahu chiefs to see me as one who graciously relinquished one of my best men in order to supply them with a chief ready to lead. It's not worth my time to chase Kumahana down—he's finished."

"But if you release Kahahana, and keep him close…as an ally of your court…" I was finally starting to see Kahekili's reasoning.

My brother did not let me finish. "Exactly! Our cousin who is close to our court is married to the chiefess of Kauai, my *hanai* son will rule over Oahu and Molokai, and I have Maui, Lanai, and Kohoolawe."

"And when my son inherits Hawaii from his father…" I said, for I wanted to make sure Kahekili was not leaving Kiwalao out of the picture.

He nodded. "That is your part. See to it that it is so."

# Sixteen

## 1773

Rumors flew back to us from Oahu like a great frigate bird returning
to shore. After the chiefs and *makaainana* staged a bloodless upheaval,
Kumahana was dispossessed. Some said that on a moonless night he left his family, stole a canoe, and paddled alone across the channel to Molokai where he disappeared into the mountains and was never heard of again. Others believed that
the Oahu chiefs permitted him to gather his family, load his canoes, and leave
the island he had ruled in broad daylight. They swore he headed in the other
direction—across the Kauai Channel—and claimed that his wife's family took
them in. They said on Kauai he was allowed to live out his days, but was stripped
of his position and reduced to the status of a commoner, the price a dethroned
chief paid. If this were true, then everyone knew the Oahu chiefs had been gracious enough not to strangle him--all the better to offer up a perfect body as a
sacrifice. All things considered, if he was alive, he was lucky.

"I can see no reason why you continue to stall," I said to my brother. "Why
don't you just send Kahahana to Oahu? The chiefs asked for him specifically."

"I have ..."

"After all, he is the son of *Alii* Elani, a well-respected chief of the Ewa
district."

"...my reasons."

"But the island is without a chief. What if someone else rises up and takes over while you dally?"

"The short answer is that they have no one capable." Kahekili sighed. "You don't understand, do you? The longer I wait, the more they will think I value him and that I am giving them a prize. Then, when the time comes for me to ask for canoes and troops, the chiefs of Oahu will have a strong reason to reciprocate. In fact, if I play the game right, they will not be able to deny me a single thing I ask for."

He had planned his moves so far in advance of anything I had imagined that there was nothing I could say, so I stayed silent and kept my peace. The more I mulled it over, however, the more I could see changes coming—chiefs were aging, new men were rising up to power. I did not want to see Kahahana inherit an island and my son left out—after all, the two young men had been raised side-by-side at Kahekili's court for the last few years. Kahahana was to go to Oahu—that was clear—when Kahekili finally decreed. What could I do to further my own son's cause? He was the heir apparent of Hawaii and due to inherit directly from his father—of that there was no question. It was only a matter of Kalani stepping down. After all, I thought, Kalani has been drinking *awa* heavily for years, which ages a man before his time. Surely he can't have too many more years.

Kahekili announced he was releasing Kahahana and his beautiful young wife, Kekuapio, to rule Oahu. Truly she was as beautiful as he was handsome; their children were sure to be the finest in all the land. Then the answer came to me. It was time for Kiwalao to step into his destiny as well. He was not a warrior so much as a diplomat. If the islands were to be under one ruler, diplomacy would be of the utmost importance. Kiwalao was perhaps eighteen years old—certainly old enough to marry—and there was only one perfect enough for him, his sister Liliha. The family had been waiting for the next generation. It was time for them both to step up to their sacred duty.

# Seventeen

## 1775

My husband Kalani was always scheming, looking for a way to out-maneuver my brother, Kahekili. I tried to keep abreast of his ideas, but living at Hana and having to rely on court spies meant that sometimes Kalani fooled me and formed plans behind my back. I learned eventually that when there was peace too long, Kalani was up to something, but that learning did not come without trial and error on my part. Kalani arrived in Hana on the pretense of checking on the fort at Kauiki.

"Why did you bring so many warriors?" I asked. "You're coming to a land you already hold," I said. "Why bring all these men? They should be planting sweet potatoes in the uplands in order to feed their families this coming year."

"The women can work while they are gone," Kalani scoffed.

"And who will care for the children?"

"Children eat," he shrugged. "I told the women to make them work too—those that are old enough. They need to know how to use their digging sticks to plant. The young boys can carry calabashes of water. They can grow strong as they care for the plants."

I sighed. Like so many times before, when he got an idea in his head, there was no sense in me trying to shake it loose. As he reminded me often, he was chief, and a wise wife knows not to argue with the man who has say over the life and death of his people.

When he found all well at the fort, he sent his men up the leeward coast to Kaupo, which had been the land of my father, Kekaulike, and which he had for years planted in sweet potatoes. At the first sighting of Kalani's army, runners headed up Kaupo Gap, across barren Haleakala Crater, down the other side of the mountain, through the village of Makawao, and across the peninsula to Kahekili's court at Wailuku. Fortunately, my daughter, Kalaniakua, who lived near Kaupo, was visiting her uncle's court at the time or she might have been killed or, worse yet, captured.

The people of Kaupo, primarily dryland farmers and fishermen, were hardly prepared for war. Kalani's troops surged upon the villagers, lighting their thatched huts on fire, pulling up the precious sweet potato vines, stealing what food there was, and breaking down the fishpond walls. In their fury, Kalani's warriors unmercifully beat the brave farmers about the head with clubs. Kalani led the brigade's ultimate insult to the innocent people of Kaupo when he laid the terrorized villagers on their backs in the fields and urinated in their eyes.

When my brother heard about the destruction in Kaupo, he was enraged that the simple farmers had been attacked and dispatched his well-trained soldiers right away. The brave men from Maui caught Kalani's troops in the uplands and bore down upon them. It was here that Kekuhaupio almost lost his life. He was chased down the mountain into the fields they had just ravaged. Some of the Maui people reported that it was as if the very vines knew Kekuhaupio was the enemy and reached out to grab his leg, causing him to trip and fall. Before he could untangle the vines and release himself, the Maui warriors swarmed him. The only reason he he lived to tell the story was because his student, the young warrior Kamehameha, lunged into the middle of the fray and wielded his mighty club in order to save his instructor.

Even Kalani's life was in jeopardy as the Maui men flooded down the hillside below the Kaupo Gap. Kalaeokailio, a Maui chief, caught Kalani and whirled his battle club over Kalani's head as a sign of victory. Why that chief didn't go ahead and smash Kalani's skull in that day, I'll never know. Kalani, slithery eel that he was, slipped out of the man's grasp and sprinted for his waiting canoe.

When Kalani's men saw their chief heading for his canoe, they did not hesitate and beat a hasty retreat. The Maui men defended their homeland, pursuing the Hawaii men. Those who did not make it to the canoes in time were caught and slain, their mangled bodies left exposed where they lay.

Later, when the stories were told, as of course they were on both sides, Kekuhaupio bragged about Kamehameha's bravery. Of course he would; he had trained Kamehameha. But what surprised me even more was hearing that Kahekili relished hearing about the brave young warrior who had saved Kekuhaupio in the sweet potato field. Even though destruction had fallen upon the people of his island, when the hero's feather cape was described, Kahekili bragged. "Kehuhaupio's savior can be none other than my own son, Kamehameha."

# Eighteen

## 1775

And so it was that Kahahana and his wife left Kahekili's court, my brother driving a hard bargain for the young man the whole time. At one point Kahekili even suggested he keep Kahahana's wife for himself—as a guarantee that Kahahana would be allowed to rule without interference. That didn't make any sense to me. It wasn't so much that Kahekili did not trust the chiefs of Oahu to let Kahahana rule. After all, were they not the ones who had come to Kahekili to specifically ask for him? Could it be that my brother was smitten? He had lived with only two wives before he became ruler—maybe he wanted a young woman to keep him from aging too quickly. What I really thought, though, was that he used her as leverage—the longer he made the Oahu chiefs see his reluctance, the more power over Oahu he appeared to have. In the end my brother reluctantly relinquished his hold on the young woman and allowed her to accompany her husband. Kahahana set up his court at Kahaloa, near the wizard stone of the same name, on the sandy shores of Waikiki.

I waited patiently for Kahahana to become established on Oahu, and then I sought an audience with my brother to talk things over. Always my gracious host, my brother saw to my every comfort. Once we were settled on our mats, I began, "I am anxious to cement the relationship between Maui and Hawaii."

Kahekili nodded.

"You know that my husband Kalani will not give up his island as easily as Kumahana."

Again, he nodded. "What is it that you propose?"

"What I have in mind will, hopefully, prevent another war."

"By all means, tell me your idea. It is not I who attacks your husband's island, but he who attacks mine," my brother said. "My people are tired of your husband coming over here, stealing their crops." Kahekili shifted on the mat. "Please, I would be grateful if you could tell me what to do since you can't seem to keep your husband from pissing in my people's eyes while he burns their houses."

His harsh words hurt, but he was right—I had not been able to stop Kalani.

"Liliha and Kiwalao are both of age. If the two are married, not only do we have a new generation in our family, but that child will be of high birth." I hoped my brother would finish my thought, thus making it his idea, but he did not.

Instead, he waited patiently.

"That child would seal our relationship with Kalani's court. He wouldn't dare attack his grandchild."

———————

*K*ahekili called the young couple to court immediately. It came as no surprise to either of them. They had known since childhood they were to marry and produce a sacred child for the family. Truth be told, they both admitted they had been anxious for the opportunity. They were wed in the sacred *Hoao-Wohi* rites, signifying the union of two persons of exalted rank.

I did not send word to Kalani to ask permission for the ceremony. My reasoning was that his seed was only one fourth of the equation. I was the mother of both Liliha and Kiwalao, therefore my stake in their marriage was half. Their respective fathers were half-brothers from Hawaii, Keoua and Kalani—or perhaps just Kalani—it mattered not. Keoua had claimed formal rights of parenthood, but he had been dead a long time. I knew Kalani would have to admit that Keoua would have been thrilled for the two to bring forth a sacred child. All in all, I reasoned, Kalani could hardly disapprove, and if he did, it was entirely too late.

And so my children, who loved each other deeply, lay down under the sacred *kapa*. They both not only understood their obligation to the family, but also their responsibility from the political perspective of keeping peace between the two islands. Peace brought prosperity to the *makaainana* and therefore to the royal household. The only result of war was obliteration.

Looking back, perhaps I should have returned to Hawaii to counsel with Kalani. Maybe he was jealous because he had not been consulted. But perhaps that had nothing to do with it—he had been planning his next battle against my brother simply because that's all he knew. Kalani's thoughts—and perhaps his dreams as well--were filled with spears and clubs. It was simply in his blood to plan an attack. But, any misgivings I had concerning his love of war I pushed down, wanting to only think positive thoughts about this new alliance.

# Nineteen

## 1776

When I returned to Kalani after seeing to the marriage of my children, he was still disheartened and humiliated by the trouncing he received at Kaupo, having returned to his lands in Kau like a dog with his tail between his legs. Every year he was sure he would gain more Maui ground, and every year it ended up costing many lives. But my husband was never one to rest if he perceived there was a grievance to right; to him, there was always some reason to seek revenge. To those ends, he worked tirelessly while I basked in the glory of my children's nuptials. When I told him the news, he hardly listened. Instead, he stayed up until the golden hours of dawn, planning and plotting with his chiefs. Try as I might to convince him of the sanity of peace, there was absolutely nothing I could do to change his mind. He refused to listen to reason. Even the marriage of his son to Liliha was useless as a token of peace.

"You are a Maui traitor, just like all the others. You think you're very clever, don't you? You sat there in Hana, day after day, waiting for the chance to deceive me," Kalani spit out. "You'd betray me to your brother in a heartbeat."

"How dare you say that," I shot back, defending myself. "Have your people not prospered while I've been with you? Did I not give you a son that has been raised to manhood? A son that you will pass on your lands to?" I flung up my hands in frustration. "What more could you possibly want from me?"

"Your brother's land," he said with a grin, as he looked me straight in the eye. "And I intend to get everything that your brother has. I remain a *puhi niho wakawaka*--a fierce and fearless warrior."

And from that moment on, Kalani's every waking hour was dedicated to the defeat of Kahekili. At times, I blamed myself; other times I knew that Kalani was just being himself, and that no one could have stopped him. For a whole year, through the pounding seas of winter, through the planting and harvesting of a meager sweet potato crop, all he thought about was my brother and how he could conquer his land and claim Maui for his own. I could have told him from the onset that he would fail.

Kalani was clever, yes. Cunning? Shrewd? Absolutely. But he did not understand his adversary.

Kahekili was patient and indomitable. There was nothing but death that would stop my brother, and even then I wasn't so sure his spirit would not grab a club and rise to fight again.

Two hardheaded men, and there I was in the middle.

Daily, I prayed at my altar for some resolution. I asked for the volcano to pour lava from the mountaintop to wipe out the village, for a tempest to sink Kalani's fleet of canoes, for a pestilence to wipe out his troops. I was tortured because what I was praying for would bring disaster down on the *makaainana*, but I was desperate. And, perhaps, in the end, that is why my prayers were not answered. The gods, in their infinite wisdom, did not wish to destroy those innocent people. I came to the realization that in some way or other, we would all die anyway—that what was to be, would be. There was no need for Pele to spew lava, no need to open Laamaomao's calabash to bring the wind to sink canoes. There was no need to pray for pestilence to wipe out the innocent. Besides, my prayers seemed to have grown wings and taken flight, heading out to sea, following the albatross that would not return for years and years. Maybe never.

---

*W*hile I spent my time praying, Kalani drove those in service to him--in short, everyone--to do his bidding. He sent men to the uplands to harvest trees for canoes. When the trees were brought back to the shore near the village, Kalani harassed the canoe carvers, "Go faster! You can work longer if we bring in torches so you can work at night." Farmers were badgered to plant extra sweet potatoes so there would be enough food for his legions. When they protested that they were working as hard as they could, he pushed them harder. "You need extra help? What are your wives doing? Where are your children? Everyone should work!" Fishermen were pestered into hauling in enormous catches—more than we could possibly eat. Their wives toiled long hours cleaning and drying the catch, for they did not want any to go to waste. Kalani had no idea how much food was really available. On the barren lava fields of Kau, the women could not depend on the ferns of the forest to feed their children. Ever practical, they secreted half of everything in the caves so that there would be enough food to last while their men were away at war.

# Twenty

$\mathcal{B}$ack and forth between Maui and Hawaii I went, trying to broker peace between the two chiefs. On Maui, the priests hoisted the god Lono on the standards and circled the island in order to collect taxes during the Makahiki season while my brother was busy formulating his own plans.

"Oahu is like a fine hen--ripe for plucking," Kahekili said. "It is time for me to make my move."

"*Auwe!*" I lamented, perhaps too loudly. "Not another war!"

"Shhh… I knew you would say that. No, not another war." He looked around as if suspected there were spies stationed just outside the door. Then he scooted nearer to me and whispered his plans so that only I could hear. "I plan to do it peacefully if I can. I would rather save my men to fight your husband, for I know he will come again." Kahekili waved even his retainers away. When we were quite alone, he said, "I sent word for Kahahana to give me only one thing on Oahu--the whales that wash to shore at the mouth of Kualoa valley."

I gasped. "Kualoa? Surely you know what you are asking from him."

My brother smiled—of course he knew. "I plan to claim my prize."

"If you claim the ivory…" I mused.

"…he has to give me the valley as well," he finished my thoughts and added his own. "And relinquish the bones of his ancestors."

"But Kahahana has been there only a short time," I argued. "And things seem to be going well for him. Why would you want to upset them? Give the young man a chance. He has been loyal to you."

"It's true--he has been loyal so far. But so far he hasn't succeeded in giving me the little I ask for."

"But he assured you he'd spoken to the chiefs on Oahu. If they didn't want to give it to you then there isn't much he can do about it. It really isn't his to give-- you know that as well as I do." I sensed there was something else my brother was not telling me, so I probed a little deeper. "And why would you ever think the Oahu chiefs would give you their most sacred valley? Would you give away our sacred valley, Iao, the place where our ancestors are buried? Don't be silly. Of course you wouldn't. And neither will they."

"It was I who sent him over there to rule. Don't you see his refusal as a sign of disrespect?"

"Kahahana? Disrespectful? No. Most definitely not." I shifted on the mat, surprised that I was being put in the position to defend Kahahana. "He tried. What more can you ask of him? He's still a young man. Maybe after he has ruled the island for a few more years you can try again."

Kahekili's face stiffened as if I had slapped his cheek. "I don't want to wait for a few more years. If I wait, he will gain strength and it will be harder to fight him."

"Fight him?" I gestured toward Oahu. "No!" I pointed in the opposite direction toward Hawaii. "Fight him!" I shook my head in disgust. "Fight! Fight! That's all you think of. You are as bad as my husband! Maybe the fates will see to it that someone else makes the first move—it doesn't have to be you."

He shrugged and nodded acquiescence, but his surrender was temporary.

I saw my brother as he was: a man in his prime—but with no years left to wait. In truth, he would wait for nothing.

He paused for a minute, "If he will not send me ivory, then I will send to Oahu for warriors. And to send warriors, he has to send canoes. Surely he wants to keep me as an ally."

I was silent, knowing that my hesitancy would signal my sincere disapproval more than the tone of my voice. "What for?"

"To beat Kalani. What else? My *kahunas* have assured me victory. This final battle will be the last time your husband and I meet."

# Twenty-One

## 1776

*O*nce again, my husband called and I returned to his side. The god Lono, of the peaceful Makahiki season, was put away and Kalani's special war god, Kukailimoku, was lifted into place in front of the altar. The appropriate human sacrifices were offered and right away the war god's red feathers bristled in the breeze. Then the gods unleased a torrent of black clouds that came boiling over the hills. The heavens opened up and dumped rain. Lightening rent the air and thunder cracked overhead so loud it rattled my teeth. I huddled in my grass *hale* for days, trying my best to stay warm and dry while the storm crashed all around us. After several days, food was running low. Thankfully the storm finally blew itself out.

Kalani paced throughout the tempest, anxious to carry out what his priests perceived were the hungry god's request. As always, he was prepared to go to war. His men tried to talk some sense into him. They pleaded for time in the fields to repair the damage the torrents of water had done to their meager sweet potato crops and the *kalo loi*, but Kalani could not see past his own nose and insisted they use their digging sticks to practice for battle instead of tending to their fields. There was grumbling among the *makaainana*, but what could they do? When the chief requested them, they were bound to do his duty. Like his war god, Kalani was not a forgiving man so no one dared rise up. To be a victim of his anger was sheer folly and a clear signal to him of a man's willingness to be sacrificed.

All his scheming and strategizing enabled him to launch his biggest offensive yet. Since Kalani had accused me of being a traitor, I decided it was high time to act like one. At the risk of my own life, I sent a messenger to Kahekili to warn him war was brewing. I think the messenger must have drowned in the rolling sea, or been caught by the guards and offered up quietly, for I never heard from any source that Kahekili had received word. In the end, I realized my brother hardly needed information from me; Kahekili was as clever as they came and scarcely needed saving. He understood his foe far better than I ever did. He had already surmised Kalani would not rest until he tried again. It troubled me that mine had been the act of a desperate woman, and in the end I had probably caused the death of the messenger, rather than saved others.

Of course Kalani insisted Kiwalao and I accompany him to Maui. "Gather up your belongings and be prepared to leave at dawn," he ordered.

"But that goes against the advice of your *kahuna*, Holoae. In fact, everything you are commanding goes against your priest. What are you thinking of, Kalani?"

"It matters not what I'm thinking of, woman. Just do as I tell you."

"Kalani…" I said, but stopped because I was talking to his back. He had turned and walked away. Once again, he refused any argument I might make. I knew the consequences of not following his orders. He was ruthless to all, and I did not expect to be exempt. If he would go against his *kahuna's* advice, he certainly wasn't going to follow mine, even if I was his sacred wife. Why had he decided to take us? Was he so sure of himself that he wanted us to witness my family's downfall? Did he not trust us to stay alone in his court? Did he think we would commandeer the nearest canoe and head up the opposite side of the island to warn Kahekili? I never knew his reasons—I only know the outcome.

———

e landed before noon, without resistance, in the Honuaula district of Maui.

Our canoe landed at Keoneolo, but Kalani's fleet of war canoes stretched over two miles along the beach to Makena at Honuaula. The country people, knowing the devastation Kalani had caused in Kaupo, headed for the hills when the guards warned of our approach. Since the villages had been abandoned, there was no battle to be fought; nothing for Kalani to do except to have his men tear up the sweet potato patches and *kalo loi* they could immediately find. Kalani's warriors killed the few men they stumbed across—those that had not followed their women and children into hiding places in the hills. Kalani didn't even bother to burn the villages. He had no reason to tarry. He gave the order to head straight to the isthmus. I was worried—what could my brother be thinking? Surely he had been warned. But my brother had sent no resistance. Absolutely none.

Even though I tried not to let on, I was worried. Had the messenger I sent before the storm not made the crossing? Did my brother not suspect the danger? Where were the guards in the hills? We had only seen a few souls during our brief stop at Makena, and none since then. Whenever Kalani turned his back on me, I scanned the uplands to see if I could spot runners heading toward my brother's compound miles away, but there was no apparent movement. I searched the landscape for fires or smoke signals that the guards might have lit to warn of danger, but there were none. It was as if the island had been deserted—swept clean of elders, women, children and fighting men. No bird called warning, no hawk circled overhead.

Because Kahekili had not sent troops to thwart his progress, Kalani's arrogance knew no bounds. He swaggered as his feather cape dragged through the dirt, freely giving the battle cry, "Onward to drink of the waters of Wailuku!" Instead of saving his best men for the heat of the battle, he sent his finest men, his Alapa regiment, through the swamp and across the plain to attack whatever got in their way.

Back behind the lines—in front of my son, Kiwalao, and I-- Kalani chortled at the thought of slowly roasting Kahekili over the coals in his own *imu*, bragging how he would use my brother's bones to fish for *ula* at his favorite fishing grounds in Kau.

Kalani, of course, kept himself and his court miles away from the danger, safe in the rear at Kiheipukoa. All day Kalani strutted up and down our camp, crowing of his apparent success. "My Alapa, the strongest fighting men in the land, are now drinking the waters of Wailuku," he boasted, as he thrust out his chest. "Everything about the mighty Alapa legion shouts of their victory!" As must have been his plan from the beginning, Kiwalao and I were subjected to his constant bragging: his troop's superior training, their superb mental acuity, their willingness to die for their chief, the excellent weapons his soldiers had fashioned out of *koa* wood and shark's teeth.

I was so sick of his boasting that I used my sacred *kapus* to retire to what little shade I could find. I had my attendants massage my head in an attempt to stop the pounding behind my eyes. When I was away from him for a moment, I was able to see clearly and understand why he'd brought us. It was so that he could have this time of bravado and relish his moment in the sun.

Little did Kalani's troops know that the Maui army was lying in wait. Just as Kalani's *kahuna* had predicted, his army walked right into the trap. Kahekili's men surrounded their enemy, luring them into the net, and then drawing the strings tight around the neck, choking them off from retreat. Almost all of Kalani's eight hundred men, his famous Alapa, were massacred in the sand hills in southwest Kalua. I say 'almost' because two men escaped. Whether they were terrified and ran, abdicating early and not being nearly as brave as Kalani thought, or whether the Maui army allowed them to escape in order to carry the news of the slaughter doesn't matter.

When the two soldiers staggered into our camp, I awoke from a restless sleep and stumbled out to see what the commotion could be. What was left of the men's helmets drooped over their eyes and blood streamed down their faces. Their hands were weaponless as they bowed before their chief. They were no longer Kalani's proud Alapa. They did not utter a word. Their demeanor and sorry state spoke far louder than any story they could have told.

"My chiefs?" Kalani asked.

"Dead," the first man moaned as he answered.

My finest troops, the Alapa?"

"Gone, oh Heavenly One. All gone. Their bodies lie exposed in the sand hills."

The second man admitted, "We are the only survivors."

The *mana* drained from Kalani's proud face. He sank to his knees, burying his head in his hands. Tears flowed in rivers down his cheeks. He let out a mournful wail for the dead.

It was sad to see him—it really was. I joined Kalani in wailing, yet we cried for different reasons. It was not that I was sad for Kalani, but rather I was sad for all the souls lost that day. I wept for the men's bodies that had been left where they lay on the battlefield in pools of blood. I cried for the women who were left alone without husbands. I mourned for all the children who would be without providers, without the guidance of their loving fathers. I keened for mothers who had lost sons, sisters who lost brothers, lovers who had lost their beloved.

The news passed through his remaining troops like flames blown by a gusty wind.

The warriors hurried to their chief, clinging to the belief that he would guide them. Faced by his troops, his moment of intense grief passed and he rose from his knees. Kalani asked the survivors, "What about Kahekili?"

I could not believe my ears! Kalani's best troops had been decimated, and yet he was still determined to go to war. Kalani's wrath against my brother had, up to this time, only been smoldering. "Tomorrow we shall drink the waters of the Wailuku!" he shouted. His call was taken up by his army and rolled off the hills. Then, as his anger rose, he fanned the sparks to flames. "And rest in the shade at Hakuawa!"

"Come, my son," I said as I grabbed Kiwalao's arm. We skirted the clamor and settled at the edge of the remaining troops.

"What should we do, mother?"

"What can we do? The only thing I know is to pray. Pray for the lost souls, and for those that remain. And, perhaps the most important prayer of all, pray that Kalani will come to his senses. Pray for a quick end to this war."

I did all I could for the spirits of the dead on both sides—those brave men who fought for the honor of their chiefs and for their land. I did not rest easily that night.

———

*K*ahekili rallied his warriors before dawn. Some he placed behind the great sand hills of Kamaomao, others he hid at Waikapu. He knew his men would lay down their lives in order to protect what lay behind them--the sacred valley of Iao where the bones of our ancestors lay in peace. He guessed Kalani would not expect him to follow the same battle plan two days in a row, so that is exactly what he did. He drew the enemy in to him and then tightened the net again.

The next morning at Kalani's camp the air pulsed with shouts of men preparing for battle. As the rest of the army headed out that day, proud old warrior that he was, Kalani stood at attention as each battalion marched past him. The men's bodies gleamed with nervous sweat as they heaved their spears high above their heads and cried, "To the waters of Wailuku!" To which Kalani answered, "Rest in the shade of Hakuawa!" The men advanced across the isthmus that divided Maui in two: the great mountain of Haleakala on the right, the slope of Kapilau Ridge on the left, and behind that the West Maui range. Kahekili could not have placed his net in a more favorable place. Like mullet drawn to the fishpond, Kalani's army was baited and caught in Kahekili's snare.

Who would have ever thought that sand could provide such an effective cover? When Kalani's unsuspecting troops neared the spot where the Maui warriors were hiding, spears and stones rained down from every direction. Terrified, Kalani's men ran. In their hurry to escape, they tripped over the mounds in the ground which were the bodies of their dead comrades hastily covered with sand. That made the Hawaii warriors easy targets. The once brave men turned as a school of fish—now rushing here, now there—once they realized the ruse, they also realized there was no escape. The bodies piled up as thousands lay dying where they fell on top of their comrades.

———

*K*alani had shown a brave face to his soldiers, but after he sent them off, he insisted we retreat offshore to watch the battle from the safety of his battle canoe. His plan was to quickly raise the sail and speed out to the open water between Maui and Lanai should a hasty retreat be necessary. It was a far cry from his bravado of yesterday. Kiwalao and I strained to see what was happening onshore. Kalani cowered in the bottom of his regal canoe, his head in his hands, but peering out between his fingers whenever he heard a sound other than the gentle lapping of the waves against the side of the craft.

Kalani's men fell like fish stupefied by *auhuhu* poison. It was such a resounding defeat that I almost felt guilty telling him when he finally raised his head to ask.

Almost—but not quite...

"We shall all be killed!" he whined as he rose to his knees in front of me. "Go to your brother and ask for peace."

"My brother? He would not grant peace to me—certainly not when I am associated with you."

"But you are his sister," Kalani whined. "The sacred one."

"You can't be serious. To him, right now, I am the enemy. If I were to leave this canoe, I would be slain, the same as you. If we would have come in peace, with love in our hearts as I have come to him many times before, then we would have been welcomed to his court with open arms. But now..."

"But you must do something," he pleaded. "Look! They are coming!" In the distance we could see what was left of Kalani's tattered troops lurching toward the shore. This time Kahekili's army would surely be following them.

"*Auwe!* I tell you, there is nothing I can do."

"There has to be *something* you can do," he pleaded. "He is your brother. If you do nothing, we will be killed."

I knew the only thing that would save us would be if we sent our son, Kiwalao, to surrender for us. But even in his desperation, it would not be wise for me to let Kalani think that anything was my idea. I had to watch my words and not put him on the defensive or the plan that I had just thought of would not work. "The only thing that might work..." I began, and then hesitated, as if in deep thought. In a way, it saddened me to see the once proud warrior shriveled up in a ball, shivering so pathetically. "Maybe if we sent someone else to talk to him." I looked down at him for a hint that he had heard me. "If we could only think of someone who is of higher rank than Kahekili." I waited for Kalani to snap at the bait.

And waited.

And waited… watching as his retreating troops drew near. Convincing him was going to be harder than I thought.

"My son!" Kalani cried finally. "But surely you don't mean to send Kiwalao. He's but a boy…"

"He is showing signs of manhood. How many years now?" I counted on my fingers. "He is old enough."

"What if Kahekili kills him? He is my heir apparent!"

"If Kiwalao doesn't try, none of us will live," I reminded him.

"At least his *kapu moe* could buy us some time… the soldiers must bow down."

I quickly saw Kalani's scheme: he was willing to send Kiwalao, but not necessarily to broker peace. No--certainly not peace, for even in the face of defeat he merely wanted time to hoist the sails on his war canoe so that he could escape. That old scoundrel would put anyone on the line to save his own hide, even our—my--beloved son. There was one thing he was right about though. Kiwalao's *kapu moe* would stop the fighting—both sides would be obligated to bow down—the Hawaii men because Kiwalao was his father's son, the Maui men because Kiwalao was a son of Maui and they would honor their chief. But I had to send a clear message to my brother so that he would know the young man wasn't being sent to deceive, but rather that it was safe to trust him. This plan would only work if Kahekili understood I was behind the plan. "But I refuse to let Kiwalao go if that means you intend to leave him stranded," I said, stamping my foot down hard, letting him know that I had seen though his intentions. I was not ready to reveal my whole plan yet —I had to play the fish on the line a little longer. "Either we try to escape before we are captured, or you join Kiwalao in making peace. Which will it be?"

"Is there nothing else we can do to assure his success?" Kalani nervously pulled at the feathers on the edge of his regal cape, panicked at the thought that simply sending Kiwalao into enemy camp might not be enough to stop the slaughter.

"Why is it left for me to bail you out?" I shouted. My husband's fear was playing right into my hand and I pretended an idea came to me. "Wait! Why didn't I think of this before? We shall send the twins!"

"The twins! Yes!" Kalani brightened. "We'll send the twins instead of Kiwalao."

He had no idea that the twins, Kahekili's younger half brothers, had been sent to Kalani's court years ago to assist me in keeping their eyes on the youth, Kamehameha. If the twins, Kameeiamoku and Kamanawa, accompanied Kiwalao, Kahekili would understand that I was behind the truce and that his nephew truly came seeking peace.

"You must send all three—the twins and Kiwalao," I insisted. "Do you want this plan to work, or don't you? Need I remind you that Kahekili would roast you and use your bones for fishhooks?" I wanted to make sure Kalani understood the situation and that he had no doubt I was speaking the truth. "My brother would delight in using your head for a spittoon—or a place to piss." My words hit their mark.

Kalani cringed, and then signaled to the watchmen on shore to paddle out. "Take Kiwalao and the twins to seek peace," he instructed.

I nodded. "If you want to live, I really don't see that you have any choice."

I waved to the three emmisaries as they started out across the plain. Kiwalao was just getting a growth spurt, but still only came up to the twin's shoulders. However, he looked every bit a chief dressed in his splendid red and yellow feather cape. The twins shielded him, Kemanawa carrying the royal feather *kahili* high so that all could see and bow down, Kameeiamoku carried Kiwalao's spittoon instead of his spear, signaling peace, not war. As soon as the men on both sides saw the royal emblems, they laid down their weapons and prostrated themselves in front of their supreme *alii*. Even though the men of Maui would have loved to continue fighting, for they were winning, they understood that the sacred son, Kiwalao, was in their midst. They prostrated before him, and lay, face down, beside their foe.

———

*L*ater, the twins told me of the meeting. They knew, of course, that Kahekili heard of their route to his court as soon as the first guard in the hills spied Kiwalao entering the battlefield. While they were crossing the isthmus, Kahekili gathered his *kahunas*, royal women and children to his court. As his guests arrived, Kahekili dared not rise, for Kiwalao was the more sacred. Instead, Kahekili rolled over on his mat, letting Kiwalao approach and sit on his chest. They rubbed noses and wailed for the men who had been killed in battle. The king honored his nephew by not speaking to him directly, but by addressing the twins. "If you two needed to see me, you could have come by yourself. Were you not afraid to walk through the battlefield? What if your chief had not been recognized and accidentally slain?"

Kamanawa answered, "We did not believe our chief would be killed. Everyone cherishes his sacred robe—yellow with the red shark's teeth. In truth, if we had not come we would have been killed, the same as if we had left the chief at the shore."

Kahekili, of course knew the reason they had come to court, but he wanted everything out in the open. "Then why are you here?"

"The chief has been sent to ask for life. If Kiwalao dies, our royal brother should kill us also," Kameeiamoku bowed as he answered.

Kahekili considered the implications of their request for a moment. All waited for his reply in total silence. "There will be no death. Let the battle cease." Then he asked, "And what of my sister?"

"She is with her husband, Kalaniopuu at Kiheipukoa. It was she who sent us."

Kahekili smiled. "She has done well. Take her *poi* and mullet. Ask her to join me at court--and invite her to bring her husband."

The two men, Kahekili and Kalani met. True to his word, Kahekili allowed Kalani to return unharmed after Kalani promised he would not attack anymore.

Kalani's promise lasted for a while, but deep in my heart, I knew it was a lie.

# Twenty-Two

## 1778

The watchmen on the hills started the signal fires, reporting that a single canoe was crossing the channel. I hope it is Liliha and Kiwalao returning, for she is near her due date. I have been praying for their homecoming so that she delivers our next chief or chiefess here on the island of her birth, Maui, safe within the walls of Pihana where I can be the first to touch my grandchild.

"Light the torches and take them down to the beach. Stay there and help the canoe land safely," I ordered the men.

"No matter who is in it, my chiefess?"

"No matter who. The guards are on alert. There is only one fire, so there is but one canoe. There are many more of you than there are of them."

As the men left the walls of the compound, I turned to the women of the court. "Prepare a place for Liliha. Spread new mats. Clean the birthing stone. Make sure we have plenty of *kapa* cloth and fresh water. Hurry!"

The ladies bustled about, eager to follow my orders. Some carried calabashes down the hill to Iao stream, filled them and carried them back. Some went to the storehouse and grabbed bundles of *kapa* while others spread mats for fresh flooring. When all was in place, they gathered around the perimeter of the *hale papa*, the women's hut, and began to chant.

In the meantime, I went to my altar and prayed to my *aumukua*, Kihawahine. I bowed before the wooden idol. "I come, oh ancestor of mine, to ask for the protection of my daughter, Liliha, whom you know, and for the child in her belly. The child is *niaupio*. She is of sacred birth from her own half-brother, Kiwalao, both children of my own blood. They are all pure, my goddess, the lineage remains unbroken and strong. Bring us a healthy baby--either a manchild, the highest ranked in the island and the next ruler, or a new chiefess for our court. Your wish alone awaits us." I stood silently for a moment, then bowed again and left the enclosure to stand at the gates of the compound, gazing out over the sea, hoping to catch a glimpse of the canoe in the moonlight.

Torches flickered on the beach. The women's soft chants soothed the air. The scent of *maile* wafted on the gentle night breeze. It was a time of watching and waiting, a time for me to collect my thoughts. I sighed as I leaned against the lava-stone wall, taking in the power of the *mo-o*, and looked out over the bay. "It is my grandbaby coming," I whispered to myself. I cocked my head when a gust of wind blew onshore, straining to hear. "I just know it. I can feel it," I said to the retainer who came up beside me.

Suddenly I doubled over as a deep pain shot through my belly. "Yes! It is the labors pain of my daughter birthing my grandchild!" I looked up at the full moon. "Hina, mother in the moon, I beseech you. Watch over the children of my loins. Bring them safe to me." Then I sat on the birthing stone high above the shoreline and chanted with the women. There wasn't anything else for me to do but pray and wait.

The moonlight and the surf and the chanting lulled me into a meditative state. I faced the sea in the direction the canoe would come and closed my eyes for what seemed only a minute. When I opened them again, I saw the canoe rounding the headland and coming into the bay. The canoe, in full sail, seemed to be flying over the surface of the water. I whistled a warning to the men on the shore. One man waved a torch back and forth, signaling those in the canoe to cross over the reef directly in front of him. The men dropped the sail, picked up their paddles and turned the craft toward the island, surfing the breakers and bringing the canoe swiftly to shore.

I saw the woman in the canoe slump down. A man—my son—I would recognize him anywhere--stepped out of the canoe, picked the woman up in his arms and ran up the hill toward Pihana *heiau*. I started down the path to meet them and then stopped, realizing I would be of better use once they got to the top of the hill—it wouldn't do me, or them, any good to be climbing the long hill behind them. I turned and hurried back to the compound. Out of breath, I waited beside the woman's hut. Soon Kiwalao bolted through the entrance, Liliha cradled in his arms. "In here," I directed as I drew back the *kapa* cloth that had been placed over the opening. Kiwalao laid Liliha on the mat.

"Oh mother... I'm so glad..." Liliha sighed.

"Now leave," I said, turning to my son.

"But I..."

"Go! This is woman's work," I said as I pushed him away. "But stay near. Your child won't be long."

"Light!" I said to the women and they brought the *kukui* nut candles. I peered under Liliha's robe when the next contraction came. "Soon—soon," I said to my daughter, soothing her with the words women understand. "Use the breath of life—*ha*! Liliha rolled on to her side. "Do you want up?"

"Yes—to walk."

"The birthing stone is prepared. We will walk to it. Kiwalao!"

Kiwalao rushed in and helped his sister/wife to her feet. He helped her out the door and to the birthing stone, then backed far away. The woman chanters fell silent.

Liliha had no more gotten settled on the rock, her legs up on the sides of the natural throne, than she had a contraction. Her straining tore a rent in the clouds. The moon and a multitude of stars shined down on us. I knelt in front of my daughter and felt between her legs.

Another contraction and I saw the head crowning.

"*Ha*—push!"

Then the shoulders...

"*Ha*—push!"

I caught the girl child in my hands—the next chiefess of the islands and the holder of the sacred goddess, Kihawahine. I held the baby up and wiped the white membrane from her nose and mouth. The tiny one whimpered.

"*Ha*—breathe," I implored, bringing the child's face to mine and blowing my breath into her. The baby took a big gulp of air and cried. "Here is your daughter, Hina," I said as I held the child up so that the moon could see the next born, a goddess like herself.

One of the retainers came with *kapa* and held it out to clean the baby. Then they handed the child to Liliha to suckle and hold near her heart. The woman went back to the group and the long genealogical chant began. "*Papa* the Earth and *Wakea* the Sky begat..." It would take several hours for them to chant all the names in this new child's family, and by the time they got to the end—to the part where her name would be added—the cord would have stopped pulsing and the *kahuna* would have cut it, proclaiming her of our sacred lineage.

Liliha's afterbirth passed. Kiwalao took the cord to the sacred *pio* place for blessing and buried it, and gave the child her name, the first among many names given to the next sacred one. In time, most would know her as Keopuolani.

# Twenty-Three

## 1778-79

*W*hen we first heard about the white men coming to Kauai on the big ships, it was while Kalaniopuu was attacking Maui again. Which time? I lost count long ago.

The Lono priests declared the ships with the billowing white sails to be the return of their god. Me? I never did believe that story because I never really thought that Lono would come back. Why? Because when I looked at the long threads of the story, it was basically about a man who promised he would come back to a woman. Never mind that she was a chiefess, never mind the fact that they had lingered together for many months, never mind the fact that she was pregnant with Lono's child. Every time the story was told, I maintained, "He's never coming back. She might as well face it. That story is as old as the mountains." But just like a woman, instead of finding a man who would treat her right, she did what women have always done: she worshipped him and made him her god. Soon she had convinced others to do the same and they formed the holy order of Paliku, based around his promise to return.

Whether they were emmisaries of Lono or not, the white man stayed until the ships were resupplied with food and fresh water, and then sailed away. Thereafter, the storyteller, Kauakapiki, made a name for himself as he traveled from island to island embellishing on his tale to anyone who would listen. He claimed he had seen the ships up close, and declared they were *heiau* floating on the sea. He maintained that the masts were the oracle towers of the temple and that the white sails hanging from them flapped like manta rays. He said there was a long stick at the front end of each ship that was the navigator, keeping the ship from ever getting lost at sea. He described the round holes in the hull as the large eyes of the *kahunas* that could divine everything. He said the ships were overflowing with priests, their skin fair and their features sharp. They wore something like *kapa,* but they were covered from head to foot. He told of fire flaring from their fingertips and smoke pouring from their mouths as they smoked from minature bowls. I thought it was like the caldera of our volcano goddess, Pele, but I kept my mouth shut as I listened to his stories. At each telling, the tale stretched just a little bit, and then a little bit more, and then a little bit more—just like the sacred knotted cord kept in secret in the *heiau.* Soon our entertainer from Kauai had the men from the ship speaking in the way of the gods in a language no one understood. He said they walked the path of the gods in sandals that covered their feet but were made from the hide of animals. He said they were eager to accept sacrifice and supplication—the same as our gods do—and procured an enormous amount of pigs, sweet potatoes, *kalo* and, particularly, fresh water.

"What did they offer in trade?" I asked.

"The lesser priests have secret enclosures in their coverings," he said as he answered my question. "When they tuck their hands between the folds, they pull out small pieces of iron as gifts for our women."

"Iron?"

"Yes. When the women make like the gods with the lesser priests on the ship, afterwards they receive a nail that they take home to their husbands. Some of the women think the lesser priests intend to stay, for it seems they are dismantling their ship from the inside, one small piece of iron at a time."

With that, I couldn't bear to listen anymore—it was all too much. His story had grown wings and, like Io the sacred hawk, taken flight, circling ever higher. Of course he would embellish his experience--he was a story teller. He received many accolades and much attention from everyone. That much I would allow him. But as to the actual truth? That, I could not say.

I know there is at least two sides to every story, so I requested others input and listened to what they had to say. My cousin Chief Kaeo of Kauai, sent Kaneakahoowaha and Kaukapuaa who had also seen the ships and walked among the men/ gods. The two confirmed that the strangers were completely covered, just as Kauakapiki had described them, so evidently that part was true. That fact helped me to see that they were not gods of our land, for everyone knows the skin breathes better with only simple garments and long exposure to salt air, cleansing rain, and the warmth of the sun.

These two tellers of truth from Kauai seemed to think the foreigners were merely men—men like any other, for the most part. They stated the fact that the men had not washed ashore during a storm, like others years ago who had been absorbed into our society, but had come here of their own free will.

After that report, people talked among themselves, mulling over the details, as they understood them. In the course of the debate, facts were changed until those who thought they knew were likely to have warped the story into something else entirely—all in an attempt to make some sense of it. Some said they were the men the old prophetess Kekiopilo said would come: the white men who rode large dogs with long ears, though no one ever claimed to have seen one of the long-eared dogs. Some said they were just men from another country--for, after all, hadn't our own people come from another place --Kahiki--mentioned in legend? And wasn't the only way to arrive here by sea?

I said, "Yes. The only way to arrive here is by sea unless they drop from the air like frigate birds." When I shared my thought that men could drop like birds from the air, it frightened people so that I stopped saying it, reminding myself that some of the visions I have at the *heiau* are for me alone and not my duty to repeat.

There were those who feared that if the white man's feet were allowed to touch the shore, they would possess the land. The people who were afraid counseled their chiefs to gather the warriors and kill every last one of the white men immediately, before they took over and became a plague upon the land.

What I knew was what the people of the Temple of Kane and those before the Altar of the Supreme Being believed, which was the part of the prophecy not everyone seemed to be paying attention to. In their haste to explain the newcomers to their land, the priests were paying attention to the first part of the prophecy--that of the white bird sailing across the water--but they had forgotten the last part, and their forgetfulness ultimately caused them not to heed the warnings.

When I consulted the priest of Io, he shook his head despondently. "Do the people not remember the prophecy?" he asked. "It says that if the day ever comes when the child of the Divine Lightening Bolt returns under the guise of Lono, it will be one hundred lunar years before the ancient line of sacred *alii* vanishes from this land."

Since that is the lineage from which I am a *pio* member, it meant the decline of my family, and since my family acted in the role of caretakers of the people, it meant the decline of all—every single last one. That realization brought me such sadness I cannot even begin to describe.

Finally, I went to the source—to the one who would know beyond all doubt whether these beings were gods or men. I sent for Lelemahoalani, Chief Kaeo's wife's daughter, the woman who was given as a tribute to the chief white man, the one we later would come to know as Cook. She told me, "The lesser priests do not cry out like our men when they make like a god with the women."

"They don't cry out? It is natural to cry out in pleasure."

"They cry out, but not in pleasure. They groan, as if spilling their seed caused them pain, not pleasure."

"Why do you suppose they do that?" I asked.

She shrugged and had no answer. She told of her time with Cook, saying her father had given her strict instructions to spend the night with him and look around carefully so that she could discover the truth. She went with Cook into the bowels of the *heiau*—down to the head priest's *hale*. She knew the way to approach a man and began caressing him, as is our custom. Quite unlike anything she'd ever witnessed before, he bolted upright, grabbed both her hands, turned them over, and stared at her fingernails. Then he seized her by the wrists, hauled her out of his cabin and up the stairs into the moonlight on the deck. He pulled out a sharp knife from under his shirt and waved it near her face. She trembled, terrified lest he slit her throat. Then he gripped her fingers, one-by-one, using the knife to cut her fingernails down to the quick. "The pain I could endure," she said. "He cut them so short that he drew blood. Why? Why did he cut my nails? Why did he need the blood?" she asked me. "He didn't catch it in any container—he just let it drip on the boards of the *heiau*."

In answer to her question, I said, "Why is any human sacrifice ever done? In order to get the *mana*."

"Yes, that's exactly what it felt like." She held her hands up so I could see the damage he had done. "See? My fingernails still have not grown back." She fretted about the harm that would come to her, and perhaps to her whole family, for everyone knows the *kahuna ana ana* could cast a death spell with the clippings from just one fingernail, never mind her blood that had dripped on the wooden deck of the floating *heiau*. When Cook had finished cutting her nails, he simply swept the clippings into a little pile and flicked them off the rail into the ocean, seemingly not the least bit concerned about their latent power. As he was putting his knife back in its sheath, she looked overboard and watched her fingernail clippings drift away on a swell. "What was I to do?" she asked.

After all this time I could tell she was still fearful that someone would recognize them for what they were. "Perhaps they will mix with the sand, and even if they drift to shore, no one will recognize them," I said in an effort to offer comfort to her.

She told me that before he dragged her back downstairs, there were other things he was fretting about. He hauled her around behind him throughout the ship, barking what seemed like orders to the other priests, but since she did not speak his language, she couldn't be sure. She could only guess his commands by his tone of voice, and by the way the other priest/ men responded to him.

Then I probed with the question I had been dying to ask. "Then he is the same as all men?" I pointed to the area between my legs.

She laughed. "The very same and it all looks the same way too, although I'd take one of our strong men over that weakling. Our men have such imagination when they make like the gods. But he did not choose to be a god with me, even when I offered. A god would not refuse a chiefess—and certainly a man would not refuse a woman. But, even when I offered to use my hand, he seemed to be in pain—as if being a god was more of a chore to him than a joy."

Then I knew for sure he was but a man—but not one to be trifled with, especially if he was exhibiting pain during the most pleasurable gift the gods had given their children. Men in pain generally stir up nothing but trouble. I certainly had learned that lesson well from living for years with my husband, Kalani.

What was I to do?

I went back to see the sacred prince of Io, Kaleimamahuihoapilikane. He saw how concerned I was, and after we spoke, he ordered the temple closed so he could have solitude to communicate with his great god. I waited for several hours. When he came out of the temple, I saw the haunted look in his eyes and could tell he was disturbed. He told me how he carefully performed the sacred rites, forgetting nothing, skipping over not a word, until he came to the *Hale Uaia,* the room where the sacred coconut fiber is kept—the one that ties the chiefs of today to the ancient land of *Ka-Kapa-Hanau-Molu,* and then through these ancients to the beginning of us all. He said that the cord is always strung taut, but when he entered the room—even in the dark—he could see that the cord was limp. He backed out of the room, left the temple, and came directly to tell me.

"The cord is stretching, like the stories Kauakapiki is spreading," I said with a flick of my wrist, hoping to dismiss the whole matter to rumor and gossip.

"Alas, my fathers are departed to the endless night and the bones of their sons are scattered on alien reefs," he lamented.

What he said chilled my heart. Much as I wished the words he said were not true, in the deepest part of my being, I had to admit that they were the same thoughts I had as I prayed at my own altar. "The gods are never wrong in their guidance," I said.

"Then we have lost our way," he said. "Isn't it strange how just a few men can change the balance of what always was and turn it into something that cannot even be imagined?"

"I know the *mana* won't die in my lifetime--I am too close to old age."

"In the end, you will see the beginning," he warned. "And like me, even with all our prayers and *mana,* neither of us will have the power to fight it."

If I admitted my inner truth, I could feel my *mana* slipping away, little by little, like the hole a rat nibbles in the bottom of a calabash. "I can't bear to think of what will happen to my people. How will they survive without those with *mana* to guide them? I have dreams and visions that bother me deeply."

"What do you see?" he inquired.

"I see men and women staggering under the weight of some kind of oppression much worse than anything I can imagine."

"Do you see a person?"

"It is never a presence I can see—only one I can feel—the weight of four times four times four hands pressing down does not adequately describe it. It is as if the people are deaf—for I call out to them, but they do not hear. And they are dumb, for even under constant pressure, they do not cry out in pain. The *lois* dry up, the leaves of our brother *kalo* wither, and the stalks turn brown, as if there is drought. Breadfruit rots on the ground and the people do not bother to pick it up although they are starving. The coconut trees lay flattened on the ground, the dried fronds rustle in the breeze, gasping their last. I step over the downed trunks and walk to the shore. The sides of the fishpond are destroyed; the water is brackish and muddy. Nothing stirs—not a fish, not a bird. I am the only living thing. I sit down on a fallen tree trunk and weep. My tears dry up before they hit the ground. The ground is not dirt, but a hard gray substance, as if the lifeblood leached out and left just a pale color. I wake up frantic. To convince myself I am awake, I leap up and go to the entrance of my hut. I am relieved to hear the stream babbling and see the first light of day breaking through the leaves."

"So it's all just a dream?"

"All is just as I had left it the night before, but I have a restless sensation that haunts me. Something is dying. All the prayers I say, all the begging I do helps not a whit. I am immobilized. I cannot stop it. I don't even know what I am trying to stop. It's the most helpless feeling I've ever had."

"Have you told anyone else about this?"

"No, I cannot tell my husband Kalani about it. He will call me a silly woman and tell me to forget it. Apparently he never feels helpless. Even when he loses a battle, he is ready to muster more warriors and go back to fight again. It is all he knows: fight to the death. How can I explain to him that I am in a crusade against an enemy I cannot see? At best, he will call in the priests and order them to find out who is praying me to death. A man will be sacrificed. I cannot bear the thought of that. I do not wish to see another life lost."

"I see…" muttered the priest, but there was no solace, other than the fact that one other person knew. "*Haole*," he declared. "The men without *ha*—breath."

"Yes," I said. "Without spirit." By telling him, I knew it would not stop my visions, nor help me sleep at night, but what could I do? I could not carry the burden alone. I hoped maybe something would come of it.

He and I sat and wailed together, our cries rising above the wind blowing down sacred Iao valley, past our dear ancestors, who were silent in their caves and powerless to help.

From then on, I kept my dreams to myself and prayed they would drift away on the outgoing tide. But they did not go—it was rather that I got used to them. From then on, I carried a burden on my back, and after a while, I forgot I was carrying it. It became a part of me—that melancholy—that spirit that fed off me, that hitched a ride on my every thought and wiggled into every dream until I could not remember a time I didn't have it. That thing that I could not name became a part of me—something I forgot to want to shake off. I didn't know if anyone else noticed that it had engulfed me, although at times I saw my daughter, Kalaniakua, looking at me in a way she never had before. Maybe she was just noticing that I was getting older… I was, of course, but it was the weight of the thing that aged me. It bent my back and settled in a deep well in my heart, taking its toll on me long before my time.

# Twenty-Four

## 1778

*I*n day-to-day living, things were as they always had been. The plover sailed out from the cliffs and returned at dusk. The tide washed in and out. The moon waxed and waned. Women gathered *lauhala* and wove mats while their sisters pounded the bark of the *wauka* to make *kapa*. The fishermen threw their nets; the hunters carried home pig; the canoe builders carved *koa*.

Once again, Kalani spent the winter months regrouping for his assent on Maui. When the Pleiades set in the morning sky, and the time of Lono was put to rest, Ku, the war god, came to the fore. Kalani ordered us to board the canoes and we went right back to Maui—to Mokulau, just south of Kaupo, where my father, Kekualike, had rebuilt the *heiaus* of times long past.

As we sailed toward the leeward coast of Maui, the condition of the land was clear. Where there had once been verdant terraces in my father's time, where the fan of mineral rich soil from the volcano's flow had been a sea of green vines, now the land was bare.

Kalani turned to me, his eyes wide in shock, "Where are the fields?"

"They are gone. The *makaainana* have not fully recovered from your last raid," I said calmly. "Maybe now you understand what happens when there is continual war. The farmers are conscripted as soldiers and die in battle, leaving the women and children to do the best they can."

Still Kalani, stubborn man that he was, would not admit that any of the help-lessness of the people had been his doing. In his rage at not finding more food, he ordered his warriors to tear up the small fields of newly planted sweet potato crops and torch the *hales*, leaving the survivors desperate. Not content this time to merely urinate in the men's eyes, he commanded his warriors to bash in the farmer's heads, leaving their brains exposed and their bodies to rot in the potato patches where they fell.

As soon as Kahekili got word that the Hawaii troops had landed, he sent his army to drive them away. I knew my brother must be furious with me for not be-ing able to better control my husband. After the first day of battle, I snuck away from Kalani in the evening when the shadows would hide me. Fortunately for me, one of the Maui chiefs recognized me and let me enter their camp. I begged the Maui men to take word to my brother of my deep sorrow at the loss of our countrymen and the food source. I pleaded with them to tell Kahekili I was pow-erless to keep Kalani in check and there was nothing I could do.

After he had done as much damage as he could in Kaupo, Kalani's troops sailed across to the small island of Kooholawe. There was not much of value, but he tore up what little he found and sailed back to Maui, landing further up the coast at Lahaina. This time Kahekili had guards posted. They had been keeping a close eye on Kalani from their watchtowers in the hills. The warriors from the westside defended their territory and forced Kalani away from land and back out to sea. He retreated across the Auau Channel and landed on Lanai. In order to conquer the island, Kalani cut off the people's water supply and then proceeded to ravage the land thoroughly, taking out his anger toward the Maui farmers on the people of the neighboring island. Lanai is a small island—the devastation did not take long. Kalani set sail once more, heading around the north side of Maui and landed at Honokohau where he helped himself to the people's provisions, for by this time ours were running low. Landing, attacking, then retreating to his war canoe became Kalani's successful battle strategy. He thought he had finally figured out a way to best my brother, but in fact, all that did was keep us out to sea most of the time. He was smart enough not to venture near the coastline at Wailuku, thereby dodging the stronghold of Kahekilii. But when he landed at Hamakualoa where there was fresh water and sweet potatoes, he was surprised to find Kahekili's army waiting for him. Kalani was once again routed. He retreated, but to prove his point, he went ashore in the Koolau district and established a stronghold. To further rub salt into the family's wound, Kalani called on our son, Kiwalao, to lead his troops.

———

*A*fter I called for him, Kiwalao presented himself to me, hanging his head and sighing, "I know what all this means, but do I have to? Why can't I just live peacefully on both islands with my wife and child?"

"Look at me." When he lifted his face, I saw how he had aged. His jowls hung slack like that of a sow fattened for slaughter. It was clear he was a man begging to be relieved of his pressing responsibilities rather than a chief who would soon rule. How was I going to get this pampered child to accept his duty to his father? How could I warn him that this was just the first in what would be a long line of obligations? "You will rule one day. You are the heir apparent of Hawaii—and you could have this island as well when your time comes. Your uncle, Kahekili, has great faith in you. But until your father steps down or is killed, you must do as he asks."

"But he's making me fight against my uncle! He is the man I swore my alligance to," he moaned as he touched his tattooed shoulder and bowed his head.

I thought of the priest's prophecy from so long ago: that I would be the mother of a ruler. Without a doubt, Kiwalao was the one to fulfill the prophecy. I had to think of something to say to him that would help him make sense of the situation. "Think of how it would look to the chiefs of Hawaii if you refuse to fight. You have no choice. Conduct yourself properly, kill as few as possible, and you will return safely."

"And what about you?"

"I have been with him this whole campaign." I sighed. "I long to take him back to Kau. Believe it or not, even the solid ground of the barren lava sounds like a blessing now. Like you, I have no wish to make war—not against my own people—not against anyone. Ever again."

"So you have to fight against your homeland too?" Kiwalao raised his head again and looked me in the eye.

"There are many things I've had to do in my life that I did not wish to do. My obligation is to the people," I said. "I pray, daily, as should you, for the divine intervention of the gods."

# Twenty-Five

*R*umors reached us that the ships of Lono had been spotted coming down the windward coast of Maui, traveling the same path that Kalani had just traveled. Within a few days, the guards at our camp in the shade of the cliffs at Uli near Wailua spotted the white sails rounding the point at Pauwalu and drifting toward us. They anchored offshore at Haaluea. At that moment I thought my prayers had been answered, for surely Kalani's curiosity about the white man would divert his attention from the daily skirmishes. On the other hand, I knew there was a strong possibility that the answer to my prayers might also mean nothing would ever be the same again.

By this time Kalaniopuu's health had begun to fail. He had become shaky on his feet, his skin was scaly from years of drinking *awa*, but he still was in complete command of his men. He went behind my back and devised a plan to take a small party out to trade with Cook. When he returned from the ship, I railed against his deceit. Later, after I had calmed down, he told me that he felt it was the chief's duty to make an offering to his god, and that his gift of a few pigs and breadfruit had been accepted. He also showed me the coveted pieces of iron he had brought back.

"A dagger," I snorted. "As if the men need another way to kill each other." I started to walk away but then turned and said, "You are nothing but a meddlesome old man."

He did not disagree. "I left Kamehameha and Kekuhaupio on board Lono's ship, but then the ships sailed away."

"How could you?" I screamed. "That was just stupid. You let your nephew and your best warrior be taken away? What were you thinking? What if they get hurt, or worse yet, killed?"

"*Auwe*! My best warriors," he slurred. He dropped his empty *awa* bowl on the mat. He pressed his back against the *hale* pole and slid down until he could stretch out his skinny legs.

"They may be strong men, but they are two against how many?"

"Kamehameha volunteered to stay," he said as his head drooped. He rested his chin on his chest. "He said he'd look around and report back."

"I'm sure he has something else on his mind."

He glanced up at me through bloodshot eyes. "Always suspicious of him, aren't you?" He closed his eyes. It would not be long until he slipped into an *awa* dream from which he could not be roused.

"I raised Kamehameha. I know him," I argued. "He's there because he sees some sort of advantage."

"It's always advantageous to be near the god Lono," he whispered.

I was going to say, 'That white man is no god,' but I held my tongue. Why upset the old man? If he wanted to think the white men were gods, he wasn't the only one being duped. I looked down on him and realized how he'd aged. He used to be a strong, virile man; now he is old and rummy with *awa*. Even though I knew I might provoke him beyond his endurance, I was not ready to let the subject drop and chose to risk it. "And how will they return?"

"They will escape, if necessary."

"How? Dive off the side of the ship and swim in shark infested waters?"

"Do not forget that Kamehameha's mother ate the eyeball of a shark, not the other way around." He cracked open a red-rimmed eye. "Besides, they have a canoe." He closed his eyes then and drifted to the end of his tether.

I knew beyond a shadow of a doubt that Kamehameha wanted to rule. He would fight to the death for it, I was almost certain, else why would he have spent years training so hard? And, my son Kiwalao, even with many loyal troops, may not be strong enough to stop him. But the priests said I would be the mother of a chief, I reminded myself.

And, he is my only son. I rolled over on the mat, afraid that in his *awa* stupor Kalani might be able to pick my thoughts out of the air. Restless, I finally got up and sat in the opening of the *hale* in the waning moonlight. Maybe Kamehameha won't return I thought, but this wish I decided to keep to myself.

———

*T*he next afternoon the lookout announced Kamehameha's canoe returning. That night everyone gathered in the compound and listened to his report. The information he brought back primarily had to do with weapons, but what I was interested in was the cure to the people's disease.

"Do these men still have the same disease the women of Kauai have?" I finally was able to ask.

"These are the same gods," Kamehameha said. "They have brought disease, but now there are two names. There is the old disease we already know, *kaokao*, the one they call syphilis. Now there is a new disease *pala hao*, gonorrhea."

"Our *kahunas* have been trying to treat it." I said. "Is there a cure?"

"I asked, but the answer is no. None."

While the men discussed weapons, I stared at the firelight and tried to reason things out. If this was really the god Lono, then why had he brought disease with him? Wasn't he supposed to be a god who bestowed blessings, not one who brought curses to his people? I knew that the women on Kauai who had slept with Cook's men had passed the disease on to their husbands and lovers, who passed it along, until the whole island chain was suffering. The priests named it *kaokao*, the disease brought about from lying with the gods, but now there appeared to be two diseases—similar, but different. Who could believe that lying with a god would bring such devastation? Not everyone wanted to believe that the gods carried such sickness. Blame was scattered around like birds dropping seeds to grow a new forest, but blame never grows anything productive. Instead it pitted wife against husband, lover against lover. It was all traced back to the ships, and to a disease the *kahuna lapaau* had no cure for.

What did I believe? The same thing I thought from the first time I heard about it.

These intruders are men, not gods. No god would be cruel enough to spread disease among the people who worshipped him. It just didn't make any sense to me and I couldn't understand why others didn't see it.

Sensing my displeasure and worried that perhaps I would not be able to hold my tongue, Kalani dismissed me and moved the council into the men's house where they talked into the night. I listened as much as I could, but intermittent squalls blew through and the rain drowned out their voices. Even the little bit I could hear was washed away by morning.

———

*B*y the next evening the chiefs had discussed the matter to death. Finally, Kalani was ready to share the information with me and came to seek my advice. "Kamehameha wasn't able to amass anything solid," he said. "And the chiefs couldn't seem to piece togther anything to come to a definite decision."

I doubted that Kamehameha was telling his uncle or the chiefs all he had seen, but I knew better than to put it to Kalani in those words. I couched my speech, pointing instead to Kamehameha's inexperience rather than his cunning. "Can you trust the report of such a young man?"

"Kekuhaupio was there too. He is well respected at this court. If he had something different to say, he would have said it. He is a man of sound judgment, don't you agree?"

It wasn't that I did not agree with Kekuhaupio's judgment, but he had also been the man entrusted with the training of Kamehameha, plus the fact that Kamehameha had once saved his life, so my feeling was that he might be inclined to agree with the young chief. I could see where further questioning of Kalani would lead me, so I let it drop and tried a different angle. "But do you believe this white man is Lono?"

He sighed. "What *I* believe hardly matters. Whether he is a god or a man is of no concern to me. It is but a short time until the start of the Makahiki. The god Lono will rise at the *heiau* and we shall see. What *is* will be revealed by and by. Now hush."

Cook's ships stayed offshore for several days. Kalaniopuu allowed some canoes from his camp to go out to the ships to take the food and water the white men requested; since it was not Kalani's land, he could not give permission for the white men to come ashore. Then the white men asked for a large quantity of sugar cane, which was also provided. We spent the night around the fire trying to figure out what they could possibly do with so much cane.

"Maybe they've discovered a cure for the sickness they brought," someone suggested.

I thought that was a reasonable idea, so the next day I prepared some cane. I asked the *kahuna lapaau* to apply a poltice to a man that was sick, as an experiment, but the compress did no good.

Kalani gave orders that when the next canoes went out, the men were to go on board and observe exactly what the white men were doing with the cane. The report came back that they had covered it with water and let it ferment for a few days, and then brewed a foul-tasting drink they called alcohol, which they consumed in large quantities.

"Did it cure them of the sickness?" I asked, ever curious as to how I was going to treat this new disease.

"It made them stupid and they couldn't walk straight. They staggered around the ship and fell down. One man leaned overboard to vomit and fell into the water and they had to throw a rope overboard and pull him out before the sharks got him. In their haze, they begged for women." I realized we must have sent out the wrong kind of cane: the white man had drunk too much red sugar cane, the one we use as a potent love medicine. Instead of curing the disease, it would in the long run, no doubt, make it worse.

After having consulted the stars, never mind the fact that the ships of their god were anchored offshore, the Lono priests declared it was time for Kalani to be sequestered to begin the ceremonies for the start of the Makahiki. It was time for the war god, Ku, to be put away, and for Lono, the peaceful one, to reign.

I had not heard from my brother, Kahekili, for quite some time, but I knew he would be glad for the season of war to end. His men could be put to better use planting *kalo* and sweet potatoes than jousting against Kalani. Just before the men went into the temple, Ulamaheihei, a trusted young chief from my brother's court, arrived and spoke to me in private. "Your brother asks you to watch Kalani's every move, as usual, and also to keep an eye on the white men's ships."

"Do you believe the ships are from the god Lono?" I asked.

"Of course our Lono priests think that. The rest of us…" Being a very cautious man, he did not finish his thought, careful that his words, like the frigate returning to the nest on the evening breeze, sailed back only to him.

"I don't care about the white men's ships," I said obstinately, hoping that by telling my opinion I could get some indication of his thoughts, or those of my brother.

"As always, we need someone to keep an eye on the chief," he repeated, reverting back to his original goal. "We need someone who can keep Kalani from being led astray. And we need someone to keep an eye on the young warrior, Kamehameha, who we hear has already traded heavily for iron."

"How can you know that?" I was astounded that he knew things about Kalani's court that were, at best, rumors.

"We too have sent men to be with the god." He smiled. "And your brother gets reports on the wind." His voice lowered as he became serious. "You need to see that Kalaniopuu takes his men and goes home—and your brother requests that you, as always, accompany him."

"As always, I will obey my brother's wishes," I said. I was silent for a minute but did not move from my mat. Then I inquired, "But what about you? What do you think of the white men at our shore? Is the one they call Cook the god Lono? I want to know what you think."

"Me? I will lead my chief's warriors home as he has instructed me to do and we will then celebrate the Makahiki."

Clever man, I thought. He dodged my question as neatly as a warrior sidestepping spears. No wonder my brother had chosen him as a messenger.

The next morning, Kalani and his legion lined up on shore to wave as the men on the ship lifted the anchors and sailed down the coast. When the ship was out of sight, the chiefs and the priests retreated to the *heiau* for a ten-day retreat. Ku was put to rest and Lono, the peaceful one, would be our god for the Makahiki season.

———

*L*eft alone with my thoughts, I had much to mull over. I remembered the question my brother had asked the last time I gave him the excuse of Kalani's warrior nature. "If he wants to fight, why doesn't he start at war with someone on his own island?" Kahekili had asked. "Better yet, why doesn't he just stay home and plant sweet potatoes and take care of his people? He comes over here and tears up the crops, and then I must take up the spear and turn to Molokai and Oahu for food, forcing me do the same thing he does."

I agreed with my brother. How could I explain to him that Kalani did not have the word "enough" in his vocabulary? Instead I said nothing. I didn't bring up the fact that our father, Kekaulike, was the one that had gone to Hawaii years before and started trouble in the first place. Even though I was silent, my brother knew what I was thinking: I wanted peace above all, and my duty was to keep Kalani quiet--if I could.

"Men get killed. Women have no husbands, *keiki* have no fathers. Why is he doing that to his own men, never mind doing it to mine?"

Again, what could I say? Should I have said, 'This is the way of this man?' or could I have said, 'This is the way of the warrior—to fight the strongest.' Or maybe I should have said what was deepest in my heart? 'This is the way of all men.' That is the truth I have observed. Men fight. Women want peace. I was raised to know that my duty is to the *makaainana*. Where there is peace there is prosperity; where there is war there is slaughter, then famine. No mother wants to grieve when her son is killed; no wife wants to lament the loss of her husband; no sister wishes to mourn for her brother. But I dared not say these things out loud. I simply had to sit and wait, hoping that enough steam would rise from Kalani's smoldering vent, and that it would be enough to relieve the pressure in order to prevent an explosion.

I also worried about the white man. Had the god come back? Or is it as some have suggested, that he is simply a man from a different place? He came to

Kauai and left. He returned to Maui, but did not come ashore. What kind of god would not claim his rights to land on the eve of his season? I was left with the same thing I was always left with: men's secrets…who could ever figure them out? Maybe Kalani was right: what is will be. Certainly Ulamaheihei is right. In the end both men are doing the same thing: keeping their own counsel. They know that time will pass and things will come to fruition. The prophets counseled me to pay attention to what the wind brings in the clouds, to what falls from the sky as rain, and most of all, to observe what blows to shore from the far reaches of the horizon.

# Twenty-Six

## JANUARY 1779

After the god Lono replaced Ku at the temple, Kalani ordered all of us into the canoes. The fleet crossed the channel between Hawaii and Maui and sailed down the leeward coast.

"What are the white men's ships doing at Kaawaloa?" I asked as we neared Kealakekua Bay.

"I sent the white man the long way around the island—the way of the god Lono--and told him he'd find good anchorage when he got here," Kalani chuckled. "I'm glad he followed my orders."

That was just like Kalani—ordering a god to do his bidding. "What kind of a god has to ask for directions to the place where the people make offerings to him?" I asked.

"A god who doesn't know the way," he answered with a mischevious grin.

"So you think…"

He waved me away. "As the ruler, I take command." He wasn't about to reveal what he thought—not to me, not to anyone.

We landed on the north side of the bay, at Awili in Kaawaloa and stayed near the home of my husband's close friend, Keaweaheulu. Before we even got settled in, Kalani left to pay an informal visit to the ships. I was concerned that he left in such a hurry, but in a way it was a good thing because when he came back that night he was upset and came to see me.

His usual habit was to prop himself up on the mat and lean against the *hale* pole, his scrawny legs and feet stretched out in front of him. He had his coconut bowl in hand and I knew soon his head would be hanging to one side in an *awa* stupor. Tonight, however, he placed the bowl on the floor and paced back and forth. "They're out there," he mumbled. "They're out there."

"Who's out where?" I asked, impatient for the details.

"The women. The ship is overrun with our women. They're trading their bodies to the white men—and for what? For trinkets—for those pieces of glass, for the cloth that rips so easily, and for nails."

"For nothing, basically," I said, shrugging. I tried to remain calm and unattached, but my heart sank. I knew as soon as the women swam back in the morning they would bring the white man's illness to the village. The thought made me sick to my stomach.

"What we trade in return--water, pigs, sweet potatoes, breadfruit--at least can be eaten and will sustain life. What they give the women in return is nothing that can sustain life. Those women are trading away life!"

"You are right, my Kalani," I said, surprised that for once I agreed with him. I wanted to quiet him so I said, "What the white man has to offer sustains nothing."

"I forbid it! I forbid the women selling themselves like that," Kalani declared, and then stumbled across the mat.

I jumped up and grabbed his arm before he fell. I eased him down and stretched his legs out for him.

"We know what happens when they sell their bodies—they get those diseases," he muttered. "They bring it back to their husbands. Our *kahunas* have no way to cure them."

It was hard for me to hide my enthusiasm. Maybe his concern for the women would be the thing that would convince Kalani to send the white man away for good.

"What are you going to do about it?" I asked as I massaged his skinny legs.

"I will send my warriors out in the canoes to bring the women back," he said. And with that, he kicked my hands away, scrambled to his feet, and lurched out the doorway into the night. He woke everyone in the village as he called for his strongest soldiers. After the men were on their way, I guided him back to his resting place by the pole. I helped him sit down so he would be in less danger of hurting himself.

"You've done all you can do for one night, my Kalani," I cooed. "Let the men do as you ask while you lay beside me as in the days of old." The thought of the days of old always calmed him. He curled up beside me and we were able to get a few hours sleep.

The next day, after the men brought the women back to shore, Kalaniopuu called all the people in the village to his court. He asked me to go with him as he walked among them. I understood his reasoning: my *kapu moe* would force them to prostrate themselves, but it would look as if they were groveling in the presence of their chief. "You are forbidden to go to the ships!" he thundered. "Any woman who goes to the ships will be killed. Go home to your families." And to the men he said, "And any man who sends his woman out to the ships will be her death companion."

———

*S*urprisingly, Cook agreed with the ban, and it lasted for a day or two, but then Cook demanded that his men be allowed to come ashore to fill the wooden water casks and Kalani agreed. The first thing the white men did was build a stone dam and change the stream's flow in order to make it more convenient to fill the oak barrels. Altering the flow caused disturbances both upstream and downstream, but as it turned out, that would be the least of the trouble.

I sat on the stone bench near the opening of my *hale* where I had a perfect angle to watch the men. I was astounded that it took several men to roll the empty barrels up the hill—any of our men could have carried that barrel by themselves. Perhaps the disease they carried accounted for their apparent weakness. Once the barrels were behind the dam, all they had to do was wait for the water to fill them up. Of course they abandoned their work the moment they heard the women giggling in the bushes. In the end, the power of the white man's baubles proved too strong. None of the women were willing to listen to a doddering old man, even if he was their chief. His threats were like him: at best, feeble.

I protested, but Kalani reminded me, "The men on those ships have been without women for a long time. If our women take care of these men, they will not make war."

"*Auwe!*" I said. "When has the sweetness a woman offered ever stopped a man from making war?" I stomped my foot. "When did it ever stop you?"

"Never." He smiled. "What the men are getting now is more valuable than you can imagine."

"Which men are you talking about—ours or theirs?" I was disgusted with the lot of them. "What could be more valuable than healthy people?"

"The white man's metal."

And so, at the village across the bay, at Kahuloa, and even under Kalani's nose at Kaawaloa, the white men who had been starved for sex after their time at sea took turns coming ashore. Their pockets were full of nails that they had pulled from the hull of their vessels. Evidently lust was a stronger incentive than the risk of a sinking ship.

"What are the women doing with the nails?" I asked.

"Giving them to their husbands to melt down in order to fashion weapons."

"Once again, it comes down to killing." I didn't know whether to be sad or angry.

In the end, I held both emotions in my hand at the same time and heard them rattle against each other like *ili ili*, the smooth stones used in the *hula* to mimic the sound of water chattering with the rocks at the shoreline.

Coming back to their husbands, the women spread the rumor throughout the village that each night the sailors hauled the full casks to the deck and dumped the fresh water into the sea so that they would have to row to shore the next day in order to fill them up again.

In due course, long after the white man had sailed, many bastard children were born to the women and raised by their families. They were called *opala haole*--foreign garbage. Those children did not inherit the gracefulness of our people, but instead the shameless greed of the *haole*, those who were devoid of spirit.

———

One morning we were summoned by the priest to come to the Lono temple across the bay at Hikiau. Cook also came ashore and met us at the landing. The head priest of the *heiau* wrapped a red *kapa* around Cook's waist and led him inside the walls of the temple. Kalani and I followed the priests and were seated inside a large circle of stones. In the center were twenty poles, and at the top of each pole, a human skull. After reciting the opening ceremonial chant, Cook was seated in the place of honor. The head priest hefted the sacred knife over his head in order to slit the throat of the pig he was about to offer as a sacrifice. It was hard for me not to chuckle when I saw the look of terror pass across Cook's face. Although protocol demanded that he not move, he unconsciously rubbed his neck as he looked up. I was sure he feared he might find his place of honor beside the sacrifice. To Cook's relief, the priests merely anointed his head with pig fat and blood while they muttered their prayers. Then the *kahuna* had to push Cook up the ladder as they climbed the oracle tower. Another prayer was offered. It seemed to me that Cook/Lono stumbled through the ceremony, merely mimicking what he thought appropriate and doing as little as he could to fulfill his role in the rituals. The priests seemed confused by his hesitancy and cut the ceremony as short as they dared, releasing him from his godly duties. Cook bolted out of the *heiau* and down the hill, heading for his ship as fast as he could.

I looked at Kalani to see his reaction, but his face remained fixed as stone.

The priests of Lono had just collected the yearly taxes and, instead of giving a portion to the chief, freely shared their bounty with the white men. Day after day they kept their word to their god Lono/Cook and sent hogs, sweet potatoes, bananas, and *kalo* out to the ships. When asked privately, the priests admitted they realized they had welcomed a very hungry god whose appetite seemed insatiable. Kalani, for his part, plied Lono/Cook with feather capes, helmets, finely woven mats, and *koa* bowls. In return, Cook gave my husband one shirt made from the cloth that rips, one sword, a few mirrors and some barrel staves.

It broke my heart that Kalani could not see how little he was being paid for all they took. He never would have accepted such trinkets from any of his chiefs, but then the men of the islands produced things that people could eat and use. When I could not stand it any longer I confronted Kalani. "What are you thinking? Do you see how the white man is taking advantage of us?"

"It is not what I think—it is what the priests think," he answered. "The head priest assures me the white man is the god Lono."

"Never mind what they think. Whose land is this anyway? What is important is what you think. The question is, are *you* certain?"

"I've told you before--it is what *they* think. How do I know? They supply their gods with pigs and food, so it might be so. It cannot be for trade, for they receive nothing in return. At least I've gotten something," he said as he proudly held up a cracked mirror.

I grabbed the mirror from his hand and turned it so he could see his fractured face. "Look! Can you not see? What they've given you is broken."

Kalani saw my distress and promised me he would stay away from the ship. I wondered what strange hold this man--who could be a god--had on my husband. Kalani's god was Kukailimoku, the one they called the land grabber. Nevertheless, it was apparent to me that Kalani was infatuated with Lono/Cook. He could not stay away from this god/man any more than the women could stay away from the white sailors, or the sailors stay away from the women. Whatever was to be traded, or bartered, or eventually stolen, there was much activity between the two villages and the ships.

One morning a young chief asked permission to enter my *hale*. "My chiefess, you asked me to tell you when I saw any strange movement or heard any rumors. Kalani is on his way to the ships. His retainers tried to detain him, but they could not. He is putting on his royal feather cape now. You have asked him not to go there, but he persists. What can he be thinking?"

I smiled. "Ah the question on every woman's mind—what is her husband thinking?"

"The chiefs have tried to stop him, but failed. They sent me to summon you because you are the only one who can stop him." When I did not move, he pleaded, "I speak for everyone. We are as desperate as you to keep Kalani from going to the ship. The chiefs have grown tired of Cook's demands--demands that grow higher each time he has contact with the Heavenly One."

"Kalani thinks he can leave for the ships because I am sworn to seclusion during the day by my *kapus*. He thinks I will not know," I muttered as I tied my *lei niho palaoa* around my neck. "Go back to Kalani and stall him as long as you can. Then see that he goes down the main path to the canoe."

"But... the canoe?"

"Hurry," I said, shooing him out the door. "Do as I say. If you are right, then we do not have much time." The retainer left my *hale* and ran back to Kalani's compound. As soon as he was out of sight, I took a shortcut, scurrying down the hill and did the only thing I could think of to do. If it worked for Kiwalao to stop a battle, I reasoned it would work for me against Kalani, for even the chief had to follow the rules of the *kapu moe*, the prostrating *kapu*.

Out of the corner of my eye I saw Kalani amble down the hill toward the canoes, helped by a chief on each side. The rest of the chiefs and some warriors followed closely behind. And there, in the middle of the trail, he found me lying on my back on the ground, stretched out where the path narrowed between two coconut trees. I had chosen the spot carefully. There was no way he could go around me; the only thing he could do was step over me. Even though he was chief, if he honored the *kapu*, he dared not. When his chiefs saw me, they quickly fell to the ground, for my *kapu moe* demands my head always must be higher than theirs. Since I was lying on my back, they all had to drop to their bellies, faces to the earth, eating dirt. Kalani stopped short and stood above me for a moment, reviewing his options, which as I had planned, were none. It was unthinkable for him to be deterred from his chosen course, and yet he dared not touch me, the one of *niaupio* birth. He turned to order his men to remove me from his path, but they were all face down behind him, honoring my sacred *kapu*. He could not move. But, as supreme ruler, he could not admit that I had deterred him from his chosen route. I smiled up at him, waiting for his wrath. But he did not speak. His only option was to turn around and return to his compound. The ruse had worked this time, but I knew it would not work again.

A day or two quietly passed, but then Cook summoned the Lono priests, asking them to fulfill yet another demand. This time he insisted the astronomers from the ship be brought ashore. He wanted them to build something he called an observatory near Hikiau *heiau*. When he explained what it was, we understood because our navigators are masters at studying the stars. In fact, that is how Lono got to the island the first time. Believing we finally could find common meeting ground, the priests were glad to accommodate the men, and sent their *kilos*, their seers, to help them. Soon the *haoles* erected canvas tents, using one side of the sacred temple to secure their tent poles. I protested that they were desecrating an important shrine, but my husband told me Cook was pressing his men to work diligently, and that he thought it meant they would be leaving soon. In fact, Kalani said the priests assured him that Lono/Cook would be leaving when the Makahiki season was over, just as he was supposed to. So sure were the priests of the departure date that they allowed the men to bring pieces of the broken floating *heiau* ashore to repair.

---

*T*ension mounted day by day. The priests had given the *haoles* food from their storehouses to supplement what the hunters and farmers also provided, but with 200 extra men to feed daily, the priest's bounty was dwindling at an alarming rate. The white man refused to eat dog, and they had already eaten most of the chickens. The priests sent out the hunters who had to range farther and farther into the uplands to bring back pig.

It was bad enough that the food supplies were running low, but every day it was a new complaint from Cook, and the problem of how to fulfill the demands were finally laid at Kalani's feet. Cook further accused our men of swimming out to the ships under the cover of darkness and pulling the nails from the sheathing on the sides of the ships. No doubt that was true. In our defense, Kalani told Cook that it had also been reported that his own sailors snuck down to the bowels of the ship and pulled nails out from inside the hull in order to pay their gratitude to the women for their favors.

"Does he not know how to get his men to do his bidding?" Kalani asked. "What kind of a god is he?"

"Maybe the craving he has unleashed is some sacred power we know nothing about," I suggested. "Do you think the white men are capable of using prayers against us like the *kahuna ana ana* use when they pray someone to death?"

Kalani scoffed, "Now they're getting to you too. You're *pupule*--crazy."

"I thought you said they were leaving soon. When?" I asked, for that was the question on everyone's lips: the gossip around the house fires at night, the grumbling of the hunters as they trudged through the uplands in search of pig, the cry of the villagers when the priests ordered them to strip the coconut trees for the foreigners, leaving nothing for their own families.

Kalaniopuu could stand the uproar no longer. He was tired of dealing with the constant conflicts between the white sailors, the native women (who were being offered less and less for their sexual services) and the complaints from the *makaainana*. On trading excursions during the day, the men that were allowed on board stole knives from the ship's kitchen. Others tore metal barrel staves from the oak casks that held the ship's supply of fresh water while the white men were cavorting with their wives in the bushes. At night, our men continued to swarm the ships and steal as many nails as possible until finally Cook was forced to have guards on watch at night.

In the predawn hours I prayed the ships would sink in the harbor. It would take longer that way, but eventually the wood would be submerged in the water and the sailors the sharks didn't eat could be incorporated into the village and take care of the children they were producing. When I thought of it like that, then I wished for the men to swim out and steal the white man blind, the sooner the better. When I told Kalani my wishes, he sent an emissary to the priests to find out exactly when Cook planned to depart.

# Twenty-Seven

## January 1779

*I* never thought I would be grateful to see the time of Lono coming to a close, for that meant Ku and the time of war would be upon us, but this time I welcomed the change of the gods and the closing ceremonies if only to take some of the pressure off the *makaainana*. And, furthermore, to take the arrogance out of some of the priests who had grown accustomed to having the physical presence of their god near.

Word came that one of Cook's men, a man/god called William Watman, fell ill on the ship. Watman was brought ashore by the white men who were guarding the observatory. They propped him up against the temple walls and watched over him as they went about their calculations. After a few days he seemed to rally—gaining strength from the *mana* of the *heiau* I assumed—and he asked to be taken back to the ship. Later that evening Watman died.

The next day Kalani called for me. "What is the proper protocol to honor a dead god?" he asked.

"Lono passed on to the depths of Po?" Astounded, I asked, "How can that be? People die and turn into *aumakua*—that's happened in my family—family gods, but that's different. Lono left, but he came back eventually. I've never heard of a god dying."

"No—no—it wasn't Lono that died--not Lono. The one they brought to shore," Kalani corrected me.

"Maybe he was one of Lono's high priests, then. Priests can die. But would a returning god die when his season is coming to an end? Unheard of!"

"Cook told the Lono *kahunas* he had traveled with Watman for twenty-one years," Kalani said.

"Twenty-one years? That sounds like man time, not the time of the gods." I speculated, "Maybe they were *aikane*."

"Maybe so. Cook insisted that Watman was not a commoner or a slave and he did not want him thrown overboard to be eaten by the sharks like normally would happen to a white man at sea."

"If they feed the sharks, then they must sacrifice to the same *aumakua* as some of our own people," I said, thinking that for once I understood the white man.

Kalani shrugged. "Apparently not. Instead, Cook wants his man to have what he calls 'a proper burial' on shore."

"Oh—I see. They want to strip his bones in the *imu*."

"No. When that was suggested, Cook was horrified. Then he finally got the priests to understand that they want to bury the body at the base of the *heiau*."

"The *whole* body?"

"Yes. Without stripping his bones. Can you imagine? The *kahunas* are shocked. They're stalling, saying that they have never had to deal with a dead god before and they are unsure about how to proceed. I thought it best to assemble the chiefs and talk it over."

I looked down the hill and saw canoes landing. "Your priestly contingency has just arrived."

"I need your help. I want you to come to the council. No one knows what to do. The chiefs have been gathered, and now that the Lono priests are here, we can begin. After the *awa* is chewed and the first cup drank, then you can enter the council."

———

*W*hat could I do? I knew nothing of the white man's ways, but obviously we were to be involved in the disposal of the body. I hoped the answer would be revealed to me if I just stayed patient and listened.

At the appropriate time, Kalani sent for me. The priests welcomed me and then explained the dilemma of the deceased man/god to the *hale* full of chiefs. "The Lono season is almost over," they said. "Lono will, of course, be returning next year, as he always does."

"But, this is the first time he has come in person," a chief spoke up.

"Actually, the second. He came to Kauai, and now here, so we can be assured he will come again," the head priest reasoned.

"Or the third time," someone else spoke up. "He came the first time and said he would return. And then kept his promise—twice, in fact."

All the Lono priests agreed that, indeed, Lono was a god of his word.

"But the problem is what to do with the disposal of the dead body," I countered, bringing them back to the matter at hand.

"Body?" the chiefs muttered.

"Yes, Lono has died," I said.

"How can that be? How can it be possible for a god to die?"

"Not Lono," the head priest corrected, then he glared at me for stirring up trouble. "One of the minor priests passed over, not the actual god."

"Still the question remains," I said. "What to do with the body…"

"We always roast the meat, strip the bones, and place them in the caves," Kalani said. "Or in the *Hale o Keawe*, if they are lucky enough to be members of *my* family."

"Since he died at sea, maybe he could be tossed overboard. The shark *aumakua* will see to it that his body is eaten," a chief suggested.

"The man who speaks for Lono, Cook, told the priests that only common sailors and slaves are fed to the sharks," the head priest informed the council. "He says the *haoles* bury their dead in a hole in the ground."

"Whole? You mean with the meat still on the bones?" a chief asked.

"What about the spirit? Does it linger?" Kekuhaupio questioned. Since it was his village that was closest to the *heiau*, everyone understood he was thinking of the welfare of his people and did not want a wandering spirit slithering around his village causing mischief.

"Maybe the white man's spirits are different," a lower priest offered. "After all, they are *haole*—without breath—without spirit."

Silence fell over the council as the chiefs and priests considered that idea.

"His body has not been damaged in any way," another priest said. "He does not have marks on his neck from being strangled. Nor has he been drowned."

The chiefs muttered among themselves. One young priest suggested he might possibly be a candidate for sacrifice, but that idea was immediately scrapped when someone remembered that if the spirit left the body on its own accord, the sacrifice would not be valid.

"Maybe it's different if the god Lono is actually present," offered another priest.

"Perhaps Lono considers him an appropriate sacrifice. Maybe in this way we can be certain that Lono will return."

"That must be so," all the priests nodded in agreement, glad they had worked their way out of this dilemma and come to a better understanding of their god. Even though Lono had come back every year, a burial might guarantee his return, and it would certainly put the priesthood in a higher standing.

"Just to be sure, though, I think we should also offer a pig," Kekuhaupio said. "In case the man's spirit gets hungry, he'll have something to feast on and leave us alone."

Everyone agreed that one fat pig could be spared for the service. With the protocol agreed upon, the chiefs walked the Lono priests down the hill to the canoes. There, below the cliffs of my late husband Keoua, they all decided it was to their advantage to include a white man in their temple and were united in their plans.

---

The men on the ship came to shore and spent the hot afternoon excavating a hole in the lava near the side of the temple. They stretched all of Watman out--flesh, bones, brains, and intestines. A roasted pig and some vegetable offerings were thrown in the grave on top of Watman and rocks thrown in to cover him in hopes that the village dogs would not dig him up. For three nights the priests honored Watman as they prepared to close the temple of Lono at the end of the Makahiki season. Meanwhile, the white men erected a marker with two pieces of wood crossed near the top and placed it on the grave.

Afterward, the Lono priests put the *kapu* sticks around the whole area occupied by the *haoles*. Within that space nothing was to be touched. What a strange way to enter the land of Po, I thought. I had never heard of such a thing, but there are many things that these *haoles* do that we do not understand.

The next day Cook's men ran out of firewood. Rather than make an arduous trip to the mountains to cut trees and then not be able to burn the wood because it was green, they cast their eyes on the pointed fence poles that surrounded the *heiau*. At first it seemed they were just interested in the fence, and asked the priests if they could tear it down. The priests were once again in a bind, and came back across the bay, seeking council with Kalani to discuss the latest issue.

"We don't want to refuse our god anything, even if we don't understand it," the priests whined.

"If Lono wants the wood, you should give it to him. A new fence will be easy enough to rebuild," Kalani assured the men.

"Maybe he will leave then," I said. Kalani glared at me. I could tell he was losing patience with me, but I continued, "The Makahiki will end soon. Lono will depart and the time of the white man taking all they desire is near its end."

The priests sailed back across the bay and told Cook he could have the fence. Cook must have felt their hesitancy because he tried to barter by offering two hatchets. The priests, highly offended after the fine ceremonies they had held for the buried god, never mind the fence they would have to rebuild, threw the hatchets on the ground in digust.

Cook, desperate for dry wood and determined not to be intimidated by the refusal of his offer, gave the order for his men to dismantle the fence and load the shore boats with what he considered seasoned firewood. His men hesitated. "You dare disobey my orders?" he chastised them as he picked up one of the hatchets. He hacked away at the first fence post, and when it toppled, had it carried to the boat. After they dismantled the fence, Cook decreed that the shoreboats could make another trip because they might as well take the tall, weatherworn carved images as well. The first to be hacked to bits was the high-crested god Lono himself.

While Cook's men were busy chopping the fence posts, the priests ran to the canoes and once again paddled across the bay to Kalaniopuu's compound. "The white men are taking apart the temple of Lono," they cried.

"You agreed they could take the fence posts," Kalani answered.

"Yes, but now they want the carved wooden idols," the priests complained. "We did not agree to that."

At first Kalani did not believe them. "Why would he do that? No god would do such a thing." When the priests did not answer, he asked, "What more can he possibly want?"

"We have given him everything he asked for: meat, fruit, vegetables, and women," the priests insisted. "He is most demanding, this god Lono."

"Are you entirely sure?" I asked as I stumbled to my feet. "Maybe he is taking his own symbol because he does not plan to return." When I reached the opening of the *hale*, I was astonished at what I beheld. "My husband! You must come and see for yourself," I said as stood outside the doorway and looked across the bay. "They have broken down the fence and are making off with the…"

Before I could finish my sentence, Kalaniopuu ordered everyone to the canoes.

The first load of fenceposts had already been taken to the ships. When we arrived, the priests were standing in the hole where the fence used to be. Kalaniopuu looked on, astonished, as he saw the largest statue, the guardian of the Temple of Lono, being heaved on a blazing fire in order to cook the *haole's* mid-day meal.

# Twenty-Eight

The Hawaiian priests, reckoning time by their observations of the group of stars that began and ended the Makahiki season—the same stars the white men referred to as the Pleiades—finished the closing rituals to Lono at Hikiau *heiau.* The fence had been stowed away in the bowels of the ships, along with salted pig, coconuts, sweet potatoes, and barrels of fresh water. In their wake, the white man left the carcass of Watman buried just outside the *heiau* to watch over the people instead of the wooden idol. Finally, Captains Cook and Clerke raised the sails on their ships, *Resolution* and *Discovery,* and left Kealakekua Bay.

Even the priests admitted they were glad their god was gone. It had been a long, trying time. The priests all agreed it was much easier to please a god when he was not physically present. It was, as they said, less trouble to bow down to a wooden diety that consumed relatively little, rather than to men who required much. When Kalani went with his *kahunas* to check the priest's storehouses, he found them almost bare.

"There is much work to do," Kalani said to his high priest. "Your priests and this village will soon be desperate. Send the fishermen to the sea and the farmers to the uplands to plant sweet potatoes."

"And the hunters?" the priest asked.

"They are exhausted from supplying the god. Let them rest. They have killed many pigs, and the pigs will need time to breed and grow. Let the hunters remain in the village." Kalani told the priests to declare a strict *kapu* over the whole area, urging people to take some time to regroup--and then return to their former way of life, the time before Lono blessed their village by eating all their food, bringing disease, and impregnating the women.

The morning after the ships departed, Kalaniopuu thanked his friend Keaweaheulu for his hospitality. Kalani loaded the canoes with the women and children and sent them off. He declared that the rest of us would travel overland. We began the long trek across the hills to Kau.

It was clear to me, as it was to all the chiefs, that Cook was not Lono. I insisted that he was not any god; that he was simply a man. Why, then, did Kalani persist in his belief long after everyone else had given up the idea? At first I couldn't figure it out, but then, as we slowly traveled down the coast, I took a cold hard look at my husband. I saw him as I had never seen him before. I thought of our years together. He had taken me for his sacred wife and I married him because I had no choice. Kalani had been a strong warrior--virile and full of himself—a prize for any woman, just as I was a prize for any man. We had both been full of *mana* and in our prime. With Kalani, I had my sacred son, Kiwalao, heir apparent. The years had aged both Kalani and I—him more so than me, for he was much older. Now he was a scrawny old man, his skin scaly and his eyes red from the constant drinking of *awa*. His hands shook. His footsteps were uncertain and he relied on his spear more for balance than as a weapon. In truth, he was fighting a different battle now, and there was that word again--feeble. Although he would never admit it, his attendants watched out for him without being obtrusive--seeing that he didn't stumble and fall, seeing that he had help standing or sitting. Because his thinking was slowed, it was easy for them to anticipate his every wish. Suddenly I gasped: I was married to a grandfather—someone who had passed the prime of life. Once I realized what the reality was, I tried to guess what he was thinking. If I were Kalani, I would be feeling very special if one of my gods came to take me away, or even if they just returned to reassure me on my march toward death. In my days upon this *aina*, I have seen much bloodshed and carnage, the sacrifice of many young men going before their time. Here is the chief—not a god, a chief--one who has survived many crusades, crossed the channels more times than he can remember--and yet he must step across the threshold to the land of Po the same as every man. The gods have brought him to this point and have not taken him yet, so he must take some solace from the fact that Lono showed up to help him, to pull back the veil between the two worlds and welcome him. The more I thought about it, the more I realized that idea would be hard to abandon, even with all the evidence to the contrary. My husband looked into the mist but failed to recognize what he saw. Maybe in his old age he wanted assurance. He knows his bones will be secreted away. His legacy is assured. Our son will be ruler of this island. What could there possibly be for him to worry about?

———•———

*C*ook and Clerke sailed north. After just a few days at sea, a storm came up off the coast of Kawaihae and broke the badly rotted foremast on the *Resolution*. Cook turned the ships around and straggled back to Kealakekua. They had been gone less than a week.

———•———

*A*s soon as the runners caught up with us to inform us of Lono's return, Kalani did not hesitate, even though all his advisors pleaded with him. Even his favorite wife, Kanekapolei, could not persuade him. Kalani set his jaw and I knew that stubborn man was determined and had but one thing on his mind. He turned in his tracks and soon his steps lightened.

"It is as I have feared all along," Kalani told me as we hurried back the way we came. "I didn't think he would follow the ritual because things seemed so confused at the end. But he was merely feigning and is, indeed, a formidable foe. Lono left, and then returned—just as the ritual prescribes. What can he be doing but challenging my right to rule? He knows I have my war god with me. It is my duty to defend the land from invaders. As long as I have breath, I will not give up the right to my lands. It matters not to me whether I must fight a man or a god."

# Twenty-Nine

We saw the company of men heading for the mountains on our way back to Kealakekua Bay, but they were so far away we did not know their mission until we got back to Kaawaloa. The priests immediately came across the bay to welcome their chief. The *kahunas* told us Lono/Cook sailed right into the bay and expected the same hearty welcome he had received upon his first arrival. When the canoes didn't come out to trade, Cook came to shore and strolled right past the *kapu* sticks as if he hadn't seen them. He told the priests the reason he returned was because a mast had cracked on one of the ships. Then Cook demanded a party to take his men to the uplands. In the past, when the men were asked to go to the mountains to get a log to build a canoe for the chief there were proper sacrifices made at the temple before the trip, and a human sacrifice made when the tree was cut—the life of a man for the life of the tree. Instead, Lono/Cook picked a few native men and sent the party off to the mountains. That angered the men's wives, who were afraid that without the proper sacrifices at the temple, their men would not return safely.

While the men were gone, the wives made good use of their time, returning to the ships, along with the few men who were trading, in order to steal as much as they could. I understood the women's outrage. Kalani listened patiently as Cook complained that the thievery was even worse than before. One night we watched from across the bay as the huts near the *heiau* went up in flames. Red flickering shadows were cast all the way across the bay. Certainly the villagers would not be burning down their own houses, we mused—it had to be at the request of Lono. But why would Lono be torching the village? Why did he mean to harm his followers? This was not the god of agriculture, the god of plenty, the god of peace that we knew and loved. No one had any answers.

Kalani paced throughout the night, muttering over and over that it was Lono's way of making him mad enough to fight because his people were being abused. It was clear to him that he would have to fight the god for the right to rule. For once, he remained true to his *lua* training, and stayed sequestered, praying and gathering *mana*. It was well known that the man who struck the first blow would give away his power and lose the battle.

———

*I* finished my prayers and was letting the morning sun warm me as I sat outside near the opening of my *hale*. I looked out across the bay and noted that a number of shore boats were being launched from the white man's ships. One cutter went toward the village on the other side of the bay; the others headed toward our compound at Kaawaloa. Cook landed only one shoreboat, leaving the others a rifle's distance offshore. Accompanied by a couple of his sailors, Cook rushed up the hill to Kalani's compound. After catching his breath, Cook barked at the first guard he saw, "I demand to see the chief!"

Two of Kalani's men stepped forward and asked Cook to wait until their chief had finished his meal, then politely offered the white men something to eat. Cook refused their courtesy. Kalani's men did not appreciate Cook's beligerant attitude and retreated inside Kalani's compound, leaving Cook to pace back and forth at the entrance. Kalani was no longer vigorous in the morning. This time the chiefs used it to their advantage and slowed things down.

I could hear the chiefs telling Kalani not to rush, to go ahead and finish his meal, for they understood that the time had come for their chief to fight for his right to rule the kingdom, and certainly a chief could not fight on an empty stomach.

The same ritual had been performed for eons, although never by such a frail man. Usually the chief had to dodge a few spears hurled in his direction. Certainly at his advanced age, no one would insult him by throwing a spear anywhere near him. There had never been a time when a chief had to fight against a foe that had a sword hanging from his belt and a pistol shoved in the waist of his pants.

Everyone thought that because I'm in tune with the sacred, I can see into the future. Yes, I am in touch with the sacred, and I can see into the future—but it is more than that: sometimes I rely on plain common sense. I knew there was going to be a problem simply because the white man was around. For one thing, the white man had never brought so many boats that far into the bay at one time before, even when he had filled them up with food or filled his empty casks with water, and I could see no empty casks in the boats. In fact, the only boat that had landed was the shore boat Cook had been in; the rest waited offshore. Then I understood Cook was using the same battle strategy the chiefs used to make sure there was always a canoe waiting for Kalani in case of retreat. What I didn't understand was why Cook sent one boat to the other side of the bay.

I raised my hand to shield my eyes from the sun glaring on the water. What I saw stopped me cold. Metal gun barrels glinted in the sunlight. All the white men were armed. On the far side of the bay I saw Kekuahuapio donning his red and yellow feather cape as he and a companion made their way to his canoe at the shore. Kekuahuapio was a seasoned and astute warrior. If he sensed trouble, there probably was. His man pushed the canoe off the beach. The man raised the sail, caught the wind, and they sped across the bay toward our village.

Meanwhile, Cook had finally gained an audience with Kalani. This was one time I was glad for Kalani's poor hearing because the translator had to shout, and thus I did not have to strain to hear. I sat perfectly still, my eyes on the bay, but ready to rush to Kalani's aid should he need help.

"One of my shore boats is missing," Cook reported. "The rope was cut clean through with a knife--obviously it would have been a knife I traded with you."

"I know nothing about your boat," Kalani answered, not rising to the accusation. "I thought we agreed you would set a watchman every night."

Cook cleared his throat. "He must have fallen asleep."

When the translator finished, the chiefs burst into chatter and laughter. Some said Cook must not be a very good captain and needed to train his men better; some said it was the nature of the white man to be stupid. A third said he would bet a *koa* dagger that either chief Palea or some of his warriors had gotten revenge for the beating Palea had suffered when he attempted to steal the forging tools from the ship the day before.

Cook constantly asked the translator what the chiefs were saying, but the translator did not offer much information, saying the men were speaking too fast and he could not understand. That, of course, was not the truth, but rather a lie the man told in an attempt to keep the peace. I concluded that the version of the story that likely would be closest to the truth would be the one that included the most stealing. I wished Kalani would ask about the huts that had burned the night before, but that was not mentioned.

"Enough of this talk," Cook shouted. "I demand an explanation!"

Kalani countered innocently, "I know nothing about it."

Then Cook's attitude shifted abruptly. His voice softened. "Kalani, my old friend, if you do not believe me, come with me out to the ship and see for yourself."

It was not that Kalani did not believe Cook about the stolen boat—to him it was just another case of the men stealing from the ship. I knew Kalani would be willing to go with Cook because it was clear the time had come when the chief would be forced to fight Lono. In the past the chief, representating his war god Ku, defended his right to reign by dodging the spears thrown by the usurpers. This time it seemed the fight was to be on the floating *heiau*. So be it. All the chiefs understood the ritual. Although in the past Kalani could have been killed by a spear, he was a skilled warrior and the chances of him losing the contest were slim. But never had a chief had to fight the actual god, Lono, in what we assumed would be hand-to-hand combat. But we knew the white man never used spears—they used guns that hurled pieces of metal, and those would be much harder to evade. And because he was old and feeble, Kalani's step was slow. To me, it hardly seemed a fair fight. Did Lono plan to take the land once and for all instead of just being a seasonal visitor?

Kalani nodded and his retainers helped him to stand. Brave old warrior that he was, he intended to carry through with the challenge and accompany Cook down the hill. I thought my heart would leap out of my chest. As many years as I had lived with that hardheaded man, I found that, in his moment of truth, I had grown fond of him and did not wish to see him defeated, especially by foreigners to our shore. This land was his—not theirs—and I could not imagine it being any other way.

The chiefs convinced Kalani that, according to protocol, he would not be ready to embark on such a serious journey unless he was prepared for battle. They led him back inside his *hale*.

I silently thanked them and edged off my doorstep and snuck toward Kalani's *hale*, being careful not to be seen lest my sacred presence cause the warriors to have to prostrate before me. I hid near Kalani's *hale* and could hear the chiefs formulating a plan as the retainers took their time wrapping Kalani's feather cape around his shoulders. They handed him the spear he would use to deflect the spears thrown at him. His warriors armed themselves with long *koa* spears, daggers, and war clubs edged with rows of shark teeth as they prepared to defend their chief. Kalani, surrounded by his warriors, was escorted back to Cook, who was still pacing in front of the compound.

BAM!

The shot startled us all. Everyone turned and saw smoke curling up from the white man's shore boat in the middle of the bay. The man in Kekuhaupio's craft slumped forward, his head on the bow, his arms dangling over either gunwale.

I rushed down the hill and reached the landing just as Kekuhaupio's canoe bumped on the rocks at the shore. "My chiefess," he said as he bowed his head. I peered in the canoe and saw the man drenched in blood. Kekuhaupio raised his head and shouted to Kalani, "No Heavenly One!"

I glanced over my shoulder. A long line of chiefs, shields and spears in hand, came behind Kalani. When Kalani heard his old war chief's shout, he stumbled on the rocky ground. The men on either side of him held him steady until he could regain his balance. Not trusting the white man, I glanced in the other direction and saw the men in the shore boats paddle a little closer, but still maintain their offshore positions.

"Stop!" Kekuhaupio shouted as he leaped out of his canoe and splashed through the shallow water. "It is not safe on the sea! Kalimu is dead! Go back, O Heavenly One! Go back!"

Right then I knew Cook's presence was a trap. Kalani did not stand a chance. I bolted up the hill to my husband and grabbed his arm. "Oh Kalani!" I cried. "There is danger. Come with me. Let us go back."

Kalaniopuu stopped.

I pulled on his arm, forcing him to turn toward me.

Kalani's red-rimmed eyes swam in confusion--he did not understand where I had come from or why I was there. His legs gave out and he sat down on the ground. "Why is Cook here?" he whispered in my ear as I bent over him. "Why are my warriors circling around? They should have prostrated in your presence. Protocol has been broken."

"Kalani, please. Come with me," I begged, as I tugged on his arm and pulled him to a standing position again.

Seeing that I had gotten the old man to his feet again, Cook grabbed Kalani's other arm.

What could that white man have been thinking?

No one—absolutely no one—touches the chief.

It could mean only one thing: battle!

Kalani's *lua*-trained warriors swooped down on Cook. Chief Kanaina-I-Kalumano-I-Kahoowaha was standing at the perfect angle to swing his long club between Kalani and Cook. The blow came down squarely on Cook's forearm. With lightening speed, Cook drew his sword with his other hand and swung around. Kahoowaha stepped back, but not soon enough. Cook sliced his face from temple to chin. Blood spurted over all of us from the gaping wound.

Kalani lost his balance again and I needed both hands to keep him upright. Immediately two chiefs grabbed Kalani's elbows, picked him up, and whisked him away,

I trotted behind them as fast as I could but I had to stop half way up the hill to catch my breath, for I was no longer young. Out of the reach of immediate danger, I turned, knowing I must watch the battle to the end so that I would know how to guide my husband in the days to come.

Cook yelled for his men to make for the boats. With his long *koa* spear, one of the warriors lunged at Cook. Cook dodged the spear and pulled his gun out. He fired, but even at such close range, he missed. He fired again and that shot brought down the warrior. Then the men in the boats started firing, killing more of our men. Cook screamed at his men to stop firing, not because he didn't want them to shoot, but afraid he'd get hit in the crossfire.

By this time Kahoowaha caught up with Cook. With blood dripping from his wounded face, he gave a war cry and bashed Cook over the head with his mighy war club. At the same time, another warrior stabbed Cook in the back with a *koa* dagger. Even from where I stood, I heard Cook groan as he fell. He died like a man, and not like a god.

Four other sailors were killed that day before they could escape to their boats, but it was clear the most important one was dead: the one who masqueraded as a god. For that, if for no other reason, he deserved to die and be sacrificed at the foot of the *heiau* he had desecrated.

I struggled the rest of the way up the hill and reached Maunaloia where I gave Kalani the news: Lono had returned and was beaten by the war god, Ku.

Kalani was ecstatic. He sang the praises of his chiefs when they marched into camp with Cook's body along with the other sailors. As they prepared the bodies for sacrifice, everyone asked the same question: now that they had killed this idol snatcher, would Lono appear next year? Would he come in his usual form, or the form of a man as he had done this year? Who could even begin to imagine what this god would do next?

I had other thoughts, but did not express them: what would the people do now if they believed that their god Lono had passed? Were we to live under the constant command of Ku, the war god, all year long? Would we never again have a season of peace? When we lived under Lono, the men planted crops. With Ku, there was the possibility they would they always be away at war. It certainly was a big gain for Kalani who worshipped war above all else, but what about the *makaainana*? How were they to survive? And if they didn't survive, how were we, the *alii*, to survive?

After the priests had prepared the *imu*, Kalani opened the ceremony, offering Cook's body to his war god, Kukailimoku. I shivered when I saw the war god's feathers bristle at the sound of the drums. Even if the sacrifice was not of a god, but of a man, the man had been a leader, and that was what counted in Kalani's eyes. Kalani prayed to Ku, and then left the rest of the ceremonies up to the priests, assuming they would do what was right.

The priests did not, of course, but were careful not to let Kalani know.

———

*C*ook was eviscerated. His body was then wrapped in banana leaves and placed on the hot rocks. More banana leaves were piled on top. All the time his flesh cooked, the dickering and squabbling among the chiefs for the choicest parts began. The priests accidentally left Cook's heart and liver lying exposed on a rock, forgetting them in the fracas over the other body parts. Some say that hungry children snatched Cook's heart and were seen roasting it over a fire. A dog made off with his liver. Others claimed a great price was paid for one of Cook's hands, which was fashioned into a fly swatter. His intestines were stretched out to mark off an arena for a cockfight. The long bones were used for the feather *kihilis* named Ililiwa and Kaikoo. The arm bones were wrapped in white *kapa* and held at Hale Mana at Pakini. Kamehameha was awarded Cook's hair. After the meat was stripped from the bones, Kalani ordered what remained of the flesh to be charred all the way down to ashes, thereby putting an end to the bickering.

Because the chiefs only wanted unsullied body parts, that which had not been claimed was taken out to the ship. The remaining hand was presented to Clerke, who identified the scar between Cook's index finger and thumb, a blemish not befitting a god and an imperfection that none of our men wanted in their possession. The men said Clerke was happy to get whatever remains of his captain he could. There was much we did not understand about the white man's ways, and were grateful that he did not open fire with the ship's big guns. But we never did understand why--after he had asked for what was left of Cook's body--he threw the bundle of Cook's remains overboard. Presumably, it was as I had suspected all along. Cook was a man of the sea and his blemished hand fed the shark god.

# Thirty

After the white man's ships sailed away, things settled down. The kind people of the region had fed us—and the white men—far too long. They were out of food and it was past time for Kalani and his court to move on. I suggested to Kalani that he send his warriors home to Kau to tend to their fishnets and plant sweet potatoes, but keep the court at Kealakekua Bay a little longer in order for him to rest. It was clear the commotion of defending his island had aged him. I was surprised that he agreed to my plan.

After a few days, Kalani regained some strength. Instead of heading to Kau, which I was sure he would want to do, he surprised me by heading in the other direction. Evidently a change of scenery and people was just what he needed to clear his mind of the muddle of recent events.

Actually the farther up the coast he traveled--first to Kainaliu near Honuaino, then to Keauhou, then to Kailua—the more he relaxed. I hadn't seen him so happy in years. In fact, he changed in profound ways. Most noticeable was his generosity.

"Extravagant," said those who had to provide for him, for he had been known for his miserly ways all his life.

I can best describe his transformation by saying his heart seemed to open up. Why? Maybe he felt he had gained status at Kealakekua by defeating Lono/

Cook. There was no doubt his men were loyal and had defended him. Maybe he was just glad that the stress of the conflict between Lono/ Ku was over and he wanted to celebrate. After all, he had bested a god—killed him, actually. Or at least his men had. Maybe he was getting senile… Who can say? At any rate, I admit that I enjoyed it too. It reminded me of the joyous days at my father's court, or the light-heartedness of my elder brother, Kamehamehanui. In my quieter moments I grew melancholy and wished Kalani could have enjoyed more days like this during our earlier years, but then that would have meant we would have been celebrating victory over my own people from Maui. Realizing that, I decided to be glad for what we had now.

Kalani surrounded himself with *keiki*, clapping along with them when the marrionettes performed. He summoned everyone to court to dance for him, particularly delighting in the *kalaau* and *alaapapa* hulas. Some of the *makaainana* were stunned when he got up to dance, others laughed because they had never witnessed such lightheartedness in their chief, he being somewhere in the neighborhood of eighty years old. His legs resembled scrawny sticks, his knees and elbows were stiff and did not bend all the way, but still he was a quite good dancer. Well, maybe not good, but enthusiastic, which was almost the same.

Kalani's frivolity and kindness ended as famine crept across the lands of Kona. Instead of making the decision to divide what was left among the people so they could husband their resources and begin again, Kalani seized everyone's property.

"Is the old chief mad?" the people asked. "Has he lost his mind?"

I wondered about it myself, but there was no use to ask him. He was having too much fun.

"We, along with your people, have nothing to eat," I scolded him the day I looked in the storehouse and found not enough for the court, never mind enough for the people.

"Well, then, we'll just move. It is the prerogative of the chief," was his reply.

The *makaainana*, tied to their homeland, were left destitute. For my part, I was upset, but I could do nothing. Kalani was having the time of his life, seemingly without a care in the world. He gathered up his followers and proceeded up the coast. The merry court, dancing and singing the whole way, moved north to Kapaau in Kohala, where we settled for a time at Hinahahua. Every morning after I rose, I stood just outside the opening of my *hale*, hoping to be lucky enough to catch a glimpse of Haleakala across the channel before the clouds gathered and hid the great mountain. I longed for my homeland. I was so near, and yet so far.

One day I could stand it no more and approached Kalani when he was at the height of his merry-making. "My dear husband, we are so close to my homeland. Please allow me a visit to see my brother and our son in Hana."

To my surprise, he readily agreed. "You wish to leave all this? Then you may go, but as usual, you are still under my command and must return as soon as I send word."

"Of course, my Kalani," I replied. I tried to remain earnest in my devotion to him, but I'm sure he could feel the joy I felt: a chance to see my beloved son and my daughters…I couldn't wait to get home to Maui.

# Thirty-One

"How is your husband?" my brother Kahekili asked. "I hear he is aging."

"Truth be told I've never seen him so content. He is enjoying the dancers."

"If he has young girls to dance for him, how could he fail to be satisfied? I hope that he is also well fed. Perhaps he will finally see the value of providing for this own people and not robbing others," my brother said. "How long will you be staying?"

"I wish I never had to leave."

My children and grandchild were near and I delighted in the gentle breezes of Hana. I felt safe and secure because my brother kept an ever-watchful eye across the channel. Surely Kalani was too old now and was finished with marauding.

For a time, all was quiet…

"The winds have changed," my brother informed me. "They bring rumors from across the channel. He's at it again. Why?"

"Perhaps the chiefs are tired of providing for Kalani's lavish ways," I guessed. "Some were concerned that he seemed too happy and they worried he was senile." I was tired of always having to answer for my husband's conduct and my voice rose in frustration. "How should I know?"

My brother shrugged. He knew I had little control over Kalaniopuu.

"Perhaps it is because that's what they do over there," I said, finally expressing out loud what I'd held inside for years. "I've never seen such discontented people. They cannot seem to enjoy the simple pleasures of living." I stood and paced the room, no longer able to keep my thoughts to myself. "Always they complain: there never seems to be enough, or if there is enough, it is not the right kind, or it didn't come yesterday, or they think of someone else who has more. Whatever it is, whatever they have, whatever they think they want, they are never satisfied."

"Nor am I," Kahekili said, dismissing my grumbling by changing the subject. "I spent some time with Kahahana on Molokai recently."

"How is the young chief doing?"

"I have managed to turn him against his own *kahuna*."

"Isn't his priest Kaopulupulu?"

"*Was*. He *was* Kahahana's priest." Kahekili grinned. "But he will be a priest no longer. I was informed that Kaopulupulu was the one who advised Kahahana not to give me the whale ivory that washes to shore at Kualoa."

"Or the sacred valley of their *alii* if you were allowed the whale ivory..."

Kahekili waved away my interruption. "Kahahana believes *me*--his uncle--the one who raised him." Kahekili leered. "You know that my pure blood runs thicker than the shallow stream of a priest." He rolled over on the mat to gaze out the doorway. "And, while I am waiting for Kahahana to kill his priest, I will send for canoes from Hawaii."

"Hawaii?! Surely you don't think that anyone on that island will support your ventures."

"Kahahana has gone back to his own island and will soon make some decisions that will be very unpopular with both the chiefs and *makaainana* on Oahu. It won't be long before his people and the chiefs turn against him."

"You are scheming to invade Oahu?"

"I am, now, one step closer."

# Thirty-Two

## 1780

The strong *Apaapaa* wind from Kohala carried the news across the channel: the chief from Puna, Imakakaloa, and Nuuanupaahu, from Kau, were protesting Kalani's extravagant ways the loudest. Soon their protest turned to outright rebellion. I hoped I would not be called to negotiate peace. Fortunately, Kalani's *kahuna* foresaw an end to the difficulties with Nuuanupaahu, claiming Kalani did not need to start a war against the dissenter—that blood would spill another way--and that he would personally see that all was set right. With Kalani's permission, the priest retired to the *heiau*.

Several days later, while Nuuanupaahu was surfing, the *kahuna* sent several sharks to kill him. Actually those present said Nuuanupaahu almost made it to shore before a shark jumped out of the water and tore off his hand. Somehow the brave man rode his surfboard all the way to shore, sharks pursuing him all the way, following the trail of blood. In a few days, and in great pain, Nuuanupaahu died.

Kalani celebrated the chief's death, for then that left him with one less enemy. Others reported that Nuuanupaahu was killed in battle, a more honorable way for a warrior to die, although a foe was never named.

At any rate, killed by a shark or by a spear, he was sacrificed at Mookini *heiau* at Kohala. Since I was not there, but on Maui with Kiwalao at my brother's court, I knew that whichever way the story went, Kalani retained control, either through his warriors or through his priests, and had once again smelled the sweet fragrance of blood. As soon as I heard the news I knew that I would soon be returning to Kalani's side.

# Thirty-Three

## 1781

*K*alani moved his court to the Hamakua coast on the eastern side of the island and then descended into the sacred valley of Waipio to rebuild the *heiau* of Moaula. When he was settled, he sent the chief Kamehaiku to Maui to bring me back to his court. Kiwalao was summoned too, and given the direction that he should prepare for a permanent stay. Not wanting to be separated from his wife and child, Kiwalao convinced Liliha to join him. The joy of being together eased the burden for all of us.

I marveled at the beauty of the sacred valley as our paddlers waited for permission to land at Waipio. The steep cliffs rose sharply on either side--sheer drop-offs to the flat valley below. The waterfall Hiilawe towered over the back of the valley. Kalani's warriors escorted us to shore. As I stepped onto the black sand beach, I thought back to the night, so many years ago, when I first set foot on this island. So much had happened since then—a lifetime—and I could hardly imagine what would be next.

Even though I had heard reports of Kalani's failing health, when I saw him I was shocked. Was this the same man that torched whole villages as he rampaged through the land, leaving the defeated starving and their fishponds destroyed? Was this the warrior who had urinated in the eyes of the survivors? It hardly seemed as if it could be so. As he hobbled toward me on the beach, my heart melted in pity. How could this be the same man? But then, face-to-face, I saw that fire still smoldering in his eyes. I knew that with only a puff of wind, the spark could flare into a murderous rage at any moment. I had seen it many times before. The warrior in him was still alive, and if he could no longer do the deed himself, he had proved there were plenty of chiefs and priests who would gladly do his bidding.

Kalani was on the beach as the canoe landed. He escorted me to the *hale* that had been prepared. I was surprised when he did not leave, but rather seemed anxious to talk.

"The *heiau* will be finished in a few days," he said as he settled down on the mat and stretched his legs out.

"Another man will be sacrificed," I muttered, and then caught myself. My back had been turned to him, so I hoped he had not heard. I turned toward him and said loudly, "Oh?" hoping that with a show of eagerness, I could cover up my first remark.

"I've sent runners to every corner of the island..." he said.

He seemed so enthused that I was sure he had not heard me, and I sighed in relief.

"...to gather all the chiefs...."

The glint in his eye brought me up short. I realized I had grown too relaxed on Maui, and I warned myself to be more careful.

"... for the dedication."

"Dedication?" I finally came to my senses. It would serve me well to give him my undivided attention.

"Yes," he said. "There is something important I want to talk over with you."

I was stunned. In all our years together he rarely talked anything over with me—he had always acted of his own accord and I had been left to deal with the repercussions. Curious, I said, "Yes, my Kalani. What is it you wish?"

"Our son."

"Kiwalao?"

"Yes." He turned and waved away the retainers. "Outside," he commanded. "And keep a close watch." He scooted closer to me on the mat. In a low voice he said, "I am going to declare our son heir apparent. That's why I'm calling everyone here. He has been with your brother on Maui for a long time. I have hardly seen the boy—who is now a man." He glared at me. "I can only assume you've been preparing him to lead. Why do you look so surprised?" he chuckled. "You've always known this day was coming."

"Yes, Kalani," I assured him. "You and I both know he has trained with the best." Of course, to me 'the best' meant my brother, Kahekili. "Our son has known since he was a small boy that he would rule over this island one day." It was the time I had been waiting for all my life. My family's dream of dominance throughout the island chain was finally coming true: my cousin, married to the chiefess on the island of Kauai; my brother guiding us from Maui, with Molokai and Lanai already under our control; my son the chief of Hawaii. It would merely be a matter of time before my brother would succeed in bringing the weakening Kahahana of Oahu under his sway. My son was young enough that he would be able to rule for many years—maybe as long as my brother Kamehamehanui had. All the stars seemed to be in alighment and the prophet's words were coming true: I would be the mother of a chief. The thought made me so excited I wanted to throw my arms around my husband's neck. But something stopped me, and I glanced at him. What I saw brought me crashing back down to reality.

"My bones tell me that I am old," he whispered. His lips quivered and his *awa*-rimmed eyes blinked back tears. "I need to trust that you will take care of my bones."

Never had I seen the old warrior so vulnerable. So, this was it. He was relinquishing his power not only to his son, but also to death. Death, the rival he had toyed with for so many years, the adversary he had stared in the face and defeated time after time had finally taken a step closer. It was clear that Kalani knew he had no defenses to stop Death's advance. As much as I wanted my son to be chief, I suddenly realized that I, too, was marching in the same direction as Kalani, and that one day I would be faced with the inevitable. A lump rose in my throat and tears, coming from I knew not where, flowed down my cheeks. "Of course I will care for you, Heavenly One. It is my duty as your sacred wife. It would be my honor."

*I*n the days that followed, preparations were made for the ceremony that would transfer the rights of the title of chief to my son. Pigs were slaughtered and prepared for the *imu*. Every morning the men climbed the long trail out of Waipio valley and combed the forest to gather dry wood for the *imu* and the night fires. At dusk, they trudged down the steep trail, their backs bent under their heavy burdens. They dumped their loads on the growing piles by the *imu* pits. The farmers harvested *kalo* from the *loi*. The rhythm of the steady pounding of *poi* echoed off the cliffs during the day. The *poi* was left to sour— just the way Kalani liked it.

As each chief arrived, he waited with his court at the top of the cliff near the village of Honokaa. After dark, the chiefs stood at attention. Their shoulder-length capes, covered in designs that signified their lineage, reminded everyone of the able armies that guarded their chiefs, and ultimately Kalani. Each chief lit his warrior's torches, one by one. When all the torches were blazing, he led his procession down the precipitous trail to the valley floor. The chief's camps spread out across the mouth of the valley until it seemed that every last place was filled. During the day mock battles were fought, each man attempting to outdo the other in displays of strength and agility. If a war broke out now... I squelched the idea. No one would dare go against Kalani--not now. Not when my son was so close to being made ruler and fulfilling both our destinies.

Kalani had been kept busy during the day rededicating the *heiau*, and at night we watched the procession of chiefs descend until all were accounted for. Then Kalani held a feast. When all his chief's bellies were full, he draped his red feather cape around his shoulders to ward off the cool night air and called for quiet so he could address the multitude. "I am prepared to turn over this island to my son Kiwalao upon my death," Kalani announced. "He shall be my successor in government. He shall have the honor of offering up the sacrifice to dedicate a *heiau*. Whatever ivory from the whale that drifts ashore shall belong to him, and he shall wear the sacred *lei niho palaoa* and be allowed to speak at any council."

Even though Kalani was old, the chiefs knew he hadn't changed; he would piss in their eyes if they dared speak against his decision, or at the very least, he would die trying. The chiefs respected—or feared—Kalani. No one spoke against Kiwalao. It was a bittersweet moment for me: my husband admitting his frailty and my son being given the mantle of the land. Daring to think beyond the present moment, I relished the possibility that maybe my life had not been in vain; perhaps I had fulfilled my family's wishes and brought peace between the islands at last. I dared to dream of flourishing fishponds. I pictured *kalo* trembling in the lush *loi*. Yes, this could be the end of war and the beginning of peace and plenty for everyone, just as it had been told in the legends before the age of constant bickering. I dreamed the men would put down their war clubs and the priest's horrible human sacrifice on the altars of the *heiaus* would become a thing of the past. I dared to dream of the legacy I would leave behind: one of harmony and contentment throughout the island chain. My name would account for much in the *oles* that the chanters would sing about this propitious declaration.

Then Kalani turned to face his nephew. "My war god, Kukailimmoku, shall go to Kamehameha."

I was not the only one who gasped. Kalani was up to his old tricks and had duped me--and his chiefs--one more time.

"His duty is to serve his chief well," Kalani smiled and nodded to his nephew.

My vision of peace shattered. I saw the flash of mischief in Kalani's eyes. He gloated because he had slipped this one past all of us--the chiefs as well as his sacred wife. The only one who did not seem surprised, of course, was Kamehameha.

Kalani's declaration buzzed through the crowd, drifting back to the soldiers that had not been able to hear Kalani's proclamation. As I glanced around the circle of men, I saw one chief's eye catching another. In those few moments, in those subtle glances, alliances were formed. The chiefs immediately understood the implications of Kalani's decision. My son would have to fight for his right to rule. The land had been handed to him, but he would have to establish his right to keep it, and he did not possess the war god. It had been handed over to the man who would now be his adversary, even as he had sworn his allegiance to protect him. On Maui, the right to declare a ruler would have elicited no conflict—our line had been passed down for generations, but on this island, they fought for every scrap.

Kalani had every right to make Kiwalao chief—there was no one in the land who could claim his sacredness. Although his father was a chief, his sacredness was primarily due to the fact that I was his mother. If Kiwalao would have been more like his father, he would have been a man of strong character, but he was not. That is to say, he had a strong character, but not the sort that made him a warlord. He had the ability to be a leader among men, but only if those men were men of peace. He would not be one to rule with the fist of death. Rather, my son had the gentleness of a man raised in the Kaiaulu trade winds of Maui. I raised him to know his destiny to rule, but he never had the stamina, nor had he really ever been capable of asserting himself as a warrior. Furthermore, he carried the tattoos befitting a chief of Maui, not of Hawaii. At that moment, I had to admit to myself that I had spoiled and indulged him. I saw my mistake, but it was too late to start over. As much as I wanted my son to rule, I knew he had not established himself at Kalani's court. Even though I had done my duty and spent time in Hawaii, living for years under Kalani's stern rule and austere court, I could see I had not done enough. I had selfishly wished for a more peaceful life among my own people on Maui, and the same for my son as well. 'Let him fulfill his duties as the keeper of Io and learn the ways of governing different from his father,' I had prayed. Although those prayers had been answered, I saw that the answer had come, as everything always does, at a price. I raised my son to be a diplomat, not a warrior. He had shown his diplomacy to everyone when he put on his yellow *o-o* cape and walked to his uncle's court to bring peace, saving his father's men after the slaughter in the Sand Hills on Maui. After that, Kiwalao had grown insufferably pompous. He thought it was something special he alone had done, rather than the fact that it was the heritage and the *kapus* that the men honored by bowing down.

On the other hand, controversy had swirled around Kamehameha from the moment his mother announced her pregnancy. Since Keoua was married to Kekuiapoiwa, he had claimed fatherhood, but his son's paternity had always been in question, some people going as far as to declare that the baby's seed rested with my brother, Kahekili. Some said that it could only have been my brother because both were men of temperment, born under heavy rains, lightening and thunder in the month of Ikuwa. After Kamehameha came to Kalani's court, he had been brash and bold, just as my brother, and I sensed then that he would stop at nothing to get what he wanted.

Above all else, it seemed it was clear that the time had come for Kalani to step aside. If he did not name a successor, it would not be long before the chiefs would rise up against him. It was much better that he made his wishes known now while he still weilded the power to carry them out and help our son establish his monarchy. I wished for peace among the people, yet I could see nothing but warfare and more bloodshed coming from Kalani's decision. My only hope was that, when the time came, Kamehameha would honor his uncle's gift and stand behind my sovereign son. If Kamehameha would do that…maybe….

But my heart told me he would not.

# Thirty-Four

## 1781

After naming his son heir apparent, Kalani dismissed the chiefs and sent them back to their respective homelands. Most were satisfied, but his old adversary from Puna, Imakakoloa, was not.

In private I said to Kalani, "My Heavenly One, I'm afraid you've made a grave error."

"How so? Don't tell me that you're not happy that your son is ruler over this island? Didn't I, your heavenly husband, fulfill your prophecy? My royal seed was spilled on your fertile ground. We had a son. I rule the island and I made him heir apparent. What else do you want from me?"

"Of course, Kalani, I am happy. So is our son—after all, he's only getting what he was born into—what he deserves. We both know there are none with as high a rank as our son."

"Exactly. This was the basis of our marriage. It was agreed on years ago."

"That is not where my disagreement lies, Kalani. I am concerned that your nephew, Kamehameha, will take advantage of him."

"What are you worried about? Kamehameha is not in a position to do that. He was given the war god, and implicit in that agreement is his duty to support Kiwalao. There is no problem."

"But what if he doesn't? What if he rises up?"

"You are worrying like a mother," he scoffed.

"Yes, I am a mother—the mother of your son!" I realized I was raising my voice, and quieted myself, the better to win Kalani's favor. "What if Kamehameha's head swells up and he begins to think he is something he is not."

"It's true, Kamehameha has a strong personality. But you must trust me. He is my nephew and I know his mind. What he says he will do, he will do."

"But… how can you be so sure?"

"Because he knows he's lucky to be given what he got. He's worked hard for the honor—he is a fine warrior. But he also understands that I am his savior. My brother died, leaving him without even an empty promise. You heard my brother on his deathbed, begging me to take the youngster to my court. I gave him the inheritance his father did not have the power to leave him. Take my word for it-- he is grateful. He told me so himself when I visited his court in Kohala." Then he planted a spear I could not dodge. "If you don't like it now, then all I have to say is that you shouldn't have left for Maui. You might have been able to influence my decision then, but now it is much too late. Be done with it."

I felt the flames of anger scratch the back of my throat. "I am taking Kiwalao back to Maui," I declared.

"Leave then," he said with a shrug. "I am still your husband. When I send the canoe to fetch you, both of you will come."

Once again, I had no choice. I swallowed my feelings, bowed, and said, "As always, my Kalani."

———

*D*espite what Kalani claimed, my presence had little to do with my ability to temper my husband. Even before I left, Kalani's thoughts had immediately turned to war. After the chiefs left Waipio and went back to their districts, Kalani's court headed down the Hamakaua coast and stopped at the full fishponds of Waiakea in Hilo. Kalani figured he could easily subdue the rebellious chief, Imakakoloa, who complained Kalani had demanded too much food and tribute from his people in the Puna district, and refused to provide for him. Kalani consecrated the *heiau* Kanowa in Puueo to his war god and then began his crusade to hunt for the rebel chief through the Puna area to the south. The struggle against Imakakoloa lasted much longer than Kalani anticipated, for Imakakoloa was a very popular chief and his people fought long and hard.

Kalani's step faltered, his eyesight dimmed, yet the *makaainana* understood him well enough to continue to respect him. He wanted to return to his home district of Kau, so his court left Hilo and slowly climbed to the summit of Kilauea and skirted their way around the steaming maw of Halemaumau crater. Then they crossed the barren lava fields of the Kau desert, finally reaching the southern region of the island. They stayed for a time at Punaluu, then Waiohinu, and settled at Kamaoa. In the meantime, Kalani's army continued to battle Imakakoloa's troops throughout Puna. Eventually the rebel's troops were beaten, but Imakakoloa evaded capture. Ever loyal, the people of Puna hid their chief for over a year.

Kalani grew impatient and tired of the chase. The long battle had been costly in terms of manpower, resources, and time. He prepared to rededicate the *heiau* at Pakini near the southern tip of the island to his war god and was determined that Imakakoloa be the first sacrifice. Kalani called his chiefs together and asked which warrior was brave enough to bring home the enemy. Puhili, seeking the Kalani's favor, volunteered. Kalani told him to use any means necessary.

———

As soon as Puhlili crossed into Puna district he called for his troops to light their torches. Starting in the uplands and moving toward the sea, village by village, they burned the people's homes to ashes, laying waste to the Puna district as punishment for hiding their chief. Kalani figured that since Imakakoloa was so popular, he would surrender before he brought down his whole district, or better yet, that the terrified *makaainana* would surrender their chief when they grew cold and hungry enough. It wasn't just war against the enemy chief; Kalani had declared war against the people of Puna as well.

Puhili knew that Imakakoloa had hair that reached to the ground and that the rebel would be easy enough to recognize if he could just find him. Eventually a fisherman, tired of seeing his homeland laid waste, told the chief where to find the dissident. Puhili had not counted on finding Imakakoloa on an islet off the coast. Instead of surrendering to save his people, Imakakoloa was only willing to sacrifice his hair. Puluhili found his enemy with his hair cascading over the hands of a sorceress holding a knife. Given just a few more minutes, the rebel would have been shorn, the hair burned in the fire blazing at his feet, and Imakakoloa would have permanently escaped.

# Thirty-Five

## 1781

*A*s soon as Kalani received word that Imakakoloa had been captured, he sent for Kiwalao and I. The longhaired Puna chief was brought back to Pikini, tortured for several days, then ritually killed and left out in the blazing sun for two days. Even as we approached from the sea, we could smell his putrefying flesh.

The first chief to welcome us was Kamehameha. He ran down to the canoe and greeted his cousin. "We will be conducting the sacrifice together," he informed Kiwalao. "I can hardly wait." Then he excused himself, claiming he had important duties to perform. He seemed to be everywhere at once as he bustled about the compound--now at the *heiau*, now at Kalani's side, now overseeing the men tending the fire, then helping the priests place the first layer of rocks in the *imu*. Since Kamehameha seemed to be in charge, I sent for him and requested that my hut be moved so that I was upwind of the stench.

Kiwalao, however, did not have that luxury. His stomach had always been delicate, and his *hale* was downwind of where Imakakoloa's body lay rotting in the heat. Because the sacrifice was being held in his honor, Kiwalao had to attend to the priest's every wish, but even the sight of the women preparing food nauseated him. I insisted he drink water, but he could not even keep that down.

My son was miserable. The priests came to his compound and chided him for not helping them prepare the base of *kukui* shells for the fire.

"Can you not see I am sick?" he asked.

"This man is yours to sacrifice," the priests insisted. That being said, Kiwalao could hardly refuse their further orders, no matter how bad he felt. "Rub Imakakoloa's eyeballs with fish oil," the priests demanded. "We want them glistening like those of a shark in deep water."

Poor Kiwalao. When he came to my hut to get away from the stench, he told me the smell of rotting pig had been hard enough for him when he had to officiate during other sacrifices. The constant reek of a decaying man's body was unbearable to him. The fact that the priests insisted he touch Imakakoloa's opened eyes positively horrified him.

———

The chiefs had been gathering for days. When all was ready, we were called to the temple. On the most important day in his adult life— the human sacrifice of a chief so that his father could make him ruler over the island—Kiwalao was pale and shaking. Even though he was in great distress, he understood the importance of his duties and conducted the service with great solemnity and care. Was he being deliberate because he did not want to make a mistake in protocol, or because he was so sick he could barely stand up? I watched with pride as he placed the spotted pig precisely on the altar. Then he carefully placed the banana stalk on the other side of the pig. Next came the fruit. Everything was going along according to the prescribed ritual. The ceremony was at its zenith and I thought he might actually get through without mishap—he was so close…

Then that upstart Kamehameha broke protocol by stepping in front of Kiwalao, picking up the rotting body of Imakakoloa, lifting the dead man over his head, and offering it to the god. As if that were not enough, Kamehameha immediately took over. He declared the service finished and released the *kapu*. Before the priests could stop him, he dismissed the assembled chiefs. And just like that, the ceremony was over. Not one chief raised a hand to stop him. Although some expressed shock, others were no doubt secret accomplices.

No one could ever remember anyone having done a thing like that before. The rumors at court flew. Those that were satisfied with Kalani's original decision to make Kiwalao ruler and Kamehameha his military advisor accused Kamehameha of rising up against the one he was sworn to defend. Others claimed his act was one of treason against the gift his uncle had bestowed upon him as the keeper of the war god. Some said he acted independently by interrupting the sacrifice himself. Others said the lesser chiefs, hoping to gain favor by starting a rebellion, put him up to it. Everyone knew that by him offering up Imakakaloa, he was claiming rule of the land and going against his uncle's wishes. Some were not willing to be so hasty to judge, trying instead to find the middle ground, seeking a position that would place them in a positive light whichever way the wind blew. They reminded everyone that Kiwalao and Kamehameha were the sons of Kalani and his younger brother, Keoua, and therefore should be treated, if not equally, then at least with equal respect.

Keoua had been gone for a long time. I did not see what honoring the dead had to do with anything. The chiefs did not know the two young men vying for the honors of the island as I did. Not for a moment did I believe Kamehameha innocent. He had been raised to rebel—it was in his blood—but I dared not speak my thoughts out loud.

I let the chaos swirl around me, but I tended to side with those that said Alapai was right years ago when he advised the chiefs to pluck the *wauka* plant before it sprouted. Although I did not agree that Kamehameha should have been killed at birth, I did know the story of his mother, who during her pregnancy, had craved the eyeball of a chief. At the time, Alapai did not wish to sacrifice one of his men, so to stop her cravings, he gave her the eyeball of a tiger shark. He watched her swallow it whole and claimed she never knew difference. After a boy was born to her, the priests predicted he would be the killer of chiefs.

It was obvious to me that Kamehameha thought his time had come. Perhaps it would be better to kill him now before he caused any more problems, but I was never one to demand putting a human sacrifice on the altar, no matter what the reason might be.

When Kalani heard that his nephew had gone against protocol, he was stunned, then angry. But most of all, he was disappointed. He had been certain Kamehameha would be thrilled to be keeper of the war god. It was, after all, the warrior spirit in Kamehameha that Kalani, a seasoned warrior himself, recognized and admired. He felt his nephew's disloyalty to our son was a disloyalty to those that raised him, as well as ignoring the warrior's duty to be in service to his primary chief, whoever that might be.

"How could he do that?" Kalani wondered aloud. "I gave him the highest honor I could. My own brother's son… How dare he betray me!"

I wanted to tell him that I was not surprised. I did not tell him how the rumors were flying, nor did I tell him how I had seen Kamehameha strutting around the court like a rooster. I knew that was not the thing to say to Kalani—not then--not ever. I learned years ago that as his wife, even one of my stature, I had to be cautious about meddling in the Keawe family business. Somehow I managed to keep my mouth shut.

Kalani leaned on his staff as he paced up and down the *hale*, ranting. He peeled back layer after layer of anger as if he were skinning a freshly killed pig. After ranting, he eventually tired and fell into a heap on the floor, "What am I to do with him?"

Honestly, I felt sorry for the old chief.

He shook with fury, but also with grief. His nephew, the one he loved at times more than his own son, had broken his heart. "What shall I do? Do I let him remain here at my court and act like it's nothing out of the ordinary?"

"As mad as the chiefs are at him, no. You dare not do that. No one will accept that for a moment, especially not the priests," I said. I thought I saw a way to salvage my son's right to rule, and possibly to take care of his usurper. "Kamehameha's actions have gone against protocol. And his actions have greatly inhibited Kiwalao's ability to assume his right to establish his rule." I watched Kalani to see if my words were being accepted. When it seemed like he was listening, I continued, "The one sworn to protect our son has risen up against him."

Kalani hung his head, and then shook it as if he were trying to clear his thoughts. "That young bastard! Why is he making things so difficult?" He sat down on the mat next to me and sighed. "Kamehameha broke his promimse to me. He has no gratitude."

I had never heard the proud old warrior speak like this. Part of me wanted to go ahead--let the chiefs have their way and kill Kamehameha. It pained me deeply to see Kiwalao betrayed. But then I remembered my mission to my brother's court: bring peace. If there was one thing I had learned about living on this island, it was that one killing had the potential to open the way to all-out slaughter. Who knew when the bloodbath would end? I comforted Kalani by rubbing his neck and shoulders in order to calm him before I spoke. "If Kamehameha stays here, the chiefs will kill him for sure," I said, acting like I was thinking out loud. It would not do for a wife to let on to her husband that she was about to out-maneuver him. "That is obvious. We both know how angry they are."

I paused, checking to see that Kalani agreed.

He was silent, but nodded.

"And then there are the priests, who have threatened to pray him to death."

Kalani jerked his head up, shocked that I would mention such a thing.

"Yes, my Kalani. That's what I have heard. They say they will kill him with-- or without--your permission." I let that option sink in. "Clearly Kamehameha's life is in danger." In my heart of hearts, I would have had the priests do it—it might not have been such a bad thing--but once again, I was drawn back to the side of peace. Maybe it would be better to let the two young chiefs fight it out later—after Kalani was dead. Then even though they would be in battle, their fate would be in the hands of the gods, and I already knew the outcome: my son was destined to rule.

"Maybe I should strip him of the war god," Kalani muttered.

"Take that away and you take away his power," I said. The old man is craftier than I gave him credit for. Why hadn't I thought of that?

"But that will never do," he said quickly. "Once a man lays his hands on the war god Kukailimoku he will not give it up willingly." Kalani understood better than anyone the power that god held over its keeper. He sighed and then struggled to his feet. "I cannot postpone things any longer," he said. He called for his nephew.

When Kamehameha approached the compound, I was sitting against the wall, facing the door. His feather cape was wrapped around his broad shoulders, but he came unarmed and alone.

"You should have not gone against protocol," Kalani barked at Kamehameha after the young man entered and bowed before his uncle.

I say that Kamehameha bowed, but it was not a sincere bow, merely a formality.

No flicker of regret showed on Kamehameha's face for even a second. For all the trouble he had caused, Kamehameha seemed to take the matter rather lightly. Instead of groveling, he hung his head slightly but did not prostrate himself in my presence, again going against protocol. His body spoke his truth, even though he remained silent. One glance in his eyes told me he was not the least bit remorseful.

"You must go." Kalani said.

"But…" Kamehameha began half-heartedly.

Kalani held up his hand. "If you stay here, the chiefs will kill you."

"I am a warrior." Kamehameha raised his head and looked boldly into his uncle's eyes. "I will fight!"

He was no son of gentle Keoua's. I knew from that moment on that he would never back down. He might wait patiently, for he was still young and could let time pass. In fact, at this point, he had all the time in the world. In his bravado, he had just declared himself an enemy of my son. I would never trust him again.

"And if the chiefs don't attack you, then the priests…" Kalani continued.

"Anyone!" Kamehameha interrupted. He pounded his fist into his palm to make his declaration clear. "I will fight anyone!"

"You cannot fight the *ana ana* curse once a *kahuna* has spoken the spell of death," Kalani warned. "Better men than you have tried…and failed."

"Who? I have never…"

"To be a chief you have to know your history--and your enemies. My wife's father, for instance."

Kamehameha glared at the old man, no doubt thinking him senile.

"And your father, for another."

Kamehameha hesitated. He knew his uncle was right. He swallowed the words and tried another tactic. "But you are still the chief, and you could…"

I understood that Kamehameha had made a grave mistake. Once Kalani's mind was made up, arguing would only serve to harden his heart.

Kalani hobbled over to Kamehameha, his eyes filled with tears, for he truly did love his nephew. "*Auwe!*" he wailed.

The years flashed before me. I recalled how Kalani had risked his own life to bring the young man to his court, something Kamehameha had never really understood or acknowledged. Kalani had just tried to tell him, but it was clear that in the brashness of youth, Kamehameha did not yet comprehend the sacrifices made on his behalf. I wondered how Kamehameha could be so arrogant. As is often the case of those who have not yet lived enough days, Kamehameha showed only haughtiness; there was no gratitude for Kalani's deeds in the past, or any empathy for the pain in Kalani's heart.

"You are the child of my beloved brother. I could strip you of everything— your land and your war god, but I will not. I have left you the war god—that is your wealth. Take your god and go to your lands in Kohala. You have betrayed your father and you have broken my heart. The only thing I can do for you now is save your life. I am old and I will see you no more. I banish you from this court. Be gone!"

# *Thirty-Six*

## 1781

After Kamehameha had been sent away, Kiwalao asked permission from his father to return to Maui. He was allowed—but only for long enough to prepare his sister/wife and daughter to move to Kau permanently. I, too, wanted to see my daughter and granddaughter, but my request was refused. Kalani said he could not stand me being away from him that long. I knew it wasn't that any love was lost, for I was not his favorite wife, but rather that he had grown dependent on me. I don't mean he was dependent on me to help him run the day-to-day affairs; he had become dependent on me physically, even though he had retainers to do his bidding. His emaciated body folded in on itself. Like a tree growing on the windward side of the island, he had become hunched over against the constant onslaught. He stooped as if he carried a great burden on his back, for in truth, the responsibilities of being a soverign weighed heavily on him. Really, that had been the case for years. He had paid dearly for his reign. His stubbly beard and hair—what was left of either—totally white, with not even a fleck of color. Feeble, but not yet without his senses, he was still the chief, and everyone bowed down. In his old age, his people grew to love him more because they feared him less—he no longer had the strength to be the terror he once had been.

News of good *ahi* fishing was reported at Kaaluulu and Paiahaa, and so he moved his entire court to those prime, but desolate, spots. The lack of fresh water with which to bathe soon began to wear on Kalani and he became even more irritable than usual. His years of heavy *awa* drinking were once again taking their toll. His scaly skin, parched as the landscape, cracked into brittle patches. His eyelids drooped, making him appear half asleep. The whites of his eyes, red and veined, looked like Pele had dragged red *ohia* blossoms across his corneas. In the ever-present wind, it pained him to blink, which made him him seem stupid when he was most assuredly not.

As soon as his *hale* was built, he sent the men for fresh water that bubbled up from the lava tubes extending into the bay. Every day the *makaainana* took their calabashes down to the shore and dove down thirty or forty feet to the cracks in the rocks where the fresh water rippled. Struggling against the tides and currents, they held the mouth of the calabash over the openings and let fresh water fill the container. Placing their hand over the mouth of the gourd, they planted their feet on the bottom of the bay and shoved off, kicking for their life as they dragged the heavy gourds to the surface. Then they body surfed down the face of the breakers to shore. When they had filled two gourds, they tied them to either end of a stout pole, slug the pole across their shoulders, and picked their way across the scorching lava beds to Kalani's compound. Other water gatherers went in the opposite direction--to the caves in the hills. There they placed the calabashes under drip spots and left them for several days, coming back when nature had filled them. Either way, there was hardly enough fresh water for all those in Kalani's court to drink, let alone the luxury of bathing.

Kalani's skin itched, and he was loath to soak in the tidal pools near the sea. Instead of the healing properties of salt water clearing up his skin, it only made him scratch more. Nor did he want to soak in the brackish water of the fishponds. He declared that nothing but fresh water would do, and demanded that his seers find abundance--the more, the better.

One night around the fire, Naonaoaina, a *kahuna puuone*--one who was skilled in the confirmation of the earth's surface—began the story, "Once in olden times…" and proceeded to tell the legend of Lono's dog drinking from a spring that bubbled out from under a rock named Kailioalono. Pele, the volcano goddess, was scouring the land and had caught the dog lapping near the rock. As she was likely to do, she turned the dog to stone. The *kahuna* intimated that fresh water could be found if they could but find the rock formation of Pele's stone dog.

The moment Kalani heard that there might be fresh water in the area he was determined to have it. Young and old, farmer and fisherman—he sent everyone out to dig for water. Another old *kahuna,* smaller than most men (a 'throw-back' to the time of the *menehune* some called him; others claimed *eepa*) scuttled into court one morning and warned that water would not be found in the shallow wells the people were digging. "If you want water, you have to dig deep. It does no good to dig everywhere," he said fluttering his fingers about to demonstrate. "It does no good to dig *around* the dog. Dig deep *beside* the dog."

Who could blame the *makaainana* for digging the holes half-heartedly? It was hot in the blazing sun. They spent more time wiping the sweat off their brows than they did jabbing and poking their wooden digging sticks into the cracks in the hard lava for the benefit of their chief. After many days of merely scraping the surface, the people wearied of their task and refused to listen to the wisdom of the old *kahuna.* Kalani, never a patient man, gave up and called off the effort. He brought the diminutive man in front of the court, told him it was his fault they had found no water, and ordered him killed.

"Kill me, Oh Heavenly One, if that be your wish, but I die taking with me the secret of the dog of Pele."

Kalani, always willing to prove his point, had the man hung.

After that, Kalani wearied of the effort to find water. He was ready to move on and told his retainers to pack up the court. The priests declared fishing season over and call for a *kapu* for conservation purposes.

The day before we left, Kiwalao returned, alone, from Maui. He was shocked when he saw how quickly Kalani was failing. "He stumbles," were his first words to me.

"The old chief needs you," I said. "And my daughter?"

"They were not quite ready to travel when I decided to return. Liliha said to tell you she would come after she conducts the ceremonies of the next full moon."

———

*K*alani, not nimble upon arising, was finally ready to depart at mid-morning. With the sun beating down upon our backs, we began the trek out of Kau, hoping to find more water along the Kona coast. We had not traveled far—just a few miles—when we arrived at Pakini, the *heiau* where Kamehameha had transgressed against Kiwalao. It was as if the spirits were waiting for us. At a spot near where Imakakoloa had laid rotting in the sun, Kalani came down with squatting sickness, *maiokuu*. Suddenly fever gripped Kalani and sweat dripped from every pore. He dropped in his tracks, insisting he was being prayed to death. It was hard to tell if those were his more lucid moments or if he had succumbed to a fever-induced delirium. The *kahunas* traveling with us prayed, of course, but ultimately said there was nothing they could do. Some of the retainers argued with the priests, insisting that his adversary had been the dwarf. If it was the *eepa*, the *kahunas* swore they were not powerful enough to tangle with the little fellow because he was now working his magic from the land of the dead. Others claimed the disease was caused by his old enemy, the Puna chief. In one of his lucid moments Kalani overheard his *kahuna's* explanation and let out a thunderous roar, denying both the dwarf's supremacy or Imakaloa's presence. Upon the obvious rejection of the meddling dwarf and the dead chief, the *kahunas* then suggested the sender of bad omens might be Kamehameha, who we had not heard from since he had been banished from Kalani's court. I thought that might be a possibility, although I was loath to mention his name to Kalani, knowing how deeply he had cared for the young man over the years. It made no sense to me to upset the old warrior now. He had met the ultimate foe, and his was a losing battle.

# Thirty-Seven

## 1781

It was the time of Kaulua, perhaps—maybe a little later. The white men called it their month, January; others said April. Some were not even sure of the year—1781 or 1782. I know not when, exactly—time slipped away from me as I cared for my husband in his final days. It was all I could do to keep an air of calmness over the court. As difficult as he had been to live with, as cantankerous and mean as he had been, and as cruel, as austere his court, still...he and I had walked together as he fought for and ruled the island for twenty-nine years—a long time for any chief, but particularly for the volatile island of Hawaii.

As I held his bony hand, I thought back over our time together. My husband, Kalaniopuu, could never leave well enough alone. Such was his way. He was a strong, brave warrior who wanted nothing less than to rule over his island, and any other land he could. In his day, he had no equal—that's the bragging right every woman wishes to make for her husband, thus elevating her own position. In my own case, however, I could say that marriage with me, the sacred queen of Maui, assured him rule over his island and certainly that of our son, Kiwalao, who was attempting to follow the path his father had carved out for him. I thought back to the day I first landed at Kau, so frightened and alone. I came from the windward sides of Molokai and Maui—from the tropical jungle, with the *Noe* rain that kept the land cool and the winds of *Holoua* that stirred up white- caps on the ocean. Even though he had been born on Oahu, Kalani's heart was in the stark, windswept lands of Kau. The lava that flowed down the cliffs from Pele's caldera scorched everything on its way to the sea's desolate shore. Like the lands both of us came from, we were total opposites. It wasn't that I wanted to marry him; it wasn't that I didn't want to marry him—it was simply the thing that was done. I was the sacred womb from which chiefly spirits sprang. I gave him a son with strong *mana*, but different from his father's. Kalani preferred the son his brother claimed, Kamehameha. By the time Kamehameha was grown, just like his uncle, he thought everything was his—all he had to do was reach out and take it.

Kalaniopuu--that stubborn man--no matter how many times he was beaten, still would not give up. I told him he would never win against my brother, but he didn't believe me and set about to prove me wrong. How many times had Kalani tried to take Maui? So many, over the years I'd lost count. Every time I turned around he had hatched another scheme, conscripted and trained more warriors, built more canoes, and headed off for Maui. Kahekili, weary of having to defend his lands and people, would exclaim, "Not again!" and then send the spies back to me with the message to keep my husband on his own island. I knew my brother thought I put Kalani up to it; that I egged him on, but I swear I did not. There was simply nothing I could do. I told my brother. "He is as hard and unchanging as the rock at Kaueleau in Puna." What drove my husband? Greed for land and dominance over the land and its people—that was part of it, undoubtedly. It is said that every man dreams of dominance over others—that it is simply the way of men. He loved everything about war: the planning, the scheming, the build-ing of canoes, the combat, the bloodshed, even wailing over the dead--he loved it all. He cherished his feather cloak of power, his shark tooth weapons, and his long *koa* spear--although as he grew older, he made sure he tucked himself safely behind the line of battle. Most of all, I think he loved ordering men to die for him. Soon all that would be over, and I had visions of the peace that lay ahead between my brother and my son. In the end, the two would be able to unite the island chain.

Kalani lingered for days, restless and weak. Nothing I did comforted him. My prayers for his easy passing were useless. The only relief I could bring him was to bathe his open sores and hold his head in my lap, stroking his thin hair as I would a sick child. I sucked up water in a hollow reed and dripped it between his chapped lips, but even those drops were of no consequence. He could barely open his mouth. When he did, his breath—his *ha*—smelled putrid, as if his insides were rotting. The reek of death hung heavy in the air.

"Send for my son," he mumbled when he opened his eyes, begging me for help.

Kiwalao, ever dutiful, came to his father's side at once.

Kalani, drawing upon his last strength, barked out his final instructions, adamant in his request, "Place my bones in *Hale o Keawe*. I want my bones to lie with my ancestors."

"Of course, Heavenly One. I promise. Our son promises." Over and over again, I assured him as I wiped the sweat from his brow. I stayed by him morning and night as he grew weaker, and then less and less coherent. Finally, fever sucked the last of his *mana* from his bones, and death rattled his lungs.

———

*H*is passing affected me much more than I could have ever imagined. I thought I was prepared—he was, after all, a warrior. He could have been killed in any battle. And, surely I was aware of his aging, bent frame. But is one really ever prepared for the finality and the changes it brings?

"Your father is gone," I told my son when I called him to my side. "You are now the ruler, but before you can claim your lands, you must go to your father's younger half-brother in Hilo. Stay with your uncle until I send for you. I've sent a runner on ahead—your uncle, Keawemauhili, will be waiting for you. But take your best warriors with you—just in case someone decides to start trouble."

"Oh mother…you make too much of it," Kiwalao said, waving me off.

I stomped my foot. "I know exactly what the chiefs are going to do. I've seen it since I was a child. You, my son, have not." I sat down next to him and spoke softly so that if any retainers were listening, they could not hear. "Once the other chiefs hear Kalani is dead, they will start grabbing for what they want: land, titles, favors from you, the new ruler. Do not tarry—you must leave immediately.

Soon the red fish will come, and everyone will see that Kalani is gone. Go now, before the taint of death is upon you."

"What about you?"

"As soon as you are safely gone, I will announce Kalani's passing," I said. "I will remain here. It is my duty to take care of your father's bones."

———

*J* waited until Kiwalao and his men had disappeared over the top of the ridge, and then sent a message to the *kahunas* at the *heiau*. I'm sure when the *poi* pounders spied the men heading north, they had a good idea; surely when the *kapa* beaters saw the priests rushing from the *heiau* to Kalani's compound, they suspected. When I stationed guards all around the compound, even those in the sweet potato patches understood. Perhaps the wood gatherers in the upland forests heard the priest's mournful lamentation carried on the wind. Their Heavely One was gone. Everyone stopped to mourn. The men began the wailing durge as they trudged back to the village from the *loi*, from the uplands, from the fishpond. Were the men keening for their chief, or for the struggles they knew were coming? Like a school of fish scooped up in the net, the *makaainana* would soon be paying with their lives in the battles between *alii* chiefs who coveted more land.

No one dared touch Kalani's body but me, his sacred wife. While my retainers wailed, I moved to the corner of the *hale* with the head priest to plan the next few days. "We will send messengers throughout the island to carry the news and call the chiefs to gather," I said loudly, but then whispered, "We need to shelter ourselves behind a long burial and grieving process so that we can give Kiwalao time to adjust to his new role."

The priest murmured. "I understand. It shall be as you wish, my chiefess." He raised his voice so the retainers could hear, "The process of preparing our chief, the Heavenly One, shall extend as long as needed to see that he is properly placed with his ancestors." Then, quietly to me, as if he were expressing extreme condolences, "Even the men who dig the hole so we can roast the body shall be instructed to take their time. The young man who wishes to rule will need every minute we can spare him." He stood up and left my side to begin preparations for the ceremonies.

I felt great relief once I was assured the priest was on Kiwalao's side and that we would proceed slowly. I stepped back to Kalani and wailed for I know not how long. Surprisingly, in those moments, I found myself loving that man more in death than I ever had loved him in life.

I began my next job as Kalani's wife—cleaning his gaunt body. I washed him from head to toe, missing not a spot. When I finished, I sent again for the priest. When he returned I was certain he would tell me he had instructed his men to begin digging a hole for the *imu* to roast Kalani's body.

Instead, he said, "Kalani is already so thin that it would be easy to postpone burial. It won't be a problem to take out his intestines and then allow the body to bake in the sun. That way we can make sure that no one will be able to steal his bones and use them as fishhooks."

"But what about *Hale o Keawe?*" I asked. "That was his desire—to have his bones placed among those of his ancestors."

"Of course, my sacred chiefess. Again, that is no problem. It will take several passings of the moon before the body will be ready for placement. After the proper procedures, we can perform the final service there. Then we can be sure all his bones are in the *kaai* and tucked away safely with his ancestors."

And then I understood. The priests were truly on our side and had devised a plan to draw the proceedings out as long as possible.

---

As soon as the chiefs across the island heard the news, they came to Kau to pay their respects. For a time even the wind stopped blowing and the sounds of wailing hung in the still air. Every evening a different voice was added. The priests followed protocol exactly. "Post guards around the *hale* where the body lays," the priests said. "At a time like this, with all the chiefs present, we can't be too careful." Anything the priests asked for--anything at all--I approved without question.

Even though they put on a good show, I suspected the chiefs weren't spending every minute wailing. I presumed they were holding secret meetings and forming daring liaisons. The custom after the old chief died was that the new ruler would divide the land. Those in his favor prospered. Those that were not in his favor lost their holdings. If Kiwalao had been present, they would have pestered him from sun up to sun down and then long into the night. Even though some time had passed since Kamehameha had broken protocol and been banished from Kalani's court, some chiefs still held a grudge and I knew it wouldn't take much to fan their anger into flames. They were not so quick to forgive and forget, especially because they thought Kalani had shown the young chief favor by mere banishment. If they had had their way, they would have placed Kamehameha beside the Puna chief, Imakakaloa, and sacrificed them both. Some still wished to go to war against Kamehameha, vowing they would urge Kiwalao, as would be his right, to take away the precious war god Kamehameha had been given. Over the last few years Kalani, who knew his chiefs well, had assured me that nothing would ever stem the tide.

Surprisingly, Kamehameha was nowhere to be found. I wondered if he even knew his uncle had passed. Quite honestly, I was a little perturbed that he had not even sent an acknowledgement, much less shown his face. It was true he had been banished from court, but to not acknowledge his cousin as chief was, as some of the others were quick to point out, disturbing. And to not acknowledge his uncle's death was just plain rude.

The longer the priests took praying over Kalani's body, the more I valued their station. Of course that meant more of everything for them: more status, more goods, more honor. "Everything should be done exactly according to protocol," I assured them. "Do not rush through anything."

"My chiefess, the whole process could take several moons," the priests informed me in front of the body of chiefs as we played the waiting game. "Maybe longer…"

"Then so be it." I said. "I will have nothing left undone, nothing is too good for my husband." Any time I could buy for my son as he established his rule was time well spent. Perhaps some of the chiefs suspected our ruse, but there was nothing they could do to hasten the process. If they hoped to gain anything in the land division they knew was imminent, they needed to remain silent and show their respect.

One very dark night the drums sounded. All the chiefs gathered inside the *heiau*. The priests set the *kapu* and the sacred fire was lit. Guards surrounded the perimeter of the enclosure and all of the chiefs would be sequestered inside until the ritual was complete. When the priests were assured all was in place, they packed Kalani's intestines in many bundles along with the intestines of the pigs that had been sacrificed. The priests carried the bundles to the shore where Kalani's most trusted warriors waited in canoes. When each canoe received its bundle, the priests shoved it off the sand. It was a moonless *Muku* night, so it did not take long for the men to disappear from view. They paddled out to the deep ocean where they chummed the water and called the sharks to feast. They did not return until long after sunrise. After the canoes were lined up on shore, a new *kapu* was ordered for two more days. Everyone was ordered to close the huts and remain inside. Only after the priests assured us no entrails had washed ashore, only after the proper prayers were said, were the people allowed out of the *hales* and the *heiau* again. Only then did I send for Kiwalao to return. I told the runner to take the long route through Puna, both going and coming back.

# Thirty-Eight

## 1782

The chiefs waited, some impatiently, for the *kapu* to be lifted and then for Kiwalao to return. Each chief had his own agenda, of course, and was quick to seize any scrap of rumor or innuendo to further his individual claim to more land. The windward chiefs, led by Kiwalao's uncle, Hilo chief Keawemauhili, returned with him. The rulers from that area had plenty of time to ply Kiwalao with their desires concerning the coveted Kona districts on the dry side of the island. The Kona chiefs, quite rightly, were worried sick. What if Kiwalao acquiesced to his uncle's demands and gave away their lands? On the surface, the wailing for Kalani filled the air, and prayers for his soul's safe journey shook every waking moment, yet underneath ran a river of in-fighting the likes of which I had never seen. I likened the wailing to the crusty surface of rock we walked upon, and the infighting of the court like the river of molten lava that coursed through the hidden tunnels underground. Like the burning magma, the rumors occasionally seeped through a crack and erupted into the topside world. Both Kiwalao and I were worn ragged listening to the whisperings and veiled threats: who was planning war against who, and where, and when. It made me appreciate how much responsibility Kalani had shouldered, keeping all the greedy, land-snatching chiefs in line. Once more I understood that it had been a bad idea to bring up my son on Maui; that I should have raised Kiwalao among the chiefs of Hawaii. It was my fault that he did not know the desires, weaknesses and inner thoughts of each chief's mind as his father had. And yet it was much too late to do anything about that—and there was no one that I trusted enough to ask for guidance. To make matters worse, my son had been completely swayed by his uncle, Keawemauhili.

Kiwalao had inherited the title of chief; it had been handed to him--like everything else in his life. Unlike the older chiefs, he had not had to battle for his position. In truth, he was an innocent young man and his nature was not one that demanded authority. He was *alii*, but he did not understand that he would have to show the chiefs that he had the confidence to step up and claim leadership over all he surveyed.

The chiefs of Kona paid their respects to me and then announced that they were going home to their own lands. When asked why, they admitted that they felt were threatened and were heading back to their people to prepare for the invasion they were sure was coming. Their hasty departure played into Keawemauhili's hand. He wasted no time in turning Kiwalao against the leeward chiefs.

Kiwalao sought my counsel. As he entered my *hale*, confusion clouded his face. "Who should I believe, mother?" he asked as he sat on the mat beside me.

"Tell me what you've heard, and who you've heard it from, then perhaps I can be of help to you."

"I've heard that the Kona chiefs left because they disrespected my father…"

"Did the Kona chiefs ever rise up against him?"

"No," he admitted.

"Go on. I know there is more."

"And that by leaving they were being disrespectful to you…"

"But they came to me and told me they were leaving and why. They showed me no disrespect," I said calmly. "What else?"

"…and that by their leaving they were being disrespectful to me."

"Did they come to you and tell you they were leaving?"

"Yes."

"Did you grant them leave?"

"Yes."

"Then there was no disrespect." I could see that he was still troubled. "And what else?"

"That by leaving they were showing disrespect to my uncle."

"Ah… there you have it. Keawemauhili is the source of your information, isn't he? He put these ideas in your head."

Kiwalao nodded.

"And what else did he say against those chiefs?"

"That they left because they are planning a rebellion against me. And that they will come back to destroy me." His face broke out in a sweat and he wiped his forehead. "He also said that a smart ruler would go on the offense and attack them first."

"Why invite disharmony?" I asked, shocked that his uncle's thoughts had so thoroughly invaded my son's psyche. I wrapped my words carefully around the weeds in my son's mind and attempted to pull them up, roots and all. "What sense would there be in attacking those chiefs? Your father is not put away yet. And you mean to tell me that you are already thinking about war? The truth is, it sounds exactly like something a disgruntled chief would say in order to start something. There is no rush to go to battle. Besides, the family is still in mourning."

"But the chiefs left…"

"They left because they felt threatened."

"Threatened? By who?" His brow furrowed in his confusion. "By me?"

"Yes—you. Think about what you're saying. What did you just ask me? It sounded to me like you were ready to pick up your spear." Then I stopped, sensing that gentle persuasion would help turn his mind around better than launching a verbal attack. I lowered my voice and put it on a more gracious, diplomatic course. "Look at it from the Kona chiefs angle. If you were them, and heard the rumor that the windward chiefs coveted your lands, wouldn't you go home in order to protect your land and prepare your people for an attack?"

"Yes, I guess I would," he said and then fell silent, considering his course of action. "Then you think they mean me no harm?"

"Whether they mean you harm hasn't been determined yet. They mean you no harm *today*." How was I going to get this young man to understand that one day they would all rise up against him and he would have to fight for his life? "You are going to have to make up your own mind, but I caution you not to let your uncle sway you so. Don't be blinded by the mist that haunts the long trail."

I saw his brow wrinkle and I knew he didn't understand. Then I spoke as plainly as I knew how. "Don't be deceived. You have a lot to learn, my son."

"My uncle reminds me constantly that he is the only man among the chiefs I can trust. He says that our common blood binds me to him."

"Your uncle is only your father's half brother. I am your mother. My blood is strongest of all." Disgusted because I could feel my son slipping away from me, I spat out the words I'd been thinking since Kalani's death. "And you? You are like the plover that can't find its way home because you're being blown about by a strong wind."

Keawemauhili's posturing and maneuvering wore on all of us. I'd hoped Kiwalao would take the time the priests were granting him to come into his own mind, but after I lost my temper and called him a wayward plover, he no longer sought my advice and kept his opinions to himself. I had lost this battle against Keawemauhili, but I was sure there would be others to come. All I could do was pray for peace among the chiefs--something that, in the long run, I knew better than to expect.

Keawemauhili courted the priests, calling on them for questions of protocol and seeking their advice at all hours. He flattered them when their spirits flagged, wooed them when he sensed they were exhausted. Kiwalao could not see that all the rumors circulating through the court had their source in his uncle. The remaining chiefs became restless as they watched Keawemauhili daily gain more power and control over my son. Keawemauhili grew bolder and bolder. Like a child, Kiwalao did not understand his hand was filled with tasty morsels and innocently fed his dog of an uncle, who stole scraps from Kiwalao's open palms. Keawemauhili spoke against all the leeward chiefs, and in particular, Kamehameha, whom he accused of rebellion, bringing up his dismissal from Kalani's court every chance he had. That master manipulator created opportunities to sow discord where I thought it expedient to remain silent. Thinking back on it, I can see now that Keawemauhili must have felt he'd been passed over at Waipio when Kalani had handed the war god to Kamehameha. After all,

Keawemauhili was Kalani's younger half-brother, and he had made it clear that he desired the war god, Kukailimoku, for himself. He kept the court, and my son, in constant turmoil.

———

*O*n Maui, the first thing Kahekili did when he heard that Kalani had passed was to begin the campaign to take back the coveted lands of Hana in the southern district of Maui. Kiwalao was in no position to marshall much of an army because he had his hands full with the squabbling chiefs of Hawaii. He sent troops to fight, but paid little attention to the outcome of their battles. What should have been an easy rout for Kiwalao's troops dragged on.

"It is not necessary to keep Hana under your control," I told him. "It is ultimately land that belongs to Kahekili. There is no need to fight. He will not back down."

"Nor will I," Kiwalao said, feigning braveness, and the battle continued.

The day came when Naeole, the lone survivor of the outpost at Hana, limped back to Kau in a bedraggled state. When questioned, he told how an old man, a commoner, had grown tired of the strife and had told Kahekili the secret to winning.

"What is it?" asked Kiwalao, anxious to learn any tips of warfare he could, now that he was the head of an army.

"Very simple," Naeole said. "They cut off the water. They must have dammed the streams at night because one morning there was no water—not even a trickle. Then it took no time at all. The crops began to wither. Like the plants, our people trapped in the fort at Kauiki were dying of thirst. Then it was easy for Kahekili to send his men in and slaughter everyone. I am a seasoned warrior, but I swear, my chief, never in my life have I seen such carnage."

"And you?"

"In this case, Kahekili told me to be sure to tell you that he let me escape so that you would understand there is no reason for you to return to Maui."

———

By pretending more grief that I actually felt, I was able to draw out the mourning period several months in order to buy more time for my son. The priests aided me as much as they could, but finally they came to the point where they couldn't postpone the inevitable any longer. They assured everyone they had guided their dead chief's spirit safely to the land of Milo, and now it was time to deposit the king's bones in *Hale o Keawe* at Honaunau on the leeward coast. The priests had carried out their job. It was time to see if Kiwalao could keep the chiefs in line. Unfortunately, even after months of bickering, Kiwalao had still made no decisions about land divisions, or if he had come to a decision, he had made no announcements.

Truthfully, I had never seen the chiefs be so patient, and I kept wondering if my son was really as blind as he appeared to be. Could he not sense their dissension? But I dared not ask. Instead, I tended to the requirements of the priests. I did nothing to disturb the peace or to draw any attention to myself, for after all, even though I had been Kalani's sacred wife, my blood was still that of the Maui clan, and I did not want the long arm of any disgruntled Hawaii chief to stretch across the channel to my brother's court.

As soon as he determined that the priests were preparing to leave for Honaunau to place Kalani's bones with his ancestors, Keeaumoku, the instigator, left. The guards reported that he had headed for his worthless land at Kapalilua on the leeward coast of the island, near where the canoes had to pass by on their way to Honaunau. I had not trusted Keeaumoku for years. He had never had the makings of a diplomat; everyone knew he was a chief who always counseled war. To that hothead, the solution to any problem was simple: a dead man was no longer an enemy.

Second to leave was Kamehameha's old fighting instructor, Kekuhaupio, a chief who watched over the coveted Kona land of Keei. The guards reported that instead of following Keeaumoku's footsteps and heading over the hills to his lands, the old warrior headed up the side of the mountain past the crater at Kilauea, taking the shortest way possible to Kohala where Kamehameha lived. Even the most ignorant servant at court figured out Kekuhaupio was traveling that most dangerous route in order to be the first to reach Kamehameha. We had not heard from Kamehameha for almost two years and had no idea what he was thinking. I hoped his lack of communication meant that he was choosing to support Kiwalao. But as soon as Kekuhaupio left, I knew that whatever Kamehameha had been thinking no longer mattered. Like my son, he was still young enough to be easily swayed. My suspicion was that Kekuhaupio intended to fan the embers into flame and raise Kamehameha's ire. No spears had been thrown, yet it was clear that the battle over Kalani's former island rule had begun.

When the people saw Kiwalao and the priests preparing Kalani's canoe, they readied their own canoes to make the trip up the coast to accompany their chief on his final journey. I had never seen so many canoes--not even in times of war. Keawemauhili insisted that his *peleleu* canoe, draped with red feather capes, lead the floatilla.

The priests carried Kalani's shrunken body to his canoe. Only his emaciated face showed above the bundle of white *kapa* his body was wrapped in. He was placed in a sitting position and tied to the mast of his war canoe, guarded by the *kahilis* Eleeleualani and Kauakaahonua, and flanked by two death companions. The woven sennit basket that had been fashioned to hold his bones was tied face up, across his lap. The eyeholes on the *kaai* were vacant. Only after his bones were placed in the basket would the mother-of-pearl eyes be attached so that he could see into the other world.

My handsome son draped his yellow and red feather cape across his shoulders and stationed himself at the front of the platform on his own war canoe under the *kihili* Hawaiiloa, and two kapu flags, Kaiwakulpumoku and Kaukalihoano.

As I prepared to board my son's canoe, Keawemauhili changed his mind and ordered all of Kalani's wives to travel overland instead of riding in the canoes. Although Keawemauhili was sure I would protest, I surprised him and yielded to his decision without a fuss. In that, I even surprised myself. When I gave it some consideration, I thought an overland trip was a good idea for several reasons: one, if anyone decided to attack in order to steal Kalani's body, I preferred to be far away; two, because if one of us were killed—either Kiwalao or I—the other would remain and could establish some semblance of control; and three, I wanted time away from the arguing factions so that I could have some peace and quiet. This would be the first time in many moons that I would be separated from my dead husband and the *mana* his body still held. Away from him, I could mull over all I had seen and make plans for the future.

The double canoes were launched and they waited for the others beyond the breakers. Last to leave was Kiwalao, who waved to me and then spoke to his navigator. The sails were raised and caught the wind. The convoy turned as one and headed up the coast.

After the canoes left, the palaquin carriers hoisted all of Kalani's wives on their shoulders and, with our retainers trudging behind, began the long climb up the hill out of the rugged plains of Kau. I was able to keep the trail of canoes in sight as they rounded the southwestern promontory, but after we reached the top of the hill, the path entered dense jungle on the southwestern side of the island and I could not see through the thicket. It felt like we fell far behind the canoes, or perhaps I was more anxious to get there than I realized. At any rate, I speculated we traveled only half the distance as the canoes on the first day, which worried me a great deal.

That night, I dreamed of bones wrapped in two bundles of white *kapa*. I knew one bundle belonged to my husband, but I did not recognize the other bundle. At dawn I awoke with a start and asked for the swiftest runner in our group. "Find Kiwalao." I had no idea what I would do if it were discovered the canoes had been attacked—what could I have done from land? But I desperately wanted to be assured the second bundle in my dream was not my son.

We had begun our day's march when the runner returned several hours later. He was exhausted, but with the good news that the *makaainana* had seen the *waa* floatilla pull into the bay at Honomalino in the south Kona district. He assured me there was nothing to fear.

Later in the day, reports came that Kamehameha was on the move, traveling with many men from his lands in Kohala overland in our direction. The spies said they could not get a clear look at the size of Kamehameha's army, fearing if they got too close they would be captured and killed. They had not been able to name the chiefs because no one was wearing feather capes, but it was reported that they were all carrying more than one *koa* spear. Surely no man would embark on such a journey without some protection, prepared to defend himself if neces-sary. The absence of flowing feather capes seemed to suggest they were traveling with peaceful intentions. I knew, however, the idea of Kamehameha coming with so many weapons signaled he was prepared for battle. As soon as the other wives heard, rumors flew. Some surmised that since Kekuhaupio had headed in Kamehameha's direction, we could assume he had urged Kamehameha to come to *Hale o Keawe* in order to honor his uncle. It would be, after all, the right thing to do, and Kekuhaupio, although a fearless warrior, was also a man of honor who had served Kalaniopuu well all those years and would surely want to pay his respects. The wives argued that the old warrior had been able to encourage Kamehameha to come peacefully and pay respects to his uncle. I was among the few who speculated that Kamehameha had come with less than honorable intentions. It was clear to me that Kamehameha would use the excuse to honor his uncle, but he would also travel with his power, Kukailimoku. All those years with Kalani had taught me that when the feathers were ruffled on that war god, men were quickly roused to battle.

We settled into camp early. I fully expected to hear that the canoes had reached Honaunau, but when the runners returned they reported that the fleet had sailed quite a bit farther—near Kailua, in fact. What could Kiwalao be thinking? Was he waiting for me to arrive before he came back down the coast? There would be no need for him to delay in landing the canoes—we had agreed to meet at Honaunau, but not necessarily to arrive at the same time. He should have known better. And then it dawned on me that his canoe was not in the lead—Keawemauhili's was in front. Immediately the crafty Hilo chief's ploy was clear: it was exactly as the Kona chiefs had feared all along. Keawemauhili had Kalani's canoe lashed to his vessel and Kiwalao, the heir apparent, following innocently behind. The farther up the coast they traveled, the more land could be claimed. If no one stopped him, that sly dog could have Kiwalao, as the new ruler, lay claim to the whole Kona coast. Then, Keawemauhili would surely receive some of the spoils when Kiwalao divided up the lands, and not shed a drop of his Hilo warrior's blood.

———

*O*n the third day of slow, dusty travel, I smelled rain before I saw the dark gray clouds rolling across the sea toward us, the harbinger of the thunder god, Kanehekili. In no time at all, we heard his thunderous footsteps marching toward us. Soon a cloudbank blocked out the sun. The wind rose and the heavens opened up, dumping rain down in sheets. It took only moments for everyone to get drenched. The palaquin bearers hurried as fast as they could through the driving rain, desperately looking for shelter. The carriers stopped, claiming it was too dangerous for them to bear us over the wet ground, afraid they would slip on the mud and their sacred women would tumble out. Besides, they moaned, the clouds had enclosed us in thick fog. Even though we were following a well-worn path, they were fearful of losing their way. That was it, of course—they were fearful—and there was nothing for us to do but halt and wait out the storm. After my feet were firmly planted on the ground, I huddled under the broad leaves of the temporary shelter the men lashed together out of wet banana leaves and shivered in the chill of the uplands. The downpour had come so fast the men didn't have time to gather dry firewood, so there was no way we could dry out or stay warm. To me, of greater concern was Kiwalao. My hope was that he was not lost at sea in the midst of the deluge, and I prayed for his safety. Then the winds increased and ripped the makeshift roof of banana leaves off the shelter the men had cobbled together. I could no longer worry about my son's safety or the security of my husband's bones; instead, I wrapped the soaked *kapa* tight around my shoulders and prayed that I would make it through the night.

I must have slept—although I could have sworn I was awake all night--for I opened my eyes when I heard the first birds of dawn. At some point during the night the wind had shifted and the storm had blown itself out to sea. The horizon was dark in the west, but behind us the sun was coming up and a bright morning rainbow spread across the entire sky. Scouts had been sent out as soon as it had stopped raining, and upon their return, they assured me Kiwalao's canoe was safe in the bay at Honaunau, and that we were actually much closer to that area than any of us thought.

———————

*A*fter the difficulties of the storm the evening before, the journey down the trail to Honaunau, although slippery and slow, was without incident and we arrived a little after the sun's zenith.

Kiwalao came to the edge of the compound to greet me. As he escorted me to my *hale*, he whispered, "I have to talk to you."

"Alone?"

He nodded.

"I will send for you," I assured him as I patted his arm. "Let me bathe this mud off." With that he smiled, bowed low, and left me to freshen up. For yet a moment I wished to relish the last hours of hypnotic rocking on the shoulders of the palanquin carriers, the song of birds in the bushes, the sugar cane rustling in the trade wind. All that was a tender memory as I washed the muck off and prepared to tackle the complexities of my son's court.

When I sent for him, Kiwalao came at once. Before he'd even gathered himself, he burst out, "Kamehameha is coming."

"So I've heard," I said in a calm voice so as not to frighten him more. "Has he sent word of his intentions?"

"Not yet."

"And what does your uncle say?" I asked, even though I already had a clear notion of what Keawemauhili had probably advised. "To fight?"

Kiwalao nodded. "There is discord between us. Did you see the storm?"

"See it?! I suffered last night—every bone in my body aches. It was cold in the uplands on the side of that hill. I had my cloak wrapped around me tight and there was no dry wood for a fire. I worried about you. I was afraid when I lost sight of the fleet. What happened? Sit beside me and tell me all about it," I said as I patted the *hala* mat.

"Oh mother, the second day was horrid," he said as he lowered himself and stretched out his legs.

At the moment he crossed his legs, and I interrupted him to say, "The way you're sitting reminds me so much of your father."

"Are you even listening to me?" His temper flared.

Again, I thought, like his father, but I brushed those memories aside and said, "Yes. Yes. Of course I'm listening… go on."

"Keeaumoku and his party came down from the hills and were waiting for us at Kapailua. They paddled out and asked if they could board my father's canoe, saying they wanted to pay their respects."

I stiffened. "You know how I feel about Keeaumoku," I said. "Although his actions do not surprise me."

"Nor I, when I stop to think about it, but when we came around the point, his presence startled me. We could see his men on the shore. We had little time to think or improvise any sort of plan. He must have had a lookout on the point, because his canoe was in the water before we saw him and he was paddling out to meet us. We could not refuse his request, so we joined our canoes together side by side—Keawemauhili's, father's canoe, and mine. I think my Hilo uncle would have fought right there—on the water--but out of respect for my father, he did not. After Keeaumoku viewed the body, he asked where we were taking it…"

"What kind of a question is that?" I interrupted. "Everyone knows your job was to carry out your father's wishes to lie with his ancestors here at *Hale o Keawe* at Honaunau."

"Yes, I know that was the plan, Mother. But when Keawemauhili heard Keeaumoku's question, he seemed irritated and spoke up before I could answer. He snapped at Keeaumoku, 'We are taking him to Kailua. There we will disembark and bring him overland to Honaunau.'"

"*Auwe!*" I cried. "It was as I suspected. Do you understand the implications of Keawemauhili's remarks? Any land the dead chief touches immediately becomes his. That's one of the main reasons you needed to travel by sea. Your uncle is stirring up trouble. He knew that his remark would further unsettle all the Kona chiefs."

"Yes. I'm sure that was precisely his intention. Of course, Keeaumoku left us right after that, and his messengers were spotted heading toward Kohala. I'm sure they were sent to intercept Kamehameha's army."

"Yes, Kamehameha--and the other Kona chiefs. *Auwe!* Stirring up trouble where there doesn't need to be any." At that moment I could see the rumors fluttering like flocks of birds scattering across the leeward side of the island. "Tell me about the storm."

"After Keeaumoku left us, my uncle untied my canoe from the floatilla. My father's canoe was still lashed to his canoe, so that he resumed his place as the lead canoe. He kept angling farther and farther out to sea, riding the outgoing tide instead of sailing close to shore. In no time we were almost out of the sight of land. I knew my canoe was seaworthy, but I worried about all the people in the smaller vessels that were trailing us. It took me some time to catch up with my uncle, but finally I was able to pull alongside his canoe. I asked him why he was traveling in that direction and was so far offshore. He laughed and said that after Keeaumoku's visit, he thought it expedient to remain at sea and give the overland party time to arrive at Honaunau. I couldn't see how he would know when your party arrived because we could barely see the tip of the island. I think he was just trying to scare Keeaumoku…"

"And provoke him by heading farther up the coast…"

"I didn't know what to do, mother. My uncle was obviously not going to change his mind. Suddenly the clouds gathered, the skies darkened, and the wind came up. Something told me to reach over and lash my father's canoe to mine. We were all together then, and I had no choice but to follow." He shook his head. "At first my men thought maybe it was a passing squall—one that would soon blow over."

"I don't think I've ever seen a storm gather so fast. The angry clouds—the wind and rain…"

"It was terrifying." He stood, imitating the storm as he paced. "For a time the seas dashed over the platform. I jumped to my father's canoe and wrapped my arms around the mast and held on to his body. The waves tossed the canoe from side to side, from front to back, but the vessel rode the waves." He stopped suddenly and quieted, a tear coming to his eye. "And then the strangest thing happened, mother. I heard my father's voice. At first I thought it was coming from the clouds, and I looked up. Then I thought maybe he had regained his life and I leaned over him in order to hear his words…but I knew that was not possible. Then I realized it was as if he were speaking directly into my ear. "Honaunau," the voice said. "Honaunau."

"Good, my son."

"Then it was like I knew what I had to do. I figured if I could at least keep my father's canoe close to mine, maybe I could get them both turned around. It was hard to see anything in the rain and waves. But once I had that thought, then I was no longer afraid. It was like I was being guided…"

"You were," I assured him, for then I understood.

"At that moment, the lashing that held my father's canoe to Keawemauhili's canoe broke apart."

"And as you headed back to Honaunau, the storm abated," I said, not waiting for the details, but rather finishing his story for him.

"Yes. I did not think of the safety of my uncle at all—just for the safety of the body of my father."

"When did Keawemauhili arrive?"

"Many hours later. He said his canoe got caught in a current and the storm pushed them farther out to sea. The skies settled down upon them, enveloping them in darkness. They had to wait until dawn when the storm finally blew itself out to know which direction they should sail. His men were finally able to get the canoe turned around and paddle back to Honaunau."

"There were many smaller canoes with you. Did you lose anyone?"

"No, mother. The men in the smaller crafts were smart. When the saw the dark clouds gathering, they did not follow us. They stayed close to shore. We did not lose one canoe; not one life."

"That was your father turning you around. The storm was his temper. He never had any trouble making his wishes known," I said smiling. "He was a forceful man—even now his spirit still gets its way. It will be best to put him in the house of his ancestors so that he can be at peace."

Kiwalao sat down again in the same way as before, with his legs stretched out, in the way that reminded me of Kalaniopuu. We sat in silence for a time and finally Kiwalao said, "I feel my father's spirit close to me."

"Yes. I feel him too," I said and patted my son's hand.

"Now that his body is here and now that we are all gathered, the priests want to conduct the ceremony as soon as possible. They said to tell you that they want to put my father's bones away before any trouble starts."

"I agree. Can they be ready by tomorrow?"

"That's what they wanted me to ask you. They have prepared the *imu*."

"Then they may light the fire whenever they are ready."

Kiwalao gave the order and the fires were lit. The priests declared a *kapu*. Kalani's dried out body was roasted just long enough to prepare the bones. With all the respect due him, the *kahuna* placed his *iwi* in the *kaai,* the sennit basket, and then they attached the mother of pearl eyes so that he could see the world from the other side. The *makaainana*, those brave souls who had followed Kalani's *iwi* to their resting place, wept and wailed as he was carried into *Hale o Keawe*. My husband's bones were finally safe with his blood relations. After the ceremonies were complete and we stepped out of the compound, a full double rainbow appeared in the west, signaling that Kalani had crossed over to be with his ancestors and was at peace at last. I wished I could say the same for the land he had ruled over and for those left behind.

# Thirty-Nine

## 1782

It was not many hours after we had returned from *Hale o Keawe* that a scout dashed into camp. Kiwalao called me to his side before he listened to the messenger.

"I came as quickly as I could," the man said. "I had to be careful. I swam with the sharks across Kealakakua Bay."

I glanced at Kiwalao to see if he understood the meaning behind the man's words. It was true that the man's hair was wet—maybe he had dodged the many tiger sharks in the bay. Or did he mean the sharks—the chiefs—who had come overland? Either way, I braced myself for the news.

"Kamehameha has arrived at Kaawaloa."

Kiwalao gasped in alarm, but I was not at all shocked and merely nodded for the man to continue.

"And he is followed by many men who carry spears, daggers, sling stones—they are fully armed."

Kiwalao thanked the guard and dismissed him, then turned to me.

"You seem surprised," I said. "Did you not expect Kamehameha to come?"

"I hoped not..." he said meekly. "But I knew..."

"Of course he would come," I interrupted. "He would be foolish not to honor his uncle." I stood and went to the doorway, looking out at the sea.

Then Kiwalao asked, "What do you think my father would do?"

"Your father would not wait for any more news," I said. "He would summon his warriors."

"That's what I thought." He fell silent and bowed his head for a moment. "But my father is no longer with us. What shall *we* do?"

It was not appropriate for me to tell my son what to do. He was a man now—and the heir apparent. The best I could do was present the truth. "Keawemauhili will want to fight right away," I said. I hoped that the recent storm had shaken Kiwalao up enough so that he would learn to trust his own advisors and not his uncle.

"Yes," he said. "I imagine he will…"

I felt relief that my son was finally starting to understand the ways of his uncle, if not all the Hawaii chiefs. At least he had placed the right name with the correct assessment. Maybe the death of his father had been harder on him that I imagined; maybe he had just needed time to come to his senses; maybe he would have the makings of a leader after all; maybe…

He stretched out full length on the mat and rolled to his back. "But I do not want to fight." He lay there for a moment, and then sat up quickly. "I shall visit my cousin Kamehameha tomorrow," Kiwalao declared.

"What?! You will do no such thing," I shrieked. "Are you mad?" Then I gained control of the protective mother instinct in me, and in a quieter voice reasoned with him. "It's just that I worry for your safety. What if he attacks you?"

"He swore in front of the priests to defend me. He will not make an attempt on my life," he answered with assurance.

"We have not heard from him in two years," I argued. "What makes you so certain that he intends to keep his promise?"

My son's jaw was set in determination. I had seen the same look on his father's face many times. There would be no dissuading him. "Send a messenger," I begged. "Ask Kamehameha if he wishes to view his uncle—he was, after all, the man that raised him." I saw Kiwalao's jaw relax a little and realized he was listening to me. "If that's what he wants—simply to pay respects—then the priests can no doubt be persuaded to unseal the door." Now that my son was paying attention, I wanted at all costs to keep the peace. "We can offer the priests payment of some sort—they always bend the rules when there are gifts to be had." The more I talked along this course of reasoning, the more I liked it myself. "Surely they can make up a prayer that will allow a late-comer to view the remains. After all, it is a long trek from Kohala…"

Kiwalao cut me off. "I do not want to wait until tomorrow. Thank you for you time and your wise counsel, mother. I know what I must do."

After he left, I went to the doorway and watched him stride down the hill. If I hadn't known he had just left, I could have sworn a younger version of his father had materialized from thin air—his step lengthened and his head thrown back in the way Kalani often strutted when he had made an important decision. I was beginning to realize that when Kiwalao wrapped his arms around his father's body during the storm, he must have become infused with Kalani's *mana*. Only time would tell…

First Kiwalao went to the priests and requested that they devise an appropriate ritual in order to reopen his father's tomb for the visiting chief, Kamehameha. When he had their assurances they would comply with his orders--and no doubt welcome the gifts he promised--he picked his most trusted warriors and set out in a fast canoe across the bay to Kaawaloa where Kamehameha was encamped.

The whole time he was gone I prayed at my altar for his safety. Maybe his surprise visit would keep him alive. Maybe Kamehameha would not be so ready to fight if he saw that my son did not come with an army, but rather came to extend the hand of peace. After all, Kamehameha had accepted the war god and made the promise to defend my son. Maybe my prayers floated across the bay and helped lay a soft *kapa* blanket of peace over their meeting. At any rate, within a few hours, Kiwalao returned. I so wanted to run down to the beach to greet him, but I remembered the dignity of his new office—that he must be treated like a chief and not my son—so I sent for him.

"We talked," he reported. "I told Kamehameha that maybe we both would die because our uncle was urging war, and I invited him to pay respects to my father."

"Well, that was an honest assessment," I said. "What did he say?"

"That he would accept my invitation and would pay his respects tomorrow."

little after daybreak the guards sent word that Kamehameha and a few of his men had crossed behind his father's burial cave and were heading toward Honaunau. When Kamehameha and his retinue reached the compound, Kiwalao's younger half-brother, Keoua Kuahuula, joined Kiwalao in welcoming Kamehameha. The young men braced their arms on each other's shoulders and touched foreheads to breathe in each other's sacred breath. Then they sat down and wailed for their dead father/uncle. Kiwalao treated Kamehameha with the utmost respect—something I feared I would not have been capable of. I kept my distance, hiding behind the excuse that I was a widow still deep in mourning, even though it had been six months since my husband's passing.

The priests, bought off with the promise of future offerings, opened up the burial *hale* again and conducted another ceremony--one without quite as much pomp as the day before, but still they made sure the rites were enough to impress Kamehameha so that he would not feel he was being overlooked as a late-comer. At the end of the ceremony, Kiwalao again commanded that his father's orders be followed, declaring in front of all the chiefs that he was ruler over this island and that Kamehameha, as holder of the war god, had promised to protect Kiwalao.

Kamehameha behaved himself, showing grief and wailing over his uncle with the proper amount of regard. As to his sincerity, one could only guess. However, it was not Kamehameha that betrayed my son that day, but rather it was the Kona chiefs who felt that by Kamehameha's show of respect, they were somehow losing ground. In fact, they had lost nothing, but neither had they gained. On the other hand, there was the greedy Keawemauhili who had not been able to wrangle all he wished either. They all had exactly what they had started out with the day before, and indeed the year before, but of course that didn't seem to be to anyone's satisfaction.

When the second ceremony was finished and Kalani's bones were permanently sealed away, Kamehameha made immediate preparations to return to his lands in Kohala. However, the seasoned warrior Kekuhaupio held him back, insisting that it would be proper to extend an invitation to Kiwalao for an *awa* ceremony that very evening before they returned to Kawaihae. Kamehameha hesitated, but when Kekuhaupio added that it would be easier for them to travel in the light of day, Kamehameha relented and agreed to his role as host of the chiefs. Kiwalao, hoping to establish peace in his court, and to secure Kamehameha's promised support, accepted the invitation and sailed to Kaawaloa as the sun set.

I only heard about the commotion when Kiwalao returned sometime before the cock's crow. When his canoe landed he saw my *kukui* nut candles burning and guessed I was worried, although I pretended to be just arising from the mat and did not tell him of my sleepless night spent in constant prayer for peace among the chiefs.

"From the beginning," Kiwalao reported, "Kekuhaupio appeared anxious. It was he, not Kamehameha, who seemed to be ordering the evening activities. In fact, it was Kekuhaupio who insisted that Kamehameha be the one to chew the *awa*."

"Why would he do that?"

"I tried to ask Kamehameha myself, directing my question specifically to him, but before my cousin could empty his mouthful of *awa* to answer, Kekuhaupio spoke up and said that it was Kamehameha's duty to serve me."

"Well, that's right. It *is* his duty."

"That's what I thought too. I figured it was as good a time as any for us to be setting that precedent in front of all the chiefs."

"Quite right," I said. "So? What was the problem?"

"Kamehameha spit out the *awa* and filled the first bowl which he handed to me. I could see that he wasn't finished filling the bowls yet, and I didn't want to sit around holding the only one, so I passed it on to my *aikane*, Kuikuipua. I figured he would pass it along to the next man in turn until everyone had a bowl and we would all drink together in good faith. I meant no offense."

"Offense? What was wrong with that? Who took offense?"

"Kekuhaupio. I had no idea Kamehameha had chewed it especially for me. All the chiefs were there—in my mind, all the bowls would be the same, signifying unity. Kamehameha finished his prayer and was filling another bowl, taking no notice, when Kekuhaupio jumped up and knocked the bowl out of Kuikuipua's hand. It went flying. *Awa* splashed all over those sitting closest to me. Kekuhaupio shouted, 'This man has insulted us! The *awa* was chewed not for the chief's *aikane*—not for a commoner--but for the chief himself and no other!' He kicked the bottom of Kamehameha's outstretched foot and insisted, 'We will go to Keei!'"

"*Auwe! Auwe!* Oh my son...."

"Then Kekuhapio said, 'I will not be a party to this insult!' Before anyone could stop either of them, he pulled Kamehameha to his feet and pushed him out the door."

"Gone before anyone could detain them?"

"Gone before anyone really understood what happened."

"Did no one follow them?"

"I think Kekuhaupio thought there would be a fight right then because he shoved Kamehameha out the door before him. That grizzled old warrior was ready to cover Kamehameha's back. No one wanted to fight Kekuhaupio and risk losing their life, especially over a bowl of *awa*." Kiwalao went to my door. The half moon was setting and sparkled on the calm sea. "We all stayed and finished the *awa*. It was the black *awa* from the upland, already chewed, and ready to drink. Why waste good *awa*? I figured if they wanted to make a fuss, let them. What had been done was done. At that point, there was nothing anyone could do to stop them."

"Did the chiefs speak of Kamehameha?"

"No one said a word until after those two left. Then of course, that was all they talked about." Then Kiwalao turned to me and asked in all innocence, "But mother, what was the offense?"

"You were wrong to have passed the bowl."

"But, I...."

"Your intentions might have been good, but you should have kept it for yourself. You are now the chief, and pass the *awa* bowl to no one, especially not at a gathering of the chiefs."

Kiwalao hung his head.

"But there was wrong on the other side as well. Kekuhaupio might have taken offense, but he was wrong to speak out."

"I'll admit that I was wrong. But, mother, which is the bigger offense—to offer a bowl of *awa* to my *aikane*, or to hurl insults at me, the supreme ruler?"

"Yes, I see your point."

"What kind of host invites me to his house and then leaves? If anyone should be insulted, it is I."

"Did Kamehameha rise up himself?" I asked.

"No—only at the insistence of Kekuhaupio."

"No doubt Kekuhaupio planned all along to cause trouble. You passing the bowl gave him the excuse he was looking for. Yours was a mistake of protocol. You are yet a young ruler. There was offense on both sides."

"But, mother, I don't see…"

"You must understand that Kekauhaupio is one of the Kona chiefs who is afraid he will lose his land."

"But he has lost nothing. As far as I'm concerned, everything should stay the same as it was."

"Ah, yes…but neither did he gain. If those are your thoughts—to leave the land holdings as they were--that's your decision." I glanced at him to see if he understood. Why would I expect him to? He was the Kalani's son. He'd been handed his lands and, up to this point, had not had to fight. "Did you see any sign of movement when you came home past Keei?"

"No," Kiwalao said as he yawned. "He will not attack this day."

I did not trust Kiwalao to have seen clearly—his mind was dulled with *awa* and lack of sleep. Nor did I trust his assessment of Kekuhaupio, that cagy old warrior, or his young protégé, Kamehameha, who held the war god.

"Besides, mother, we cannot be attacked here. It is a place of refuge," he said as he stood up, stretched, and then left for his own sleeping quarters.

Kekuhaupio was no doubt awake, the same as I. It was the hour before dawn—the time when the soul takes its last flight into the land of dreams. But after that night, only the foolish would have been caught dozing.

———

*L*ater that morning, when my retainer brought me food at the usual time, I could hardly wait until she set it down. I was famished.

"My chiefess, the same as you, there was another person stirring last night," she whispered as she set the calabash in front of me. "That Hilo chief, Keawemauhili."

Instantly I was on guard. "Have you told Kiwalao?"

"He has yet to open his eyes."

I dared not speak the words that crossed my mind. Was Kiwalao alive? Had last night's *awa* been poisoned? Is that why Kekuhaupio knocked it from the *ai-kane's* hands? Were all my son's men...? Panic seized me and I choked back the tears. "He's not....?"

Although she dared not look at me, as a mother herself she sensed my distress and quickly assured me, "The chief, young Kiwalao, is sleeping soundly, my chiefess."

"Then leave me be. I must think." Things were not settled on this island, or in my mind. I paced as my thoughts raced. I was fighting with myself long before the chiefs had raised a spear at each other. My son is too trusting of his uncle, I thought, and it is entirely my fault. I never should have sent him to Hilo when his father died. At the time, I never would have dreamed that Keawemauhili would have stirred up so much trouble. But, I should have known...it was just plain stupidity on my part. Except, where else could I have sent Kiwalao? I knew he would be safe in Hilo at his uncle's court; Keawemauhili had plenty of men to guard the new ruler. Yet of course he would have seen Kiwalao's gullability... of course any of them would have tried to sway such an impressionable young man, and take advantage of him in his hour of grief. And of course they would have tried—any of them—to enlarge their landholdings. I had raised Kiwalao to put stock in blood relations because the Maui court depended on pure blood, whereas the Hawaii chiefs put more stock on the blood that spills on the battlefield than on the kinsmen's blood that binds. These chiefs did not know my son—he had not been raised with them. As a young man he had run away to my brother's court and had the thunder markings of the king of Maui. But why didn't he know he would have to fight to save his kingship? He had heard the stories of my own brother Kamehamehanui, who had to fight his half-brother for the right to rule. But to my son, it was just a story told around the court fire at night. Those people had long passed into the darkness of Milo and were but a dream to the young boy. My family had ruled for so many years on Maui that the thought of any chief rising up against my brother Kahekili, Kiwalao's mentor, was unthinkable. I would have thought my son understood the difference: the chiefs of Hawaii were not like my family on Maui. Maybe it was that Kiwalao had the over-confidence of youth—yes, that was it! Did he not know that the chiefs would fight over land? Why could he not see that a war was brewing? Why was he being so stubborn? I sent word that I wished to speak with him.

But Keawemauhili got to him first, forcing his hand. He insisted that Kiwalao declare, once and for all, the division of land. Kiwalao, sick to death of the squabbling, said, "Divide it, then," and waved him off as if the decision to be made was of no consequence. And then he added, almost as an after-thought, "But when you do, do not forget my cousin, Kamehameha." Kiwalao had played right into his uncle's hands. Of course Keawemauhili had no inten-tion of sharing anything with anyone and took the choicest Kona lands for him-self. Then declaring he was sole spokesman for the chief, he handed out what little remained to those who quickly changed sides and feigned allegiance to him. When Kiwalao heard the complaints and protests that the division had not been fair, he went to his uncle.

Keawemauhili reprimanded him, saying, "If you would not have me take what is rightfully mine, then you should have divided the land yourself."

There was, afterall, truth to that statement.

One of Kalaniopuu's younger twin sons, Keoua, openly confronted Kiwalao, hoping that by asking him about specific lands, he could get Kiwalao to see the error of his ways. Seemingly Kiwalao did not understand that, at the very least, he should have been the one to announce his decision to leave the land divisions the same. When he delegated the task to his greedy uncle, of course the chiefs were disgruntled. But the fact that Keawemauhili plucked the land away from everyone caused great upheaveal. Keoua tried and tried to show Kiwalao that he was not pleased, but finally had to abandon his queries and pointedly asked, "Are we—both you and I--to have nothing more in this new division of lands?"

Kiwalao's answer--that his half-brother was to receive nothing new, but rather retain only his father's old lands--did not sit well.

Keoua gathered his few men—for he had come to pay respects to his father and had not brought enough men to fight. He left Honaunau in a huff, heading for his home in Kau while the afternoon sun still glared upon the sea.

# Forty

*I*t was peaceful for only a couple of days, then Keoua returned from Kau with his warriors. Instead of stopping at Honaunau to pay his respects to Kiwalao, his half-brother and new ruler of the island, he headed straight for Keomo, ostensively for high diving. But everyone knows that a diver does not wear feather capes and helmets to the water, nor does a man dive with sling stones tucked in his *malo* or gripping a long *koa* spear. And as for Keoua's sacred *lei niho palaoa* necklace getting wet... unthinkable. The excuse about diving off the cliffs was just a ruse to get to a village near the shore. Keoua had sent very clever scouts who had learned that most of the men of the village were at Keei surfing and their women and children had gone along as spectators. The only people left in the village were men too old to raise a hand to defend the young women too pregnant to travel or the young mothers who stayed behind to nurse their babies. Finding no resistance, Keoua's men cut down a large number of coconut trees. One of the young mothers left her baby with her sister and snuck away to warn the village. When the three caretakers of the grove heard that their trees were being descimated, they hurried back to defend the trees and the village that depended on them. The three men were no match for Keoua's warriors and were killed straight away and taken to the *heiau* to be offered as sacrifice. Another five men who had come to offer help were taken hostage.

Even after he took the life of those three men, not enough blood had dripped off Keoua's spear. He still wasn't satisfied, and ordered his men to find the villagers who were hurrying to defend their home, but were still a couple miles up the beach at Keei.

Some said that it was a good thing the villagers were not present when the trees were cut down, for in his anger, Keoua would have slaughtered everyone. They said that it was better to lose some coconut trees and a few men than a whole village. Others said it was simply a show of might on Keoua's part: that trees were safer to attack than warriors. Still others said Keoua was displaying his anger at Kiwalao for not awarding him more land. It was his way of seeking revenge. Others claimed pretension on Keoua's part--that only a *naupio* chief had the right to cut down the livelihood of the village. As usual when people try to assess blame, all were right to some extent. The problem was that the trees were on land claimed by Kamehameha, not Kiwalao. So if Keoua's objective was to seek revenge against Kiwalao, he'd missed his mark. Some said that Keoua had to have known whose land he was on; others said he was just on a rampage and it wouldn't have mattered where his feet landed. All agreed that with so many chiefs in one place, war was inevitable, and that, once again, the blameless *makaainana* had unfortunately gotten caught up in *alii* events.

———◆———

"What am I to do, mother? When Keoua cut down the trees, he killed three men and brought in five captives. He insists I offer all the men up as sacrifice on the altar."

"Your younger half-brother is spoiling for war. He smells blood and cares not which camp he fights. If you fail to offer up the bodies, then prepare to go to war with him and potentially lose the homeland that you share with him in Kau. If you offer up the bodies, then he will accept that as a sign you do not wish to fight him and he will point his anger elsewhere."

"Where?"

"Undoubtedly Kamehameha. Keoua killed those men on land Kamehameha inherited years ago from his mother. Since Kamehameha is nearby, he will have to defend his honor as chief over that land. Certainly the Kona chiefs will join him. They will feel a threat to his land is a threat to theirs and they will most assuredly defend their land."

He stopped brooding to consider. "If that's the case, then one of them—Keoua or Kamehameha—will have to die." He brought a water gourd to his lips.

I could see that he was finally beginning to think like a ruler. "Maybe a battle between the two of them would not be such a bad thing. It would be to your great advantage if one of them were dead. Maybe that's what Keoua's offering—to do the killing for you. He is your younger half-brother, closer to you by blood than the Kohala chief, who is merely your cousin."

He sipped and wiped his mouth. "If I accept Keoua's offer, could I sacrifice the three that are already dead and let the other five live? It's a shame to kill five good men."

"That would only anger Keoua more. If you accept the sacrifice, you'll have to accept all he brought, dead or alive. He's testing you."

We sat in silence for a bit, but finally I could stand his indecision no longer. "Surely you are not seriously thinking of engaging in war with your half-brother?"

"It's the captives..."

"Which is better? To have five more men killed or an entire army of your own?"

"When you put it like that..."

"Offer all of them up as death companions for your father at Honaunau. Keoua will be satisfied, and the men--both living and dead--will have been put to good use."

Of course Kiwalao's offering of all the men at the *heiau* split the faction wide open. Keoua was, for the time being, satisfied to fight Kamehameha. Keawemauhili offered the support of his warriors from Hilo, hoping that by joining Keoua and defeating the Kona chiefs he could gain the land he coveted. During the night, some of Kamehameha's warriors deserted, changed sides, thereby swelling Kiwalao's ranks. Who knows what caused them to change sides? Maybe they decided to support their ruler after the sacrifices had been made at Honaunau; maybe they talked it over and came to the conclusion that Keoua and

Kiwalao offered a more united front; maybe they thought they would stand a better chance of surviving under Kalaniopuu's sons.

Whatever the reasons, the first skirmishes started the next morning. Having the majority of warriors on his side inflated Kiwalao's confidence and he began to strut like a cock at daybreak. I so wanted to remind my son that we'd seen his father strut just like that before the Battle of the Sand Hills when I'd had to send Kiwalao out to beg my brother Kahekili for our very lives. But by now I could clearly see that Kiwalao had been taken over by his father's spirit. What had been a scared young man turned into a warrior spirit. I had seen the same spirit in Kalani. Like his father, he was swept along in the glory of battle. "Go back to your altar, mother," he said as he waved my warnings aside. "I will have none of it."

My heart sank. As I walked back to my compound, I tried to think of some way to save him. And then it came to me--if I couldn't talk some sense into him, maybe his wife and child could intervene. I sent a messenger in a canoe to fetch Liliha from Maui—to hurry to her brother/husband's side.

# *Forty-One*

## July 1782

*I* had hoped to talk to Kiwalao before he left that morning, but he was up and gone from his *hale* before I finished my morning prayers—not that I really knew when one prayer ended and the other started, for I had been at my altar most of the night and was still there at dawn.

I was afraid for my son and the fate that seemed to be rushing to meet him. Recently I had seen Kiwalao squint his eyes and wrinkle his brow the same as his father. I knew that look. The night before I had reminded my son about the times his father had failed to heed the warnings of the priests; of how he had lost battles and large numbers of his warriors, and how Kalaniopuu would not listen to anyone he perceived stood in his way. I wished that Kiwalao had inherited more of Kalani's craftiness and less of his obstinance. It was Kalani's cunning, and ultimately, his understanding of men that made him a strong leader. But unfortunately Kiwalao seemed to have taken on all Kalani's weaknesses: his stubbornness, his arrogance, and his boastfulness. In truth, my son was becoming a braggart. The battles Kiwalao had fought up to that point had been nothing more than posturing on both sides. I wanted to tell him he had no right to his new-found swagger until he had achieved a real victory. How sad that those were the thoughts I held about my son on the morning the real battle began.

When the sun was high overhead, Kiwalao sent a messenger, telling me of his victory in the morning.

"They have been fighting for how many days now?" I asked the messenger.

He counted on his fingers. "Seven days, my chiefess. This day makes the eighth."

"I wish to go to the battlefield this afternoon. I wish to see my son."

"It is a few miles up the coast from here, and there are no canoes," the messenger said as he glanced over his shoulder toward the battlefield. "Kekuahupio has directed the fighting to the rough *a-a* lava flow not far from the *heiau* at Hauiki in Keei. Do you know it?"

"Yes. I know the area—and so does that seasoned warrior. He knows it like the back of his hand." I felt a heaviness settle over me. I rose to pace the floor, but it was as if an anchor was tied to my legs and pulled me back down. "That crafty man knows every stone, every gully, every crevice of that place. That is his land and he has walked it many times. He knows the best place to stand to throw a *pololu* spear and the best place to pick up a spare stone for the sling."

"Even though smaller, Kamehameha's army is well equipped," the messenger added.

"As I would expect them to be," I interrupted.

"And today many have returned."

"Returned? I thought they deserted to Kiwalao's army," I said.

"Some joined Kiwalao because they were hungry," he answered. "Others who wished to stay with Kamehameha went to the mountains for pig. Still others raided the people's fishponds. When they all returned two days ago, Kamehameha's army feasted. Now they are rested and well-fed."

I did not like the information this man was telling me. Why was this the first time I had heard the truth? I certainly had not heard this from my son, who bragged every day how the battle had been going totally in his favor. I should have known better than to believe him. He sounded too much like Kalani. I was sure my fury at my son showed on my face even though I tried to remain calm.

"Yet…" he hesitated.

"Yes, go on," I insisted.

"That battlefield--in my opinion, seems to be a land that is better suited to a smaller army, such as the size of Kamehameha's. It is not a battlefield for the size of Kiwalao's army."

"Kekuhaupio is a smart man, a skilled warrior, and a seasoned battle leader. He picked his spot well. And Kiwalao? What of my son?"

"He is busy at this moment, my chiefess. He is at the *heiau* finishing up the sacrifices for those that were killed this morning. There were many…"

"And the priests? What have they said? Has no one read the auguries?"

"Oh, yes, they have been read regularly. The priests were consulted last night, again before the battle started, and just now." He glanced up at the sun. "When the sun was high overhead—just before the latest sacrifices."

"Well? What, specifically, did the priest Kalaikuiaha say?"

"All the priests have said the same thing: that the flood tide was ours in the morning, but that it would turn after mid-day. There was mention of major chiefs being slain. The priests all advised Kiwalao to postpone the fighting until tomorrow."

"So he will be here soon?" I looked up, hopeful that Kiwalao would leave the battle and come back to Honaunau.

"No, my chiefess. I'm afraid not. He could not be dissuaded and has gone back into battle. That is why I have come… to tell you. Kiwalao looks exhausted. I fear these days of battle have been very wearing on him."

"*Auwe*! Has he not learned anything?" My head dropped to my chest and I prayed for his safety. "So like his father," I muttered under my breath. Then I turned my attention back to the messenger. "And what of Kamehameha?"

"All the chiefs have been accounted for. We have seen all the feather capes, except Kamehameha. We are fighting the Kona chiefs, led by Keeaumoku, who is currently leading Kamehameha's troops. When I left to come here, Kamehameha still had not been seen. The good news is that some of the Kohala warriors who were fighting on Kamehameha's side fled after the morning fighting."

"Much to their dishonor," I added. "And Keoua? Surely he will be of help to his brother."

"Keoua has had the canoes in position just off-shore all morning, just in case the priests were right and a retreat is needed."

I knew what all this posturing meant: even though his half-brother will fight on Kiwalao's side, and take the spoils of battle if Kiwalao wins, the one who had cut down the coconut trees and started this fight in the first place had taken a safe position off-shore and left Kiwalao alone to rally for his lands.

The rest of the afternoon I prayed. I say I prayed, but my prayers were fretful and, I fear, incomplete. Since there were no available canoes to take me to the battlefield, there was little I could do. I thought of striking out on my own across the fiery *a-a* plains. I felt I needed to warn my son—to plead with him to come back to the place of refuge, to wait and fight another day. But, instead, I stayed to pray. My son, following in his father's footsteps, had lashed himself to his father's bones in more ways than one. I had seen it on his face several times recently—the way he defied me, and the way he defied the priests, who were, after all, merely the mouthpiece of the gods. Like me, the elders could warn him sternly, but had no accountability over his actions. Like his father, Kiwalao thought he knew and was all-powerful, but in fact he was blatantly shaking his fist in the face of the gods.

I could only hope that the priests had been wrong. Maybe they had made a mistake… they were, after all, men, not gods. They had only said that a chief would be killed. They had not specifically said Kiwalao. I found myself praying, as any mother would, that some other chief would be lost—not my son. I hate to admit it, but I first prayed that Keeaumoku would be the one to lose his life. Certainly he had shown himself to be an untrustworthy man—changing sides whichever way the wind blew. Would the world lose much if he were slain? Or Kekuhaupio? His hair was turning gray—he had lived his life. Why not take him—one who has already lived and fought? Or why shouldn't the gods take Kalani's half-brother, that rabble-rouser, Keawemauhili? What would it hurt if he were no longer stirring up trouble for his nephew? Hadn't he caused enough trouble? Or what about Keoua? He was the one who cut down the coconut trees. If the gods chose anyone but Kiwalao, things would be much quieter all the way around. "Take one of the skilled warriors," I begged the gods. "Take several, in fact—in skill they would more than make up for my son, but please not my son--not the shining light of both Maui and Hawaii." I knew it was futile to bargain with the gods, and yet I found myself doing just that: presenting my case as if I could reason with them and convince them that my ideas were worthy of consideration—a case to be at least mulled over for a day or so--if not actual acceptance. "If he is allowed to live and reign, my family could be the catalyst to unite the islands. His cousin is already the ruler of Kauai," I reminded the gods. "My brother could overtake the rule of Oahu easily…and the islands will be united under one family." Surely the gods could see there was potential for peace and reconciliation; that there would be no more cause for war. The *makaainana* could go back to providing for their families and not have to pick up their spears to fight the chief's bloody wars. Their lands would flourish, their families would be well fed, and prosperity would come to all, *alii* and commoners alike. Maybe my fondest wish could come true: I dared to dream of laying Kalani's war god, Kukailimoku, to rest with the bones of the chiefs in *Hale o Keawe*. Could the gods not see the benefit of my plan? Surely they would consider such an idea. Would the sacrifices the priests offered from a healthy populace not be to the god's benefit as well? I pleaded for them to chew on my ideas, as the chiefs chewed on the *awa* root. I begged them to turn it this way and that and see that a small sacrifice and a certain victory was all that was wanting.

When the guards announced that canoes were spotted heading toward our bay, I stepped to my door and recognized Keoua's red and yellow cape. My bones told me that I while I had been praying for one thing, the gods had been busy delivering another.

While the line of canoes waited beyond the breakers, Keoua's canoe came to shore. I hurried down the hill to the beach. He jumped out of his canoe, splashing through the shallow water toward me. He bowed, and then delivered his news. "I cannot tarry, my chiefess. I must head for the safety of my court in Kau."

"My son?"

"Dead."

"*Auwe!*" I wailed and clutched my heart. A searing pain shot through me and I fell to my knees in the sand. I opened my eyes and looked down at my hands, sure that I would see blood oozing between my fingers, for it seemed as if I had been stabbed by death's dagger myself. "And his body? His *lei niho palaoa*—his sacred necklace?"

"He has been taken to a *hale* at Keei." Keoua said as he bent over and reached for my elbows to pull me to my feet.

"Kekuhaupio's?"

"Yes, my chiefess. He and Keeaumoku were both taken there."

"Keeaumoku is dead?"

"No, he lives. It was he who dealt Kiwalao the fatal blow. Kiwalao wanted to save Keeamoku's *niho lei palaoa*."

"The sacred necklace, Nalukoki…" I shook my head.

"Yes. Keeamoku was down, and so wounded we thought he could do no harm. Surely he was about to die. Kiwalao moved toward Keeaumoku, intent on saving the necklace. From a distance a woman saw Kiwalao's cape and launched the stone from her sling. It caught Kiwalao on the side of the head. Our chief fell to his knees, unable to move. With his last ounce of strength, Keeaumoku crawled a short way to Kiwalao, raised his shark-tooth weapon, and slit Kiwalao's throat."

"*Auwe*! Oh my son…. My son…. "

"I am sorry. I thought you should know. They are surely after me. I must flee."

By that time, all those at camp had heard my cries and hurried to my side. Keoua handed me over to my retainers. As he turned to leave, I thought to ask, "And what of his body? His *niho lei palaoa*?"

As he splashed through the foam toward his canoe, he turned and shouted, "We both know that Kamehameha will be the one to perform the sacrifice."

It was then that I became aware the winds had stopped blowing. I blinked. The color had gone from my world: the sun was a throbbing white mass, the sky dark gray, the clouds lighter gray. The fronds of the coconut trees drooped. For me, at that moment, the whole world stopped.

I knew that if it ever began to spin again, it would never be the same.

Suddenly I realized the danger Keoua had put himself in by taking the time to stop and tell me the news. Although he was at the sacred refuge, these were times of war and he was a chief. He would not be safe until he was far away. And, speaking with him any longer would not change a thing—it would not bring my son back. I waved to him and said, "May the winds carry you safely home."

In the past few months I had worn the feather cape of grief easily. I could slip it on and off as needed. But now it was as if the cape had draped itself around my shoulders and encircled me. I could not lift my feet. The imaginary cape dragged behind me as I shuffled across the sand. What was real and what was in another realm? I could not tell. My feelings were too big for me. They owned me, instead of me owning them. For once, I had absolutely no control. I stumbled and I realized I couldn't see. There was nothing to light my way. I was enveloped by a blindness darker than night. And in that darkness, a hand reached out to tug on mine. The hand did not release its grip and pulled me down. Down. Down I plunged--head first--into the pit of grief.

My retainers, sensing something wrong, hoisted me up by my elbows and rushed me up the hill to my *hale*. They stretched me out on the mat, each one trying their best to comfort me, fussing over me like mothers cooing to settle a baby. "Leave me alone!" I scolded. "All of you!" They scurried out the door like brown leaves dancing across the compound, blown about by a gust of wind.

I reached out in the half-light for my calabash. I rubbed my eyes and blinked repeatedly, hoping to restore my sight. I wanted so much to believe my son's face would be there when I peered over the edge of the gourd. His smile would shimmer in the water at the bottom of the calabash and he would be waiting for me to recite the sacred prayers and restore him to his body. Soon he would be coming home, I told myself. I bent over the water and saw—nothing. I swirled the water and waited what seemed like eons for the water to still—and, still, there was nothing. "It cannot be," I screamed. "It just cannot be." I heard a woman's voice wailing; from far off I heard her moan. "*Auwe!* Alas!" The sound was louder. "*Auwe!*" It was as if the woman was right beside me. Her cries became louder. It was as if the woman was inside me. Her cries became my cries. "*Auwe!*" I shrieked. Then I threw the calabash across the room. The water splashed down the *pili* grass wall and pooled on the mats.

I shook my head to try to clear it. I had to think. There must be something more I could do. If his face was not in the water, that meant he had already started his descent into the land of Po. Milu would be reaching out his hand and tugging on him. Maybe it had been the god of the underworld's hand that had been tugging on mine. Whoever it was, whatever was happening, I knew I had to hurry. Every moment was of the essence. If I waited too long, I would never catch up; I would never be able to find him. The thought of wandering alone in the underworld terrified me, but not having my son by my side was unthinkable. Terrified or not, any mother with my powers, my *mana*, would do the same. I reached down inside myself and pulled my courage out of my *naau*. I staggered to my altar. I knelt beside it and called on all the spirits I could think of to help me find the trail called Mahiki, the pathway that the souls travel to enter *Lua o Milu*, the Land of Milu, and help me find the god of the undeworld. I had to be careful on my descent—if the spirits of the dead saw me, a living being, they could turn me to stone just by staring at me. I had to make haste for I didn't know how long ago Kiwalao had entered, and I did not know how far down the path he would be. Was he wandering alone, or did he have an escort? If he wandered alone, he could be anywhere. If he had an escort, they would be quickly following a well-worn path. Either way, my own soul was heading into dangerous territory.

I decended, stepping boldly to make deep footprints so that I could find my way back as I looked for signs that I could remember in case my footprints were erased. I had to be careful, and yet I must hurry. On and on I tramped, farther than I had ever dared go in that realm before. It felt like even my *aumakua*, my guardian goddess Kihawahine, had left me. I stumbled over my feet, braced like anchors that drug behind me with every step. I wasn't sure I could go on, yet I dared not stop. Then I just happened to turn my head--maybe I heard a sound, maybe it was his spirit calling me for rescue—I know not what, but I saw him! He was standing in front of a *hale*. I called to him, "My son! Kiwalao! My son!" He turned. I could not see his face—his shadow played in the light of the doorway. But I am a mother—I would know my son anywhere. Milu stood inside the doorway, only his ghostly image visible. I rushed up to my beloved son, longing to envelop him in my arms the way I had done when he was a babe. I wanted to hold on to him tight and never let go. But Kiwalao held up his hand and would not allow me to touch him. Gray mist--full of spirits--swirled around us. Those that were inside Milu's *hale* beckoned for us to come through the doorway. Upon hearing their voices, I was tempted and again reached for Kiwalao's hand.

"Only I can go," he said. "You cannot enter, mother."

"But my heart is broken," I exclaimed. "I felt the dagger of death."

"You felt a dagger because your heart is broken, but your heart still beats in your chest, mother."

"But I want to go with you."

The voice of Milu warned of the truth I already knew. "Kiwalao is right. You are free to join him, if you wish, but if you step across this threshold, you can never escape."

"I may not be able to stay here with you," I said. "But you can come back with me. I know the way back to the land of the living. I can help you. I can heal you."

"No, mother. I cannot. My blood has soaked into the ground."

Milu, unwilling to spend any more time listening to a mother's desperate pleas, made his final offer. "If he chooses to go back with you, your sacred *aumakua* will die."

"Think clearly, mother. It's not worth it. We cannot forsake our people like that. It is much better for you return to the land of the living, and I go to the land of the dead." He turned to glance inside the *hale*. "In fact, I see my father now." He raised his hand in greeting to the spirit I could not see. "We will be together later," he said as he smiled at me for the last time. I reached out to grab him, but my hand held only air. Like a vapor, he had slipped through the doorway and was gone.

All alone at the door of death, I had little time to make up my mind. If I chose to follow him, I could be with him for all eternity. If I stayed I must return to the living—I could not tarry at the door. If I was to choose the living, I must find my way back without turning to stone.

Then I heard a woman's voice. "Mother! Mother! Come back."

"Liliha!" I called. "Where are you?" I turned, thinking she had followed my footsteps in order to help me retrieve her brother/ husband.

"Right beside you," she said.

I felt her gentle touch on my arm. Immediately I was transported back to the land of the living—to the floor of my *hale*, and to the loving arms of my daughter.

"Why is your sacred calabash on the floor?" she asked as she looked into my vacant eyes. Then grabbing me by the shoulders, she shook me. "Where are you, mother? Come back! Come back!"

Quietly, I said, "I went to him."

"Did you find him?"

"Yes. But he would not come. He said the *aumakua* would be taken from us if he returned with me. He said it was not worth it."

"To the end, he was a chief--true to his people, mother. He thought of their well-being before himself."

And then we held each other and wailed. Grief wrapped its dark arms around both of us. We had lost one most precious to us.

# Forty-Two

## 1782

Like a shooting star, Kiwalao had blazed across the sky and then was no more. On the horizon the constellation of Kamehameha was rising. With the death of Kiwalao the battle was over and Kamehameha, with his priests beside him, offered his cousin up on the altar at Hikiau. The defeated few that staggered back from the battlefield said that Kamehameha had ordered his warriors to claim all the bodies, no matter whose side they fought on. In his greediness, he gathered in all the *mana*. In more ways than one, the wind had shifted. The gusts of the departing souls carried the stench of burning flesh, which clogged the air from morning to night.

I had not been able to bring my son back from the land of Po and sank into the crater of sorrow so deep that I might as well have been one of the burning bodies. My spirit wandered restlessly, and I didn't care. I didn't even have the energy to wail—I sat in the middle of my *hale* and rocked back and forth, as if I was quieting a baby. My granddaughter, Keopuolani, crawled up in my lap to take advantage of the rocking. Sometimes she would curl up and fall asleep; sometimes she would grow bored and toddle away when she could not pull me out of my trance. I didn't eat, I didn't drink water—I just rocked and moaned, and held my hand over the deep black hole in the place where my heart used to be.

Liliha let me mourn like that for two days and then she sat down in front of me, placing her hands on either side of my face. She glared into my blank eyes and asked, "What about his bones?"

Her directness was like a sharp slap across my cheek. She had reached down into the pit and pulled me up. I blinked and squinted, shielding my eyes from the bright light of day.

"We cannot let his bones be made into fishhooks. We must go to Kamehameha and petition for our beloved Kiwalao."

"We?" I questioned.

"Yes, you must go with me, mother. If anyone can influence Kamehameha, it is you. Did you not help raise him at Kalani's court? You were like a mother to him."

I shook my head. "I might have been like a mother to him when he was a pup, but he is no longer a pup. He is a full warrior, and to him I am nothing but a useless, withered old woman."

"What has happened to you, mother? I don't believe my ears!" In frustration she straightened her back and set her face in determination. "If you won't go, then I will!"

"You?"

"Yes, why not me? I am Kamehameha's half-sister, after all. His father and mine were the same."

"If you would believe…" I started to say, but she interrupted.

"All that is old news," she said, cutting me off. "That family claimed him. And so for the current purpose, he and I have the same father. It matters not what is said in the rumors at court. The point is that the claim has been made—he and I had the same father. That's the key that may help me convince him that the bones should be mine. I will remind him that he is my half-brother. He should respect that."

"He is likely to respect nothing," I argued, but then I thought about it for a minute. Of course Liliha was right. I could not let my son's longbones be made into fishhooks. Maybe there was some hope, after all. His father had bestowed the rule of the lands on Kiwalao--of that there was no doubt. Even Kamehameha seemingly had honored that for a little while. But Kiwalao had the tattoos of the thunder god of Kahekili. He had been branded a son of Maui, through and through. It was only fitting that his bones be tucked away in the recesses of the caves of our family at Iao. I tried to rise in order to carry out my duties as matriarch of my clan, but my feet buckled under me. Liliha grabbed my arms as I slumped down on the mat. Excruciating pain seared through my heart again. "I dare not move," I stammered.

Liliha called for the *kahuna lapaau*, the medical expert, who assessed my situation and forbade me from going anywhere. They said I needed rest and quiet. "If you can't go, mother, then I will. There is not much time. We need to begin the proper grieving rites ourselves, and for that we need the bones of our beloved." She wasted no time and marched down the hill to command the men at the beach to take her to Keei.

Keopuolani was only two years old, and really had no idea where she was, what had happened to her father, or where her mother had gone. Actually I was glad to have her near, even though I was in a weakened condition. She crawled up under my arm and hunkered down like the scrawny little hatchling she was. I could do nothing to save my son's bones it seemed, but I could do my duty to the family to protect my granddaughter, one of the most sacred souls in the islands.

And yet, in the still of the night, I worried. Liliha had left so suddenly that I had not had the chance to warn her about the possibility that Kamehameha might take her captive. She was, after all, the widow of his boyhood companion who had become his enemy. It was a custom of the land that the widow was a prize to be claimed by the conqueror. If he held her captive and made her his bride, because of their half-sibling relationship, it would elevate the rank of any child he might father by her. Liliha's impulsive act had put her in grave danger.

My retainers were worried sick and fussed over me. After a day or two I began to regain a little strength. But as the hours of waiting for Liliha stretched into days, I grew concerned and began to fret anew. I wanted to send a message to my daughter, but I could not. It pained me to think that the gods would be so cruel as to take both my son and daughter away from me, for then there would be little to live for, except the small fledgling currently under my tattered wing. For hours I stared into the water in my calabash, attempting to divine what was happening at Kamehameha's court, but it was like trying to navigate by the stars through scuttling clouds. Omens appeared and then were gone…none of them clear enough to read. Was it the calabash, my grieving state, or were Kamehameha's *kahunas* blocking my view of the future?

The village carried on as usual. The sounds of the industrious *makaainana* that usually soothed me had the opposite effect. Both the steady pounding of the women beating *kapa* and the incessant chatter of the *lauhala* weavers made me edgy. The men constantly rocking back and forth as they pounded *poi* made me want to jump out of my skin. "Everyone stop!" I wanted to shout. "Hold still! Don't move! Don't make a sound." I could have stopped them all easily enough—I could have called for a three-day *kapu*. In a flash they would have had to gather up their chickens under baskets, muzzle the dogs, and sequester the children. Peace would have settled over the land because the people would have had to stop the work of the village and huddle in their huts. I had the power to do anything I wanted, but I refrained. Why make the commoners suffer any more than they already had? Hadn't most of them, too, lost a loved one in the recent *alii* war? It was not their fault my daughter was at Kamehameha's mercy, begging for the bones of her brother / husband. Why confine them in their stuffy huts just because I was scared for my daughter's life?

And then the sentries announced a double-hull canoe rounding the point. I went to the doorway, peered out, and recognized the standard of Kamanawa, one of the sacred twins—half-brother of Kahekili. He had been sent to Kamehameha's court to serve him and also act as a liasion between the two families.

"My chiefess," he said as he bowed low at the doorway. "I came when it was safe for me to deliver a message."

"My half-brother," I said in reply, reminding him that his loyalty should remain with the family whose blood coursed through his veins, not the nephew he had been sent to watch over.

Diplomatically, yet ever the warrior, he parried the thrust of my verbal spear. "The ruler has requested that you return to your homeland."

"The ruler?" I bristled. "Alapai was the ruler of this land, then Kalani was supreme chief. Then my son, Kiwalao…"

He coughed and cleared his throat. "Then perhaps you will understand my meaning this way: the chief Kamehameha grants you the right to return to the safety of your brother's court at Wailuki."

"The chief Kamehameha grants me..." I started. That upstart, I started to say, but held my tongue. What difference did it make what he called himself? He was not *my* chief. He never would be my chief! I'm sure Kamanawa could read my thoughts, but he wisely remained silent. Then my senses returned and I asked the most important question, "Is Liliha safe?"

"It has been a trying ordeal for her."

"But she has the bones?"

If I had not known Kamanawa since childhood, I would have not noticed that his demeanor changed ever so slightly—a veil passed over his eyes like thin clouds covering the glare of the sun. He spoke slowly in order to give me time to brace myself for his crushing blow. "Kamehameha will be bringing the bundle to *Hale o Keawe* tomorrow. He will place them in the crypt himself." He could not look at me directly, but made an attempt to soften things a little to help me gain some perspective. "At least all your son's bones will rest next to his father's."

Like the deep crater at the volcano Halemaumau, I wanted to open my mouth and let my steaming anger pour out. I wanted the hot lava of my tears to run like rivers down my cheeks and burn holes in the ground as they dripped from my chin. My anger was like the clinking *a-a*—it would destroy everything in its path. I wanted to throw up my arms and hurl clouds of debris in every direction. But I was a woman, not a volcano—I did not have that kind of power. Instead, I swallowed hard. The knot in my throat remained and I knew better than to open my mouth. The blame lay with Kalaniopuu, the one who started all this nonsense by giving Kamehameha the war god in the first place. Then I remembered how Kiwalao had said, 'My father calls me' when we stood at the doorway in the Land of Po. I knew to the depth of my bones that the visions never lie to me—they only reveal what is true on all levels of reality. Again, I felt my anger rising, although in some undefinable way, it was different this time. This time I straddled the chasm. Now as it began to rise, I rode it to the surface, sensing I would need the energy it provided in the days ahead.

"As we both know, it could have been much worse," he added, bowing his head slightly. The fact that he had moved his head at all told me he was at least sympathetic.

"But Liliha…?"

The persistence of my question allowed him to move on to the rest of the business he had come to impart. He scooted nearer to me on the mat and spoke in low tones.

"Prepare to leave Honaunau tonight. It may be possible for you to meet with Liliha on the way."

"So I will not be able to complete the ceremony with my son?" I spat.

He saw my rage and put up his hand to deflect the barb I had thrown. He shook his head as if to say, 'No more.' But what he did say was, "What's done is done. My promise to you is that I will stand at the doorway tomorrow, as a member of our Maui family." He glanced at Keopuolani. "I speak to you now as a brother. Liliha has managed to escape this time because Kamehameha's attention has been diverted. It is better that you escape with the young one and go to Kahekili while you can. You do not want to tarry, for if Kamehameha changes his mind…"

"You need say no more," I said. He had made it clear. I knew our lives were in peril. Kamanawa had done what he could to see that my son was being honored as a chief of the Keawe family instead being debased at the end of Kamehameha's fishing line. Within the boundaries of what his family had asked of him years ago, Kamanawa had done what was *pono*—what was right. As soon as he sensed I understood, he leaned closer and whispered, "A canoe will come for you at sunset." He kept his head bowed as he backed out of the door.

I had little time to pack, but there was not much I wanted to take with me from this island. After all these years, I wished to leave the trappings of Kalani's court behind. I poured the water out of the calabash and stuffed it full of food for the men and Keopuolani. We left just as the sun flashed green on the evening horizon. The paddlers headed straight out from shore. A single canoe might not be seen as a threat to the sentries that Kekuhaupio and Kamehameha surely had posted on the hill above their village. Only a scout with eyes of a hawk would be able to pick out our canoe in the trembling, tumbling water. The moon rose late, making a pathway that shed just enough light to enable the men to keep the island in sight as we headed up the coast.

There are just some things a mother knows—intuition, some call it. I felt it in my *naau*, in the pit of my stomach where my sixth sense lies. In the distance we could see the fires burning the sacrifices at the *heiau*. The wisps of fetid smoke that blew past us were the souls of the dead leaving the island. Still burning after all these days… how many lives had been lost? I prayed for them all, releasing the ghosts to the land of Po. "Look for my son," I whispered. "See that he is safe. Tell him I sent you, his kinsmen all, to keep him company until I arrive."

We traveled in calm sea, the waves and wind pushing us, helping the paddlers make good time in order to put the past bethind us. Keopuolani slept most of the night, tucked in tight under my arm. At daybreak Mauna Kea and the peak of Hualalai were in our wake; the men, exhausted and famished. I hoped to be able to find Liliha's canoe, so I said a blessing, thanking all the spirits that helped us make a safe night journey, and then gave the order to take us closer to shore on the incoming tide. We spotted canoes in the lee of a deserted point—Puakea, perhaps—we did not know the name. Even from a distance—more with my heart than my eyes—I recognized the yellow feather standard from Maui. When my heart skipped a beat, I urged the men to head for the bay.

# *Forty-Three*

## 1782

The men drew our canoe up on the rocky shoreline and I gave the paddlers from both canoes the calabash with the food. The three of us—Liliha, Keopuolani, and I—moved away from the men so they could eat in peace, and so that we could be alone to talk.

Tears streamed down Liliha's cheeks as she choked out the words. "*Auwe!* Mother, I have failed. I did not get the bones. And I don't even know what happened to them. Oh mother, I am so sorry. I tried, but I failed." She fell into my arms and sobbed.

"It may be this very minute, in fact, that Kamehameha is taking them to *Hale o Keawe*. Kamanawa came to me yesterday urging me to leave Honaunau. If I had remained, I'm sure Kamehameha would have claimed both Keopuolani and I if we had attended the ceremony. At least we are safe," I said. I did not want her to think that everything was her fault. "In the Land of Po I was unable to bring him back because Kalaniopuu claimed his spirit. I, too, failed. You were the soul who brought me back." Then we held each other and cried for our dear one.

After we had consoled each other for a while, Liliha said, "Imagine my shame at having to go before the court and beg for his bones. Kamehameha acted like he was doing me a favor by even agreeing to listen to me. I've never been so humiliated--so debased--in my life."

"The wind carried the reeking smell of that fetid place," I said.

"It's a good thing Kiwalao was offered up first," Liliha explained. "Kamehameha gathered up all the bodies on the battlefield and claimed them all as his own. He sacrificed everyone on the field, never minding which chief they had followed."

"Every one?"

"Yes. His men spent several days cleaning the battlefield. He allowed no one to interfere. How many were sacrificed I don't know. Four times four times forty. My eyes burned and turned red from the smoke and my nostrils were filled with the stench of smoldering flesh."

"Kamehameha's war god got his fill," I said, shaking my head in disgust. I was almost afraid to ask the next question, but I had to know the rest of the story. "But you did ask for his bones?"

"Of course, mother," Liliha, said, her tongue as sharp as the blade of the white man's metal axe. "That's what I went there for, isn't it?"

"Let's not let our anger and grief turn us against each other," I cautioned. "Don't let Kamehameha's spirit divide us as a family. That will only make him stronger."

She sighed. "You're right, nother." More calmy she continued, "I went before Kamehameha and petitioned for the bones. I was sure he would give them to me—after all, I am—was--Kiwalao's wife and half-sister."

"No one could doubt your entitlement," I assured her. "But...?"

"But Kaahumanu showed up."

"Kaahumanu? The girl born in the cave in Hana after our half-sister and Keeaumoku had been banished from Kahekili's court?"

"That one. Yes."

"What right did she have to lay claim to my son's bones?"

"She claimed Kiwalao because her father had been severely wounded and yet had used his last strength to deal the fatal blow, thereby securing the victory for that upstart, Kamehameha."

"Huh... she has no right," I grunted. "And how old is she now?"

"Old enough to be as beautiful as her mother was at that age--a woman's full form. And every bit as clever as her father."

"Devious you mean," I snorted. "No doubt Keeaumoku put her up to it. He was always willing to do anything to be a favorite at any court, depending on which way the wind blew."

"He had to send Kaahumanu because he is still suffering. Instead of breaking the spear off and leaving it in him the way they sometimes do, he had them pull the spear all the way through. Kaahumanu brought the spear caked with dried blood to prove to Kamehameha how badly her father had been wounded."

"Anybody can show up with a bloody spear after a battle such as that. Surely you argued that you were closer in blood."

"The spear helped to convince Kamehameha, but then she said that our beloved Kiwalao was her…" Liliha spat out the word, "Uncle! Can you believe it? And she claimed that she had been promised to him since her birth."

"What?!" I gasped. "Why the family…" I stormed. "She was never…how dare she!"

"Oh mother, I don't think she really believed it herself—she used it, and anything else she could think of, as a way to get Kamehameha's attention—to let him know she was available and ripe for the plucking."

"*Auwe*! If she is as attractive as her mother was, I doubt he needed any convincing —even when he's up to his elbows in sacrificial blood. If she is indeed as clever as her father—and with her mother's wiles…"

"There is more," Liliha said. "The Hilo chief Keawemauhili was captured at the battle and taken to a canoe shed next to where Keeaumoku lay recovering."

"That Hilo *apiki*—that rascal--he was the one who started all this in the first place with his land grab. He was the one who wanted Kiwalao to give him the Kona coast—as if being Kalani's younger brother was enough to assure him a place to warm his bones in the sun. If I never have anything to do with him again…" I stammered, bitterness dripping from my voice.

Liliha interrupted, "Actually, he was of help to me."

"Oh? How could that be if he was captive? Didn't they have him under guard day and night?"

"Because he is of such high rank, his guards were afraid of him. And they felt sorry for him, knowing that when Keeaumoku recovered, he would request that Keawemauhili be tortured and sacrificed. In the dark of night, the guards turned their backs on him and encouraged him to escape. When he realized they were not going to follow him, much to my surprise, he came to my *hale* before he headed over the long mountain. He warned me that I was in as much danger as he was. 'Only you are much more valuable to Kamehameha alive than dead,' he said. He reminded me that Kamehameha had every right to keep me because my husband had been killed by one of his chiefs." Liliha shuddered. "I tell you, it made my skin crawl, and I vowed I'd get out of there as soon as I could."

"Well, then Keawemauhili redeemed himself a little," I admitted begrudgingly. "It's also a good thing Kamehameha is young yet and does not understand all the ways of the victor. And in that regard, we can also thank Kaahumanu for being so aggressive and capturing his attention. He will wake up soon enough and realize his mistake for letting you slip through his fingers. One of these days he will come looking for you. He can use his war god to fight his way to power, but with our family's *mana*, any heirs he would have by you would assure his lasting kingship. His war god, Kukailimoku is the land snatcher, but our diety, Kihawahine, is the landholder. But finish your story... how did you escape?"

"In the morning, after Keawemauhili was discovered missing, all the attention went to finding him. Kamehameha left me alone. Keawemauhili really put fear into me and I was afraid to go to Kamehameha directly, so I sent word to him through Kamanawa that I was relinquishing my request and asked permission to leave. Kamanawa must have approached Kamehameha at the right time because he said Kamehameha was so busy that he just waved my request off as if I was an afterthought."

"So, then you were free to leave?"

"Kamehameha said he would make me comfortable at his compound in Kawaihae where I could finish the mourning ceremonies. Kamanawa offered to accompany me. That's when I finally understood I was not exactly free. And so I stayed at Kawaihae a few days and then asked for a canoe. By that time Kamanawa said Kamehameha's men were chasing the Hilo chief over Mauna Loa by day while Kamehameha pursued Kaahumanu in games of *kilu* by candlelight. I owe my being here now to Keawemauhili—he distracted attention from me so that I could slip away."

"Ah, Kamehameha—caught in the web between the daughter and the father." I chuckled.

"A day or so ago, Kamanawa heard the rumor that Keeaumoku had promised Kaahumanu to Kamehameha. It was then that he knew it would be safe for me to leave the island and called for a canoe."

"And he visited me as well. It is by his steady hand that I have this canoe and these men. Although he remains in Kamehameha's court, he has seen to the safety of his sacred blood."

By that time, our men had refreshed themselves and we boarded the canoes. We hugged the west side of the island until we reached the point at Upolu. By then the sun was high and burned our backs. My men struggled across the rough waters of Alenuihaha Channel. We stopped at my old compound in Hana overnight. I cried when I stepped out of the canoe and set both my feet on my beloved island again. I looked back across the channel and felt relief. At least there was now some distance from the land where I could remember nothing but sorrow. We left the men to eat and rest as much as they could, and then I slept the night through, the first solid sleep I'd had in weeks.

In the morning, I thought of sending a runner over the mountain to my brother to tell him of our arrival, but then I figured why bother? In the time it would take the man to run up the coastline, climb the gap at Kaupo, trudge across the desolate crater of Haleakala and descend into Makawao, we would be rounding the bay at Wailuku where we would be safe and protected in the heart of my brother's lands.

# Forty-Four

*I* thought with the family together and tucked safely in the bosom of my brother's court at Wailuku, we could all settle down—that things would be the same as they had been when my brother Kahemahemanui had been the ruler. For a few days, the sound of an industrious village was music to my ears. As I was preparing my altar and saying my morning prayers, my brother, Kahekili, never one to let things rest for long, called me to his side. "Don't get too comfortable here—and don't bother to unpack your things."

"I have no idea what you're talking about. My things? Where am I going?"

"We," he said and then smiled as he rubbed his tattooed arm. Then I cringed as Kahekili, like Kamehameha, reached over to run his fingers through the feathers of his own war god, Kanehekili, the god of thunder.

"Bring your retainers with you. And of course include your sacred calabash. In short, don't forget anything that you will need for an extended stay."

"My sacred calabash no longer tells me," I said. "I can no longer see into the future like I once could."

Kahekili blanched at that news, then recovered.

"So, this is it? You are preparing to invade…" my voice trailed off when I saw his grin. "But what about your *hanai* son, Kahahana? Do you plan to go to war against him—the very one you put into the position of power?"

"What better person to defeat? The one I know so well." He sat up on the mat and called for his retainer to bring him water. "I met with him on Molokai. Instead of using the poison god on his body, I used a subtler method." A sly grin parted his lips and his eyes danced with his perceived cleverness. "Instead, I poisoned his mind against his own *kahuna*." When his retainer handed him the gourd, he drank slowly, and then wiped his mouth with the back of his hand.

I dared not speak until he dismissed the retainer. "You poisoned the young man's mind against Kaopulupulu? How did you ever manage that?"

"By utilizing the services of his *kahuna's* brother." Kahekili chuckled, hardly able to contain his amusement. "I had every intention of sending my troops to Oahu, but Kaleopulepule talked me out of it. He asked me if I was interested in carrying out a plan where I would not have to waste manpower. Of course I was intrigued. Why kill men when it is not necessary?"

"Why indeed?" I said, hoping that he understood my sarcastic tone.

"That crafty *kahuna's* plan worked better than anything I could have thought of, actually, because I simply had to convince Kahahana that his *kahuna* had been lying to him."

"And so you lied…"

Kahekili shrugged. "I told him that his *kahuna* had offered me the sacred valley of Kualoa years before, but that I had graciously refused. I told Kahahana I had not taken it then because I had been saving it for him when he was old enough to rule."

I couldn't believe my brother had stooped so low. "That young man spent years at your court. You raised him. And now you will unseat a young man that you raised as your own son?"

"*Hanai* son. Let's make that clear—he is not my blood. When the chiefs of Oahu asked for him, I played my hand well, making it seem as if he were hard to get. But, the truth is, I put him in place precisely to do that," he said. His face took on a firmness I had never seen before. "In return for his rule on the island, all I asked for was the lands of Kualoa and the whale ivory that washes up on the shore. Kahahana did not see fit to give me the means to make *lei niho palaoa*. If I cannot have those two small things—the valley and the ivory--then I will conquer him and feast from his prized *kalo* lands. Not to mention that with Oahu comes the whole island of Molokai and all their wealth—and their powerful *kahunas*--as well."

If I had learned anything as my hair turned gray, I had learned that once a chief's mind was made up, there was no use arguing.

"Soon, my dear sister, all the land will be ours," he said with a sweep of his hand, extending it in the direction of Molokai and Oahu. Then he called for his new *kahuna*, Kaleopulepule. The moment I glanced into the priest's face, I knew I could never trust him. Did Kahekili not see the lines of anger that were chiseled in the priest's forehead? Kaleopulepule sensed my intuition and disinterest. I honestly think Kahekili had in mind to match me with his *kahuna* so that I would keep an eye on him, for the reason he was in my brother's court was that he was a traitor. Had he not just betrayed his own brother and the land of his birth? I could easily see that my brother needed someone close to the priest in order to keep a careful watch and make sure his allegiance was secure. However, I wanted nothing to do with the priest and did not try to cover up my feelings. When my brother saw my reaction to the priest, he dismissed him. Then, thankfully, Kahekili seemed to put the idea out of his mind. Without saying a word, I had made it clear that I was no longer willing to be traded as a prize. Brother and sister we were, chief and sacred chiefess, but I think he understood I would no longer stand for that much manipulation from him.

# Forty-Five

*I* had not been around my brother for a long time, and I noticed how much he had changed. He had always been clever and cunning—that wasn't it—not exactly. Now he had turned wily. I had seen that same look on my husband's face when he had come to battle Kahekili at the Sand Hills and lost his army. I had seen the same look on my son's face not so long ago. Kahekili was no longer a young man. If he was going to make his mark and rule all the islands, he could not waste any more time. So far his plan had succeeded—Kahahana had fallen for Kahekili's ruse and had orchestrated his own priest's death. It was time for Kahekili to make his move. He announced, "I'm going to ask Kamehameha for canoes."

"Why on earth would you think Kamehameha would help you?"

"He probably won't," Kahekili said, and then smiled. "But he has enemies on his island and when they hear that he won't help me, they will."

"You're expecting help from…?"

"Hilo, for certain. Keawemauhili was willing to help Liliha escape. He has no use for Kamehameha. He will want any ally he can get and will be willing to help me so that I will have to help him."

"You have a point…"

"And from Keoua in Kau--he was the one who started the uprising that got your son killed." He sat back, sure of himself. "This is where I need your help. You were married into that family and you still have influence over them. I need you to convince both of those chiefs to help me."

"Why would you think they would help you if they have not thought to join together themselves?" I wanted him to know that his plan wasn't going to be all take and no give. "And what would I have to bargain with? They will expect something in return."

"I will help them bring down Kamehameha."

"But you will let the other chiefs fight him first." I had made a statement rather than ask a question. It was clear the devious old swindler was up to some new tricks. He intended to have the Hawaii island chiefs weaken each other's forces for him so that he could save his own warriors for the final battles, thereby perhaps defeating them all. "It is the same ruse Kamehameha used to bring the whole Kona coast under his command at Mokuohia."

"If it worked for him, it will work to defeat him," Kahekili said. "Simply by asking Kamehameha, I will force his hand. Either he will be on our side or against us. The lines will be clearly drawn. My spies tell me Kamehameha's strength, and certainly his arrogance, is growing. I have sent Alapai Maloiki and Kaulunae, the younger brothers of his head warrior Keeaumoku, to Kamehameha to ask for canoes."

"Then what do you need me for if you have already acted?"

He smiled.

"Tell me, do you really need canoes? You could make your own…"

"And wait," he interrupted. "Or I can go to Hawaii, ask all the chiefs for canoes and warriors and see who will support me and who will refuse. That tells me what I need to know. On Oahu, Kahahana is young and his rule untested. The spell that my *kahuna* cast on him is working. Although the chiefs on Oahu begged me to send him to rule, I heard he has begun to treat his people badly. He will crumble as soon as I invade Oahu."

"It sounds like you are prepared to invade Oahu whether you receive help from Hawaii or not."

"Of course."

"And what if you do get the canoes from Hawaii? You'll stir up trouble on that island."

"Pitting one chief against the other, yes." The twinkle in his eye was enough to tell me he was actually having fun planning the young chief's downfall.

"And what if the other chiefs expect you to send warriors in return?"

"Oh, don't ever think I would put myself in jeopardy. I am not like your husband, Kalaniopuu. I would not promise something I could not do. I have warriors to spare and they are the best trained of any chief." Kahekili shrugged. "My only problem is that I lay awake at night coveting the fertile lands on Oahu." He stood and reached for my hand to help me up. He had no more need to talk about it. He had laid out his plans and expected me to not only accept them, but to pray to the gods for a swift conclusion in his favor.

———

*O*f course Kamehameha refused to send canoes, just like Kahekili knew he would. Kamehameha's reply was straightforward and harkened to the bitter days after Kalani's death: if he had been given the southern regions of Hawaii--Hilo and Kau—he would gladly have sent canoes to help defeat Kahahana on Oahu. But since Kiwalao had not awarded him those lands, he said he refused on the grounds that he would need his canoes and warriors to defend his own territory. Kahekili knew that was a lie. We both knew that in his minor skirmishes since he had defeated Kiwalao, he had smelled slight whiffs of victory and he would not be willing to be at the bequest of Kahekili or any other chief. It was, as Kahekili guessed, the chief of Hilo, Keawemauhili, and of Kau, Keoua, who promised to send canoes and warriors in order to secure the forces of Maui as their ally. That they would ask for warriors to go against Kamehameha had already been anticipated, and Kahekili sent canoes and warriors right away. In his mind, the sooner a battle started on Hawaii, the sooner there would be a victor, and if he was very lucky, Kamehameha would, at the very least, lose power.

As soon as Kamehameha was driven back to Kohala, the chiefs of Hilo and Kau returned the favor and sent canoes and warriors. Kahekili worked with his new men only briefly. They did not need to be whipped into shape;

their bravado was fresh from victory on Hawaii. Kahekili wasted no time as-sembling his own forces and headed up the windward coast of Maui in route to Oahu. Not trusting his new *kahuna* to give him enough *mana*, he stopped at Molokai to gather strength from the powerful priests on that island. While he was at it, he raided the fishponds, saying he needed to feed his army, but every priest and chief knew it was to impress upon them his might and right to rule.

Kahekili hadn't been on Oahu long before he sent a canoe back to Maui and implored us to join him. He wanted his son, Kalanikupule, to come to Oahu to help, and all of us—Liliha, Keopuolani, and I--to accompany him. I suspected Kahekili just wanted our *mana*, but I had agreed that I would do as he wished in exchange for his protection, so we boarded the canoe and went to his court at the coconut grove of Ulukoa in Waikiki on Oahu.

Once again I watched and waited while Kahekili drove his troops this way and that, chasing the shadow of the former Oahu chief, Kahahana, the young man he had helped into position. Although the people of Oahu were not at all certain they still wanted Kahahana as ruler, they were not certain they wanted Kahekili either. What they knew for sure was that they did not want another war, for war meant death of their loved ones and destruction of their homes.

Three battles were fought, but none were decisive. Finally, in frustration, Kahekili went to the battlefield himself. He divided his troops into two sections: one he sent behind Puowaina and the other he commanded from Kahehuna and Auwaiolimu. The bodies piled up in bloody Kaheiki stream. On the ridge facing the valley of Pauoa, the Oahu troops became confused. Sensing defeat, Kahahana and his wife, Kekuapoi, fled to the upland forest. After their chief deserted them, the Oahu warriors were free to lay down their weapons. The prophecy of Kaopulupulu had been fulfilled. The *makaainana* had had enough. What they wanted most was peace. Their once productive lands were barren and their families were hungry.

Dismayed at being overrun by Kahekili and frightened for their well-being and their chief, the *makaainana* hid Kahahana from Kahekili and his Maui invad-ers, causing Kahekili much frustration. What he wanted more than anything was to offer up his *hanai* son as a sacrifice to his war god, but Kahahana's game of hide-and-seek dragged on.

"This reminds me of Kalani chasing Imakakoloa all over the Puna district," I said to Kahekili one day when he was grousing about his scout's inability to track down the errant former ruler.

"No good ever comes from the people hiding a chief. Don't they know that?" Kahekili replied as he called for his retainer to wisk the flies buzzing around his head.

I saw an opening and attempted to reason with my brother. "The people of Oahu have been through enough. Leave them alone and do not punish them for hiding their chief. Instead, honor them for their loyalty. You may need their loyalty if you ever succed in catching Kahahana."

He interrupted, "Not *if*—when. *When* I catch the him!"

"When..." I bowed my head in his direction, humbly correcting myself. "Catch him then, and leave the people to their *loi* and fishponds. It will always be as our parents taught us: you will prosper when the *makaainana* prosper."

My brother huffed. "I did not call you here to lecture me." He was silent for a moment, then turned to me and snarled, "You seem unhappy. What is it you want?"

"I have lived my whole life under the thumb of the man who thought the islands were his to conquer. I dreamed of my peaceful home on Maui and longed to have my family united again. But I see that you are no different than Kalani." I surprised myself at my outburst, but as long as I had started, there seemed to be no end to my tirade. "The truth is, I am sick of battles and soldiers. I detest sharktooth daggers, long *koa* spears and war gods whose ruffled feathers call for yet another sacrifice. It makes me sick to my stomach when I think of a soldier's blood poisoning any more streams."

My brother was stunned.

Even if I had not agreed with his plans, I had always reluctantly supported them. I had never spoken to him like this before. "You asked what I want? This is what I want: I want to go home to Maui," I continued." If I never have to go anywhere ever again, I will be happy."

"It is not possible," he said sternly. "I need your *mana* here with me." And then softening a little, more to shut me up than to comfort me, he said, "After Kahahana is captured, then, I promise, you can go home."

———

*I* prayed for a speedy resolution, but the gods acted like they didn't hear me. I had forgotten they had their own timetable. The hunt for Kahahana dragged on and on. For well over a year—maybe two, for I lost track of time--the people on Oahu hid their chief, his wife, and *aikane*. Kahekili spread his men throughout the villages on Oahu, spying on the *makaainana's* comings and goings, but they refused to reveal the little band's hiding places deep in the mountains. All the spying did nothing to endear Kahekili to his new subjects. Eventually the rumor came to court that Kahahana's wife had contacted her brother, Kekumanola, asking for help because they were destitute and starving. To hear of Kahahana's suffering was music to my brother's ears. Kahekili wasted no time in sending a runner to Kekumanola's compound in Ewa to offer fishponds stocked with mullet and a fine *loi* if he could convince the traitors to surrender. Unfortunately for the fugitives, the brother's greed overshadowed his loyalty to his sister and his former chief. It wasn't exactly surrender that the man provided. It was capture. But, to Kahekili, the nature of the deed was of no concern. What he cared about was the act of finally apprehending his wayward *hanai* son. In the end, the brother managed to save his sister's life, but Kahahana and his *aikane* were killed and brought to Kahekili to be sacrificed at Papaenaena *heiau,* at the base of Leahi, the crater the white man called Diamond Head.

Kahekili then moved us to Kailua, on the windward side of Oahu. I had a feeling he intended to move slowly up the coast and eventually take up residence in Kualoa—the valley he always had his eyes on. Before he could begin that maneuver, though, his spies reported a plot by all of the chiefs of Oahu to assassinate Kahekili. My younger brother always relished turning an invasion back on an invader. Never one to let a rumor go unfulfilled, he swiftly planned a massacre. He sent out his loyal followers across the island. In one day he had every ranking Oahu chief and their chiefesses annihilated. His deed shocked everyone into complete submission. His message was clear: if they kept him from claiming the bones of their ancestors at Kualoa, he would satisfy himself with the bones of the current chiefs. Kahekili had all the bodies brought to him at Papaenaena where he kept the priests busy with sacrifices. After that gruesome day, one of Kahekili's chiefs, Kalaikoa, wishing to prove his loyalty, built a *hale iwi* at Moanalua. There he spiked the skulls of the former chiefs on top of their long bones, decorating the top of the fence surrounding his compound. More than twenty heads served as a grim reminder lest anyone forget: Kahekili was the undisputed ruler of Oahu.

It broke my heart that the men had been sacrificed, that so many families had been set adrift, that, once again, so many lives had been lost amidst such brutality. It was not the way we had been raised. Hadn't I always been told to keep the peace?

How had things gone so despicably wrong?

After the blood had been wiped off his hands, Kahekili called for me. "As I promised, I have something for you. I'm giving you a new husband. His name is Kaopuiki and he has agreed to take you to Olowalu and care for you in the place of refuge, where you will be safe."

"Olowalu? But I am not in danger."

"No. Not now. But there may come a time… until then. You said you wanted to go home to Maui, so enjoy your new home and husband. Make him happy— and he will make you happy. He has promised me." Kahekili was proud of himself for having found me a suitable mate—someone who agreed to watch over me, someone who was loyal to my brother and not a hindrance, someone who actually asked to be associated with a sacred chiefess and was willing to honor all of my *kapus*. Did my new suitor want a seat at my brother's court? Most assuredly he did, but he would settle for being husband to his sister. Those that weren't born into high ranks were drawn to power, seeking it and yet not understanding the full implication of the responsibilities that went along with it. After a lifetime of being in the center of the ruling court, I was ready to step aside. I was tired and wished to retire to my *hale* where I could perform my duties as chiefess privately. In the past couple of years my life had been turned upside down. I wished to be back on my home island where there was peace, where I wouldn't have to travel anymore. All I wanted to do was gather my daughters and granddaughter around me and live a calm, simple life.

"And you will come with us?"

"No. I must remain here and establish my rule securely on this island. I am sending my son, Kalanikupule, whom I trust, to rule Maui in my place."

# Forty-Six

*K*ahekili was true to his word—we were all together on Maui. He moved Liliha and Keopuolani, along with his son Kalanikupule, to his old court in Wailuku. He sent my new husband and I to the safety of the secluded valley of Olowalu. We settled in and for a time all was peaceful. But I knew when my husband, Kaopuiki, the man who never shuffled faster than a snail, came running up the path from the beach that he had to be bringing bad news. Before he had even entered my hut I asked, "Now what?"

"Humuaula," he said. He dropped to his knees and bowed low as he came in the doorway.

"Humuaula?"

"There's been…" he hesitated as he attempted to catch his breath. "The men…"

"Here." I patted the mat and signaled to my retainer to being him water. "Sit."

He crawled toward my retainer, keeping his head below mine, and welcomed the water gourd he was handed. He gulped the refreshing draft. After he poured some down his back, he raised the gourd to his lips again. The last of the water trickled down his chin and dripped on his chest, mixing with his sweat. He wiped his chest with his hand and set the gourd on the mat beside him. "Humuaula is where they whipped the men."

"Whipped what men?" I asked as I picked up the empty calabash and waved it at the retainer, ordering her to fill it. She scuttled out the door. I turned my attention back to my husband. "What are you talking about?"

"Where the white men whipped the men." He raised his eyes to look at me. "And now the white man is coming here."

"The white man is coming here? You mean coming to trade?"

"No."

"Then why? What could the white man possibly want with our little village?" I rose from the mat and stepped to the doorway to make sure the retainer was filling the gourd from the stream. Satisfied that the young girl was hurrying, I turned back to my husband. "The white man only wants food and fresh water to fill their barrels. The people on this island trade a bit with the white man now and again. It's simple: the white man comes, gets what he wants, and then goes. What is the problem?"

"Men were whipped because the white man wants to know who took their boat. Someone from our village was named."

"What!? Why would they tell them that?" I knew the answer to the next question before I even asked, "Did anyone from the village do it?"

He dared not look at me in the eye. "N-n-no," he stammered.

"No? If the answer is no, then why?"

"I don't know." He shook his head, still not daring to look me in the eye. "Maybe because we're the *puuhonu*, the place of refuge, and they figured they'd come here and be safe…"

The reality of the situation began to dawn on me. I did not know my husband well yet, but I suspected he was circling the truth, otherwise why would he not be able to look at me? "Let me get this straight. Someone *stole*--the white man's boat?"

He nodded, but turned his head. "And they killed a man."

I sat down on the mat before I fell down. My thoughts raced. "It's one thing for one of us to kill our own kind—there are ways that can be worked out--*hooponopono*—to make things right. But there is much more danger when the white man gets involved." I remembered the blood that had been spilled over Captain Cook. Try as I might, I never had been able to wipe the vision of that day out of my mind. My heart raced and I clutched my chest. I whispered, "Not the white man...not again...not another bloody scene...not more death..."

"Don't blame me!" Kaopuiki shouted at me. "I didn't do it!"

Clearly my husband was as afraid as I was. His way of showing it was just like a man—by getting angry. I saw that it was imperative I remain as calm as I could. "Do you know who stole the boat? Who killed the white man?"

Kaopuiki fell silent.

"Well?" I spoke sarcastically and immediately regretted it, knowing that my tone of voice could easily escalate into a shouting match that would get us nowhere. "Are you certain the white man is dead?"

He nodded.

"Do you know where the body is?"

He tucked his head to his chest.

"I'm taking that as a yes."

The retainer returned with the water. I dismissed her after she handed my husband the water gourd. While he drank, I paced from one side of the hut to the other. "You have the body?"

"No, not exactly..."

"Tell me."

"We have the bones."

"*Auwe!* You have the bones? This white man's body has been cooked in the *imu* and his bones stripped of the flesh already?"

"We were hoping he wouldn't be missed. "

"You..."

"Not *ME*."

"Someone stole a white man's boat and then killed him—and you hoped he wouldn't be missed?" I whirled around and faced him. "There aren't that many white men! Of course he's going to be missed. What's the matter with you?"

"What is one white man?" He shrugged. "He wasn't even a very good watch man. He should never have fallen asleep. Maybe he had been drinking the white man's poison—alcohol made from sugar cane." He shrugged. "I don't know. At any rate, he got his boat stolen..."

"Of course he got his boat stolen—it was him against how many others?"

"Five," Kaopuiki said, then looked guilty.

It seemed obvious to me that he had to have been involved--he knew too many details. "Five against one. I doubt that you could defend yourself against such odds."

Kaopuiki started to say something, then thought better of it.

"If we're not careful, more men are going to get killed, and this time it won't be white men—it will be men from our own village." I racked my brain for a solution as I glared at my husband. "What are you going to do about it? I do not wish to see another man killed—*haole* or not."

"What can I do?" he shrugged. "The man is dead, the boat ..."

"*Now* you tell me the rest of the story," I yelled. "What else could possibly go wrong? A white man was killed, his body cooked, the flesh torn from his bones, and no doubt fed to the sharks by now." I stared at him. "Is that the truth? Is there more?"

He nodded.

"Let me guess. The boat has been stripped?"

"Just like his bones." Kaopuiki hung his head.

"Is the whole truth out now?"

"There is nothing more to tell." He sat still.

I was so angry that if he had moved, I swear I would have killed him. I, the sacred chiefess of this island--the one everyone regarded as a calm, dignified, sensible woman, a woman of incredible power—and here I was, ready to commit murder myself. How could things have gone so wrong? I stared out the doorway and across to my *loi*.

"What are you going to do?" he asked, timidly.

"I don't see what other choice I have," I said, over my shoulder. "I declare the *kapu* of the burned grass. For three days no one approaches the white men's ships."

"But, what about the trading?"

"Absolutely no trading. Stay away from the shore. Stay away from the white man. Stay away from the white man's ships."

"What shall I tell the men to do?"

"Tell them to tend to their brother, *kalo*, in their peaceful *loi*. Maybe some sanity will return to them while they are there."

"*Kalo*? They don't want to be up to their knees in mud in their *loi*. They want to trade," he started, but when I turned, he saw the sternness on my face and thought better of arguing with me.

I was seething inside and could not bear to look at him. I turned back to the view across the stream. "Maybe it would be a good time to send the men up to the hills to hunt for pig. Get them far away from here." Setting the *kapu* had calmed me down for a moment and I found the patience to try to reason with my husband. "I know the men want to trade, but I've been through this before and it did not turn out good. My husband, Kalaniopuu, ruler of Hawaii, almost got kidnapped and men on both sides were killed when the white man came seeking revenge about a boat. I saw it all—that scene still haunts my dreams at times. If our men are stupid enough to ask, you can tell them why there is a *kapu*. You should only have to repeat two words: Captain Cook. Everyone knows that story and they will understand the reason. If they don't understand, send them to me and I will tell them the story of that bloody day." I looked him straight in the eye. "I have spoken. The *kapu* is set. No one goes near the beach or the white man's ships. If the gods are smiling on us, this will all blow over. If the white man can't make contact with any of us maybe they will think better of it and go away. Under the circumstances, it is the best we can hope for."

Kaopuiki sighed. "The men aren't going to like the idea of not trading with the white man—it's where the good deals come from these days."

"One thing you need to learn, new husband of mine, is that when a *kapu* is set, there is nothing to do but go along with it. I only hope three days will be long enough for the impending storm of the white man's wrath to blow itself out," I said. Now that my mind had been made up and I had come to at least a temporary solution, I sighed, letting my breath carry the stress away. I focused solely on my husband. "And you…"

He flinched.

"You will see to the careful wrapping of the white man's bones, and then you will return the bones--and anything that is left of the boat--to the white men."

"Me? Why me? *I* didn't steal the boat," he argued. "*I* didn't kill him."

"*You.* You married me because you wanted the responsibilities of a chief. Now, *act* like a chief." I am a chiefess, but I was also his wife. And I had shamed him. He may have had the title of chief—a minor one at that--but I am *alii*. He had no choice but to do my bidding.

"And what will you do all this time?"

He was lucky I didn't grab the calabash and throw it at him. Instead, I calmed myself and said, "I want to be alone. Go spread the word about the *kapu* and see that the sticks are put in place at the beach. It would be best to do it yourself—that way you will be able to assure me that it has been done. Do you understand? There will be absolutely no trading and no fishing. Maybe the white men will not try to come ashore when they see the warning of the crossed *kapu* sticks. Display them prominently. Somehow they seem to understand that much." I called for my young retainer and said, "Follow me." I stepped out of my hut, and then stopped and said to my husband, "Don't disturb me. I am going farther back in the valley--to *hale o papa*. The women's *heiau* is the only place I can be left alone to pray." Without looking back, I left him and walked up the path to the stone temple. I set my own *kapu* sticks and drew the veil down around myself, hoping my prayers would calm things down. It was the only thing I knew to do.

I awoke before dawn and bathed in the stream in the back of the valley. When refreshed, I returned to the *heiau*. I knelt before the altar to speak to my gods, as much to talk to them as to hear myself think out loud. "Kihawahine, *mo-o* of us all. The white man has come to our shores and we are now in times we fail to understand. Their ways are not our ways; their gods are not our gods. They came to us across the water and my husband, Kalaniopuu, wanted so hard to believe the god was returning, but I feared he had been deceived and the white man was not a god. Cook was just a man—blood and bones--the same as any man. Now the white man returns to our shores again and again, and each time there is trouble. Sometimes the trouble goes away when they depart, but other times the trouble lingers because our people spread sickness among themselves. Now it seems trouble has come again from the white man and his ships. Goddess, what else can I do? I put a three-day *kapu* on the men from going out to the *haole* ship. I was not the one who stole the small boat, nor was I the one who killed the watchman. But evidently five men from this village did—or they are being blamed by those that did. At this point it doesn't matter. What our men desire above all is the hard metal that comes from the white man. It is harder than whale tooth, harder than *koa*, harder even than the stone that comes from the quarry on the top of Haleakala. Sometimes the metal is made into knives so that the men can more easily stab each other; sometimes it is melted into small or large pebbles they call bullets so they can destroy each other from farther away. To me, it is just one more thing for the men to take into battle and kill each other with. Rumor has it that Kamehameha, the holder of the war god Kukailimoku, has a stockpile of hard metal that he got from trading his island's sacred feather cloaks to the white man. For all I know, that's what he did with my son's cape. It sickens me when I think of it. When he was alive, I begged Kalani not to give Kamehameha that war god. 'It will only bring us more trouble,' I said. And I was right. Now, since Kamehameha has metal, all the men must have it to defend themselves from him. I have told my brother, Kahekili, that no good will come from the white man. They are too volatile and not at all understanding of our ways. We trade them our water and our precious food, and what do we get in return? Cloth that rips at the slightest tug, not strong and durable like the *kapa* the women beat; shiny glass--the only use we've been able to find for it so far is as a signaling device and we already had fire and the voice of the drums for that; and the most precious of all--these metal objects. And now, I fear, it is much too late. When I questioned my husband yesterday, he knew they had the watchman's bones—not body—bones--for he knew the man had been cooked in the *imu* and the flesh stripped and fed to the sharks. *Auwe!* When I look in the calabash I sense an ill wind has already started blowing, sent by the white man. I see *hales* burning. I see sharks circling in a feeding frenzy. I feel the rain of the people's tears beating on the ground. Even though, at the moment, all is calm, I feel the presence—and the destruction—that follows in the wake of the white man."

———◆———

*I* wanted to keep to myself during those three days of *kapu*, but it seemed there was always a question of protocol that my husband brought from the men at the beach. I wondered how many questions the men really had and how many my husband made up so that he could keep an eye on me. The first inquiry was, "I understand the men aren't supposed to trade with the white man, but could they prepare for trade?" Then, "Could they fish at the beach if they promised not to engage in trade?" Then, "Did you mean for the *kapu* to involve all trade? Could they trade with each other as long as no white man is involved?" And on and on it went.

It made me tired. I wanted the whole world to stop. I prayed for the people to come to their senses. Things had gotten too lax. When I was a girl, if the *alii wahine* said 'stop,' everyone stopped. Quiet settled over the land and after a few days of quiet, people regained their balance.

Now there is not that sense of balance. The world was tipping at a dangerous angle and it had become a daily struggle for me to stand upright. It was as if a tiny bug burrowed inside my ear and gnawed away at my center. Other times it felt like a veil was being pulled over my eyes. I squinted, struggling to see clearly. It seemed the many breadfruit trees in my *ahupuaa* grew coconuts instead. It was as if dogs squealed when offered scraps of food and pigs barked warning. The people seemed no saner than the animals. There didn't seem to be anything I could do to restore order--certainly not since the coming of the white man.

They were, I sensed, men without a soul, without the sacred, without *ha--* breath. They breathed the air but did not stop to draw it in, to take it to the marrow of their bones. They breathed shallowly and were always on the move, always traveling and trading and scuttling off here and there, bringing nervousness to the land that I had never experienced before. The very air around them vibrated, sending off sparks that had the potential to ignite into a raging fire. Seemingly, they were blind to it all.

The white man did not stop to grow their own *kalo*, to plant their own breadfruit trees, to raise chickens or hunt wild pig in the uplands. They were not connected to the land in any meaningful way. They did not even paddle their ships, but instead raised their sails and skated over the sea, passing from one island to another, pulling up the anchor and then dropping it again so fast the natives couldn't keep track of all the white men's ships in the island chain. They were on the sea, but they were not *of* it. Their exploring seemed to have no real purpose other than to make marks on flimsy pieces of parchment and they would move on to the next place. They did not know the land: they did not sit on the rocks or under the trees, nor did they bathe their feet in the streams. The only thing they cared about was depleting the villages of food, filling up their barrels of water, loving the women for a night and then pushing them overboard with some trinket in the morning, leaving them to swim among the roving sharks on their way back to shore.

All these thoughts were interrupted when I heard someone coming up the path. Again. What little peace I had since the previous interruption was gone. I heard my husband's voice.

"Kalola…I hate to disturb you, but…" He waited for a moment, and upon hearing no serious objection from me, came to the doorway and knelt.

I rolled over on the mat to face him. "Is this important? Is it really necessary? Or is it one of those pesky questions you could figure out for yourself?"

"No, my sacred one. This may be the biggest question of all."

I sat up and nodded.

"The white man…" He watched me closely, making sure to keep his head down and his feet firmly planted, in case he felt the need to make a quick escape.

"I knew it!" I exploded. "Always the problems are with the white man!"

"Well, yes," he said quickly. "And…no."

"No? How can that be an answer? Yes… and no?" My sarcasm dripped like sweet sugar cane juice down my chin. "No? What do you mean?"

"The white man…" he began again, and when I didn't stop him, he continued. "The white man…"

"Yes, we've established the white man. The question is, which white man?"

Kaopuiki nodded. "The one on the ship coming from Humuaula. Yes, that very one—Captain Metcalf, he is called, on the ship *Eleanora*. He let it be known among the people that he wants to trade, and that there is a reward for the return of the boat…"

"But there is no boat," I interrupted. "Your men…"

"Not *my* men."

"All right—*the* men—have already dismantled it. At least that's what you told me the other day. Is that still correct?"

"Yes, it was torn it apart."

"And the wood?"

"Burned." He hadn't meant to answer my questions so clearly, but I had found that leading him gently made his answers just slip out. It was better that I found out from my husband than some poor *makaainana*. It wasn't likely that I would order anyone killed—I had never been known to do that—but these days were different, hence people were different. I was *alii*, and I could invoke a law any time I felt like it—whether it made sense or not. But, what was I thinking? It scared me when I realized I was starting to think like the white man myself. That would never do.

"Yes, the boat is gone," he said, "But there is good news."

"There'd better be." I turned over so that my back was to him. I gave him the advantage of a head start should I find his news displeasing. I knew he was only the messenger, although I wondered, sometimes, how much he maneuvered behind the scenes. "Go on."

"And there is a reward for the return of the watchman."

I bolted upright and spit into my empty coconut shell bowl. "Who is dead. And whose bones are in as many pieces as the boat. What kind of good news is that?"

"Well, I have an idea."

"You have an idea…" I repeated slowly, trailing off, unable to find anything positive in his information. "What sort of an idea?"

"Well, it's true that he is in pieces, but at least his bones weren't burned. I mean, he could be placed in a sennit basket. We could take him to up to the cliffs…"

"He is a *white* man! He will not go to the cliffs with my ancestors!"

"Then perhaps we could give him back to Captain Metcalf, and collect the reward. Maybe all he wants to do is take care of the bones of his men—the same as we do for our men. If he has the bones, then he can do with them as he will: bury them in a high place—not in our cliffs, somewhere else—dig a hole on the beach, or throw them overboard…"

"Throw them overboard? They do such a thing?"

He nodded.

"Do you know that for a fact?"

"For a fact—no. But it's what I have heard."

"You. Have. Heard. We all have heard many things about their strange ways. It is said they only have one supreme god, like our Supreme God, Io, the one whose name is not mentioned. Who knows what to believe?" I considered my husband's idea for a few minutes and then said, "I see, though, that this may be the best we can do, under the circumstances. Perhaps this Captain Metcalf may be a man to be reasoned with after all."

"I knew you would see it that way, my chiefess. I'll see to everything." He backed out of the doorway on his hands and knees.

"The finest sennit basket," I yelled out the door after him.

"The finest," he echoed as he stood and bustled down the path toward the village.

The man's bones weren't at rest yet, although with any luck, they soon would be.

No one's bones want to be handled so much. It isn't good for anyone, living or dead, to be unsettled in their bones.

I was exhausted and stayed in my *hale* the rest of the day. I closed my eyes and listened to the stream, hoping the peaceful sound of the water slipping over the rocks would calm me and slow my thoughts down. Let the men figure out what to do with the white man's bones. I didn't want to make it my concern. I rolled over on the *lauhala* mats to nap, hoping my husband could be trusted to deliver the bones to Metcalf along with a groveling apology sufficient so as not to get himself killed. All I could do was watch and wait, but I knew I would get no sleep this afternoon—it was too hot and I could not quiet my thoughts.

I sat up, wrapped the *pau* loosely around my breasts and went down the steps to the stream. I sat on my favorite rock and lowered my feet into the water. Immediately my body cooled down. I loosened my wrap and let it fall to the ground. I slipped off the rock into the deep pool that had been built only for me, a place to get away from the cares of the world. I looked up through the trees on either side of the stream and saw puffy white clouds rolling across the blue sky. It had been a game of mine since childhood to look for pictures in the clouds. Some thought I foretold events from cloud watching. That may have been the way it seemed to others, for I often knew of events before they happened, and certainly others, like my oldest daughter, were trained as *kilos*--seers--but I knew in my heart it was simply a way for me to relax. I hoped the clouds carried the answer, but they whirled about, buffeting each other in confusion, the same as my thoughts.

Another day passed and I remained in seclusion at the temple, praying. The only person who dared approach me was my husband, and he was wise enough to spend little time near me, and much time with the men of the village, seeing to the white man's bones and the boat keel. For he seemed to be in luck and part of the boat had been discovered.

The last evening of the *kapu*, I sat in council with the chiefs and the men of the village. Glib speaker that he was, my husband tried to get other men to take his place. Delivering the bones to the white man was a dangerous proposition, the men argued, and better suited to his position as the husband of a chiefess. Each man explained why he should not be the one to go out to the white man's ship. Most men relied on their expertise in one area or another: the most agile coconut tree climber, or the expert fire starter. One man boasted that he always carried the heaviest load of firewood. They listed their responsibilities to their wives and children, their productive *kalo* patches, their fine net making skills— anything they could think of to place the burden back at the feet of Kaopuiki. To hear the men tell it, the village would be plunged into certain ruin should anything happen to any one of them. In the end there were only five men who had not laid claim to some specialized corner of communal life.

"Where are the men who stole the boat and killed the man in the first place?" I asked, hoping that someone would innocently name names.

"They are deep in the mountains," someone whispered.

Sticks were drawn and the law of chance decided the matter, which every-one agreed was what the gods wanted all along. The more the men discussed the matter over bowls of *awa*, the more they recognized that the right man had been chosen. They praised me, their chiefess, for my prayers in seeking the infinite wisdom of the gods. And, ultimately they decided, all was well and exactly as it should be. Someone had to pick the short stick, and the burden was placed right back in the hands of the man who was trying to shirk his duties—my husband.

Kaopuiki felt otherwise, but it was of little use. The job had fallen on his shoulders. The men went back to their *kalo* patches, back to mending their fishing nets, back to cooking for their families, and waited for the morning when the *kapu* would be lifted.

———

*A*t daybreak I arose and bathed in the stream. After my morning prayers, I ordered the *kapu* sticks taken down from in front of my hut. As soon as the retainer removed the sticks, I heard shouting and walked down to the beach. Several hundred men from every village along the western shore had gathered. Their canoes, loaded with pigs, chickens, coconuts and breadfruit were hauled up on the beach. Upon my arrival, the men dropped to their knees, in honor of their sacred chiefess. I strolled past the men until I was upwind of them, then I turned and put my hand to my mouth so that my voice would carry down the beach. The men did not fully prostrate themselves, remaining on their knees, but at least they quieted to hear my voice. "We no longer float in the calm," I began. "The Koolau wind blows." They knew my reference to the wind meant a storm was brewing, and that it was my way of warning them. I pulled up one of the *kapu* sticks that had been planted in the sand and tucked it under my arm. "I have consulted the water in a calabash, I have prayed at my alter, but there is nothing I can do to halt the destruction."

The air vibrated with tension, but it was not the tension of those preparing for battle. Instead, I sensed the men longed to be on their way to the ship. The white man's goods made them deaf; their ears only wanted to hear the words that went with trade. Anymore, they were not interested in my prophecies. They had forgotten how to listen to the voices on the wind. I had done all I could do to save the people. I could not fight their greed for the white man's goods. "When the bones have been delivered to the Captain, then you may trade," I said as I pulled up the second *kapu* stick and tucked it under my arm next to the first one. My heart was heavy, for in the early hours of prayer, I had been shown the vision of what was to come.

# *Forty-Seven*

## February 1790

*I* saw Kaopuiki's shoulders sag as he picked up the sennit basket with the white man's bones and the piece of wooden rudder. The basket can't be that heavy, I thought, however I understood that he was feeling the weight of the people. Everyone was anxious for Kaopuiki to go to the ship and fulfill his mission, for the sooner he took care of this nasty bone-and-boat business, the sooner they could trade. As he walked to the shore and placed the woven basket and the rudder in the bottom of his canoe, he glanced at the men huddled in the coconut grove. For his sake, I hoped the thieves and murderers would finally declare their guilt and step up to take responsibility.

But they did not.

I watched my husband inch the canoe into the water. The waves lapped at his ankles. Surely a brave man would step up. I waited, but evidently those huddled under the trees and their brothers on the beach were cowards. What had happened to the fierce warriors of my brother's generation? Then it occurred to me: there were plenty of brave women who fought alongside their men. I needed to be an example to my people. I broke my daytime *kapu*, ran to Kaopuiki's side and jumped in the canoe. The men came out from their hiding places and cheered when they pushed our canoe from the shore.

As we pulled along side the ship, the man they called Metcalf smiled as he leaned over the rail. Kaopuiki tried to hand the basket of bones and the boat's rudder up to the translator, hoping that simple act would be all that was required. "Tell them to come up," Metcalf instructed the translator with a broad sweep of his hand. "Bring the presents directly to me."

There seemed to be no doubt--we would have to board the white man's ship.

Kaopuiki lashed the canoe to the ship and then climbed the rope ladder that had been lowered over the side. After he was aboard, he leaned over the railing and I handed him the basket and the boat rudder.

I had intended to remain in the canoe, but a white man came halfway down the rope ladder and reached for my hand. After I scrambled up the ladder, I saw the basket and rudder piled in a heap near my husband's feet in the middle of the deck.

My husband pulled himself up to his full height to show his bravery, although I suspected he was shaking on the inside. All of us were silent for a moment, no one quite knowing what to do. Then the translator broke the silence by instructing my husband to pick up the sennit basket and present it to the Captain.

Kaopuiki picked up the basket.

Metcalf strode across the deck and accepted his present. "What have we here? Have you brought me some tasty morsel as an apology for shutting down the trading for three days?" Captain Metcalf rubbed his palms together in anticipation. His long skinny tongue snaked out of his mouth as he wet his lips. "What is this?" he said as he turned the basket over, trying to find some way to open it. "What could it possibly be?" He brought the basket up to his nose and sniffed.

The Captain's actions seemed strange to me. Was he trying to emulate our greeting of *ha*, breath, as we touched foreheads with each other and took in each other's spirit? I had never seen any white man do something like that before— and certainly not in regards to a dead man's bones. I had heard of many strange things the white man did; maybe this was no different. I glanced at the translator, looking for some sign, but he seemed undisturbed.

The woven basket, about two feet tall, was shaped somewhat like the dwarf that Kalani had killed years before, sans arms and legs. "This delicacy is all for us...

if I can just get it open," Metcalf mumbled as he poked at the figure, attempting to find a rent in the weave. Finding none, he twisted the narrow neck. "It's about time they opened up their store houses again," he said to no one in particular.

The white men crowded around their Captain, eager for him to share his good fortune. The bones rattled slightly when the Captain shook the basket. He turned it around and stared into the mother-of-pearl eyes.

"It's the watchman, sir," the translator said quickly when he saw Metcalf stick his finger under one of the eyes in his attempt to tear it out.

"The watchman!" Metcalf sputtered and dropped the bundle of bones as if it was full of hot coals. "What?" He moved menacingly toward Kaopuiki, and then turned to the translator. "How can that be the watchman? There is no body. Tell him we want him to return the body at once."

"That *is* his body, sir," the translator replied. "Well, what's left of it..."

An incoming swell rocked the ship and the bundle rolled, clattering, across the floor, coming to rest against Kaopuiki's foot. Horrified, he jumped back from the bundle as if he, too, felt hot coals.

"How dare they!" Metcalf glared at Kaopuiki. "I ask you again—where is the watchman's body?"

The translator nodded at the basket and signaled for Kaopuiki to pick it up. What could my terrified husband do? He bent over, picked up the bundle, and with his arms outstretched, offered Metcalf the bones again.

"It's the way they do it, sir. We saw this down in the South Seas. Must be the same idea here. They cook the flesh off the bones..."

"They do *what?*"

"That way the meat comes off the bone easily. Then they strip ..."

Metcalf didn't allow the translator to finish. "That's the most horrid thing I've ever heard! Who in their right mind would do such a thing? It's savage— that's what it is—inhuman and savage." Metcalf turned his back on Kaopuiki and paced across the deck, leaving my husband holding the basket.

The white man's *iwi* shifted in the bundle and I saw the wild look in Kaopuiki's eyes. He almost dropped the basket of bones, but caught himself and put them down gently. Then he picked up the piece of wood--a much more solid offering--and attempted to hand it to the Captain.

Metcalf recoiled, wary of touching anything my husband handed to him. "What on earth does he have now?"

The translator questioned Kaopuiki and then replied, "What's left of the shore boat, sir."

"Where, pray tell, is the rest of it?"

"The boat was burned so they could get to the metal. That's what they're after, sir. It's the fastest way for them to get to the metal."

I quickly surveyed the scene and assessed the danger: we were two—maybe three if we could count on the translator—against a ship full of white men. Was I the only one who noticed that the Captain had been resting his hand on his pistol the whole time? I was terrified he would pull it out and blast away. In such close quarters, I hoped he realized he would risk hitting his own men.

Keopuiki spoke to the translator. If I had known what he was going to ask for, I would have told him to shut his mouth and get in the canoe, but it was too late.

Metcalf began to pace. "Now what does he want?"

"He wants to know about the reward, sir," the translator said.

Metcalf whirled around, his face turning a brilliant crimson. He wrinkled his forehead into such a hateful stare that his eyebrows seemed locked together. He clenched his jaws as tight as his fists, then narrowed his eyes until they were but slits. He grabbed the rope hanging from the brass bell to steady himself. Then he took a deep breath. Metcalf spoke so deliberately that, even though I couldn't understand the words, I had no trouble comprehending the death toll. "Tell him they shall have their just reward by and by." He was silent for a moment, and then his demeanor changed abruptly. He smiled at Kaopuiki. "Invite them to trade. Tell them to bring out as many provisions as they can," he exclaimed as he strode toward Kaopuiki and clapped him on the back. "Welcome! Yes, welcome!"

Kaopuiki, so glad the ordeal was over and that he was still alive, dropped the rudder, and bowed to Metcalf. He grabbed my hand and we fled overboard.

As we paddled to shore, Metcalf turned the ship so that it was broadside, facing the beach. The men on the shore were so anxious to launch their canoes that they did not wait for us. As they passed us I tried to warn them—I even tried to initiate another *kapu*—but they ignored my warning and paddled their canoes laden with trade goods right out to the ship. As the canoes fought for the prime trade positions near the ship, Metcalf readied his men. I sank to my knees on the shoreline and prayed, helpless to stop what came next.

When the canoes were all huddled together near the ship, Metcalf barked his orders. The sailors dropped heavy ballast stones on the canoes. The stones cracked the men's skulls open, their brains splattering across the water. The wooden *koa* crafts splintered in two. Chickens squawked and bashed against the wooden cages in their attempt to free themselves, their soaked feathers pulled them under the water as they battered against the sinking cages. Fowl lucky enough to have their cages broken open fluttered into the sea and paddled in circles. Hundreds of waterlogged breadfruit, rendered inedible, sank next to the ship. Coconuts, resembling men's heads, bobbed and clacked against the sides of the wooden ship. The few men that survived--sometimes more dead than alive—body surfed the breakers across the reef as best they could. Swimming along side the struggling squealing pigs and squawking fowl, they dodged the sharks lured by the scent of blood.

Then the ship's cannon ports opened and the guns were leveled at the second round of traders and those who had paddled out in an attempt to rescue their wounded kinsmen and the frightened animals.

"Fire!"

The first round mangled the approaching canoes. Sharp splinters of *koa* from the canoes mixed with deadly shrapnel from the cannonballs flew through the air all the way to the beach. We ran for cover into the coconut grove.

"Fire!"

"Fire!"

"Fire!"

Maybe they ran out of ammunition, maybe they thought they had done enough damage. Maybe he could see no one left alive to fire upon. Maybe he finally had his fill of revenge. Who knows why Metcalf finally decided enough was enough? At any rate, he ordered the sails raised, the anchor lifted, and the ship sailed away.

———————

he incoming tide helped wash the bodies to shore. I sent runners from the village to each hut up and down the western coast of Maui—from Kaanipali to Humuaula, spreading the word. All afternoon dismayed women and children hurried to the shore at Olowalu.

"Could the rumors be true?" the women asked each other. Their husbands had been harvesting, hunting and fishing for three days to gather enough to trade with the white man. They had loaded their canoes and left by the light of the late night moon in order to arrive in time for morning trading. "How could it be that they will not return?"

As the women neared Olowalu and saw the blood in the water and the bodies floating on the incoming tide, they began to wail, sending warnings back to those who followed. For miles along the shore, women fell to their knees as they faced the ocean, keening for their lost loves, for their means of support, for the fathers of their children, for the brothers and uncles and sons and fathers.

Tears streamed down my face as I greeted each woman. All afternoon I walked among them, offering prayers for the lucky men who were merely severely wounded. And for those not so lucky, I consoled the widows and the children.

———

he women pulled the injured, the dying, and the dead from the bloody sea. They set up *tiki* torches as day faded so they could nurse the men in the flickering light. All evening dead bodies bobbed along on the current and eventually washed ashore, some as far away as Hekili Point, surrounded by the flotsam of splintered canoes, drowned animals, and waterlogged food. The moon rose late. By then, the old men had hobbled down to the shore to help. The incoming tide swept up against their spindly legs and they dared not wade out very far from shore. They stood knee deep in the shallows to retrieve the bodies as black-tipped reef sharks circled in a feeding frenzy, feasting on sheared arms and legs. The elderly, no longer strong enough to haul the bulky warrior's bodies, had to wait for the waves to tumble them all the way to the sandy beach. When the bodies came within safe reach, two or three old men wrestled the men's hefty bodies out of the water and rolled them up past the reach of high tide. There they stacked their loved ones like firewood. On all the bodies there was some identifying mark—most commonly a tattoo—that the men left exposed so the women could identify their men and see to proper disposal.

*Kalolopahu* the Hawaiians later called the slaughter in their chants: spilled brains.

# Forty-Eight

## 1790

All along the leeward coast of Maui, we were in mourning for our loved ones who had been slaughtered. The world as I had known it dropped away, and I retreated to the back of the valley, sequestering myself in the peacefulness, away from the comings and goings of the world. My attention went inward, as always, to prayer. I wandered to the *kalo* patch, much the same way I had as a young woman when I returned to Maui in order to get my bearings. The birds were my sentries, particularly a hawk that flew in and out of the valley daily. Because that hawk watched over me, I no longer had the need for anyone to lean on a spear to protect me. The days slipped by as smoothly as the stream that babbled outside my door.

A few weeks after the *Elenora* sailed away, rumors came that some of Kamehameha's men had captured a white man's ship, *Fair American*. He not only captured the guns on the ships, he had managed to hold hostage two white men to teach him how to use the big guns. I had no idea how important the capturing of that ship, the big gun, and the white men would be to Kamehameha.

Sequestered as I was at Olowalu, I was not at the battle of Iao, although word had come to my quiet valley that Kamehameha had landed hundreds of canoes and thousands of men on the other side of the mountains at Wailuku.

Kalanikupule and the fiercest Maui warriors did their best to stop the attack. For days the battle raged as the Maui men fought bravely.

Throughout the last day I had felt the rumbings, but I did not know it was the cannon balls from the gun salvaged from the *Fair American* hitting the sides of the valley on the other side of the mountain. I thought maybe the gods were answering my prayers to end the battle by sending small earthquakes to interrupt the fighting. I peered into a calabash in an attempt to read the omens. I swirled the cloudy water, hoping to clear it. Instead, a smell so bitter—unlike anything I had ever smelled—stung my nose and I dropped the gourd, which shattered into several pieces. The water that ran out was not clear; instead, it was thick and red. I had just seen the story unfold, and yet I did not yet know how to piece together the details.

In the end, the Maui men were no match for the artillary of the white man, the gun they called *Lopaka*, which Kamehameha's white hostages had brought to shore and used to shoot the men off the cliffs of my family's sacred valley. The warriors had been herded into the valley and then trapped, there being no way for them to escape except to try to climb the vines hanging down the sides of the cliffs, making easy targets for the mortar fire. There was no mercy shown by the warriors from Hawaii. The men were left where they fell. The river, dammed with their bodies, ran red with blood. For months after, the water that had been used to irrigate the *kalo lois* was unusable. The people complained that it was undrinkable, bitter especially due to the sharp tang of rotting flesh and battered brains.

My daughter, Liliha, and my granddaughter, Keopuolani, had been at staying at Kalanikupule's court. I knew the chiefs would see that they were taken to the plateau above Iao, thinking that they could watch the battle from a distance, but I still worried for their safety.

Kalanikupule and some of his most trusted warriors fled the battle, ran to the plateau, and shouted to Liliha, "There is no disgrace in running if you can live to fight another day." My daughter grabbed my granddaughter, hoisted the child on her back, and they all ran for their very lives.

*I*t was nearing sunset. I had been in the back of the valley, at *Hale o Papa heiau*, praying all day, not knowing if I had been able to influence the tide of battle or not, but praying anyway. Now that my calabash had broken and I could no longer read the omens, it seemed there was nothing else I could do for my people but plead with the gods. The shadows were lengthening and the early evening stars lit my way as I began the slow trek down the valley. I knew the path by heart, and I knew no one had been in the valley with me all day. Then I heard footsteps behind me and froze. Who could be coming up behind me? No one was allowed in the back of the valley—it was my private sanctuary. I had no guards to warn me, not even my little *ilio mo-o* had time to whimper a warning. I whirled around and was almost toppled over by my own people.

"My chiefess, we are in flight. You must join us. Kamehameha is after us all," Kalanikupule said as he pushed past me. Fast behind him was my daughter, Liliha. The trusted warrior Kamohomoho was carrying Keopuolani on his back, for the sacred child's feet were not allowed to touch the ground.

"Let me take her," I urged.

Kamohomoho shrugged and said, "She is slight and is not a burden."

Of course I hurried with them.

On the way down the trail Liliha told me of the massacre at Iao and the desperation with which they scrambled up the little-used trail past the caves of our ancestors, scurried along the narrow ridgeline of the *pali*, and slid down the steep muddy trail along the cliffs that skirted the waterfall at the back of the valley. She had only to say one word: Kamehameha. When that word was uttered, I understood what the ancestors had been trying to tell me in the omen of the broken calabash. I had seen the outcome of the battle.

According to tradition, we should have been safe at Olowalu since it was a place of protection, but even my husband Kaopuiki, the keeper of the refuge, could not guarantee our security and urged us to flee to the sure safety of my brother's court on Oahu. We were eager to get word to Kahekili because we knew that as soon as he heard of Kamehameha's rout, he would send troops and squelch the usurper.

"Any of our family left on the island is in grave danger," Kalanikupule warned. "Kamehameha is on a rampage, and with this victory he will not stop until he has all of us burned in the sacrificial fire. We must flee."

My heart skipped a beat. "But what about Kalaniakua?" I cried. "My sacred daughter in Kaupo is in danger as well."

"We have sent a messenger, my chiefess," the men assured me. "Her people love her. They will see she escapes before Kamehameha's men find her."

I grabbed what provisions I could carry and, I'm afraid, hindered the small band as we fled to the shore and scurried up the coast to Lahaina. Those younger than I ran ahead as I fell farther and farther behind. Panting in order to catch my breath, I sat down on a rock—I could not keep up.

Kamohomoho handed Keopuolani to her mother to carry and came back to find me. "Please, sacred one. Let me carry you." And so before I could protest, Kahomohomo hoisted me up on his strong shoulders. Me, their chiefess, the one who was spiritually responsible for the welfare of the people of her island, had to be carried like a child. My heart pounded and I struggled to get my breath, but Kahomohomo dared not stop.

We set out to sea in the dark of night with only the stars to guide us, lucky to be well on our way before the moon rose. The men's backs strained with every paddle stroke and we made good time. They brought the canoes close together when we neared Hewea Point, tarrying for a moment so the men could rest before crossing the dangerous channel between Maui and Molokai.

I was dizzy and hung on to the sides of the canoe. I felt the arms of the water parting to welcome me and finally understood my father's wish not to die at sea. With a feeble moan, I begged the men to take me back to Maui while we were still near enough.

"It is too dangerous," Kalanikupule said. "Kamehameha will find you, for sure."

"She cannot make it all the way to Oahu. It is too far and she is too…" Liliha did not want to say the word 'sick' so as not to draw the evil spirits any closer to me. She was thinking of my safety, but I could have told her the words: 'near death.'

"Then where?" Kalanikupule asked.

"Molokai," I mumbled.

"Yes! Go to Kekuelikenui. You will be safe there," Kalanikupule said. "Kamehameha's men will not suspect we have split up. Lilliha and Keopuolani can go with her to Molokai and we men will go to Kahekili on Oahu. They will follow us for they can easily guess where we are headed. They will not think to come to Molokai."

If only I had been able to make it to Oahu—to brother Kahekili. If only… but I just couldn't. Liliha laid my head on her lap.

The next thing I remember was being carried up a hill. I was terrified I'd been captured, but then I saw Liliha's face. I whispered to her, "Where are we?"

"It's all right, mother. We're at Kekuelikenui's compound on Molokai."

'Where is he?"

"He? Who do you mean, mother?"

"Kamehameha. Is he here?"

"No. Our allies on Molokai have graciously opened a *hale* to us until the men can get our own compound built in a few days. The *kahunas* have drawn a veil of protection down over the island. Kamehameha will not be able to find us here. Word has been sent to Kahekili that we are safe. You may sleep, mother."

When I knew we were safe I was able to rest. My usually strong healthy body had given out. The deep, black hole in my heart had opened up again, this time with a chasm I fear I will never be able to cross. I am no longer young. My hair is white, my bones ache, and my head throbs at times. I am weak. I can be hurried no more. Now, in all things I must take my time. My daughter thinks that with some rest I will be able to board another canoe and make it to Oahu, but every day I feel the *mana* draining from my bones and I grow weaker. I have not told her yet, but I know in my heart I will never see my brother again. Even if Kahekili sends a canoe for us, I know I dare not board it. I know something is chasing me—something other than Kamehameha—something that I am no longer strong enough to run from.

---

*I* don't know how many days I drifted in and out of sleep—two, maybe three. I'm not exactly sure what is real and of this world and what is in the other world—the one that seems to be pulling me toward it. This world I know by the fact that my daughter is here. She brings me food and tries to tempt me to eat, even though I am not hungry. I try to take deep breaths, but I cannot—I just don't have the strength. Like the thin sliver of moon setting in the morning sky, my heart flutters weakly. I eat a little; I swallow cool water when someone holds the bowl to my lips. Most of the time I just lay still and listen— there is no need for me to comment anymore. It's all beyond my ability to mold the future: all the warriors and fighting, the gossip at court, the betrayal. It's all too much for me. I prefer to be in the other world—the one where my ancestors reside and we are all at peace. I travel back and forth between the worlds; pushed and pulled in one, silent in the other. When I awake, Liliha is there, caring for me as she would a baby.

———

On what might have been the fourth day, I heard the news that a canoe has pulled in to shore carrying my most sacred daughter, Kalaniakua. She, too, was running from Kamehameha. Liliha brought her to my side. I was so glad to see her I forced myself to stay conscious as the sisters and Keopuolani gathered around my mat to hear her story.

"As soon as Kamehameha heard the chiefs left Maui, he took over Kahekili's compound at Wailuku and made his intentions known," Kalaniakua told us. "Remember that time he came to Nuu and I would not see him?"

Liliha giggled. "Yes."

Kalaniakua did not laugh. "He claimed I had insulted him that day."

"You mean that time he came to court you? You and your retainers were at the beach when he landed. He did not recognize you and did not know that he was speaking to the very one he asked for. That time?" Liliha asked.

"Yes. I told him that he could find me in the village and sent him up the hill. And then the villagers said, 'Oh no. She has gone to bathe at the beach. Did you not see her?' and sent him back. He came to an empty beach because we'd had time to hide in the bushes. It was all we could do not to giggle. He boarded his canoe and went back to Kohala. Well, he's never forgiven me for that little trick, and called for my sacrifice at Pihana."

My eyes flew open at her shocking news. "What kind of a man sacrifices a *kikilo,* a seer? He knows your genealogy. How could he think to sacrifice one who is so near the gods?"

"What kind of a man sacrifices a woman, period? Despicable," Liliha said and spit on the ground. "But you are here. What happened?"

"My loyal court would not hear of me being sacrificed. Several women offered themselves in my place. They argued, each claiming they were willing to be sacrificed for my honor. I was deeply touched and tried to disuade them, but they would not hear of anything less than offering up their own life, even if it meant their families would suffer. I held them back from their decision as long as I could, hoping that by some miracle things would change. Then Kamehameha's messenger strolled into my compound. We could not debate any longer. They gathered around me and drew straws. Poloahilani, my *hanai* sister, got the short straw." Kalaniakua sobbed. "She gave her life so that I might escape and live." She wiped the tears from her eyes and continued, "Since the man who came for me did not know me, she was accepted without question. Several of my men went along and were present at the sacrifice at Pihana. They reported that Kamehameha had been completely fooled. When it came time, she said not a word. She held her head high and walked directly into the blazing fire."

"To think of all the blood spilled at Iao and Kamehameha wanted more," Liliha said and pulled her daughter closer to her.

"Nothing shames him," Kalaniakua said. "He will leave no evil deed undone."

"It is the war god," I said. "It calls out for blood and casts its dark shadow over men's hearts." Deep in my own heart I hoped that when Kalaniopuu met his son's spirit in the land of Po, my prediction would be vindicated. He should have given both the rule and the war god to my son. That was wishful thinking on my part. It does no good to be right to a dead man.

"Kamehameha is looking for us. All over the west side of Maui he is burning the *hales*, tearing up *loi*. He's dammed the streams so that the *makaainana* are without fresh water. He and his men have destroyed the fishponds, thereby showing great disrespect to our blessed *amakua*, the *mo-o*. As usual he has hopes of scaring the people into telling him where they are hiding us. He thinks we are still on Maui somewhere. The people are putting up with the destruction because they say it is their duty to protect the sacred ones of Kihawahine who has always provided for them. Bless them—they are being sacrificed as well, yet they plead ignorance. Kamehameha is on a rampage. He has even murdered a few... just because he can."

We could no longer hold back our tears and wept for our brave kinsmen.

"He does not understand one simple thing," Kalaniakua said. "People who submit to torture will never make those who torture them their leaders by choice. If the usurper is mighty, they must obey if they hope to live, but they are merely reverting to their survival instinct. They follow only if they choose to live. Kihawahine has always brought food and plenty to her followers—those with full bellies will glady do what is *pono*."

# Forty-Nine

## 1790

*I*n my bones, I felt Kamehameha's arrival hours before the guards apprised us of his fleet of war canoes coming across the channel. When there was no place else to look—not on Lanai, which he destroyed after he tore Lahaina apart, not when he had sent Haalou to ask the great seer on Oahu if we were there or if we had fled to Kauai, not near the fishponds—only when there was nowhere else to look, finally he found us at Kalamaula on Molokai.

Before the canoes landed, I called Kalaniakua to my side—in truth, she was never far away from me—and urged her to take some men and escape, to find a canoe and get to her uncle, Kahekili, on Oahu. "Kamehameha will not be expecting to see you," I said. "He thinks he sacrificed you at Pihana."

But she would not budge. "I cannot leave you, mother. Instead, let me kill him. I can do it, mother. I can run him through." Kalaniakua ran to the guard just outside the door, grabbed his six-foot *koa* spear, and scooted back to my bedside. The guard dared not touch her; dared not tug the spear from her hands. "See?" she said as she let out a battle cry and charged the wall of the *hale*, piercing the thatch with the point of the spear. She stood back proudly, having run the shaft half way through the *pili* grass. "See? I can kill him!"

I grimaced and shook my head. "Running a spear through the neutral grass wall of a *hale* is not the same as fighting a seasoned warrior." I raised myself on my elbow. "Besides, it is not the way of our kind."

Kalaniakua dropped the spear and came to my side.

"I have no doubt that you are fearless and brave, my dear daughter. If you attacked Kamehameha, I would call you fool-hearty as well. I have seen him parry with spears since he was young. He is a warrior. It is the thing at which he excels. You would stand no chance."

"Why should I not kill him?" Kalaniakua said. "He wants to kill me."

"That he didn't know who he sacrificed is to your benefit. You are here and Poloahilani is gone. All Kamehameha knew is that a beautiful woman from the Maui court embarrassed him. He would slay us all if he didn't need us so desperately. He walks under the god, Ku—given to him by my own husband. Without the sacred women of our family, spilling blood is the only way he has of winning." I lay back down because I could see that I had made my point. "Besides, you might be lucky and kill him, but could you kill all the others? He travels with many canoes."

"No," she said quietly, and hung her head to show respect and that she had given up the idea.

To make sure I was clear, I said, "You have never killed anyone in your life. Kamehameha, bloodthirsty one that he is, has his hands stained red. It's the only way he knows to get his way."

"You are right. I will not try to kill him, if that's what you want, mother. But I insist that I stay with you," Kalaniakua said. "If I left for Oahu, it would only draw the Hawaii warriors to Oahu. Then my uncle Kahekili would have to fight him and it would cause even more destruction."

"There has been enough grief to last many lifetimes. Does our *aumakua* not promote peace and plenty? Then let us be at peace. Let there be plenty."

The kind men of Molokai were willing to protect us, to lay down their lives in honor of the sacred chiefesses of Kihawahine, but it would have been silly to waste so many fine men. Even if all the bodies on Molokai had gathered together and formed a ring around us, Kamehameha's troops would have still outnumbered them. Those Kohala warriors were fresh from victory and looting. They still had blood dripping from their hands and destruction in their hearts. It was senseless to sacrifice those who had been our saviors.

———◆———

*T*here was nothing we could do but watch Kamehameha's fleet land on the beach below our compound. In no time at all, they swept through the valley, scouring the mountains for wood and *pili* grass to build a large camp. Kamehameha did not come to my *hale* immediately. Instead, he and his warriors settled in and trained daily to show us their might. They took over the people's *loi*, their gardens in the upcountry, and the animals in their pens, leaving the *makaain-ana* without. When they had eaten all the domesticated meat, the warriors roamed the hills, coming down the hillsides at night carrying pigs dangling between two branches. The aroma of meat roasting in the *imu* spread over the village, and yet the stingy bastard—that ungrateful son from Kohala--shared none with the people of Molokai. We prayed that my brother would send relief, but none came.

Helpless, I lay in my bed, witness to it all. As the days wore on, my *mana* drained away. Although I had not seen him yet, I knew Kamehameha had asked his *kahuna* to unleash the *ana ana* prayers on me and that I was slowly being prayed to death. I asked my daughters to watch my servants carefully to see if one of them was supplying Kamehameha with fingernail clippings, strands of my hair, my spittle, or my toilet. Maybe my daughters thought I was raving in a fevered dream, maybe they believed me. At any rate, they assured me they could find no traitor in our camp. I concluded that Kamehameha was just simply draining my energy of his own accord--that he and his *kahunas* needed no spittle or hair. I was already in a weakened state, and they had all the time in the world. They had simply decided to offer up prayers of death without any aumulet of mine—it would just take a bit longer, that was all.

———◆———

*H*ampered as I am in my decimated body, I still have enough energy—and certainly enough time--to think. I have had time to see how my life unfolded. It breaks my heart to know that the traditions are beginning to fade along with me. The visions of the future that the dying seem to be privy to have shown me that the prophecies are coming true, and that things will never be the same. The *mo-o* had given us plenty—times of fresh fish and bountiful harvest; times when *kalo* thrived and everyone has eaten well. It was my duty, as the daughter of a full brother and sister mating, to see that all were cared for, that there was enough to eat, and that the rains came on time. There are no women in the islands more precious than the ones from my loins. My brother Kamehamehanui was a husband to me in order to keep the lineage strong. Our daughter Kalaniakua has been trained to carry on my sacred duties after I am gone. My daughter Liliha is young enough yet to birth a chief, and Keopuolani is the most sacred child of her generation. The oldest chants tell me so: no one but a woman from my lineage will do. It was prophesied that from my blood, chiefs would be born--from *my* pure blood and none other. But ours are not the only *kahunas*. The priests of our sacred lineage are carrying on a battle in their realm the same as the warriors do in this realm. I can clearly see now that my brother had no choice but to marry me to the chiefs of Hawaii. He had to protect our island and used me as *leho ahi,* the cowry shell that lures the octopus. My precious womb was sacred. My son was destined to rule after his father passed on, after Kalani returned no more from the upland sweet potato fields, when the stars no longer lit his way, when *awa* was not emptied from his coconut cup. It was not for me to question—it was only for me to do. When my children were born I hoped they would be able to keep the line strong, even against the prophesies of the priests that said we'd only have one hundred years. I knew the *mana* wouldn't die in my lifetime—I was too close to old age when the prophecy was given, so it couldn't possibly be me. But I had no idea that things would disintegrate as fast as they have. I was hoping, of course, that I could…somehow…by some act of cunning… stave it off. But it hasn't worked out that way. I feel my *mana* dripping from my bones like the water that slowly drips from the ceilings in the caves of dry Kau. In my dreams I cry out, "Where is the water of Kane?" But the world is silent: there is no answer.

When I cry out, Liliha thinks I am thirsty and offers me a wet rag. She lays it tenderly on my dry mouth to soften my cracked lips. I use what little strength I have to suck on the rag, but it is not enough. Like the *aina*, I am parched.

———

"My grandmother, my mother, my aunt," Kamehameha cries. "I've come to see you."

I recognize his voice without opening my eyes. I knew he would have to come some day. I open my eyes to acknowledge him, but do not speak. The less said, the better. Let him speak—he has the energy. I do not.

"I have come to ask your permission to care for your sacred daughter and granddaughter. You know they will not be cared for as well by any other chief as they will by me. I will take them with me and protect them always."

My eyes closed of their own accord; I cannot keep them open. I act like I am considering his request, but really I am fighting to remain conscious. In his presence, the battle for me is no longer on the outside anymore—it is on the inside, and I tread a thin ridgeline—on one side, life, on the other, the land of Po. The pull of his energy is so strong I can barely stand to have him near. Unlike me, Kamehameha still has both feet in this world. He can wait. I do not need to reply immediately.

"You who were like a mother to me at my uncle's court," he says, flattering me. "You who cared for me and watched over me."

I do not have the energy to stop this nonsense. I did not care for him at court. It was my husband, Kalaniopuu, who rescued him from the court of Alapai and saved his life. It was Kalani who brought him up in the warrior way, giving him the great warrior Kekuhaupio as his trainer. It was Kalani who handed him the war god. None of it was my idea. If he really stopped to think about it, he would know I was always responsibile to my own children and to my *aumakua*, Kihawahine, not to him, and certainly not to his war god. But he is full of himself and I do not even have the strength to interrupt. He is a fine orator, flattery being his main weapon against me, although his tears are wet and seem real enough as they drop on my face.

Why is he bending over me?

My *kapu moe* requires that his face be below mine.

After much too long he stopped talking and wailing and there is blessed silence.

For the moment I do not open my eyes because I dare not see my daughter's face. I know Liliha will be shattered by what I am about to say. Yet she also knows I have no choice. Kamehameha has brought his warriors who have shown their might to the village. There is no reason to bring any more of his wrath upon those who have so graciously housed our court and kept us safe as long as they have. There is no reason to put anyone else in jeopardy. Even if I said no, he will take my daughters anyway. I know the path of least resistance is the only one I can take.

"You may have Liliha and Keopuolani after I am gone," I whisper as he leans over me. "But not Kalaniakua."

My final pleasure is seeing the shock on his face when Kalaniakua steps from the shadows.

Once again she had tricked him.

I said, 'You may have the two who share your blood,' I whispered, but what I really meant was what my brother and I agreed on so many years ago--only over my dead body.

# *Appendix*

Alapai—ruler over most of Hawaii island. Uncle of Kalaniopuu and Keoua. Enemy of Kekaulike of Maui.

Captain James Cook—English sea captain. Discovered 'the Sandwich Islands". Killed at Kealakakua Bay.

Hale o Keawe—sacred house at Honaunau where the bones of the Keawe family were kept.

Io—sacred priesthood. Hawaiian hawk. Name of supreme god.

Iao valley—Ancestor burial place for Maui. Site of battle where Kamehameha defeated Maui.

Kaahumanu—daughter of Keeaumoku and Namahana. Favorite wife of Kamehameha.

Kahahana—king of Oahu. Raised at Kahekili's court on Maui.

Kahekili—son of Kekaulike, chief of Maui. Full brother of Kamehamenui and Kalola. Became ruler of Maui after his brother's death. Defeated Kalaniopuu. Suspected father of Kamehameha.

Kalaniakua—daughter of full brother and sister, Kalola and Kamehamehanui of Maui. One of the last chiefesses of *pio* rank. Wife of her father, Kamehamehanui.

Kalaniopuu—succeeded his uncle, Alapai to become chief of Hawaii island. Married Kalola. Father of Kiwalao.

Kalola—Daughter of Maui chief, Kekaulike. Wife of chiefs of Hawaii: Keoua (father of Liliha) and Kalaniopuu (father of Kiwalao). Mother of Kalaniakua by full brother, Kamehamehanui. Grandmother of Keopuolani by Kiwalao and Liliha.

Kamehameha— Son of Keoua. Given the war god by his uncle, Kalaniopuu. Became ruler of Hawaii, then conquered all the islands.

Kamehamehanui—Son of King Kekaulike by his half-sister, Kekuiapoiwanui, and succeeded his father as chief of Maui in the mid-18th century. Ruled Maui for 29 years. Father/husband of Kalaniakua by his full sister, Kalola.

Kaopuiki—Kalola's final husband at Olowalu.

Kauliaimokuakama—after the death of their father, Kekaulike, he rebelled against his half brother, Kamehamehanui for rule over Maui. Defeated.

Keawemauhili—Hilo chief. Half-brother of Kalaniopuu. Uncle to Kiwalao.

Keeaumoku—warrior and chief from the Kona district, Hawaii. Supporter of Kamehameha, Killed Kiwalao. Father of Kaahumanu.

Kekuelike—chief of Molokai who cared for Kalola and sacred daughters

Kekuhaupio—warrior who trained Kamahemeha

Kekuiapoiwa—chiefess. Mother of Kamehameha

Keopuolani—sacred daughter of Kiwalao and Liliha, half-siblings of Kalola.

Keoua (Kuahuula) younger twin son of Kalaniopuu.

Keoua (Kupuaikalaninui)—half-brother of Kalaniopuu, father of Kamehameha.

Kiwalao—son of Kalaniopuu and Kalola. Briefly succeeded his father as chief of Hawaii before being killed by Keeaumoku. Married his half-sister, Liliha and by her had a daughter, Keopuolani.

Ku--Hawaiian god of war.

Kukailimoku—god of war passed from Kalaniopuu to Kamehameha. "Land Snatcher"

Imakakaloa—chief of Puna district. Sacrificed at Pikini heiau.

Lono—Hawaiian god of agriculture.

Liliha Kekuiapoiwa—Daughter of Kalola and Keoua. Half-sister to Kamehameha. Married her half-brother Kiwalao. Mother of Keopuolani.

Metcalf—sea captain. Battle of Olowalu.

Namahana—daughter of Kekaulike. Married to her half-brother, Kamehamehanui. Upon his death, she married her second husband Keeaumoku. Their daughter was Kaahumanu.

# Glossary of Hawaiian Words

*a-a*—rough lava

*ahinahina*—silver sword plant

*ahupuaa*—a land unit running from the mountains to the sea

*aikane*—good friend, can also mean sexual companion

*aina*—land, earth

*Akua*—god/ goddess

*alaapapa*—traditional hula

*aliii*—royalty

*alii wahine*--chiefess

*auhuhu*—poison used to stun fish

*aumakua*--animal guardian spirits, sometimes from ancestors who had been transformed into guardian spirits after death.

*aloha*—love, compassion, sympathy

*apiki*--rascal

*auwe!*--alas

*awa*—narcotic drink used by the *alii*; made from *Piper methysticum*

*eepa*—person with remarkable powers

*ha*—breath/ spirit

*hale*—house

*hale iwi*—house of bones

*hale papa*—women's house

*hale uaia*—room at the heiau where the sacred coconut fiber is kept

*haole*—foreigner, later to refer to primarily Caucasian

*hanai*--adopted

*hapai*--pregnant

*heiau*--temple

*heiau luakini*—men's temple for the god, Ku, where they sacrificed, among other things, people.

*heiau papa*—women's temple where they prayed and offered food and dogs as sacrifice.

*Hokulea*—star used by navigators

*hooponopono*—ritual to make things right

*hua*—testicles

*hui*—association; club

*hula*— dance

*iliili*—smooth stones used to accompany *hula*

*ilio mo-o* —brindle dog

*imu*—underground oven

*iwa*—frigate birds

*iwi*--bone*s*

*io*—hawk

*kaai*—woven basket used to hold the bones of the chiefs

*kahili*—tall feather standards to announce the presence of royalty

*kahuna*--priests of the temples. They 'read the signs' and were instrumental in politics, giving advice to the chiefs

*kahuna ana ana*—the priest who prays people to death

*kahuna laa lapaau*--the priest who specialized in medicine and knew the healing herbs *kahuna puu one*—the priest who specializes in reading the confirmation of the earth's surfaces

*kalaau*—hula danced to the beating of sticks, one against the other

*ka-maka-huki-lani*—eyes drawn heavenward; epilepsy

*kalo*--taro, the main staple of life. The leaves were eaten and the roots pounded into *poi*.

*kanawao*—fruit from a small tree endemic to Hawaii; fecundity

*kaokao*--syphilis

*kapa*-- cloth the women pounded from the bark of the paper mulberry tree

*kapu*—taboo

*kapu moe*—prostrating taboo

*kaula*—seer who transmits oracles

*keiki*—child/ children

*keokeo*—small pebbles used as game pieces

*kiha*—lizard symbol for showing generations

*kilo*—stargazer, navigator, with the ability to transmit omens

*kilu*—games of flirtation

*kipuka*—oasis in a lava field where vegetation grows

*kikui*—Candlenut tree

*koa*—tree with its hard wood used for weapons

*konane*—game

*laho*—scrotum

*lauhala*—Pandanus leaf, used to weave sails, mats, baskets, etc.

*leho ahi*—cowry shell used to lure octopus

*lei niho palaoa*—tongue-shaped whale's tooth necklace suspended on braided human hair. Worn exclusively by the *alii*.

*loi*--the "field" of kalo. Most kalo was grown in terraced fields upland from the villages, using sophisticated stream diversion for irrigation.

*Lono*—one of the four gods brought from Kahiki. God of fertility and agriculture.

*lua*—the warrior's art of bone breaking

*mahiole*--helmets the *alii* warriors wore, made from rare bird feathers.

*makaainana*--people of the land

*maile*—a native twining shrub

*maiokuu*—squatting sickness

*makini*—gourd helmet worn by warriors

*malo*—male loincloth

*mana*--strong sacred spirit

*mano*--shark

*mele*—song

*menehune*—legendary small people

*mo-o*--the lizard goddess

*Muku*—moonless night

*naau*—intestines

*niaupio*—a child from the mating of half brother and sister

*ole*—chant that records historical events

*oo*—digging stick

*o-o*—honeycreeper bird/ a few yellow feathers from the black *o-o* bird

*opihi*—very tasty small shelled animal. Extremely dangerous to harvest due to the crashing waves

*opu*—stomach

*pahoehoe*—smooth lava

*pahu*—drum

*pala hao*—gonorrhea

*pale keiki*—midwife

*papa*—earth

*peleleu*—double canoe, sometimes used as a war canoe

*pili grass*--long grass strung over wooden frames to form huts

*pio*—a child resulting from the mating of a full brother and sister

*pono*—correct behavior/ moral rightness

*poi*--kalo, pounded into an edible paste

*pololu*—wooden spear

*puhi niho wakawaka*—fierce and fearless warrior

*pukuha*—chief's retainer who handles the sacred spittoon and refuse containers

*pule*--prayer

*pule kuni*—black magic sorcery

*puloulou*—crossed sticks with *a kapa*-covered ball on one end. Used to announce *kapu*

*punalua*—sharing spouses, as in two brothers sharing one wife

*pupule*--crazy

*puuhonu*—place of refuge

*ule*—penis

*wahine*--woman

*waimahoehoe*--funeral rites befitting a chief

*wakea*--sky

*wauka*—bark from the paper mulberry tree/ used to make *kapa*

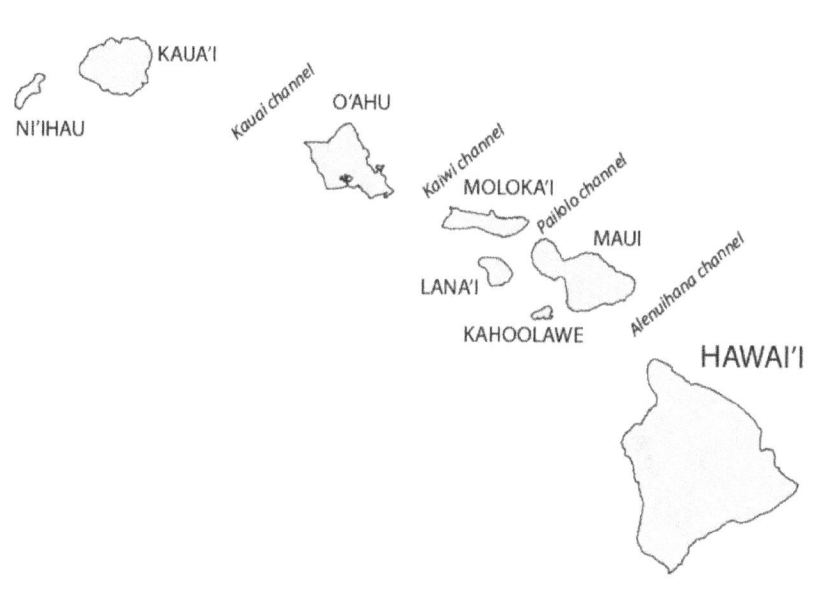

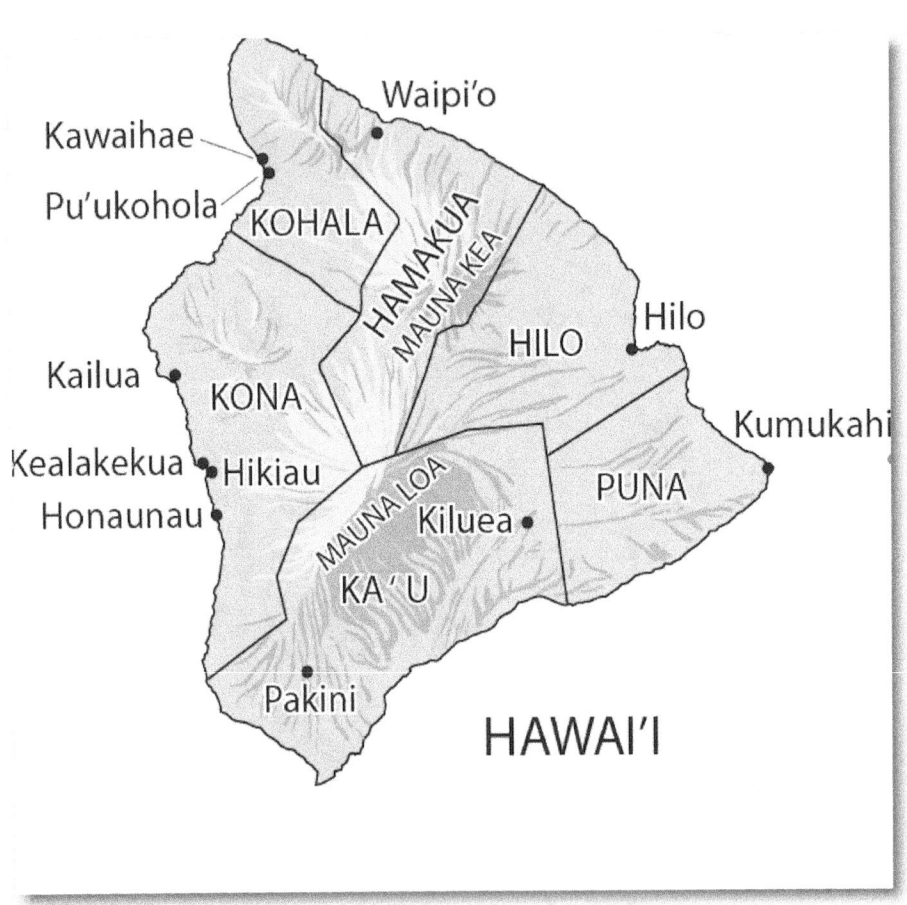

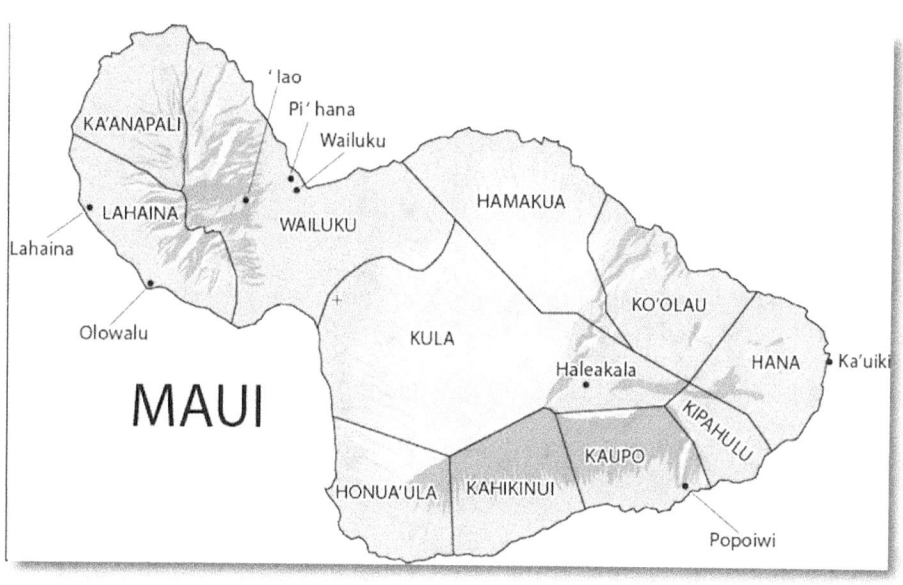

www.ingramcontent.com/pod-product-compliance
Lightning Source LLC
Chambersburg PA
CBHW051241260626
47162CB00002B/539